Everlasting Light

A NOVEL BY SHEY STAHL

Ann
thank you!

FOR CODY AND BRYNN

"SOMETIMES I'M TERRIFIED OF MY HEART; OF ITS

CONSTANT HUNGER FOR WHATEVER IT IS IT

WANTS. THE WAY IT STOPS AND STARTS."

EDGAR ALLAN POE

Chapter One

I WANT CRAZY

BENTLEY

"JUST GO ALREADY."

"Go where?" I taped up the last of my belongings into the large cardboard box and wrote my name on the side.

"With us. It'll be fun."

I never enjoyed those words. *It'll be fun.* In my experience, any time someone said those words, the night turned out to be a complete disaster.

I'll even give you an example here. Freshman year in college, the one and only time I was arrested, the night began with a boy from my calculus class saying 'It'll be fun.'

What do you know? I was arrested for indecent exposure. Nothing about the night, from the nakedness to my uncle Jerry bailing my ass out of jail at three in the morning was fun. And neither was his disapproving glance at me wearing a damn tablecloth as a dress.

I was sure this night wouldn't be any different.

The last thing I *wanted* to do was go to a party. Call me crazy, but after this last year of struggling just to graduate, I wanted to relax, finish packing up the dorm room, and head back to Mountain Brook before I started my internship.

Laney, my roommate for the last four years, wasn't having it and was hell-bent on dragging my lame ass with her to Lake Martin for the weekend.

I knew all about the parties around Lake Martin, and it wasn't my scene, especially graduation weekend. Just picture a crowded house on the lake with enough liquor to kill a person and so much noise it disturbed the entire lake. Did I mention the drugs at those parties?

I wasn't *that* girl. Not even a little bit. I rarely drank, didn't smoke, and drugs? Not unless I was sick and they were necessary for me to stay alive.

Some would call me a goody two-shoes. Well, I might have been, but I graduated with honors and had my head on straight—or at least on. We won't talk about the arrest. There was nothing wrong with playing it safe. In fact, I had my whole life planned out. I'd graduate, get a job, find a husband, settle down in a house with a wraparound deck, and have two kids.

Seemed easy enough. I had the degree part down and the job figured out. Now, all I needed was to cross off everything else on that list, and I'd be good to go. Simple enough, right?

Probably not.

"You're being a bitch and completely unreasonable," Laney quipped, kicking my box of books in her playful tantrum. "Just go with me, Bentley!"

Apparently, she wasn't taking no for an answer

"Why do you need me to go? All that's going to happen is you're going to see Gavin, you two will fight and go your separate ways, and I'll be stuck trying to bum a ride home because your ass has ditched me." I set down the packing tape in my hand. "No thank you."

My eyebrow arched in question when she gave me an innocent stare. Laney—for as far back as I could remember—always had an ulterior motive for everything, and she never exposed her plan until she had you hooked.

Her eyes widened, loops of curly blonde hair falling in her face. She knew I was calling her ass out. "I promise that won't happen."

"Don't you dare," I warned. "You promise all the time, but you still leave me!"

Eyes wandering around the small room, she scrambled to find something to use against me to get her way. "Beau will be there."

Of course he will be. Ugh!

If Laney ever wanted me to do anything, she threw Beau Ryland in my face. The story behind Beau was complicated to explain, and then, not so complicated. It was as simple as a girl in love with a guy who didn't know she existed.

I'd known Beau since I was fourteen, which was long enough that he *should* know who I am, but didn't have the slightest clue.

Beau was what some would say, oh, you know, hot!

A word like hot didn't do Beau justice. Every girl in high school drooled over him, including Laney, having moved to Mountain Brook shortly before graduation, when she first noticed him at our senior party. Though he was two years older than us, he still hung around town occasionally.

Beau had the looks with thick brown hair that fell hopelessly in baby blue eyes and the voice—as in he could sing, and by sing, I mean he was a rock star. Well, if rock stars came from Mountain Brook, Alabama, where we all grew up. He had that country edge, but he was a total bad boy too, making him completely different from your average country singer. He walked around in holey jeans, ripped shirts, and worn out black boots and usually had a guitar nearby. Did I mention he had tattoos?

Total bad boy.

Having admired Beau from afar for years, he was the only weakness to my plan, because that husband I spoke of, well, there was only one guy to fill that damn position, and it was Beau Ryland.

Just thinking his name made my heart flutter. It was that bad. It didn't matter where Beau went, rumors and sighing teenage girls followed him around. Sadly, I was one of them.

Although he was talented at sports, especially football, he wasn't some jerk face jock you usually encountered. He was a gentleman, saying hello to nearly everyone and smiling.

Whether you wanted to admit it or not, Beau had a way of drawing you in. It didn't matter that he was two years older than me; I had my eyes set on him since I was in middle school and he became the star quarterback as a freshman in high school.

Football was never his plan though, despite graduating with honors and being offered a full ride to any college he wanted. He gave it all up to follow his dream of becoming a singer. I admired that about him, being able to choose yourself over what society expected.

Wanting a set plan, I chose a degree in Human Development and Family Studies. I always found it a bit exciting that Beau chose from the heart, rather than what was the grown-up thing to do. I was never that adventurous.

Laney waved her hand in my face, creating spears of light from the afternoon sun flickering off her bracelet. "Earth to Bentley!"

Even our names went well together. Beau and Bentley. Perfection. Utter perfection.

"So you'll go?" She was waiting on my response, her wishful blue eyes pleading for all she was worth. "Please say yes. I'm leaving for Michigan next week, and then I won't see you anymore. The least you could do is come party with me."

Despite the fact my friend was moving away and I wanted to go out with her, but I couldn't stop thinking about Beau being there.

Remember when I said I had a plan? There was a problem with my plan. Beau didn't even know I existed. He also had a girlfriend, and no one stepped on Payton's toes.

If there was ever the perfect girl, it was Payton West. She was extremely sweet, so it made hating her even harder. It was like telling yourself chocolate tasted like dog shit because it was brown, but you knew damn well it wasn't true.

"So." I was trying to play it cool and picked up the packaging tape again.

"So what?"

"What does Beau being there have to do with anything?" I was never very convincing when it came to hiding my feelings or attraction to Beau, but it was still worth a try.

"Oh, I don't know, maybe because you're *in love* with him."

Tossing the tape aside, I lay back on my bed, which was now just a mattress, and stared up at the ceiling. "I need to get home and get settled before I start my internship at the hospital."

It took some convincing, but thanks to my aunt, I now had a six-month internship lined up at Hill Crest in Birmingham. It was a behavioral health hospital where I could put my degree to use.

"One weekend off isn't gonna kill you."

She had a point. It wouldn't, but it didn't change the fact I was awkward and would feel completely out of place at a party. Especially one Beau was at.

"So you'll go?" she pressed again when I closed my eyes. She knew I was giving in.

Damn her. Or in this case, damn Beau for being my weakness. "Lane, he has a girlfriend."

She sat beside me, then sprawled out, flopping her legs over mine, her sweet-scented perfume making me want to curl into her and breathe in. She always smelled like summer, the perfect combination of sun and berries.

"Stop smelling me, B." She pushed my head away, giggling, and then sat up. "Word around town is Beau Ryland is single."

I told you she was convincing.

Among the many thoughts I had right then, including flashes of what our babies would look like, was the amount of girls who would be at that party if they knew Beau was single.

"How do you know that?"

"Gavin is friends with him," Laney pointed out. "Apparently, Beau and Payton broke up last year, but they didn't tell anyone, wanting to remain friends and keep it civil."

That sounded like them. I couldn't imagine two people like them having a bitter breakup.

"Why is Beau going to that party? He's on tour right now."

The Beau I knew rarely went to parties. If he did, he went with a group and you couldn't get near him. He'd recently started touring with country singer Sam Shaver and that only amplified his hometown appeal. It was as if they all knew he was on the brink of being the next big thing and wanted in before he was famous.

Imagine trying to nonchalantly bump into him at a party when he was surrounded by at least twenty people.

Been there, done that, which just got me glared at and very nearly arrested.

So like I said, he didn't even know I existed, yet I could see it all in my head. Our babies were beautiful.

Laney moved her legs from mine and rolled to face me. "Gavin said something about him wanting to have some fun this weekend."

Fun this weekend?

What would that mean?

Laney saw me wavering and handed me a pair of boots, the same ones she'd worn to the concert last Friday night. "Let's go. You can get his attention and finally fuck him."

I rolled my eyes at the crassness of my roommate. Laney thought because she was essentially a slut, everyone should be. That certainly wasn't me.

I wasn't a virgin, but it'd been long enough I might have possibly qualified as being one. I had sex a few times with Eldon Sheets in my calculus class. We were study partners freshman and sophomore year. To date, it was my *only* relationship. If you could qualify study sessions where you had sex—and then didn't speak of it outside of that—a relationship.

Eldon never did.

I didn't budge from my spot on the bed, but I did stare at the boots. They were a dark brown leather with hints of teal and rhinestones and exactly what I'd need if I wanted to get Beau's attention.

Did I want his attention?

Uh, yes! Who wouldn't?

Trying to appear relaxed and not overexcited about going—I couldn't let her think she had won this battle—I sat up and reached for the boots. "And what do you suppose I wear. Everything I have is packed away."

Laney twisted around, her hands on her narrow hips, tapping her barefoot. "I have something around here. . . a pair of shorts or something."

"I'd rather wear jeans."

"No." Laney opened one box and then another. "You need to show off those legs you keep hidden behind sweatpants all year."

That was a true statement. I enjoyed sweatpants.

Laney dug through a bag on her bed and then withdrew a pair of shorts that covered less than my panties. No lie.

"I don't even think so." I pushed them back at her, shaking my head. "My panties cover more than those."

"Only because you wear granny panties." Her brow arched, challenging me. Laney Cutler should have gone into law, not business administration like she did. She could argue her way out of anything, or convince you to sell your soul to the devil himself without you even realizing what she'd done. "I say you're wearing them."

I placed my hand on my hip like I was going to stand up for myself, a feeble attempt I might add. "And what would make you think I'll listen to you?"

"Because you know I'm right, and you *want* to go." Drawing in a deep breath, she let me have it. "For four years, no, five years, I've watched you focus on school, and your mother. What's the harm in having one weekend for you before you throw yourself into the next thirty-something years of dealing with other people's shit and trying to pay bills?"

She had a point. A really good one. What would be the harm in letting loose for one weekend?

Glaring, I took the shorts from her. "Fine."

"Eeek!" she squealed, wiggling around. "I knew you weren't a total prude!"

Chapter Two

HELL ON HEELS

BEAU

"WHO'S GONNA BE there?"

Judging by the ten cases of beer in the bed of my truck, I knew I was in for a wild night, or they were planning one for me.

"People."

"I don't—"

"Beau, you're going. Don't try any of your usual bullshit. You're going and you're going to get laid." Wade was married and had no business being at a party without his wife.

No surprise, but his marriage of only one year was already on the rocks.

"Says who?"

Wade pointed at himself, letting go of the steering wheel. "Says me." Taking off his paint-splattered hat, he tossed it on my dash. "Chicks will be throwing pussy your way all night."

"Don't be nasty, man." I shoved him lightly. "And keep your damn hands on the wheel." Wade had picked me up from the studio in Birmingham in my truck, which I'd let him borrow for the day. I should have made him get out so I could drive—in the opposite direction of the lake.

"Well, it's about time you move on from Payton." He ran his forearm over his face and then stared at me. "Have you even fucked another girl since her?"

No way was I telling Wade that. Fuck this guy. He may be my cousin, but he thought because he was my boy I'd share everything with him, including who I slept with. More than likely because the moment he said I do, his wife stopped putting out.

Wade wanted to live vicariously through me. I didn't exactly want to tell him I hadn't been laid in months.

MONTHS!

I was never one to kiss and tell, let alone fuck and tell. Payton and I had hooked up a few times in the last year, but it was nobody's business but ours.

No matter how much fame followed me, I wasn't going to be *that* guy. If anything, with the way my career was going, that type of lifestyle was the last thing I needed.

It'd gotten me in my fair share of trouble with Payton in the past living that way. I certainly wasn't trying to get Payton back, but I was also done being with a different girl every night. It was fucking lonely living that way.

Flying down the highway toward Lake Martin where my buddy Miles lived, I looked over at my guitar beside me and then back to the road. "Who's gonna be there?"

Wade shrugged. "A bunch of girls from Auburn University. Apparently, they're having some kind of graduation party there."

Fuck. That's worse than I thought.

I stared back down at my guitar, escaping in the music in my head to distract me from the upcoming nightmare. Lyrics flashed, so I reached for the notebook in my glove box and jotted down some random verses.

I GREW UP around music. It was all I'd ever known. I'd been strumming on a guitar since I was old enough to pick one up. After graduating high school six years ago, I struggled to get my music heard on the radio. I played in every bar and coffee shop imaginable, and even stood outside on the street corner a few times just to get my music heard. Then, I fought with bar owners, record producers, managers, and even other musicians just to get heard.

Eventually, I was invited to tour with Sam Shaver, still without a recording contract or even the intention of recording an album. I was just looking for exposure. I traveled around from city to city, pouring my heart into my lyrics and performances.

I put my life and every relationship on hold for my dream, in hopes that once I made something of myself, those I cared about would still be there. I lost my girl and my friends. Then I made some new ones, but lost them too. Nearly everyone wanted to be my friend, but for all the wrong reasons.

Once someone found out you were a musician, they came out of the woodwork trying to gain your trust before destroying your life.

I had one girlfriend all through high school, Payton West. When I left Mountain Brook, Nashville bound and playing in a different bar every night, I fucked up a few times, made some decisions I wished I could take back, but I couldn't, and it ended our relationship.

We remained friends and still hooked up on occasion. I think she understood because Payton was a musician as well. She understood what that lifestyle brought with it. That didn't mean she wanted to work it out, just that she wanted the occasional trusted fuck.

"Hey, can you send Miles and Gavin a message and let them know we're on our way?"

Clearing my throat, I looked out the window, away from Wade. "Nah."

I wasn't thrilled about going to Lake Martin in general. That crowd and these university parties were exactly what I wanted to stay away from.

Even though my voice had been laced with harshness, Wade flipped his hand at me, like it didn't matter. "Stop being an asshole," Wade grumbled, reaching for his phone. "It'll do you some good to hang out with your friends for a weekend instead of being buried in your music. You know there's a life outside of that, right?"

"I know. . ." I didn't look at Wade, the same guy who'd watched me go through some of my worst moments while trying to keep this dream alive. The brutal ones where I was a drunken asshole and blaming my own faults on everyone else. Hell, that was this morning, wasn't it?

During that time, I didn't want to admit to him, or to myself, that I'd thrown anything away, especially the relationships in my life. I had let so many people down; I wasn't sure I had anyone left.

But I did, guys like Wade and Miles. No matter how often I ignored them, they stuck by me in hopes I'd see them.

They wanted nothing from me but my friendship. Never once had they asked for a favor or even money. Not that I had much of that anyway. I could barely afford to keep my apartment in Birmingham.

Wade was my cousin, but I'd known Gavin and Miles just as long as I'd known Payton, since we were probably all snot-nosed brats tearing up the streets of Mountain Brook, Alabama.

Payton, with her long brown hair and wide-set green eyes, had my heart from a young age, but times changed in the six years since we all graduated. Or maybe it was my infidelity that was too much for her. Probably that.

Squinting into the sun, I adjusted my hat and then looked over at Wade. "University party, huh? How'd you find out about that?"

"Gavin." Wade kept his eyes on the road. "He's been seein' some chick who just graduated."

Some chick meant he was just fucking around with college girls.

The more I thought about the party, the more it sounded like it might be fun. It had been months since I went out.

"You know I gotta be in Montgomery on Tuesday for a show, right?"

"So, that's next week," he blew me off. "Let loose for the weekend. It'd do ya some good."

Rolling my eyes, I shifted my gaze back out the window. Drawing in a deep breath, I thought about the show in Montgomery and what it'd mean. This was my first tour with Sam, and I wasn't sure what he'd expect from me opening for him.

The first few shows were good, but I kept waiting for him to say, "Hey, this ain't working for me."

We arrived at the lake about fifteen minutes later and parked next to a line of trucks in front of Miles' parents' house. Being their only son, he had free rein of their home and toys when he wanted.

Looking around at all the women half-naked and dancing in the beds of trucks and on the dock, I knew this weekend might be a bad idea.

My eyes shifted again to my guitar as I reached for it.

"You gonna play tonight?"

I shrugged, knowing at some point tonight I'd be asked to by someone. "I might."

I brought my guitar with me everywhere. Wade reached to the dash for his dusty black hat. Placing it over his wild mess of curly dark hair, he gave me his smile that reminded me of the Joker.

I was reluctant to move, ready to change my mind, when Miles hit my arm that was hanging out the open side window. "C'mon, boy, party's already started." With a longneck in one hand, he rubbed down his bare stomach with his free hand. "I've got my eye on some babes down by the water."

I bet he did. Miles was one of those guys who had a different girl every night, sometimes more than one in a night.

Wade laughed and grabbed the case of beer sitting between us, nodding out the windshield at a girl walkin' by. "Lookin' good."

Miles rarely had a shirt on during the summer and always had a girl or two he was working on getting with. When he achieved that goal, he'd move on to the next, girl that is.

My stare drifted from the direction of his to a blonde with long legs I wouldn't mind wrapped around my waist.

I smiled at him, snatching a beer before he took off with them. "Not bad."

Maybe tonight wouldn't be so painful.

Chapter Three

COP CAR

BENTLEY

OKAY, SO I was going to a party and Beau would be there. As I stood barefoot in my dorm room, surrounded by boxes that would be picked up later that night by the moving company, I listened to Laney in the hall talking to Gavin on the phone.

"Yeah, I'm bringing Bentley with me." And then she giggled, as if it was a joke. It probably was a joke to her—me, going out to a party.

Now, what to wear with Laney's tiny shorts? I couldn't just wear anything. I mean, Beau Ryland was going to be there. I had to, well, look like the hottest girl on the planet.

Right?

RIGHT.

Stop. He's not even going to look your direction. Just go to get a glimpse, and then go on with your life.

There, that's great. You're onto something now. Don't get your hopes up and you won't get hurt.

Slumping back against the bed, I felt hopeless. It was pointless to think he'd notice me.

"What are you doing?" I screamed at myself, and even stomped my foot. The idea of going to a party was nerve-racking in itself, then add on Beau being there, and I wasn't sure what to think, or wear.

I eventually settled on the jean shorts and a black tank top that read: Somethin' Bad's About to Happen.

It wasn't mine, it was also Laney's.

"Are you ready yet?" Laney asked, peeking her head through the open door. "Gavin's in the parking lot."

With a sigh, I turned to face her, ready to get this weekend over with.

Squealing, Laney's hand clasped over her mouth as her eyes traveled over my body. "Oh, my God! Look at you and your body. Who knew you actually had curves under those sweatpants?"

I waved my hand in her face, trying to move her out of the way. "Oh stop. I wear regular clothes to school."

"Barely. Yoga pants and sweats don't count as clothes." Her hands then cupped my breasts. "And you have tits. I never knew that."

"They're comfy." Taking her hands in mine, I removed them from my breasts.

"Still, they're not everyday clothes."

"Shut up," I pushed her out of my way, "and let's go before I change my mind and put my sweatpants back on."

"We're going."

After digging through a couple boxes, I tossed some clothes in a bag and we were running out our dorm room to meet Gavin.

THE REALITY OF what I was doing didn't hit me until we were at the lake and I saw his gray Ford parked in the field. He was here.

Gavin drove us out to Lake Martin where a guy named Miles Wheatley was having a party. Apparently, he was a good friend of his, and Miles's parents owned a house right on the lake.

With my heart pounding rapidly in my chest, ready to burst at any moment, my shaking hand reached for the door handle. I wanted to vomit and then slap myself for allowing a guy I'd never actually spoken with to hold so much control over me.

I turned to glare at Laney as Gavin watched me with amusement. "I'm only staying for tonight. I'm leaving in the morning." I had no idea how I was going to get back, but I'd find a way somehow.

"Fine, but you're getting drunk tonight and enjoying yourself."

I snorted. Get drunk and enjoy myself? Sure, I could do that, right?

There was no harm in being a college graduate for a weekend. Party. Let myself relax and enjoy life for once. Slow sip bourbon and shotgun a beer. Get high on the night and breathe in the smells of lake water and whiskey while dancing barefoot in the Alabama red clay.

I could do this.

Opening the door, country music bellowed through the field, headlights lighting up a field full of pickup trucks. Among the trucks were hundreds of people, half-naked and swaying with beer and Solo Cups in hand. Smoke swirled from around the fire near the lake, laughter and music resonating in the air.

So this was what I had been missing out on all these years?

At first, I didn't think it was much, and then I saw the crowd and heard the music. The warm breeze and the energy in the air washed through me. The atmosphere was captivating.

I could see the lake in the distance and a large gray home with dozens of college graduates surrounding it; some I recognized, others I didn't.

Most everyone was on the lawn leading down to the water or the dock, which sprawled out and curved around a swimming bend in the lake.

To the right were tents surrounding a bonfire. Though the sun was still dancing along the tree line, smoke billowed up while sparks moved and swirled as guys fussed with the logs, longnecks in hand. A fire shined, glowing brighter as we walked, and the crackling of firewood could be heard over the conversations around me.

My heart fluttered watching the scene before me. These people were relaxing. . . living, just letting go of everything and enjoying themselves. I could do that, right?

To my right, Laney wrapped her arm in mine, steering me in the direction of the house where a keg was on the deck. "Let's get you a drink."

"Maybe we could start slow, like with water."

"No." She shot me down instantly with a scowl. "We start now."

The thought of drinking beer made me want to gag. Laney noticed and elbowed me. "Live a little, girl. Look." She raised her hand and pointed near the lake to where the bonfire was. "Let's grab drinks and head down there. Gavin's down there with Blaine and Wade."

My eyes went wide. "You mean Blaine, as in Beau's twin sister?"

"Yes." Laney gave me that look, the one that begged me not to be weird. "She's here."

I was begging myself not to be weird.

Beau was not only the hottest man on the planet, but he had a beautiful twin sister and a gorgeous older brother, Jensen. I was actually surprised their parents didn't have any more kids, considering how attractive their children were. If I were them, I would have just kept having kids to populate the world with beautiful Ryland babies.

The keg was surrounded with about five guys, all laughing until Laney and I approached. Then it was all eyes on us. Laney winked at them when someone handed her two red plastic cups to fill.

I watched closely as she filled the cups to the brim, before handing me what looked to be urine in a cup and smelled exactly as I remembered beer to smell like. From the time I was five, to the day he finally left when I was fifteen, my dad drank every Sunday to the point where he passed out. Believe me, I remembered the smell distinctively.

Stepping down from the porch, I watched my boots sinking into the dirt. "I hope you don't expect me to actually drink this." I stared offensively at the cup, regretting my thoughts of shot gunning a beer.

"Humor me. At least pretend to drink it, because there's Beau—" she brought her cup casually to her lips, smiling "—and you need to look like you at least fit in with this crowd."

The mention of his name sent my heart thudding out of control. My hands shook, the beer splashing around over my fingers as I gripped the cup a little too tight.

Laney noticed and shook her head. "I can't take you anywhere."

My eyes frantically searched for him, scanning the lawn, the lake, and then I was rewarded with the sight by the fire.

Beau Ryland.

The love of my life, right there.

His body was leaning casually to one side on a log, a beer dangling in his hand and a guitar at his feet. Wearing a dark gray T-shirt and jeans with that same old red baseball hat I remembered, he was irresistible. There was a certain modesty to him, a slow grace in his movements. He was calm, attentive to the conversations around him.

I wanted to go sit next to him, introduce myself as his future wife and baby mama, and then have a drink with him. Only my nerves rooted me in place and I realized how pathetic all that sounded.

He probably wouldn't even give me the time of day.

As the sun began to sink down, I watched him and the way he interacted with everyone.

Too bad I wasn't watching where I was walking. Overgrown grass made it hard to see where we were going.

Not paying attention to my surroundings, Laney and I walked through the yard, my stare on Beau.

And then, as graceful as I was, I tripped over a log as we went down the hill. I wasn't sure what it looked like to others, but it was mortifying for me.

I did the move where I face-planted and flopped down the hill into another log. There went my beer, and me, sailing through the air.

When I landed, on Beau Ryland's lap.

On.

His.

Fucking.

Lap.

"Fuck, are you okay?" Beau gasped, his eyes wide as he helped me to a sitting position and touched my face, pushing my hair out of the way to examine me.

Well my plan for nonchalantly bumping into him worked, didn't it?

I didn't answer. I think I was in shock at what just happened, and my mind was racing.

He's touching me!

His knees were in the dirt now, kneeling before me. "Shit, you're bleeding." His head turned. "Miles, get me a towel and some ice." Someone tossed a T-shirt at him and he pressed it to my head.

The last thing I wanted to do that night was announce my presence to Beau Ryland by falling on my face. I'd imagined a calm, casual, and, hell, even sexy introduction.

Not one where he was hovering over me—along with ten others—applying a T-shirt to my head where I was apparently bleeding.

It was evident I hadn't mastered the tuck and roll.

Instead, I probably resembled something similar to my mother when she saw a spider—arms flailing, legs scrambling, and a look of pure horror.

It wasn't the first time I had ever looked at him, but it was the first time I'd seen him in person in four years. He had a manly appearance to his six-foot frame. Muscular with a defined chest and arms, I could tell he spent some time inside the gym. His hair was longer than I had seen it in the past, chocolate strands grazing his thick lashes that framed his sky blue eyes.

As I laid there, a man of pure heavenly beauty staring down at me in concern, I realized my possibility of needing stitches took any romance out of our first formal introduction.

Why are you so pretty? my dazed mind wondered.

"Can you talk?"

See, he thinks there's something mentally wrong with me. Great.

"I'm fine," I mumbled, glaring at my now empty beer, the cup magically still in my hand.

How did I not spill that?

They mistook my glare for thinking I needed another one, and someone laughed, "Get Tumbles another beer."

Beau's lips quirked into a smile, but he said nothing to them.

Nice. I got a nickname already.

Ten minutes later, I was propped against a cooler, another beer being placed in my hand, while Blaine, Beau's twin sister, performed first aid to my forehead, giving me a cheerful smile.

Blaine had been going to college at Auburn University for six years. Her majors switched monthly from what I'd heard.

"I got this," she told me, digging through a first aid kit. "I'm Blaine. I'm going to school to be a registered nurse, so this is great practice," she said, sweeping a wet cotton wipe over my forehead. With a heart-shaped face and tender blue eyes, she had a gentle touch I appreciated, given how sore my face was. "So you're in good hands."

I hope this doesn't leave a scar.

"Glad I could help you out." My tone was laced with sarcasm, but I gave her a small smile. I didn't want her to think I was a bitch.

"I thought you wanted to be a lawyer, B-Love," Miles noted, smiling at Blaine and rubbing his bare stomach before taking a handful of chips and shoving them in his mouth.

"Too much school for that." She glared over at Miles. "And don't call me B-Love, asswipe. I'm nothing to you and certainly not your B, or your love."

"You know, if you would have stuck with law to begin with, you would have graduated already."

Blaine scowled, her touch still gentle as she cleaned my wound. "Shut the fuck up. No one was even talking to you."

Miles grinned, mouthing, "She loves me," and pointing to Blaine.

My focus shifted to Beau, who was now across from us, watching his sister and me.

"I'll be back to check on you," Blaine said after applying a bandage to my forehead. Bet I looked attractive.

"Are you sure you're all right?" Beau asked, obviously concerned for my well-being. I knew then he had *the perfect* voice. It was soft, but had a shiver-inducing rasp. I knew if he ever whispered in my ear, I'd have all-over tingles that shot straight to my legs, spreading them just for him.

Breathe, Bentley. Breathe, because if you don't, he's going to think there's something mentally wrong with you or start CPR.

On second thought, don't breathe. Pretend you're dead. Mouth to mouth would be amazing.

Look at that face, those eyes! Who knew there was a shade of blue like that? So pretty.

Beau eyed me cautiously when I didn't reply. His voice and eyes had rendered me speechless. Pathetic. "Honey. . . are you okay?"

Honey? He called me honey.

I sighed, my head throbbing. I would have bet a million dollars that Beau Ryland would have never looked twice at a girl like me. He was the type of guy who caused you to literally stare in fascination that God made someone so beautiful. And had I not fallen, he wouldn't have noticed me tonight.

Maybe my incapability to stay on my own two feet was fate.

But, damn it, now he knows you're really alive. There goes your chance at mouth to mouth.

Loser. He knows you're alive; you're sitting up and clearly breathing.

As he stared at me, waiting on my reply, I wondered if he thought there might be something mentally wrong with me. Surely my inability to speak was an indication I wasn't all there.

"What?" I wanted to say more, but I was speechless at the idea of him talking to me.

"I asked if you were okay," he repeated, his brow scrunching in concentration, at what, I had no idea. "You took a pretty good fall there."

I fell for you. Oh God, don't you dare say that out loud. Don't!

"Oh. Right." Thanks for the reminder. "I'm fine," I mumbled, holding a bag of ice to my tender forehead.

Watching him for a moment, I almost began drooling. In an attempt to control myself, I lowered my eyes and rested my gaze on his hands.

Sweet Jesus, he had nice hands.

Someone called his name, pulling him away without another word.

Great, there he goes. Your chance to convince him you were meant to be together is out the window and you're left dirty and bleeding.

"Was that for attention, or did you really trip?" Laney asked, taking a seat next to me on the ground. She smelled like vodka and dirt.

I stared down at my banged up and bruised legs and realized the dirt smell was coming from me. I was covered in it.

"Not exactly something I'd do for attention, Lane."

She shrugged me off. "Uh, well, listen. . . ."

I knew where this was going when Laney sat down. She wanted to go off with Gavin. "Go." I raised my new beer. "I'm not moving from this place right here. I'll be here waiting, so if you decide to leave, you'd better come get my ass."

She grinned. "Did Bentley Rae just say 'ass'?"

"Shut up."

Giggling, she stood to brush the dust from her stonewashed jeans. "Okay, well, don't move then."

How was it fair I had to wear shorts and she got to wear jeans?

Laney left, and there I was, by myself next to the fire, surrounded by ten people I didn't know. I guess I should say ten people who didn't know me. I knew who they were. They were friends of Beau's from high school, and they were all smiling at me.

I felt uncomfortable with their stares and would have moved, but I was afraid if I stood, I'd fall face first into the fire.

The heat from the fire felt like it was sucking the air from my lungs as it warmed my face to hotter than the night's air. Orange flames swirled, flickering and dancing in the sky as I nursed my beer. The fire crackled and projected shadows on the house behind us.

The fire, like the party, was pulsing, glowing with embers that seemed to move with the rhythm of the music bellowing from the nearby stereo—it was all mesmerizing, or maybe I was a little concussed from my unintentional front handspring gone wrong.

A half an hour later, my beer was nearly gone and I heard his voice again.

"You know—" Beau took a seat next to me "—your landing was impressive."

I rolled my eyes, refusing to look at him when I felt the burn of my cheeks along with every other part of my body. "I'm sure it was. It's a good thing I landed in your lap. Or, yeah, whatever."

Stop talking.

And then I thought about close he was sitting.

Holy shit, Beau Ryland is sitting right next to me.

If I moved two inches, our bodies would be touching.

Move.

No, you should fall. Just pretend you're lightheaded and fall into him. Face first.

If I could have fallen sitting up, and not have looked ridiculous, I would have done it just to bury my face in his chest, or lap.

Lap?

Must be the beer.

"I'm just playin', relax." He nudged me with his elbow, smirking. "But hey, I'm not complaining about where you landed."

How can I? Look at you and then look at me. Ugh!

Bringing my beer to my lips, I finished it off, feeling absolutely humiliated.

"Beau!" someone called his name again. He turned, looking over his shoulder, and I did the same.

"Fuck," he mumbled, and then our eyes met, briefly. "I'll be back."

And then he was gone, again, for another twenty minutes.

When he returned, he smiled down at me, lifting his brow at my shirt, entertained. It was then I remembered what it actually said. I wanted to rip it off.

Somethin' Bad's About To Happen.

Something bad did happen.

I felt so embarrassed.

"Hey there, pretty girl." I could immediately tell that in those twenty or so minutes he was gone, he had a few too many drinks. "Are you okay?"

"Really, I'm fine," I mumbled, still not sure what to make of this. Dropping the ice bag to my lap, I stared at it, refusing to look at him.

"You look a little—" he shrugged, scratching the side of his face "—out of it."

"Well, I did fly through the air and smack my head on the ground." I straightened out my legs. "Damn, I'm going to have so many bruises tomorrow."

He chuckled softly, leaning into me as he reached inside his jacket he was now wearing. "You look like you're in pain. Here." He flashed a bottle of whiskey at me. "Try this."

So I did, because when Beau Ryland offered you a drink, you took that damn drink.

GASOLINE AND SMOKE FILLED the night, but the moon was so bright you didn't even need a flashlight to see your way down to where the water slipped up the bank. A crowd of twenty sat around a bonfire, laughing and letting go, and I was one of them.

Breathing in deep, my heart soared. I felt like I was shaking all the way to the bone from being around Beau. With his help, I'd also finished off a bottle of whiskey.

I was drinking with Beau. Like a normal person.

Only I was low-lidded and moving slowly, every thought, every turn of my head exaggerated. I couldn't tell you the last time I'd been drunk.

"What's your name?" he asked in my ear, closer than ever. We were now nearly touching.

He looked at me, the blue in his eyes seemed darker and brighter. It felt like he was trying to convince me to trust him. Breathing deeply, I watched his face. The scruff of his jaw begged me to reach out and touch it. I could almost feel the shivers I knew it would cause. His eyes remained watchful, waiting for my answer.

"Bentley Rae Schow."

Why did you say your whole name? Pathetic. So freaking pathetic.

His left arm moved to wrap around my shoulders, dragging me through the dirt so our bodies touched.

Beau winked, his smile too crooked for his own good. He was slow talking, with eyes bright and his arm wrapped around me. "I'm Beau Ryland."

What had I gotten myself into?

"I know who you are." I couldn't take my eyes off his, entranced that he was looking at me, touching me.

He didn't seem surprised I knew who he was, more than likely everyone here knew him. "Is that so?"

I nodded, the motion painful. "Uh-huh."

"Mmmm," he hummed, a smirk growing on his face and lighting up his eyes, as if he felt challenged and was accepting it. "Looks like I'm gonna have to work to impress you then."

Nope. You did that years ago.

He squeezed my shoulder after taking a drink. "I think you're in good hands tonight."

"Yes, because we know I can't walk," I teased, my own smile taking over.

"All the more reason for you to stay beside me."

Beau was interesting to me, and now more than ever because he was completely different than I assumed he'd be. The more we interacted, the more curious I became.

"You don't have to stay with me. I know you probably have friends here."

He looked over at me, sporting a smile that was higher on one side, but my eyes caught his, so blue, shadowed by the night. "I'd rather be here with you, pretty girl."

PICKING UP HIS GUITAR from beside him, he swept his gaze to mine, smiling, as if to let me know he was about to show me something. The idea of seeing him sing sent me into a frivolous nervous shake. I'd never heard him play in person before.

"Should I play something for you?"

I tried to keep my voice from sounding like a four-year-old little girl who had just received her first Barbie. "Yes!" *Shit, tone it down a little.* "I mean. . . if that's what you want to do, or, whatever."

Beau chuckled, lightly and ran his hand over the back of his neck.

I had heard him sing on many occasions, but only online. I was a frequent visitor on YouTube after the shows, trying to decipher the shaky, screaming girl, cell phone footage.

The crowd around us was rowdy and ready for something more, begging Beau to play them something wild. Apparently, there was more rock in this boy than country, and he lived for playing tunes like "Walk This Way" or "Highway to Hell."

"C'mon, man!" they would shout each time a new song came on the radio and he resisted. I wondered what it was he was resisting, because I really wanted to hear him sing.

He moved away from me, standing casually on the other side of the fire.

Blaine sat down next to me. It seemed I went from the hands of one Ryland to the next.

She was all touchy-feely with me and kept hugging me.

"He's on tour, right?"

Blaine grinned. "My brother is going to be a star, just wait. He's going to headline his *own tour* someday."

I know he will.

"Hey, Legs," someone said, handing me another beer.

Taking the cup, I recognized him as Miles, a friend of Beau's, and smiled at him. "Hey."

He was the same guy harassing Blaine earlier.

"How's the head? You seem confused if you're hanging around this guy." He leaned forward and smacked Beau, in the chest with his palm.

Beau shook his head in amusement, catching himself so he didn't step back in the fire.

Miles practically sat on my lap beside me on the log, his arm wrapped around my shoulders, pulling me against his side. I seemed to be the life of the party, since you know, I made such an entrance.

Miles was the same age as Beau. He was another football star who took very little in life seriously. From what I heard around school, he'd been mooching off his parents since he graduated, but occasionally painted houses with Gavin and Wade when he wasn't touring with Beau.

Gavin and Laney returned from wherever they had been. Gavin focused on Beau, giving him a head nod. "Play something."

Beau didn't say yes, but he also didn't say no.

And then our eyes drifted to one another with the flickering of the fire light. I wanted to beg him to play. I think my eyes did a little because he winked at me and set his beer down.

"So, Bentley, how into Beau are you? Do I stand a chance tonight?" Miles smiled, giving me a suggestive nod.

Blaine gagged. "She has better taste than to give you a chance, Miles."

"Oh stop." Miles pawed at her, like he was imitating a valley girl.

He was attractive, had a nice lean body, but he was no Beau Ryland. And I think I was taller than him, so that wasn't going to happen. Ever.

Beau tipped his head with a deep chuckle that shook his chest. "Bentley, meet Miles Wheatley." He rolled his eyes, focusing on Miles. "Hands off."

Hands off? What did that mean?

Miles smiled and moved closer to me when Beau plugged in an amp beside him where his guitar was now leaning against a log, but then he stopped and faced Miles again. "Don't even think about it, Miles," Beau warned. "She's with me."

She's with me? What did that mean?

Whistles and shouts broke out in the crowd of nearly twenty, but Beau didn't look up.

He placed the guitar pick in his mouth and talked around it. "All right, here goes nothing," Beau mumbled into the microphone, still not looking up.

If I didn't know any better, I would have thought they planned this, to have Beau sing all night. Given they had equipment and everything.

I took in the sight before me—the fire and lake behind him. It was perfect, a smeared scarlet red running wild over the night.

Removing his guitar pick from his mouth, he gave a soft smile and messed with the amp and his guitar. "Here's a little Tim McGraw for ya."

Blaine let out a scream and then raised her drink in the air, whistling at the opening notes.

Beau began to play his guitar, eyes down and focused.

As the opening notes drifted through the air, Beau leaned into the microphone and began singing.

Everyone started dancing around, feeling the upbeat tempo.

When Beau did look up, he smiled at the enthusiasm.

Blaine had me up and dancing with her, Miles and two other guys watching us closely. I wasn't paying them any mind. All my focus was on Beau.

As the song reached a crescendo, he leaned his head back, singing with passion, belting out the chorus with a roughness I'd never ever heard before. I stopped dancing and watched.

He was so alive right in front of me. It was clear to see there was a side to this guy I never expected. And how could that be? I had faithfully worshiped him for years and had no idea *this* was the way he was.

As he finished "Down On The Farm," he went straight into the coolest version of "Baby Likes To Rock It" I have ever heard with a growling edge to his baritone voice.

I was ready to throw myself at his feet in the dirt, naked, and let him do anything he wanted to me. Not that I hadn't been already, but now I was *that* girl completely. Judging by the way he regarded me, he knew it too.

My problem was, he was utterly surrounded now with women trying to get his attention. Half-naked women in their bikinis, despite the sun being set, dancing around together seductively.

When the song ended, I finished my beer and smiled up at Beau as he laughed.

I knew this moment was something I'd never forget.

"This one is mine," he said, winking at me.

My heart fluttered, knowing he was about to sing something he wrote, words he'd poured himself into. And then he sang, "*Well take a look at what's left in that sunset. Fireflies poppin' like the fourth of July, yeah, you're gonna wanna see every single thing I'm gonna show you tonight.*"

The way the night darkened everything around him but his face, made it more thrilling to hear him like this. He had a prowess and distinctive voice unlike anything I'd ever heard. It was raw, honest, and had more range than I would have initially thought after hearing him talk. He owned that sandy resonance coupled with a masculine southern drawl.

The tune was catchy, and I was in awe at the way he'd strummed his guitar, never missing a cord. His teasing smile left me speechless. I didn't know if I should laugh or stare at how beautiful he was. "*Got the perfect scene set of a moonlight glowin'. Just keep them baby blues wide open. Girl take a look around, yeah, it's goin' down. It's goin' down just right.*"

Holy. Crap.

In the background, I heard girls giggling and sighing over the lyrics. One, who'd obviously had too much to drink, even hollered out that she'd take him up on that offer, but up until the end, his eyes never left mine.

Music filled the night, the sound rushing through me as I swayed. Some reacted to the beat, while others talked amongst themselves but felt the words Beau was singing.

Once he was finished, he set his guitar down and came right back over to me as everyone clapped.

THEY TURNED THE radio back on, another catchy tune surrounding us. It was then I took a seat on the log, feeling like I'd had too much to drink and needed to sit down.

Beau did the same. His arm around me was heavy as he scanned the crowd, slowly bringing a bottle of what looked to be bourbon to his lips.

I noticed his attention was elsewhere. "Are you looking for someone?"

His eyes narrowed on the crowd. "I'm lookin' for your boyfriend. Surely you have one, and I just got his girl drunk, and now I have my hands on her. I'd be fuckin' pissed if I was him."

"Keep looking," I teased. "Let me know if you see him. I hear he's a complete asshole."

He laughed, shaking his head, his own motions just as slow. "You seem so innocent. Have you ever been kissed?" Beau asked, his attention wavering from the fire, to me. For a brief moment, he took in my face. I was stunned-stupid with shock that he would ask me that.

Is he trying to offend me? Have I been kissed? Pfft.

"Shut up. I thought you were a gentleman."

"Mmmm." *Oh God, make that sound again. In my ear please.* "Never said that. I prey on the weak."

I snorted.

"Are you going to answer the question?"

"Yeah." My eyes left his for the fire, as I nearly swallowed my tongue at where the conversation had suddenly shifted. How did this happen? I tried really hard not to let him know how embarrassed I was, working to breathe calmly.

"Yeah what?"

"I've been kissed before."

Play it cool, I told myself.

"By a boy?" His question came out with a laugh as he leaned on his arms, propping up his relaxed body. He was probably hoping it was a girl.

"Well, yeah." Trying to show him I was comfortable— though I wasn't—I leaned back on my arms, mimicking his position.

"Sure you have." The sarcasm in his voice was clear, and I didn't appreciate it, and he knew it. Looking over at him, I watched him gaze down at my position and then my chest. "And I bet you've never had sex before, have you, pretty girl?"

What the fuck? Did I look like a child to him?

Glancing around, I caught sight of those around the fire, a few watching us, others caught up in their own conversations.

"Shut up," I said, giving his shoulder a push, teasing him. "It's none of your business anyway."

"I'm just teasin' ya." His eyes caught mine, and we stared in silence. His forehead creased in deep concentration before he finally asked, "Do you want me to kiss you?"

I felt that question in my gut, like a punch. My heart bounced and then settled on a hard thumping beat. Just his presence made me so ridiculously nervous, but suddenly I felt brave.

Don't be shy and naïve. Act normal, like this happens to you all the time.

"If you want to."

Tilting his head, he stared at me in silence and I could tell he understood what I was feeling. The anticipation, the fear, and the excitement, it was all there for him to see for himself, if he wanted. I was trying to be indifferent. I didn't lean in, nor did I act like I wanted it to happen.

And then it happened.

Moving closer, he had me trapped securely against his side. I felt his hot breath on my skin, and then the tender brush of his lips.

"So are you going to let me kiss you sometime soon?" he asked, moving my hair to the side and brushing his lips down my neck, so close the warmth of his body overwhelmed me. I had never been kissed on the neck. Ever. Not even when I lost my virginity.

Then came the tingles, the tiny hairs standing on end, and a warm feeling situated itself nicely in my gut. I wanted to be kissed on my neck all night.

Screw the lips, keep kissing my neck!

"I wasn't aware you wanted to." Heated cheeks and hearts beating fast, we stared at each other for a moment. I tried moving back a little, but he wasn't having it as he kept a firm grip on me. Though he was making me wait, he wasn't about to let an inch of space come between us.

Dipping his head forward, I had his lips again. "I think you are well aware of the fact I want to kiss you, Bentley." His lips became steady as he kissed up and down my neck, sending shivers through my entire body.

"Hmmm," I hummed, enjoying the feel of him finally touching me. "I don't think I was aware of that."

He pulled back, his eyes locking with mine. His sky blue eyes sparkled as a coy smile graced his lips and he leaned in. "You knew. You did."

And at last, his lips touched mine. My body jerked at the feeling of lightening rushing through my veins as his lips fused with mine. His free hand that wasn't on my hip pulled my face securely against his as his tongue glided along my bottom lip, and I opened my mouth to accommodate. With his hand sliding into my hair, he kissed me deeper, giving me his tongue, tasting of whiskey and cinnamon.

As he surrounded me, heavy and constricting, the taste on my tongue was the only thing that mattered. It was a moment I would never forget and a feeling I would never understand.

His kisses became filled with passion, more urgent, as if he wanted more. Moving closer, his hands fused me to him, with no complaints by me.

How does he control my reaction to him this way?

And why me?

Closing my eyes, I let the sensation soak over me like rain, coating everything and encouraging me to believe this was really happening, that Beau Ryland was actually here with me. There were hundreds of women here on this lake, but because I took a flying leap through the air while I wasn't watching where I was going, I was the one in his arms, lip-locked.

With a sigh, he pulled back, and I could see it in his eyes. I could see the significance and feel his passion. He felt something for me, even if it was just for tonight.

But then it ended. He drew away, the soft and tender smile matching his eyes. "Told you I wanted to."

"Well, not necessarily," I pointed out. "You asked if I was going to let you kiss me sometime soon. You didn't say the words 'I want to kiss you.' You could tell I wanted you to kiss me, but I didn't realize you'd kiss me stupid."

He raised an eyebrow, smirking. "Kiss you stupid?"

"Um, well, I apparently forget how to speak around you, so yes, you kissed me stupid."

He winked and gave me one more kiss, this one lingering on my lips a little longer.

With a sigh, I leaned back and stared at the stars.

Despite my grand entrance, maybe tonight wouldn't be so bad. If only I could shut the fuck up and stop talking in front of him.

Chapter Four

LITTLE BIT MORE OF YOU

BEAU

WHAT WAS I doing?

Was I leading her on?

No, you're just. . . I had no answer to finish the thought.

I knew I was nowhere ready for any type of relationship, but I didn't want to let this girl go.

"What's going on with you and the hottie with the legs?" Miles asked when I was retrieving beer from the keg, one for me, one for her.

"Nothing," I mumbled, barely making eye contact. I'd known Miles since I was a kid. If I looked up at him, he'd know I had intentions with this girl. For tonight anyway.

"She looks like she took a pretty good fall there, enough that you—"

Glaring, I shook my head before he could say anything. I knew where he was going with that. He saw me kiss her and he was going to point it out, or ask where I was going with it.

Even I didn't know why I kissed her. There was just something about those eyes and the way the fire sparked against them that had me wanting a closer look.

Miles didn't let my glare stop him from watching Bentley dancing around by the fire with Blaine and two other girls. He let his eyes wander a little too long and a pang of jealousy gnawed at me. I shoved him back. "Knock it off."

He held up his palms, grinning, as he watched me grab two beers from the cooler beside the tapped keg. "Okay, I see she's spoken for. . . at least for tonight." Then he gave a nod to the house. "You can use my room if you want."

I rolled my eyes. "It's not like that."

He knew I had my eye on her from earlier when I told him to keep his hands off. Miles let out a dark laugh while raising his beer to his lips, shaking his head. "Yeah, right."

My problem was, if I didn't show interest in Bentley, one of these guys here would, like Miles.

You could be damn sure I wasn't going to allow that to happen. No fuckin' way. The idea made me want to run down to the fire and grab her, haul her over my shoulder, and lead her away like some kind of caveman.

Miles made a humming sound, as if he knew my answer of, 'It's not like that.' was bullshit. Even I didn't know if it was true, but I knew I wanted another kiss soon.

I craned my neck forward to look over at her. Watching her dance, and those tan legs, hell, I wanted more than a kiss.

"Sure, Beau, but hey—" he motioned me forward and then gave a nod over his shoulder "—Payton's been lookin' around for ya."

Fuck. I forgot she was here. Damn it. She was gonna think we could hook up, and the last thing I wanted was to be wrapped back up with her.

Payton was in Memphis with me about three months back and we fucked around for a weekend and then called it off, like we always did. She was toxic. She consumed me and my thoughts any time I was with her. And when she left, I was reminded of how lonely I was and that it didn't matter if I lost myself in her for an hour, or two. I would never escape that feeling with her.

My problem was anytime we were in the same city together, she assumed we'd get together despite me telling her I couldn't keep doing it.

I nodded and tried to walk away, only Payton spotted me.

Ignoring her, I kept walking toward the fire and Bentley, who was now watching me curiously, still dancing around with my sister. My sister wasn't exactly a social butterfly, but the fact that she instantly took to Bentley made me realize there was something special about this girl.

Watching them now, you would have thought they were best friends.

I flashed her a smile, but Payton approached me at the same time. Bubbly and smiling, I knew she was drunk.

"Hey, babe," she purred as her arm locked around my elbow and she leaned in to kiss my cheek.

Only I dodged it and tipped my head to the left so she couldn't reach. "Don't."

Payton looked offended and jerked her head back in surprise, her wild brown locks falling freely out of the black and red trucker hat with my dad's bar plastered across the front. "What?"

"We can't keep. . ." I gave a nod south, "doing that. I told you in Memphis."

She laughed, or giggled, whatever it was she did that I used to find adorable. "I didn't think you were serious."

"I was completely serious."

I started to walk away, but Payton tugged me back right before I reached the fire, her pleading green eyes finding mine. "You've never said no to me."

"I know, but I can't." Without meaning to, my stare drifted to Bentley, who was now being coerced into doing shots of tequila with my sister and her friends.

"Why now? Someone else got your attention?" She gave a quick drift of her eyes to Bentley and then back to me.

I laughed condescendingly. "Don't do that to me. You said it was over a long time ago. Just because you keep leadin' me on, isn't my fault."

She frowned, knowing there was a lot of fucking truth to my words.

"Excuse me." I moved away from Payton, her hand dropping from my arm, and then I was standing a few feet from Blaine and Bentley, who were practically holding one another up. When I reached them, both had their arms around my shoulder immediately, squishing me between the two of them.

"Uh, what are you doing to her?" I asked, looking to Blaine for an answer, noticing Bentley was so drunk now I was actually holding her up.

She shrugged, glossy-eyed and giggling. "Gettin' this girl drunk. Fuck, she's awesome!" Blaine brought the bottle of tequila to her lips, threw her head back, and took a drink. "Now play something for me."

I saw the way Bentley watched me when I played for her earlier, and I wanted that look again, the one that said she was totally captivated by my presence. For so long, I never paid much attention to the way anyone looked at me, not since Payton. It was a feeling deep inside I never fully understood until I craved the connection it gave me once I finally had it again.

I had one-night stands with the intention of getting physical pleasure, and knowing once I did, the thrill would be gone and any feeling I had toward them would be sustained.

This—what kept drawing me to Bentley—wasn't anything like that.

Finally, I felt something, a spark, a desire for something more, and it was Bentley who I saw it in. With irises so dark they resembled midnight, I found it ironic we were the complete opposite. Where I was sky blue eyes, the color of the clearest days, she had the darker ones, consuming me. It was as if I could see myself in the shadows of her eyes, my loneliness staring back at me.

I moved back, out of their grasps, and Blaine held Bentley up, both laughing. Bentley raised her hands up in the air. "I can't believe I did a flip into you!"

Her voice was loud, and right in my ear, but I laughed anyway. "I think your shirt jinxed you," I teased, winking at her.

"Maybe I should take it off." It was the first time I'd seen her flirt, with anyone, and it was most certainly directed at me. Even when I kissed her, she was standoffish and timid. This wasn't timid.

"Maybe you should." My problem when I said that was she actually started to.

I stopped her, kissing her forehead. "I was kidding. Don't take it off. . .yet."

Her cheeks instantly flushed as she stepped back, smiling, cherry-red lips calling to me. She fiddled with a strand of hair, like she was trying to think of something snarky to say.

Fuck, what was with this girl that drew me in and held me there?

Picking up my guitar again, I whispered in Blaine's her. "Take it easy on her."

She knew what I meant. One look at Bentley with a bottle of tequila pressed to her lips, she knew.

Payton had the nerve to sit down next to the fire as I began to play, crossing her legs seductively.

Fuck, this should be interesting.

Maybe I was being a dick, or I'd always been one, but I decided on something new I found fitting for tonight. "This one is call 'Little Bit More Of You'."

"It started with a sweet look and that's all it took for this old boy to get torn up and wrapped around your pretty little finger. Ever since I found you. I've been all about you. Girl, you might as well be the only girl in this town."

With the lyrics clearly directed at Bentley, Payton huffed out a breath and walked off in the other direction toward a group of men, where Miles and Gavin were now standing as well.

My gaze turned back to Bentley. She was slumped against a log, giggling with Blaine, and so far gone I was surprised she was still sitting up straight.

Once our eyes locked and I felt trapped, something stirred in my chest and I was unable to shake the feeling.

When the song was done, I set down my guitar, and took a seat next to her, the warmth of her body practically scalding.

"So, pretty girl." I drew out the words, slowly reaching for the bottle of tequila, because she was now having trouble focusing on me she was laughing so hard. "Maybe you've had enough."

Bright glassy eyes, sweet creamy skin highlighted from the alcohol—I had to laugh. She was adorable. Usually, I found drunk women annoying. Bentley didn't even come close to fitting in that category.

She jumped up, yanking me up to a standing position. Her arms flung up and around my shoulders. I definitely had no complaints, but I feared she'd fall again.

I'll catch you.

Her eyes drifted to mine and then down to my lips. "Not even close, Beau." Her lips parted, her breath faster, anticipating my mouth on hers. And then she kissed me, again—the kind of kiss that held meaning and promise of more to come. Not just any kiss, a strong, determined kiss.

I knew that kiss. The soft brush of her tongue, her sweet captivating taste.

I wanted that too. I bet she was wet and ready for me to go further.

Fuck yeah.

When I looked into her eyes, she had an expression I hadn't seen before. I had never seen the look on another girl, and I certainly didn't understand the meaning behind it. There was a field full of people surrounding us, but I couldn't look away from her in that moment.

Breathing deeply, trying desperately to keep my erotic thoughts at bay. "Come with me," I whispered and drug her away from the fire to my truck where I sat her on the edge of the tailgate.

I had to have her alone.

Standing in front of her, between her legs, I ran my nose up her throat, kissing gently. As I did that, Bentley squirmed under my touch, wrapping her legs around my waist and drawing me closer.

Kissing her sent a wave of pleasure through my entire body. I ached to lay her back, let my hands roam, and fuck her right here, but resisted, seeing how the crowd around us would surely notice.

Ordinarily, that wouldn't have bothered me, seeing as about a dozen trucks around us had the same noises coming from them. Kissing the side of her neck, I became lost in the moment until her hand found my waist, drawing me into her more firmly.

She whispered my name, a breath caught in her throat.

Fuck, I wanted to take this so much further. I wanted to lay her back and cover her body with mine. I wanted her warmth. I wanted to feel her heartbeat against mine. I wanted. Just wanted for the first time in a long time.

Needing a breath, I drew back, my eyes flickered to her lips. "Slow down," I told her, hoping she understood the meaning. I didn't want to rush this.

"I can't," she gasped, her body tensing around me.

My problem was, I had been imagining in detail everything I wanted to do to her, so I couldn't slow those thoughts down either. My mind had gone wild thinking about kissing her in seclusion, licking up the side of her neck or kissing her breast and sucking her nipples into my mouth.

I gave thought to slipping my hand down her tiny shorts and feeling how wet she would be. And then another more drawn out thought of me removing those very shorts and slipping inside of her.

Fuck, you're an idiot. Keep going.

Blood surged through me when I started kissing her with more intensity, and it went straight to my dick. I was so hard and trying to draw back, keep from pushing her further when I knew she wouldn't remember anything in the morning.

The pent-up passion had been building, and even when I would pull back, I would groan, needing more, and bringing her mouth right back to mine.

Her kisses were urgent and full of passion, igniting everything I thought I'd lost inside of me, that burning desire to live in the moment.

Her body moved against mine in a desperate way, pulling me against her, tiny hands caressing me in ways I hadn't felt in so long and unlike anything I'd felt before.

Her soft hands swept over my shoulders and down the contours of my back. I let out a groan, pulling her hard against me. My mouth moved from its place against her neck back to her warm lips, moving frantically. Lust began drowning any rational thoughts I had about this and I was scrambling to gain control.

Time seemed to stand still, nothing else mattered but the two of us on the bed of my Ford. Taking off my flannel, I let go of Bentley and then moved to sit next to her on the tailgate. Our mouths collided again, and I groaned into hers, pulling her flush against my chest, hungry lips searching for more.

Her noises, subtle but so fucking sexy, left me wanting more. She moved then to straddle me. She had to feel my erection against her. She had to. I should have been concerned at the obvious display we were putting on, but I couldn't help it. I cared about none of that as much as I cared about the way my body was responding to her.

Her arousal was evident, as was mine, but how could I take this from her?

"Bentley," I sighed, keeping her firmly in place, my hands on her hips. "As great as this feels, we should slow down." It took me a moment to calm my need and hormones, but I did and finally looked down at her.

"I want you. It's okay," she assured me, grinding herself into me. I very nearly flipped her over on the truck bed and fucked her. Every time I touched her, throaty moans escaped. I wanted to feel more of her, so much more.

It was everything I could do *not* to.

"We can't."

Emotions I didn't understand swirled in her eyes, only I recognized rejection as one of them. "Sorry," she mumbled at my denial, untangling herself from me and then laying against the cool metal of the truck bed and glanced up at the sky.

"I just don't want you to think that's all I want." My words seemed lost, she was already assuming the worst.

Nodding, she wouldn't look at me, her gaze on the sky.

Afraid I'd already offended her, I studied the stars.

When I peeked back at her, she was passed out, sleeping on my arm, drooling.

Thank God.

Twisting around, I kissed her forehead and then carried her back to where Laney was. She remained out cold.

"Oh, you found her."

I laughed, watching Laney, who was about as drunk as Bentley was. "I did. Where's your tent?"

Laney gave a nod to a row of trees where the tents were lined up. "Over there."

"Hey," Laney called out when I was a few feet away.

"Yeah?"

"Thanks for, you know," Laney waved to me and Bentley, stumbling around in the uneven ground beneath our feet, "for not being a total douche."

I squinted at her as she tied a flannel to her waist, and then brought a cup to her lips. "What?"

"With Bentley. You're the only reason she came to this party. So thanks. For being cool."

I was the reason she came? Bentley didn't seem like someone who would go to a party just to meet me. . . or had she?

With what seemed like luck, I managed to get Bentley inside the tent without dropping her. Part of me wanted to stay in there with her, but then the more noble side weighed out, knowing if I did and she woke up, I might try something.

Scratch that. I *knew* I'd try something.

Instead, I covered her up with my flannel and went back to the party where AC/DC was blaring.

Miles caught me by the fire and sat next to me on the log after I put my guitar away inside my truck. He raised an eyebrow. "Where'd Legs go?"

I snorted, unsure of what to make of her friend's comment or Miles and why he was concerned with Bentley. "Passed out."

Miles handed me a beer. "And you didn't fuck her? Free game when that happens."

He wasn't serious, at least I hoped he wasn't. What kind of jerk would do that? Well, he might. He did sleep with my sister. Most guys know sisters are untouchable. But hey, they all fucked Payton, too, so where the hell was the brotherhood there?

I suppressed a sigh, turning my hat around backward. "No, Miles, I didn't. I'm not an asshole."

Around the fire, three girls were dancing to the radio, topless, and I noticed one was Payton. She was kissing another girl, eyes locked on mine trying to entice me into joining. She'd played this hand before, mostly when she was getting desperate for me to look her way.

I'll admit, it worked when we were younger, but not now. Especially not now.

Miles chuckled watching Payton. "Hmmm, interesting." He shifted in his chair, probably turned on by it. Leaning to one side, he relaxed and glanced at me again. "Does Legs have a boyfriend?"

"I don't think so." She hadn't mentioned one, and I asked her.

Did she lie to me?

Nah, she wasn't the lying type.

"Oh, I thought I heard someone here say she did."

Shrugging, I stood, taking the beer with me. "No idea."

Passing by her tent, I had to force myself not to go check on her. I found an empty tent and noticed by the coat inside of it, it was Gavin's and figured he wouldn't mind if I crashed in there with him.

Laying back against the vinyl, I breathed in deep, telling myself to stay in the tent.

The thought was there, and then without warning, I was hard again, imagining her kissing me and the way she felt wrapped around my body.

Damn it.

Had she really just showed up because I was going to be here? "Fuck," I groaned, feeling like I'd made a mistake turning her down.

Chapter Five

GET YOUR SHINE ON

BENTLEY

MY HEAD WAS pounding, a sharp pulsing in my ears and neck to a horrendous rhythm of a growling snore.

Fucking Laney.

"I hate you," I muttered, trying to shake her awake.

It didn't work.

Though I wanted her to, there was no way Laney could hear me with the horrific nasally noises coming from her. I'd been dealing with her snoring for four years now, and I knew it wasn't about to get any better. The more you tried to wake her, the worse it became.

Laney and I slept in a tent last night—though I wasn't exactly sure how I got in a tent—and I thought about sleeping outside at one point.

I mean, seriously, she sounded like a damn freight train every time she took a breath. I wondered how she stayed alive, surely she wasn't getting quality REM sleep sounding like that. No wonder she woke up tired all the time in college.

Grumbling to myself about the inner workings of Laney's respiratory system, I got out of the tent and sat by the smoking fire as Beau emerged from his own tent without a shirt on.

Holy shit, he's here again.

Seeing him wearing nothing but a pair of jeans, I almost choked on my own saliva.

Did I mention his belt was undone?

It was, and it was a shame he was buckling it.

Damn, look at that body.

If I were him, I would walk around half-naked all the time just because I could.

When he noticed me, he quickly pulled on the shirt he had tucked under his arm and then his hat.

"Hey there," he greeted me, scratching the back of his head. "How ya feelin'?"

"Like death," I mumbled. If death was a feeling, I was sure it resembled this.

Surrounding the fire were about a dozen people sprawled out in the grass, some awake, some out cold from the party last night. Around them were beer cans and empty liquor bottles.

With the way my body and head felt, I was sure at least a few of those bottles were from me. I was surprised I wasn't one of the passed out bodies by the fire judging by the taste in my mouth. I didn't even remember getting inside the tent.

Crap, what the hell was I thinking last night?

I hadn't been, that much was apparent. Judging by my headache, torn up knees, and the bandage on my head, the night hadn't been easy on me.

Clearly confused, I peeked over at Beau as if he held the answer. He grinned wider, but didn't say anything.

What in the world did I do last night?

The look in Beau's eyes and his smile made me question if we. . .well, you know. But I was fully clothed this morning and still wearing that damn tank top. . . *Wait.* I looked down at my shirt.

Fuck. I was wearing someone's flannel shirt.

Where the hell did this come from?

I stared down at it offensively, my eyes wide, and then looked at Beau questioningly.

"How's your head?"

"Hurts."

He could tell I was wondering why I was wearing this shirt, and noted, "You look good wearing my shirt."

Can I keep it? I'll make a blanket out of it—or better yet—a pillowcase.

"How'd I get your shirt on?"

His smile faded and he glanced over at the lake in the distance where a few people on the dock enjoyed the peace before the parties started up again.

Taking a seat next to me, he bumped my shoulder in the process. "I gave it to you." He shrugged, leaning forward so his elbows were resting on his knees, his head hanging as if his neck were sore.

"Oh." I gave him a half smile, wishing I could remember last night, but it made my head hurt to even think about it.

What if we had sex and I didn't remember it? How tragic would that be?

Looking at Beau, I noticed he wasn't smiling. Had I offended him?

His hand ran through his dark brown hair, and then he put his ball cap on. "You don't remember last night, do you?"

I swallowed, heavily, feeling like my heart was going to explode. "No."

"That's a shame." And then he waited for our eyes to meet. "You don't remember me kissing you?"

The moment he mentioned it, the images of that kiss flooded my brain, and then I remembered my fall and getting so drunk I had to be carried to bed because I couldn't walk.

I also remembered attacking him, begging him to have sex with me, and being denied.

God, memories suck.

Why couldn't I have just gone on remaining clueless?

I frowned, disappointed in myself. "I remember."

"So I take it you're not thrilled by what happened?" he pressed, looking for an answer. With the intoxicated haze of last night beginning to lift, the closeness I felt to him now was unlike anything I'd ever felt before.

"I wouldn't say that, just confused." I snorted, once. "Maybe I hit my head a little too hard."

He nodded, taking a deep breath. "Well, you did hit your head pretty hard, but what has you confused?"

That you're talking to me. That you're here, next to me and so much more than I imagined you would be.

"Why you stopped us," I admitted, staring down at my hands, wishing I could throw them over my face from the embarrassment. But with my luck, I'd probably knock myself out in the process, give myself a black-eye and a fat lip to match my attractive looking gash on my forehead.

Just before Beau was about to answer me, Laney chose then to come out of the tent and made her way over to us.

Perfect timing, jerk.

"Hey," she grumbled. Sitting beside me, Laney placed her arm around my shoulder. "Thanks for coming last night."

Stop talking. Go away!

"Uh, you're welcome." I was begging her with my wide eyes not to say anything embarrassing in front of Beau. He had his cell phone in his hand now, but still, he could hear her if she said anything—like tell him I've been crushing on him since I was fourteen, or that the only reason I came to this damn party was to catch a glimpse of him.

Then I landed in his lap and he took pity on me.

See, that was it. He felt bad for me.

Damn it.

Laney shifted her eyes to the lake and then back to me, a strange flicker of emotion present. "Gavin said he'd take you back to Mountain Brook today."

"Okay." I stood, awkwardly tugging at the bottoms of the jean shorts that kept riding up. "I'll grab my bag."

"Your stuff is still in his truck." For some reason, Laney's face broke into a wide smile and she stood herself. "I'll find him after coffee." And then she took off in the direction of the house when she spotted Miles and Wade on the deck, both with coffee mugs in hand.

"Gavin's in the tent," Beau noted, my head whipping around to face him. I wasn't sure what he was thinking, but his brow scrunched in what appeared to be concentration. "You can't leave."

You're right, I can't. Marry me. Let's have babies! Before I can voice my nonsense, I whispered, "I need to go. I don't have enough clothes for the weekend."

"Oh, c'mon. Won't you stay?" His eyes slowly met mine, and I saw an emotion I couldn't quite place. "Miles has a washer and dryer. We can wash your clothes."

I didn't say anything. My brain hurt from thinking too much.

"Please?" he begged, a teasing smile spreading over his beautiful face, watching me fall in his hands, not literally, but he knew I was just about to tell him I'd stay. "I mean, what will happen if you leave? Look at me. I'm a good-lookin', charming guy, and if you leave. . ." he shook his head, letting out a slow whistle as he touched my cheek with his warm palm, "I might fall into the wrong hands. You wouldn't want that, would you?"

Still, I didn't say anything. I wasn't sure how to respond to him.

Beau's face was scrunched as if he was trying to remember something. "Why do you want to leave?"

"I don't want to leave." And then I grinned, unable to keep myself from doing so any longer. "Maybe I fell into the wrong hands?" I teased, and then heard Miles and Wade on the deck arguing about who was the best porno director.

Beau raised an eyebrow. "Still think I'm not the best pick here?"

"I really wouldn't know. You've scared everyone else off."

Liar.

I would know. I obsessed over him for years. Believe me, I *know*.

"Well then see, all the more reason for you to stay and let me show you I'm the better guy."

"You're convincing, aren't you?"

"Very much so. You should see what my charm gets me."

"Charming? Yeah, like the charm you laid on me last night?" I giggled, unable to stop myself. "If it's anything like my 'charm,' I think you're in big trouble. Because last night was the least charming thing anyone could have done."

He threw his head back, laughing.

Yep. I'm funny. Not!

I noticed Payton then, walking with Miles, her arms around his neck. "I have an idea what that charm can get you," I noted sarcastically.

Beau frowned, seeming disgusted with Payton and her hanging on Miles, and reached for my hand. "Did you bring a bathing suit?"

"No. . . ." I tripped while trying to keep up with him as he dragged me toward the house. "Should I have?"

"You can borrow one of Blaine's." He glanced back at me, smiling. "Do I need to carry you?"

"Shut up." I scowled at him. "Where are we going?"

"On the boat."

Awesome. Me and water. I would probably drown.

THE SATURDAY AFTERNOON sun was burning against my skin as we laid on the deck of the boat, my mind on Beau and my eyes on the water sparkling like diamonds in the sky I stared at last night. The ripples in the water rocked the boat in a gentle motion I found incredibly relaxing. The longer I laid there, the more I thought about taking a nap.

When Beau said we were going on the boat, I had no idea it would be him and his friends. For my own comfort, I drug Laney and Blaine with me, only they were in the water and I was afraid to move.

Soaking up the precious rays, my cup beside me was mostly rum with a splash of coke. I figured if I were going to stay, I would drink to relax me and, hopefully, not be so damn awkward around Beau the rest of the day.

I heard footsteps before I could see him, and I knew it was Beau standing there by the way my heart started to beat faster.

"Want some company?" he asked, as he sat down beside me, his hair messy under his red baseball hat.

He probably just wants some. Why else would he continue to hang around me?

He turned you down last night, smarty-pants.

Oh right.

"Sure, yeah. Help yourself. If you want."

Help yourself if you want? Just stop talking.

I looked over at him then, arms hung over his knees, watching the lake.

As we sat there in silence, Laney floated around on a raft. Wade and Miles jumped off the side of the boat. I knew what they were about to do—flip her off the raft. They were obvious about it as they snuck up on her and Blaine.

Sensing his chance, Miles flipped the raft over, dunking Laney down into the water, and untied the strings of her bikini.

She screamed, flailing around for the dramatics of it all and knocking Blaine off her raft too.

Laney wasn't fooling anyone, though; she loved this shit where Miles was paying attention to her when Gavin was nowhere in sight. I didn't like what she was doing, leading Miles on, or Gavin, but I wasn't anyone to judge her.

Beau shook his head. "They'll do anything for a little attention."

"Who? Miles and Gavin?"

"Yeah, and Wade." He let out a chuckle and then sighed, as if he was used to them doing this. "Bunch of fuckin' hoodlums."

Covering my mouth, I giggled hearing him cuss like that. I knew he did, even on those YouTube videos I obsessively watched of him on stage. Between songs, when he was interacting with the crowd, he wasn't exactly PG-13.

I once saw him take his pants off on stage and sing an entire song in his boxer briefs. Best three minutes of my life. Well, until last night when he kissed me.

Just thinking of that kiss sent my heart pounding and my tummy flipping.

Laney screamed. "I swear to God, Miles, I'm going to cut your dick off and shove it up your ass!" she warned, splashing water his direction.

Undeterred by her warning, Miles took a hold of her, taking her under water with him.

"Are they always like this?"

Beau snorted. "Yep."

"You'd think they were competing for her attention." Cupping my hands around my red cup, I took a slow drink, feeling the effects of the rum.

Keeping my attention on the water, I noticed how many people were surrounding the boat. It was everything I thought a graduation party at Lake Martin would be, hundreds of beautiful women and men, all drunk and livin' up their freedom for the weekend.

His eyes, those piercing blue ones that screamed sexy, scanned my body. "They are fighting for her attention. They've just moved on from hair pulling when we were little."

"So hair pulling only happens in the bedroom once you're older?"

Oh, my God! I can't believe I just said that.

Immediately, I could feel my face burning.

He didn't say anything, but he stared into my eyes for a long moment before chuckling. "If you're into that kind of thing." He motioned with two fingers for me to lean in closer, so I did. Then he whispered in my ear, low and seductively, "But I don't need to pull your hair to get your attention, do I?"

"No, but if you pull my hair, you better spank my ass."

Jesus, just stop talking. Word vomit. So much word vomit. I wanna die.

I think I let out a noise that was near a squeak but closer to a snort, either way, it sounded like something a baby pig would make and not at all sexy.

Was I trying to be sexy? Uh, yeah!

"I'll remember that." Beau chuckled and casually leaned back away from me, as if he was leaving me with those thoughts. When the commotion in the water calmed, I started to relax around Beau again, but still wasn't sure what to say to him. I didn't feel comfortable making conversation, in fear I'd say something stupid. Especially after the hair pulling comment.

The music was louder, mixing with the nearby sounds of boat motors and laughter.

The sun high in the sky, I soaked up every ray, remembering what it felt like not to have my nose in a book constantly.

Beau bumped my shoulder with his and then winked at me. "Am I making you nervous?"

"Yes," I answered truthfully, smiling at him. "I guess you could say that. I mean, do people normally ramble and unconsciously make an ass out of themselves around you all the time? Or am I an exception?"

I heard chuckling and noticed Miles and Wade carrying a bag of ice and eyeing Laney who was on her raft again. "If you want to keep your dicks, I wouldn't do that," I advised, but they ignored me and dumped the bag on her.

Beau and I watched Laney come around, waiting for what her reaction was going to be.

After screaming bloody murder, she shrieked out, "You fucking motherfucker from hell!" In the process of her flailing around, Miles had jumped in the water and took a foot to the face.

Blaine let out a cackle, floating around on her own raft again. "Serves the fucker right!"

When he shot up out of the water, after being submerged by her karate moves, it was evident his nose was broken.

As we watched, Miles drag himself out of the water, dripping blood all over the white seats. Beau looked over at me with a sudden seriousness as he laid back on his towel, his body glistening with the summer sun. "Are you mad I kissed you?"

He clearly wasn't concerned with Miles bleeding.

Looking down at him propped up on one of his elbows, my breath caught in my throat, thankfully, I didn't choke this time. The desire and want was obvious in both of our eyes as he looked up at me. "No? Should I be? I mean, it didn't suck, and I definitely enjoyed myself."

I'm thrilled you kissed me.

Wait. . . enjoyed myself? That sounds dumb.

"You. . .just—" he drew in a heavy breath "—didn't say anything, so I thought. . .I don't know." He shrugged, seeming nervous and it made me want to kiss the hell out of him. "Miles said something last night about you having a boyfriend."

He thought I had a boyfriend?

"I don't have a boyfriend." I gasped, blinking in disbelief. "*Laney* has a boyfriend."

Beau chuckled, rubbing his hand down his jaw, his hat concealing his expression slightly, his eyes narrowed at me. "I see. So you really did come to this party just to see me then?"

I whipped my head around, nearly giving myself a neck sprain, shocked at what he said, only to have him wink.

"Fucking Laney," I mumbled, wishing I could fall face first off the side of the boat and never surface. I couldn't even look at him. "I came because she wouldn't stop harassing me about going to a party. When she mentioned you'd be here, I might have caved."

"And are you disappointed now that we met?"

"No, I mean, I could ask you the same thing, but yeah. . ." He quirked an eyebrow at me, his smile higher on one side. "I mean, no, I'm not disappointed." *You're rambling. Shut up!* "Now that we've met and kissed, and I've made an ass out of myself many times, you've seen the worst possible side of me. And you've been nothing but a gentleman, so. . ."

Miles groaned, holding a towel to his face, and sat down next to us. Soaking wet, he wrapped his arm around me. "I think my nose is broken."

I'd never been more thankful to see him, and I didn't even like Miles, but he saved me from myself.

Beau stared at him, a slow shake to his head. "Too bad for you." Then he looked at me. "Wanna get wet?"

"I'm already wet." I looked up to meet his eyes, so afraid of what to say or do next, and then realized I should have clarified that last statement when Beau smirked, as did Miles. Fuck. "Okay."

Miles started to say something when Beau smacked him in the chest. "Shut up." And then he gave a nod to the water, waiting for me to walk in front of him. "Let's get wet."

Don't trip.

He made me so damn nervous, and when I snuck a glance at him, I saw his eagerness, every bit as intense and incandescent as mine.

"Fine, leave me in my state of need," Miles grumbled, and then took a squirt gun from next to him and started spraying Blaine with it. "Woman, get out of the water and fetch me a beer."

She flipped him off.

I smiled back at Beau, watching him as we walked to the back of the boat. Running his hand over the back his neck, he removed his baseball cap and tossed it on the seat by my towel and sunglasses.

I sighed at the sight before me—his rock-hard body, abs that begged to have hands worshiping them, and tan olive skin that made his bright eyes sparkle.

Afraid of belly flopping in front of him, I stepped off the back into the water feet first. Beau joined me fluidly, like everything was effortless for him. Probably was.

Swimming around, I treaded water, feeling the relief from the sun, watching Beau swim closer. Dunking his head below the water once, he then came back up as the waves from the nearby boats lapped at my face.

"You don't have to be embarrassed that you came for me." He couldn't even say that with a straight face and laughed. "Sorry."

It took me a minute to comprehend his sexual innuendo, but when I did, I rolled my eyes, splashing water at him. "Shut up."

Water beaded over his face as he shook his head, his eyes bright against the opaque green water and set on my mouth, watching me. "So you don't remember anything from last night?" he asked, his chin dipping below the water. He was so nonchalant about the question I wanted to dunk his cocky-ass under the water.

"I told you I remembered the kiss." Heat licked at my sunburnt cheeks, the air around me a smoldering, disorienting haze with him this close. We came together, each of us holding onto the railing on the back of the boat. "And falling and getting drunk."

"Something tells me you *don't* remember, because if you did—" he moved my wet hair to the side and kissing down my neck, holding onto the side of the boat "—you would remember how good it was." My stare went to his biceps as he flexed to hold on. "And you wouldn't be able to keep your hands off me right now."

"I remember asking you for more. . . but you told me no." My voice was barely above a whisper. No way did he hear me clearly. And I wasn't sure why, but I let go of the boat and held on to his shoulders, the position bringing our half naked bodies together.

I'm pressed against him! Yes. Don't speak. Don't say a damn word.

In the process of holding onto him, I bumped my already sore head against the side of the boat.

Figures.

Blinking rapidly, I felt the sting immediately. It'd be a miracle if I made it back from this weekend alive.

Beau rubbed the spot gently with his free hand. "The only reason I stopped you was because you were drunk, and I wanted you to remember what it felt like."

"How what felt like?"

"Me and you. . . alone. . . together." He leaned in, his wet, hot mouth making contact with my skin. I swallowed, my entire body trembling in anticipation as his hand that wasn't holding onto the boat touched my waist. "And me showing you just how *good* it would be."

Good for sure.

Snaking my arms tighter around his neck, my heart thudded painfully in my chest as every single breath he let out caressed my skin.

Is this real? Is this honestly happening right now?

Maybe I'd hit my head a little too hard last night, and in real life, I was now in a coma and this was my dream. All of it was a dream. I was imagining that—out of the fifty girls hanging around Miles' house—Beau focused on me. And now here I was, wrapped around his body like an octopus.

Can't possibly be real. Nope. Not a chance.

But… it was real. So freaking real I felt it deep in my bones and pushed me forward. Feeling brave, my legs rose, locking around his waist when his mouth found mine, gentle at first, and then not so gentle, determined and focused, deepening the kiss.

There were people all around us, in the water, on other boats, laughing and partying, but he didn't care, and neither did I. He seemed thoroughly intent on making me believe last night ended only because I was drunk. Had I not been. . .well, then maybe more would have happened?

Internally—despite thinking I was in a coma—I was doing one hell of a victory dance.

I wasn't one for opening my eyes when kissing, but when Beau moved, pressing me against the side of the boat, his grip on the rail tightening to hold the two of us, I wanted to see his face, his reactions. To be sure it was real, I wanted to see *him* kissing *me*.

Opening my eyes, I watched him just for a moment. His eyes were closed, tiny drops of water dripping from his dark lashes like diamonds.

He's so freaking beautiful.

Beau made a noise low in his throat, his hips making contact with mine when I slipped a little and, well, I slid down his erection.

Beau Ryland was hard.

And I made him hard.

Me.

Before I knew it, the kiss was explosive as he pushed his body closer, a muffled groan escaping him. Unable to comprehend what was happening, I gasped against his lips, losing myself in the kissing and grinding my center into him. I needed more, so much more.

Beau chuckled, drawing back. "Slow down, honey." His voice was strained, as if he didn't want to, but needed to. He licked his lips, and then kissed me once more, tenderly, drops of water falling from his hair onto my nose. "Fuck, I haven't been able to stop thinking about that kiss last night," he whispered huskily in my ear when his mouth moved to my neck, his breathing heavy as his eyes fell closed and he sighed. "But we have all night for this."

What's he talking about? Slow down? No way!

I couldn't think clearly enough to respond to his words. I was drowning in the scent of him and becoming dizzy and out of breath just thinking of what I *should* be doing or what would come next. I was perfectly content with where it was going, even if it was just a coma dream. I'd never been kissed the way he kissed me, or touched the way he touched me. I wasn't sure I ever would be again.

What would tonight bring?

When our mouths parted again, Beau flashed an easy grin my way. I hated the feeling that drew me to him—a familiar compulsion to just get lost in his words and the smile that teased, demanding attention. I knew I should have been more levelheaded, but he made it hard. He made me forget every rational thought, which was good for once. Every girl had that one guy they couldn't shake, or even act normal around. Beau was that guy for me.

I breathed out, long and slow, wanting so much to hide what I was feeling. I knew the type of guy Beau was, or at least what I assumed a musician would be. Everyone did. But then here he was, sweet-talking, charming, and kissing me. Now my assumption of what he'd be like wasn't accurate at all. He was more.

"You have a sweet mouth, pretty girl," Beau whispered in my ear, his hand lifting my chin, as if he was about to kiss me again. "I'm having a hard time waiting for later."

He's so much trouble.

"Why wait?" Just as I was leaning in for another kiss, Miles dumped a bag of melting ice over the side of the boat. The ice bounced over our heads like rocks and into the water.

With the heat, the ice felt shocking, enough that I let go of Beau and slipped under water.

"Whoops," Miles laughed, peeking over the side, "didn't see you two down there."

"Bullshit," Beau grumbled, moving away from me. He helped me back on the boat, pushed Miles off, and then wrapped a towel around me from behind, hugging me to his chest. "I'll pick up where we left off, soon. Promise."

I'd hold him to that promise. I would.

Turning to face him, I let the towel fall off my shoulders. "You better."

His eyes raked over my body before he sighed, shaking his head. "You are too beautiful for your own good."

He certainly had a way of making me feel that way, didn't he?

FEELING THE STING of my sunburnt cheeks, I couldn't stop smiling as afternoon turned to evening. Maybe it was from the rum in my cup, or maybe it was from having a good time.

I had a feeling this particular group partied together often, as they did in high school.

Miles, Gavin, Blaine, Wade, Payton, and Beau, they all seemed. . . close. It wasn't long after supper and I began to feel out of place.

We were back at the house and Payton kept glancing my way, her looks anything but friendly. She was nothing like what I knew in school—the sweet cheerleader who smiled at everyone and befriended the girl's no one spoke to. I guess she only befriended them when she knew they weren't competition to her.

Now it seemed I was her enemy, probably because her man wasn't far from my side.

"I'm glad you stayed." Blaine wrapped her arm around my shoulder, her gaze on the lake to our right while mine remained on Payton.

The music around us was so loud I could feel the bass thumping with my heart as though they were one beat. Over the roar of the music, it was hard to hear anyone talking, much less the distant sounds of laughter.

Around us, Payton and Laney danced with Gavin, Miles, and Wade, paying little mind to anyone else around them.

Was she trying to make Beau jealous?

I looked to Beau seated in a chair next to the cooler with his third beer in the last hour in hand, slow-drinking and watching *me*.

I smiled, my stare drifting back to those who were dancing. For someone who spent very little time letting loose, this seemed surprisingly easy for me to be here, with them. I wasn't even fazed by the obvious drug use happening around me, but

I was relieved Beau hadn't taken up a single offer pushed his way. I'd been offered weed today more than beer.

I grew up in a quiet house, one where I didn't have a lot of friends over. We had a small family and rarely got together in a large setting such as a party.

In just a day, I'd experienced a lifetime of memories from the bonfires, slow cooked southern barbeque, sweet tea and rum mix, hot nights and sun-kissed skin that made me never want to leave.

I hadn't realized how much I craved interactions like this. It made me feel like I had a depressing upbringing and these people, they... experienced things, good things that made them who they were today.

"Wanna go swimming?" Blaine asked, giving a nod to the lake, unable to watch them dancing. I really liked Blaine, her smile drew you in, pretty and fierce, but the sweetest girl I'd ever met.

My eyes drifted to the lake, the sun was nearly set, a pink and red glow smudging the once blue sky, the air thick and heavy as it dipped behind the horizon. My skin glistened, the nape of my neck damp in the sweltering heat as I looked at the bombardment of colors in the sky. The radiant glow scintillated and beamed off the lake.

"Sure." I hopped down from the railing I was sitting on, smiling at Blaine and then Beau, who was probably wondering why Blaine and I were suddenly stripping out of our jean shorts.

I didn't wait for him to say anything, or try to stop me.

Running through the warm blades of grass, we didn't stop until our toes were sinking in the red clay and onto weathered wood still hot from the day's heat. We jumped off the end of the dock into water that was over my head.

Swimming around to where I could touch, I heard Blaine laugh. Her eyes bright and wild, her wet dark hair stuck to her cheek as she swam next to me, bobbing under water until she found her footing.

"We need some rafts."

We didn't see any nearby and neither of us wanted to get out and look for one. But there was a group of guys swimming near us, splashing and trying to get us to join them on their big-ass raft. "Come on, baby, come over here," they'd coax, raising their beers in the air.

Blaine flipped them off, turning to me. "I think my brother likes you."

My face burned, as always, eyes fixed on the water. "He's just being flirty."

Is it that? Or is it more?

"He's my twin brother." She gave me a look that asked if I was that naïve. "I know when he likes a girl."

Beau and Miles came barreling into the water, flipping off the dock and sending a wave of water in our faces.

I lost sight of Beau when he went under water, but I had a feeling he was going to do something stupid, he just hadn't popped up out of the water yet.

Shit, did he hit his head?

Just as I began to panic, I felt something grab my feet and pull me under. At the last second, I held my breath.

I couldn't see anything in the dark water but had a feeling it was Beau, with the way he embraced me. I was quickly beginning to recognize his touch.

We both came up laughing, my arms around his shoulders and his face buried in my neck. Our bodies making contact, again, so close and warm.

Standing there, he let go of me and helped me back to where I could touch. "You okay?"

I nodded, still unable to stop myself from smiling.

Miles had done the same to Blaine, only she slapped him. "Stop that, jerk."

"She doesn't like him much, does she?"

"Not really. Miles is an asshole," Beau noted, shaking his head at them and turning back to me. "He fucked around a few summers back and slept with her. She thought it was more; he didn't."

"Wow, you summed that up quickly," I teased.

Beau's head tilted to one side, his eyes on mine. "Two years of bullshit in one sentence."

"You have a way with words, don't you?"

He reached out, running his fingers lightly over my cheek, his eyes searching mine. "Sometimes. And you should be careful."

"Why?"

"You're finding me charming and it's showing on your face."

I wanted to pop off with something snarky, tell him I would never find him charming, though I did, when I felt something against my stomach, and my stare went to Miles to make sure he wasn't doing anything. He was fighting with Blaine.

"Something touched me." And then I thought. . . was that his. . . "Was that your—?" I couldn't even finish my sentence; it sounded so childish. I couldn't say penis around him. He'd think I was juvenile. Would I say cock? That was the adult thing to say, right?

Beau threw his head back in a cackling laughter, knowing what I was thinking. "No, it wasn't. We're like a foot apart. I'm sure you'll have no complaints in that department, but I'm not a horse."

"Are you sure?" I asked, reaching under the water and grazing his crotch in the process. It didn't faze him one bit, even made him smile wider. Yep, I copped a feel right then and there. My hands shot out of the water. "I'll just keep my hands to myself."

Beau raised a questioning eyebrow at me, a raffish smile plastered across his lips. "Aww, don't get shy on me now."

"Seriously, what was it?" I searched the water, wishing I could see below the surface. I hated surprises and water I couldn't see through, like lakes. The fact that I was even swimming in the lake was a miracle.

"Maybe it was a gator?" Beau joked, waggling his eyebrows.

I swallowed over a lump in my throat. "Seriously? There's alligators here?"

I felt it again, this time on my calf, and screeched, which was heard by damn near everyone on the lake. In my screaming, I lunged forward and grabbed onto Beau, practically climbing up his body in the process.

He seemed to have no complaints and held me to his chest. "It was probably a bass." He breathed out, obviously affected by our closeness by the increase in his breathing and the way he watched my eyes and then my mouth, like he was begging for another kiss.

"Beau?"

"Yeah?" His breath blew gently over my face, like a warm breeze.

"Don't let me down." Fuck, there was so much meaning in that statement and he knew it.

His lips twitched into a small smile. "I won't until you ask me to."

Leaning forward, I captured his warm lips with my own, the taste of lake and beer on his lips. Once our lips touched, I lost all sense of time while clinging to him desperately. The sensations were too much and I felt the sweet tension building within.

I couldn't wait to be alone with him. I wanted to drag him off right now, but knew he was still going to play later with a group of guys who came over from another house to party with us. I would have to wait.

Beau kissed me back and then pulled away, his breath increasingly ragged. "It's killing me waiting like this." With our mouths parted, he nipped across my chest. His nose swept between the valley and the stubble on his cheek scraped across my sensitive wet skin.

"Me too," I finally said, wishing he'd kiss me again. I wanted our mouths to be welded together forever.

Miles made a cat-calling sound beside us and then wrapped his arms around Beau and me. "Can I join in?"

Beau glared as he held me in place for a moment and then slowly let me down. "Sorry, but I'm about to kick his ass. I'll be back."

Sensing he was in trouble, Miles took off out of the water, holding up his shorts with one hand as he streaked through the grass and into the house.

Beau took off after him and my eyes were immediately drawn to his muscular physique as he ran. The way his muscles moved and contracted.

Jesus. They make me this pretty?

As I stood there drooling, Blaine wrapped her arm around my shoulder, her bikini top missing. "I hate that little fucker. He took my top."

I snorted out a laugh as she stood there, completely unfazed that she was now topless and standing beside me as if nothing was wrong. I wanted Blaine to be my best friend, always and forever. I knew that for sure right then.

And then came the look as she watched Miles and Beau. The one that screamed, don't be silly, girl. "Still don't think he likes you?" she asked, dropping her hand from my shoulder when she noticed her bikini top in the water by the shore.

My eyes did that quick blinking thing where you didn't exactly know how to answer the question, so you blinked to distract the other person as you desperately tried to think of something to say. "I, uh. . . oh, you mean the kissing?"

She reached down and grabbed her top from the water, ringing it out. "The kissing. . . the attentiveness. *All* of it. My brother doesn't do that. Like ever. Not even with Payton-in-my-ass over there."

"Oh," was all I said and then wondered what Blaine thought of Payton. I was a sophomore their senior year, and wherever Payton was, Blaine was nearby. "Do you not like her?"

Blaine tied her bikini top back on as she spoke. "I used to like her. We were practically best friends growing up, and when she and Beau broke up, she acted like we did too. Wouldn't talk to me anymore. It wasn't my fault they couldn't make it work."

I felt so bad for Blaine that her best friend dumped her like that, but I also couldn't relate. I was never close with girls growing up, probably because I was so freaking awkward they all thought I was weird or snobbish when I didn't talk much.

It also made me wonder what really happened between Beau and Payton. Was I just the weekend replacement?

THE RAIN MOVED in just after the sun finally set and thirty or so people were trying to gain shelter under the covered deck on the back of the house. The guys from the other house showed up with electric guitars and drums, they had quite the set-up back there.

With his flannel from last night around my shoulders, Beau and I were in the back under the covered deck when he leaned to his side and reached for his guitar after Laney begged him to play for us.

Taking the sleeves of the flannel, I brought the fabric to my face, and breathed in deep, noticing it was a nice mixture of firewood and Beau, a fresh pine smell I would forever associate with this weekend, this lake, this moment.

The crowd quieted down when the music began. Sitting on a chair, Beau bowed his head toward his guitar, a trail of chords broke the silence as did the slow drumbeat. His right hand thumbed against the guitar as his voice carried through the air. *"I can't seem to shake this feeling. It's deep in my bones and she's more than willing."*

The song was slower than anything I'd heard him play yet, and definitely a new one. I certainly hadn't heard this one on YouTube.

When did he write it? Who is it about?

I listened to his every lyric, contemplating if the slow song was about anyone in particular when he'd say things like, *"She was slow-sippin, body swaying to the beat of my heart."*

I knew he wasn't talking about me, but how strange to think it related a little.

As I watched Beau, his head tipped back as he belted out lyrics I knew he'd poured himself into, I could feel the passion radiating from him. The energy, the adrenaline, he owned and used to his advantage.

His eyes met mine again, and his intense stare had me blushing in seconds. He licked his lips in a deliberately casual way. His head angled to one side before dropping his eyes back to his guitar. *"Kiss me under the stars. Love me and they're ours. I'll keep you safe, if you keep me wild."*

I was far enough back on the deck that if I tipped my head back, I could feel the rain that was coming down in a fine mist, clinging to my overly heated skin in the best way, like a fresh breath of air.

Looking up at the sky as I gently swayed to the music, I felt every single drop for what it was. I knew then, even if I never heard from Beau again, or this weekend didn't go any further than right now, I was okay with that. I would be anything he wanted for what I experienced now.

This was what I had been missing out on.

This life.

Beau.

All of it. Even if I never experienced something like this again. He was so much more than what I imagined him to be.

Drawing in a deep breath when the song ended, the air felt damp and I savored the way my body felt listening to Beau's voice surrounding me.

I was absolutely right, he was more.

I'll keep you safe if you keep me wild.

Did he realize how powerful that was?

STANDING BY THE fire, for the second night in a row, just as the clouds cleared for a break in the storm, I felt a familiar set of hands on my hips and relaxed, knowing it was Beau.

It was nearing ten and the party around us was raging, wild and ready for something more, as was I. Beau seemed the same, but down with being the entertainment. I wondered if he ever grew tired of this, always the center of attention and expected to perform.

"Do you get tired of singing?"

Beau's arm wrapped tighter around my chest with his lips at my ear. His tongue darted out and then he nipped my lobe with his teeth. "I'd rather be singing just for you."

My stomach was full of butterflies, my heart racing so fast. Inhaling a breath, as if I thought anything tonight would go smoothly, I inhaled a bug.

A fucking bug.

Coughing and choking, I either swallowed it, or spit it in the fire, I wasn't really sure other than it wasn't in my mouth anymore. Turning slowly, I faced Beau, red cheeked and nearly crying. "If you never want to see me again, I completely understand."

He burst out laughing, his shoulders shaking as he turned me back around. "Now why would I want that? It'd deprive myself the chance to see you, like this."

"Like what? A hot mess choking on bugs and tripping over logs?"

"I don't mind if you trip again."

"I'm starting to wonder where all this 'charm' you say you have is," I teased, only to have him growl softly in my ear and hug me tighter.

It was then I felt his heartbeat between my shoulders, his chest pressed to my back and his arms wrapped around my waist as we danced.

I could feel his heavy breath on my neck, through my hair. This feeling, the needy ache in the pit of my stomach, was better than anything I'd ever imagined. I was exactly where I wanted to be tonight, and every other night. I never wanted to let him go.

"Now what?" I asked, leaning my head back against his shoulder, feeling his even breathing against my neck when we finally sat down. I was hoping he'd say we could sneak away someplace to be alone. "Because I'm afraid to move, or breathe, or speak."

"You'll see." He spoke slow, and then kissed my neck, once.

Never stop kissing me. Ever.

"See what?"

"Shhh. . . ." He pressed his finger to my lips. "Look up, baby, and get lost."

Unsure what he was talking about, I looked up to a once cloudy sky dominated by the tumbling grays of smoky and silver clouds, and thousands of tiny lights caught my eyes. I found myself in a place where nothing else mattered. Just tonight.

The night scattered with silver stars, a surreal blanket above our heads. As one star shot across the sky, I could feel Beau's breathing against my neck and his hands on my stomach under my shirt.

The sky looked like glitter, so far away, but always bright, waiting for you to look up. In some ways, we were just like that falling star. We fell to make our dreams come true.

I'd put my life on hold through college, and now, I was staring up at the stars with a man I only dreamed I would be able to talk to, let alone be wrapped in his embrace.

Beau kissed my cheek. "Beautiful, huh?" Drawing me against his chest tightly, his voice was a low gravelly sound that left me trembling in his arms.

"It is."

The crowd around us was fading—slow and sleepy talking with drooping eyes focusing on the glint of the firelight.

The music was still loud, but not loud enough that I couldn't hear Beau whisper dirty things in my ear every once in a while.

All night, it seemed he'd been giving me curious looks, his eyes cutting and smiling, teasing even. It warmed me when he stared at me as though I was the only woman here that mattered to him.

"What are you thinking about, pretty girl?"

I bit down on my bottom lip before saying, "Nothing, you're just. . . nothing like I thought you'd be."

"And that is?"

"Vulnerable. . . ."

"Charming?" he ribbed, glossy-eyed, handing me that easy smile again, the one that seemed country, slow and sweet. There was a different side to him tonight, one I couldn't ignore but felt completely comfortable around, as if I had known him *like this*, for years.

I smiled, but didn't say anything.

"Did you really only come because of me?"

"Yes," I admitted.

"And your assessment?"

I swallowed, thankfully not another bug. "Umm. . . hot and perfect in all the right ways." *Crap on a cracker, why did I say that?* I shrugged, trying to be nonchalant, only to have him laugh. "I mean, you're all right."

"I'm just going to assume you mean somewhere in between those two answers, and with that, you aren't so bad yourself." He was quiet for a moment before replying with, "But it looks like I have some convincing to do."

SPRINGSTEEN

BEAU

"DANCE WITH ME." My hands reached down and cupped her ass, pulling her against me.

"You are so drunk," she slurred against my shoulder, wrapping her arms around my neck.

I could have tried to blame the last two days on the alcohol, saying it had severely damaged my judgment, but, honestly, it wasn't that at all.

"I'm actually not," was my only answer as we moved to the pulsing beat.

I knew what I wanted tonight, and I wanted to be sober for it. Removing my hands from her ass, I traced them up the lines of her hips—my fingers dug into the velvety skin and pulled her even tighter against my hips. She gasped and closed her eyes as though the sensation was exactly what she wanted.

She had to feel my erection against her—she had to. I should have been concerned at the obvious display we were putting on, but I couldn't help it. I only cared about the way my body was responding to her.

We danced, her hips moving against mine, only we weren't doing much dancing, but instead kissing on the deck. The rain had moved in again, leaving us all under the shelter of the back porch, well most of us. A bunch of girls were half-naked and dancing on the lawn to The Tractors.

As our kisses continued, my mouth moved frantically from her ear to her neck and down to her collarbone, then returning urgently to her lips again as if I needed her breath to breathe. I was past the point of stopping.

"Where are you going?" I reached up and touched her face when Bentley pulled away, our skin brushing again. I couldn't pry my hands away from her. Not after the teasing we'd done today.

"Out of this rain." Our eyes met, locked in a heated stare. "You can join me if you want."

She walked away, keeping my stare momentarily, before turning around. I watched her until I couldn't see her shadow any longer in the moonlight.

Tossing my beer back, I took one last look at the party.

What is it that I couldn't shake about this girl?

Maybe it was the softness in her voice or the smile. Or maybe it was her eyes, so dark and captivating that I wanted to find the depths in which I knew were there.

Commotion around the house drew my attention, Miles shoving Gavin playfully, or not so playfully into someone. They were competing for Laney's attention.

Drawing in a heavy breath, I tried to talk myself out of following her, but couldn't think of a damn thing.

Standing, I made my way into the shadows where her tent was. My eyes dropped to the ground as I approached.

Just leave. Don't go inside that tent right now.

If you do, you know damn well what's going to happen.

My rational side was outweighed by those dark irises framed by thick lashes and the need to get lost in them.

I knew for sure she would always be that girl, the one who always crept into my mind, lingered, and left me needing more from her.

I'll be anything she needs me to be.

Chapter Seven

BACKSEAT

BENTLEY

THE SOUND OF the tent's zipper slowly being opened sent my heart racing.

I tried to control my breathing, the fluttering in my chest just as heavy as my lids, my long lashes meeting my summer-kissed cheeks briefly before I stared up at the open vent in the tent, sending drops of water on my face, each one a relief from the humidity. I should have closed the vent but there was something about the rain on my skin I enjoyed.

He moved inside, zipping the door shut again before consuming the small space with me—finally alone, despite the party just outside.

The rain sounded like bullets against the canvas, and my heart beat so fast, so hard, I couldn't breathe, let alone comprehend that I was in a tent with Beau and he was removing his shirt.

A gust of wind rippled through, straining the tent against the ropes and pegs, the edges flapping wildly in the night.

Beau's shirt made a slapping sound when he tossed it aside, hitting the ground. The twang of a country song in the distance, ever so soft, ever so right, relaxing me for just a second.

He took his damn shirt off. Take your jeans off too!

No, wait for him to do it.

Dropping to his knees before me, Beau leaned in, his hands on either side of my head holding himself up.

Our eyes caught, locked, waiting, and then he gave me his weight.

When he pressed into my ribs, I let out the breath I'd been holding, my hands shaking as they wrapped around his neck, wanting to hold him so close to me he'd never be able to part.

Coasting his nose along my throat, his skin felt hot, burning mine with each pass, our heartbeats dancing. My head fell back onto the sleeping bag underneath me, my spine curving, and skin burning for his touch.

Each drop of water that slipped over my cheeks, slowly falling from his wet face, washed away my fears. Our stares locked together, blurring the torrent of emotions inside of me. His eyes were like a fantasy, every moment I'd ever dreamed about colliding inside of me, like a stolen wish granted.

"Hey, pretty girl," he drew out slowly, much like the song he'd been singing. His breath brushed against my skin, burning with his every touch as his fingers trickled down my ribs over my tank top, soft and gentle, teasing. I squirmed, trying to find his eyes in the low-lit tent, my hands shaking as I held onto his back, his breathing just as ragged as my own. I couldn't believe he was on top of me, in a tent, alone.

"Hey." I let myself get lost in him. His scent, the way his concrete arms felt around me, and the way my heart sounded with his chest pressed to mine.

With a low laugh and flushed cheeks, he slowly continued kissing me. I wasn't sure if I should move or just lay there, but at some point my body relaxed.

Closing my eyes, the night soared, too much to drink, too much to feel. The aching in my stomach was almost too much. It was a needful, distinct fire spreading throughout me, burning, prickling under the surface of my skin.

I wanted him so badly it was hard to remain calm.

Is this really happening?

Beau moved, his erection, still concealed in his jeans, hitting my center. My legs spread automatically, wanting, no, *needing* to feel the friction.

I looked at him then, eyes hooded and breathing shallow.

"How far are you gonna let me take this?" he whispered in my ear when I frantically began kissing him and trying to get my shirt off at the same time.

Would I let him?Did he want to?

Oh yeah, he wanted to, but the question remained, would I let him. We talked about it all day, but never actually said we were going to do it.

Jesus, Bentley, you don't schedule this shit. It just happens.

He bent his head down to kiss my exposed skin. His shoulders squeezed together; taut, tan muscles begged to have my hands running over them.

He was whispering and gentle with me as I panted and pleaded for more, wanting and begging for him to just do it. His hands began to work my shirt up, higher, taking my heart with it.

I wanted him to move his hand, stick it inside of my shorts. Anything to make this connection stronger. Bringing my hands up, I run them over his back, feeling the contours of his muscles as I finally answered his question. "As far as you want."

Dragging his parted lips over my neck, he moved the fabric of my tank top, working his hands over my hips and around my back. The motion, the feeling of his hands on my bare skin was almost too much to take.

Beau groaned, rocking his hips into mine, and I wished like hell our jeans weren't there so I could have felt him completely.

Damn it, get these clothes off!

Opening my eyes, I focused on his face, watching me. Reaching up, I stroked his cheek. We stared at each other, letting the connection between us soar. I'd never felt as alive as I did right then, the excitement and the fear.

It had been a while, and for that, I was ready and willing to let him do whatever he wanted. That and after his kisses today, I wanted more of him.

"You done this before?"

My stomach flipped and flopped at his words, rising up in my throat. "Yes."

I wasn't sure if he believed me, but he went back to kissing me.

It was no wonder Payton was with him all through high school, off and on. I was sure of that when we kissed. His mysterious allure was amplified by his ability to kiss.

Wanting his lips again, I turned my head, the humidity and the dampness inside the tent making my cheek stick to his.

He was kissing my neck, his spiky jaw scratching tender, sunburned skin. Tracing his lips along my collarbone, he made a slow deliberate path to my lips, which seemed to take forever.

He was moving again, his knees sliding along the ground, creating a zipping sound from denim meeting canvas.

When I finally had his lips back, they were warm and wet, sending a heady sensation straight to the pit of my stomach.

With our mouths never parting, he rose up on his knees, and I heard the clanking of his buckle and his zipper being lowered. Then his hands were on my shorts, unzipping them.

Holy crap! This is gonna happen! Okay, breath B. Breathe before you hyperventilate.

And then I gasped when he shifted his position, our mouths disconnecting. In only a few movements, my shorts were gone, bringing me back to what this was as he pulled his jeans and boxers down before returning to press his warm, naked body against mine.

The whole situation was overwhelming. Every second his lips were against my skin helped my nerves, but it also made my temperature rise and my passion for him peak even more.

Just when I thought he was going to move forward, he slid down my body again, this time his head between my legs.

Oh shit, really?

And then I thought, what the fuck do I do with my hands? Do I cross them on my chest like this?

No that's awkward.

Maybe behind my head?

No, umm. . . shit.

Down by my sides?

That's not it. Still weird, like I'm a mummy or something.

In his hair?

Yeah. That seems normal.

Shit, he's looking at me.

"Are you okay?" he asked, smirking, more than likely knowing what was happening inside my head—a whole bunch of nonsense.

"I'm fine." My voice was shaking, leaving me unsure as to if he even heard me.

Pressing a kiss to the inside of my thigh, he winked. "Don't be nervous. It's just me."

Boy, you and "just" don't belong in the same sentence. Ever.

I had no idea what to expect, because the one experience I had of someone down there was with my gynecologist. Surely this would be different. Running his tongue over my most sensitive nerves, it felt like he was kissing me.

Before long, he was pushing a couple fingers inside me and licking me with just the right motions and the right pressure.

In a very graphic description, I could tell you all kinds of things that might be gross to some and turn others on. Like the fact that I could literally feel myself dripping wetness all the way to my ass. Or that I wondered if I should have shaved a little better. Were my pubic hairs tickling his nose?

You had to admit, it was a justifiable question.

But there was the fact he was doing something very intimate to me. No one else had done this to me but him. There was just something about letting a man downstairs, trusting them in the most intimate position. Strangely enough, I trusted Beau.

With his left arm laid across my stomach, he held me in place, screaming possessiveness that rolled from him, captivating me.

It didn't take long, and my orgasm, my much needed, months-delayed orgasm, rocked me to the point where I was sure everyone on the lake knew I had just had the best experience of my life.

When I glanced up at him, he crawled up my body, his hand moved from my hair to my cheek, running his fingers down it. "That was sexy."

I had no actual words.

"You liked that?" Most of his weight shifted to rest against his arm, which was bent near my hip, supporting him.

"Yes."

He still kissed my body desperately as his impatient hands grabbed my hips a little rougher than I expected.

There was no, "Do you want to?" or "Do you have a condom?", which Beau, thankfully, had. It was just doing and heavy breathing and me freaking out internally. I wondered what he thought of me, wide-eyed and watching his every movement with rapt attention.

There was the briefest of moments, when he had his weight leaned to one side while putting on the condom, I really comprehended what it was we were doing. I wanted to look, check him out, but knew I'd be too obvious, so I stared up at the ceiling.

I just officially met him last night, and now we were having sex. This wasn't real. I was definitely back to the coma theory because no way. *No fucking way* could this be happening between *me* and Beau Ryland.

"Hi," he said when he returned his weight to me, humor laced in his words, but there was tension rolling from him. As if maybe he was asking himself the same question, were we making some kind of mistake?

I chuckled, my cheeks blazing like the fiery sun. "Hi."

I could feel him there, at my entrance, pausing like he wasn't sure. A flash of something crossed his features, and then was gone before I could decipher it. He looked. . .lost almost.

Dipping his head forward, his mouth nipped at my tender flesh, so unbelievably soothing, yet scary. His body was heavy, but I was in no position to complain. I wanted this too badly.

By the way he shook slightly, I wondered how long it'd been for him. The air seemed light as my shallow breaths against his skin.

When our bodies joined, I gasped as he entered me without warning. There was a moment, right then, where I forgot to breathe, like he was taking my breath from me. It'd been so long, the feeling of him filling me was painful at first, and then immediately replaced with what could only be described as tingles.

Drawing back, he grinned, a gentle grunt falling from his lips, baby blues shining in the night so bright my heart hurt with his beauty.

Beau moved slowly at first, his movements shaky and undecided, neither of us saying anything. I was thankful I had no words.

His smile was so tender; I'd remember it for the rest of my life. "You're. . .so pretty, honey." His hands were in my hair as his lips kissed raindrops from my rosy cheeks. "Relax. It's just me." He said again, sensing my nerves with each movement, by the way my body was shaking.

The problem was, he didn't see the significance behind those simple words.

"I've wanted you for so long." My voice sounded like the wind, ragged "I can't believe this is happening."

Stop talking.

I wondered briefly if he understood what I meant. Did he realize he was my first crush, my only crush, and now this? My eyes searched his face but never met his eyes.

He stopped mid-thrust and looked down at me, giving me a glimpse into the vulnerability he had; it was there if I cared to look. He wasn't some dream guy, he was a real person, with real problems and fears just like everyone else. "What?"

"I want you to fuck me. Like, *really* fuck me." My voice went lower, as if what I was saying was something so naughty it couldn't be said at a normal volume. "If we only have tonight, I don't want to be able to move tomorrow."

With a growl, one that surfaced from deep within, shaking me to my core, he asked, "Jesus, are you trying to kill me, Bentley? We have more than tonight."

Moving in and out as if he knew exactly what I wanted and needed, his heavy kisses gave me everything I was looking for, and then some, as he whispered my name across my neck.

His hands curled around my shoulders and pulled me into his thrusts, which seemed harder each time, my breath expelling on contact.

My mind was lost, which was a good thing. All I had now were sensations that left me weak. Curving into his body, I gripped him as tightly as I could.

Until I had a leg cramp from motherfucking hell. It hurt so badly.

"Ow," was the only word I managed to get out.

"Shit. Am I hurting you?" He slowed his motions, unsure why I was in pain.

"Fuck." *This isn't happening. What a fucking loser I am.* "No, but I am getting a cramp in my thigh and hip. Shit. Ow. Get off!"

He laughed, shaking his head while moving back a few inches off me. "Well, that's what I'm trying to do for both of us."

Great, he's going to stop all together and realize anything with me is entirely too much work, conversation and sex.

I arched an eyebrow at him touching my bare thigh, his eyes on my legs and not me. "Can you help me out here?" His ever-talented hands roamed my thighs and hips, intent on relaxing me. "Put pressure there and mas—Oh shit." He had talented hands for sure. "Yeah, that's good. Right there."

"You're wounding me here. You're supposed to say that while I'm between your thighs, not rubbing out a cramp in your hip."

"Okay, wise guy," I waved him forward, "now that you have proven yourself to be an excellent masseuse, get back between my legs."

"Jeez, you're bossy when you're horny." He reached down, checking the condom.

I could sense that my leg cramp may have put a damper in the romance. He wouldn't admit to it, but I felt the need to change it up a bit.

I reached up, placing my hand on his chest. "Let me repay for helping me out with my leg cramp."

Beau didn't quite understand the meaning behind my words until I moved from in front of him to on my knees. My hands ran up his thighs as I reached for the condom. "Do you have another one of these?"

"Yeah, why?"

I removed it and tossed it aside. "Because I have a favor to repay."

His eyes lit up. "Fuck yeah."

If there was any way to excite Beau, it would be seeing my mouth wrapped around him. His eyes dropped to my hands as they glided over him and then on my mouth replacing them.

He was all heavy breaths, dirty whispering, and soft grunts as his hips met the movements of my mouth.

I hadn't given out many blow jobs before. In fact, I'd only done this one other time, but YouTube was, again, a very informational website.

"Jesus," he moaned, moving my hair to the side to watch. He used the hand in my hair to guide me, while the other rested on mine on his bare thigh.

"Fuck, you do that so good. . .just like that, baby. . ." he moaned and then dropped his head back against the ground and closed his eyes. I learned quickly the more I swirled my tongue and brought him deeper in my mouth, like I was gagging on him and the more I reacted and the more noises he made.

Okay, so gagging myself turns him on. Awesome.

The thought that I was giving Beau Ryland a blow job was electrifying and completely unbelievable. I was pleasuring him in the most intimate way, attached to him in ways I'd never been with anyone else.

Being on my knees provided me the ability to see his face this time, his beautiful contoured face that was on the edge, moments away from pleasurable numbness.

He looked down and his hand gently touched my cheek, curling around the back of my neck. "So fucking pretty." Hooded eyes focused on me. Thick lashes blinked slowly. "Watching your mouth on me is. . . ." I took him deeper and his voice caught. "My God. . . ." He pulled me away. "You gotta stop or I'm gonna come."

Placing his hand on my chest, he pushed me back so I was laying down again, before putting on a new condom. If I could have stared at him forever, I would have as I watched him roll on the condom. He made something so simple look insanely hot.

Damn. Just damn.

"Now, where were we?" He smirked, like he was holding a secret all to himself.

I chuckled at his question. "I think it was something like this," I let my words fall short, as I reached between us and stroked him once.

"Oh, God, you feel so damn good," Beau mumbled as he slid in, his head falling forward in the process to rest against my shoulder.

Within seconds, I felt him get right back to that blissful, heart-pounding rhythm before that nice charley horse decided to show itself.

How embarrassing.

"More. I *need* more," I demanded, digging my fingers into his shoulder and tilting my head back to give him access to the sweet spot.

"That's it," he growled into my neck. "You like to be fucked, don't you?"

"Yes." I nodded against his shoulder, biting down as the pleasure already started to peak. "God, yes, Beau!"

"Say it again."

"What?" I laughed, wrapping my legs around him.

"My name. Scream it for me." He pulled back, his lips finding mine as he drew me in for a passionate kiss. His tongue lapped, swirling and curling with mine. His kisses, *oh, God,* his kisses. They could make you come before the sex even started.

"Come on." He thrust into me harder, and then again, slamming me into his movements. "Say it."

"Conceited much?"

"Don't make me beg, *pretty girl*."

Beg a little.

"Oh, God. . . Beau!"

"That's not loud enough," he hissed, demanding more, slamming into me.

I turned my head, my breath expelling with each movement, screaming in his ear. "BEAU!"

He groaned again, and then laughed, the sound pushing me further over the edge as his mouth moved over my jaw and to my neck.

Why was his laugh such a turn-on?

One hand stayed curled around my shoulders, but his right hand moved and angled my hips as he drove into me, harder this time.

"The moment I saw your long legs... I knew you'd be screaming my name."

"Why's that?" My lips were at his ear, kissing along his neck, arching my body into his.

"Because I *wanted* you to be," he said, pulling back. Beau looked down at me, his face flushed and determined, and then repeated, "I *wanted* you to be."

Everything about it was unbelievable, in the sense it was so much more than I could have imagined.

He smiled, winking down at me. "I'd ask if you could put your leg on my shoulder, but you'd probably kick me in the face."

I smiled, wanting to punch him before bringing his mouth to mine again.

Savoring the warm sensation of his body moving with mine, the heat between us was creating a sheen of sweat as we slid against one another.

Despite the fact I was burning up, my entire body was trembling.

Beau had one hand on my hip, the other wrapped under my neck driving me into his movements, which had turned passionate and thoroughly focused. I could tell by the darkness in his eyes and his flushed cheeks, he was intent on this, us, fucking me.

I kept thinking, *should I be saying anything? Should I talk dirty to him? No. Just stay quiet.*

"It was so hard to pull away from you last night," he admitted, spreading kisses over my jaw and against my neck before he pulled back to look at me. His left hand moved from my hip to rest against my cheek.

I said nothing.

Any time I felt like talking, I kissed him, saving myself the word vomit dilemma, and I didn't dare move.

What I couldn't ignore were the reactions my body was having to Beau and the angle of his hips. He knew just the right pressure to place on my center with his pubic bone and the way to move his hips.

I felt everything, and so much more.

I was so close, and all I needed was that one last push. Thankfully Beau knew what to do and arched his chest away from mine, driving into me with slow, forceful dragging motions.

Yep. Just like that.

He's amazing.

"Oh, God," I breathed out through clenched lips and closed eyes as drops of water soaked my face and a rush of pure ecstasy tore through my body. Rocking into his hips, I rode out the ripples consuming me. "Jesus. . . ." I released a long breath I'd been holding onto.

Beau's breathing changed from panting, to gasping as his movements sped. Wanting to feel him closer, I pulled at his shoulders, his arms letting go as I brought my lips to his collarbone, sliding across the sweaty and rain-soaked skin.

He stared down at me as he shook, body trembling, eyes dark and his brow with intensity.

Say something. No, don't. Don't say anything.

His breath expelled in a heavy pant in the same moment his hand squeezed my thigh, pulling me into his hips one last time as the last of his orgasm pulsed through him.

We came together, panting, his entire body rigid as the warmth crashed over us. Oh God, the groan he let out in my ear, the way his body tensed; it was all too much.

I had sex with Beau Ryland.

It took us a moment of heavy breathing before I finally spoke, rain pelting our faces. "It's wet in here."

That's random. Talk about the rain when you just had the best sex of your life?

"We should close that vent. Everything is soaked in here." Beau sighed, rolling onto his back. Neither one of us said anything for another minute, when he asked, "Was that your first time?"

I laid my head against his chest, blinking incessantly as I attempted to process what he had just asked and why.

Did I do something wrong?

As the words hung in the air, his heart beat rapidly, his breathing erratic.

"No, it wasn't."

Beau nodded, but said nothing to my confession, and rolled to bring me to his naked body, our legs tangled under the sleeping bag.

I could feel his heartbeat between my shoulders and his stomach against my back, a gentle rhythm. With both his arms around my middle, I was also glad I was facing away from him, because the way he was holding me made me smile like some kind of lunatic who just had sex with the man of her dreams.

Lifting my right arm out from under his bicep, I placed my hand over his, which was curved around the top of my rib cage. I wondered if he could feel my heart beating like crazy. I wondered if he knew how I felt about him, how I have felt about him for so long.

He pressed his face closer; I could feel his nose by the back of my ear, his scruffy jaw scratching against my shoulder. Warming my body and surrounded me, he whispered lowly, "Thank you for tripping into my arms."

Shut up, Bentley, now is not the time to say anything. Be normal, if you can.

"I should be thanking *you* for catching me after all of my graceful coordination."

I could feel his breath on my neck through my hair and over my entire body.

Beau Ryland did things to me, made me feel a sense of. . .I didn't even have a word for the way he made me feel being close to him, but he was exactly what I never thought I needed.

I wasn't sure if I could sleep that night with all the thoughts in my head about what we were doing, how I felt, how he felt, all of it, but then Beau made the lowest, quietest humming sound right by my ear, my heart thudding louder than before.

It made my eyelashes flutter and my heart soar.

"Goodnight," he whispered, his voice tickling my ear.

I hummed in response this time, and sleep found me before I even knew it.

THE NEXT MORNING, I lay there, unable to process that Beau was, one, asleep beside me in my tent with no clothes on, and, two, had sex with me.

Embarrassment didn't do this justice when I thought about having sex with Beau. The sunlight streaming in through the roof in the tent greatly overshadowed the moons reprieve from last night, and I felt naked. Even though I was, I felt almost vulnerable to this. I was petrified of what his reaction was going to be.

Drawing in a breath, I rolled a little to my right and faced him, sighing contently. He looked adorable and younger than he did when he was awake and the tension in his eyes crept over him.

I didn't want him to wake and find me staring at him like the creep I was being, so I rolled back over and stared at the ceiling of the tent. I was kinda surprised the little snoring monster hadn't come in here last night.

Oh God, what if she had? Did she see anything?

The thought made me both a little giddy and terrified.

The longer I lay there, the more I wondered about my coma theory. Had I hit my head hard enough that I dreamed I had sex with him? My head told me I was dreaming, but other parts of me, the soreness and the fact that I was still naked, confirmed maybe I wasn't in a coma after all.

Maybe this was really happening and Beau Ryland was into me.

I fist pumped the air, and then heard a chuckle beside me.

"Did you just fist pump the air?" Beau asked, peeking an eye open at me.

Fuck! Really?

"Why did you have to open your eyes right then?" I asked, peering over at him, glaring. "You weren't supposed to see that."

"So why were you fist pumping? Or is that supposed to be unknown too?"

"I was uh. . . well. . . I was just celebrating the fact I am not in a coma."

Ugh. . . You really just can't shut your mouth, can you?

He had his arm over his face, but I could see his blues watching me. Arching an eyebrow, the corner of his mouth twisted slightly into a half smile. "A coma, huh? Well, I knew I was good, but good enough to put you in a coma is a new one. But really, I'm a light sleeper."

"Uh-huh," I groaned.

When he didn't say anything, I looked at him again and he asked, "Do you remember anything about last night this time?"

"A little. Maybe you could refresh my memory."

He chuckled, his body shaking in the most adorable boyish way. "Hey, I tried to go for another round—" taking my pillow from me, he put it over his face "—but you kicked me in the balls for waking you up."

I did?

His poor balls. I should really kiss them, or massage them again and make up since they are holding my future children's DNA in them. Whoa. Slow down. You fucked him once. Don't get carried away.

Jeez. Laney had told me I was a little violent at night, but I had no idea I'd do that.

"Sorry. I like my sleep, and if I'm woken up, I'm not friendly. Laney once told me I slapped her and called her a bitch when she tried to wake me up. I've also told her to go to hell and I hated her face. I think it's a medical condition or something. I'm pretty sure I read it on the intern—" I paused, mid-word, with his light laughter. "Stop smiling at me."

"Apparently, you are talkative in the morning and unfriendly," he mumbled, his voice marred by the pillow. "We need to move this tent later. I slept on a rock all night."

With the sleeping bag pulled down a little, I had a nice view of his stomach and lower regions.

Jesus, look at him. He's. . . fuck.

The need stirred in my stomach, and I realized I had missed out on how good sex was with the right person.

"We could, I don't know, try again." My voice was timid, floating through the gray morning like a whisper.

Beau shook his head. "Give me a little bit. . .you like sleep and I'm not a morning person." Despite the rejection, he rolled over and drew me into his chest. "Now sleep with me."

He wants to actually sleep and cuddle me.

Okay, I could definitely get used to this. And what kind of cologne does he use, or is that just his natural smell? I might have to ask him when he wakes me.

"ARE YOU HUNGRY? Miles and Blaine made biscuits and gravy," Beau asked, returning to my tent as I was getting dressed. I could tell most everyone else was awake with the noise coming from the lake. Beau and I had fallen back asleep this morning and hadn't woken up until Miles was making obscene sex noises outside the tent.

My eyes lit up. I was starving.

What I feared though was when we emerged together, everyone would know he was in my tent with me last night.

They already knew that, dumb shit.

Would they stare at me? Would the girls who gave me the stink eye last night be jealous?

Part of me was okay with that, but I wasn't one for causing a scene or having anyone stare at me. My lack of walking skills the other night was a perfect example.

As I pulled on my jean shorts, I looked up at him, nervously. "Yeah, I'm hungry."

Beau didn't reply right away. Instead, his expression made me think he was deep in thought, watching me. And then he spoke, lowly, "Are you afraid they'll see you're with me?"

With him? I'm with him?

He waited, looking contemplative, but curious as to what I was about to say. "Yes." My voice was like a whisper again, soft spoken and subtle. "I wasn't gaining too many friends last night."

Raising his hands to his head, he turned his hat around backward. "Why do you care what they think?" Once again, his expression appeared lost.

"I'm not sure. Payton. . . ." I let the words hang in the air, refusing to finish the sentence, finding my hands very interesting.

"So?" Beau replied right away, his voice even and soft, assuring me my assumptions were wrong. "I'm not with her."

There. He said it. I nodded, not knowing what to say, and put my freshly-washed shorts and tank top on.

Beau tossed his flannel in my face. "You can wear that too, if you want."

Beau winked watching me button the flannel. "Stop giving me that look. I'm hungry, and if you keep looking at me like that, I'll be in here all day."

What's wrong with that? Jesus, he's hot.

We didn't say much else that morning as he helped me out of the tent, and to my surprise, no one paid me any attention. Some were drinking beer already, even though it was only ten in the morning, where others were still sleeping.

A few people were on the dock, cooling off as the sun was already beating down on us.

After a quick shower, thanks to Beau sneaking me in the master bedroom upstairs, he and I sat together on the deck at a folding table where he ate biscuits and gravy and talked to Miles, and I picked at a cinnamon roll.

Beau chuckled when the boys left, looking over at my half-gone cinnamon roll. "You sure do have a sweet tooth, pretty girl."

I rolled my eyes, licking frosting from my lip. "You have no idea," I moaned around the sweetness. "I like sweets."

"You should try my mama's apple pie then." Beau took a bite of his biscuit and chewed slowly. "It's amazing."

Flashing Beau a hopeful smile, because I really wanted to taste his mama's pie, I noticed Payton watching me, not glaring, but still watching me. I scooted away from Beau a few inches, and then realized I was wearing his flannel, again, what the fuck was the point in scooting away when it was a given I was with him last night.

"Don't do that," he said, as if I should have known what he was talking about.

I looked at him, his stare moving to mine and to his paper cup of steaming black coffee. "Do what?"

Beau gave a shrug, raising his cup to his lips. "Act like she makes you nervous," he answered, his eyes on his cup.

Uh. . . how could she not?

"She *does* make me nervous," I replied softly, continuing to pick at my cinnamon roll.

Beau smiled around his coffee cup. "She shouldn't."

Uh, yes, she should. If there were ever a perfect girl in the dictionary, it would have her face next to it.

It was so easy for him to say that, but it was another for me to believe it.

Laney came by, sitting across from Beau and me, her gaze bouncing from mine to his. "Hey kids."

"Beau!" Miles yelled from inside the house, banging the kitchen window. I looked up, laughing at his black eyes from where he was kicked in the face yesterday. "Come here."

Nodding, Beau reached for his plate. "I'll be right back."

I smiled. "Okay."

When he was out of sight, Laney grinned, wide and goofy. "You had sex with him, didn't you?"

Am I that transparent?

My smile gave me away, if my heated cheeks didn't. I was never very good at keeping secrets.

Laney gave a head nod to Payton, who was still watching me, but now talking to three other girls. "You pissed off the queen."

"Why do you say that?"

"Uh—" Laney took her cup of coffee and dumped two scoops of sugar in there, then stirred it with her finger "—because she's been watching you both all morning."

"They're not dating anymore though."

My heart began to kick, holding on to hope I wasn't getting in the way of them and what Beau told me was the truth. I knew they had something; hell, everyone in Mountain Brook knew about them. They were that couple. The cheerleader and the football player, only said football player wanted nothing to do with that life and left after high school to be a musician.

"So I take it you're having a good time?" Laney was amused with herself, sweeping her tangled hair back in a bun. "You can thank me now."

My brow arched in her direction, and then I noticed Beau standing at the table again holding keys in his hand. "I'm in charge of getting more beer. Wanna come?"

Alone. . . with Beau. . . again?

Heck yes!

I jumped up, slamming my knee on the table. "Son of a bitch!" Beau shook his head in disbelief I was this uncoordinated. "Uh, yeah, I do."

"We'll talk later!" Laney chirped.

I rolled my eyes, walking along with Beau.

Beau grinned, raising an eyebrow as he reached for my hand, in front of everyone. "What was that about?"

"Nothing."

When we were inside the truck, I was nervous, my mind scrambling and replaying images of last night.

Beau chuckled softly and grabbed my arm to scoot me closer to him, his cheek pressing to the side of my face, warm and comforting. "You were too far away."

When I didn't say anything, he started the truck, the engine rumbling to life.

"You seem distracted this morning."

"You have no idea," I muttered under my breath.

"Oh, I think I have an idea." He placed the truck in drive and winked at me.

"SO YOU GRADUATED, right?" Beau asked when we were on our way back to the lake.

"Yes, just last week." It was the first time we'd talked about me.

"What was your major?"

"Human development."

He made a face, like that wasn't what he was expecting. "Interesting choice."

"I've always wanted to help people. I want to be an independent living assistant."

"Like in a nursing home?"

"No, assisted living, there's a difference."

"Why there?"

"My mother is in an assisting living center and has no one but me who visits her. They get lonely and no one is there for them but their family, or independent living assistants, only there's not enough of them."

Beau was quiet for a minute, one hand resting on the steering wheel, the other on the back of the seat, rubbing my shoulder. "Do you have a job waiting for you?"

"I have an internship in Birmingham. I start in two weeks." I turned my head to watch him, his eyes on the road. "What about you?"

"I'm on tour right now." He paused for a moment as he passed a car in the left lane and then moved back to the right lane of the road. "Hoping that turns into something." After a brief pause, he asked, "I thought I heard Laney say you're from Mountain Brook too, is that right?"

I wanted to be like, 'Yeah, dude, and you never noticed me until I flew through the air at you like a damn spider monkey.'

But I didn't.

I nodded though. "Yes, I moved there from Jacksonville when I was seven. We actually went to high school together. You graduated when I was a sophomore."

"Oh yeah?" He leaned back, relaxing in the seat, his weight settled to one side as he rubbed his left hand over the stubble of his jaw. "I never noticed you."

"How could you have? We were never introduced and you were with Payton."

"Girl like you," Beau said conversationally, moving his arm from around me, his hand finding my inner thigh, his fingers rubbing circles over my skin just under the frayed edge of my jean shorts. "I would have noticed, had I met you."

"I, uh, had a *huge* crush on you though." Shit. I said it out loud.

His head whipped around to face me. "Is that so?"

I nodded dramatically.

"As clumsy as you are, I'm surprised you didn't fall into my hands sooner."

I wasn't laughing and glared at him.

"How come I never saw you? Who'd you hang out with?"

"No one. I was a cheerleader for a little while, but it wasn't exactly a good thing for a girl like me."

He shook his head slowly and chuckled under his breath. "I wouldn't image so." Then his face took on a more serious expression, his brow drawing together. "When did you first notice me?"

I had to think back to that first initial Beau sighting, the one that drew me in and left me with this ten-year crush, even though I'd never actually spoken to him until two days ago.

"Summer before my freshman year, I was fourteen, two days shy of fifteen. I was sitting on the front porch and you drove by in your truck and pulled into my neighbor's driveway. I didn't think much of it, but then you looked my way, smiled, and gave me a wink." I hadn't realized it, but my voice and my face had taken on an expression of a girl telling a fairy tale romance about Prince Charming.

Well, it must have been entertaining to him because he laughed. I felt humiliated that I had just told him how it happened for me—just a damn wink and I was in love.

But you had to remember I was a kid and at an age that when an older boy gave you a wink, we fell hopelessly in love with them

I frowned. "Are you making fun of me?"

He shook his head immediately, squeezing me to the side of his body. "Not at all."

"Well, it sure seems like it, you know, with the whole laughing thing. All right, so now I sound like a creep."

"No, I think it's cute. You got a dreamy little look on your face when you were talking about me. It feels good to be the center of someone's fantasy like that."

Shit, my face is burning. Hopefully it wasn't red.

"Well, you've been my dream guy ever since."

Keeping his eyes on the road, he kissed the top of my head. "I'm glad we didn't meet back then. . . ." My heart sank, and then he spoke again. "Because I probably would have been a jerk and never lived up to the image you had of me."

My heart was racing when I asked, "And now what?"

"Now I can be your Prince Charming." And then his body shook as he let out a laugh. "I got the charming part down. I just need to work on the prince part."

I laughed myself; he was so goofy. "Keep trying. You suck at it so far."

He winked. "I love a good challenge."

Chapter Eight

SOMETHING 'BOUT A TRUCK

BEAU

I WONDERED WHAT this meant. Bentley said she had a crush on me in school, but did she actually know anything about me aside from the fact I was Beau Ryland?

Did she know how lonely I was, despite being surrounded by people all the time?

Bentley and I made our way back to the house where I parked in the field behind Miles's house.

I wasn't sure what to say to Bentley this morning, or how to make her feel about what happened. Maybe I shouldn't have had sex with her.

Hell, I knew I probably shouldn't have now that she said she knew me. How'd that make me look?

At least she wasn't a virgin. I would have felt even worse about it.

But last night, it was. . . I didn't even have words for what it felt like being with her. I've had one-night stands, been with women whose names I'd never remember, but there was something memorable about last night.

Maybe it was the way she watched, like I was the wish in a dream, or the way she moved, responding to every single touch I gave her.

We got out of the truck in silence, neither of us saying anything.

Miles caught me in the kitchen as I set the beer cases on the counter and Bentley used the bathroom. "What's going on with you and Legs?"

I was tempted to leave on our way back from the store, only I'd take Bentley with me so she didn't have to put up with this shit and these guys today.

"Stop calling her that."

Because they'll never be wrapped around you.

"I'm sorry. It's just, damn," Miles watched her walk down the hall to the bathroom, "look at them."

Oh, I was, but he didn't need to be. I began to walk away when he stopped me, tossing a roll of paper towels at the back of my head.

"Hey, wait." I turned, picking up the towels and chucking them back at him.

"What?"

"We're gonna have a little fun on the boat tonight."

"Yeah, Wade said something about it earlier."

He cracked the top to a beer. "So you'll play a little too."

If I didn't know any better, I'd think the reason they have me around is to keep the party going.

"I said I would."

He laughed, leaning casually into the counter after taking a drink of his beer. "Hey, I didn't know. You seem like you're distracted."

"I'm not distracted."

Yes, you are.

"Yeah, okay." He wasn't buying it, but I also wasn't very convincing when he saw me watching Bentley as some kid I didn't know approached her. He looked young, barely eighteen, but he made her smile. Watching them, my gut felt strange. I definitely felt something for her and didn't care for the idea of another guy going up to her.

"Who's that?" I gave a nod to the kid and Bentley, who was laughing at something he said, her cheeks flushing as she glanced down at her tank top under *my* flannel.

That flush should have been for me only, because it was last night. A memory of me grasping her thigh, bringing it higher on my waist as I slid inside of her plagued my mind.

"His name is Joel. Some kid we met last night. Came over from the neighbors and didn't leave."

I wanted to make him leave. Stupid kid. I was never one to get jealous. Never really did with Payton, but I suppose I had my moments as a hot-headed kid at times.

Now was a bit different. I felt. . . possessive, I guess.

The kid left and Bentley walked back over to me, barefoot and flushed.

"Who's he?" I gestured to the kid now watching Bentley standing next to me.

Bentley gave me a curious expression, her cute nose scrunching. "His name is Joel."

"Hmm."

"Hmm, he says. What does that mean?"

"It means nothing." *Liar.* Reaching down, I took her hand in mine. "Wanna go somewhere with me?"

She looked at me, full of apprehension. "I just did."

"No, someplace else."

"Fine." Bentley rolled her eyes. "If you must force me to hang out with you."

I had to chuckle at her. She had a sense of humor for sure.

"HOW GOOD OF a swimmer are you?"

She raised an eyebrow at me when we reached the top of the rock. I borrowed a Jet Ski from Miles and took her out to Acapulco Rock. "I'm okay, why?" She was panting, having climbed up forty some feet with me.

I pointed to the water below us now. "Let's jump."

"I'm *not* jumping off that cliff, Beau."

"C'mon, baby—" I gave her a wink watching her lips "—live a little."

"I'm afraid of heights."

"I doubt that."

Her eyes widened, taking a step back. "I am."

"I'll hold your hand."

"I don't think that will help."

She had an answer for everything. "You won't know unless you try."

She knew I had a point and started to fidget. "What if my bikini falls off?"

I waggled my eyebrows, reaching for her hand. "Lucky me."

Drawing in a heavy breath, she stared at the water.

Seeing her tan skin and all the places I kissed last night had me thinking staying up here might be better, but something told me Bentley wasn't a risk-taker.

In fact, I doubted she had done much in her life, and certainly never jumped off a cliff into the water forty feet below. I first jumped off this when I was eight years old. Proudest day of my kid life back then.

Taking a seat on the rock, she crept her toes along the edge and peered over again, her arms wrapped around her stomach. "Beau, I can't do it. I'm terrified of heights. When I was in the eighth grade, we went swimming and there was a cliff they wanted me to jump off. I got up there and couldn't even look over the edge. Those assholes counted down and pushed me in!"

I took a seat next to her, nothing but water, rocks, and trees surrounding us. The view from here was rustic and rough, like something you'd see at the Grand Canyon. The way the water shined bright off the red clay and rocks, I'd rather be up here than on a stage any day.

"Sure you can," I whispered, bumping her shoulder with mine. "And I won't push you."

Taking a peek myself, it looked a lot higher than I remembered.

"Wow, I don't remember it being that high," I teased, elbowing her. "I jumped off this cliff when I was eight, you can do it."

For a second, we looked at each other, sparks igniting inside me, and I wanted to know everything about her. Irises the color of night, there was something in their depth that wouldn't let go of me, like heavy weights.

"Come on, you gotta jump sometime."

Finally, after five minutes of me giving her a pep talk, telling her it was good for her soul to face fear like this, Bentley stood. "Hold my damn hand, Beau. If I die, I'm taking you with me."

I laughed. "Nice."

With one last look, we jumped, together.

In the midst of the jump, I let go of her, not wanting to hurt her if we became entangled. It stung like hell when we landed, and I'd probably never do this again.

The nearby swimmers and boaters cheered us on when we popped back up.

Bentley let out a shriek, her face flushed and confused, and then she grinned, swimming toward me and the Jet Ski.

"Holy shit!"

I smiled, my thumb sweeping away the water on her freckled cheek. "I told you. . .I got you."

Maybe it was the intensity of jumping and her facing her fears, but with the way she was watching me, I had to kiss her.

All I'd planned on doing was jumping with her.

Instead, I was sure she made me fall.

Just before I leaned in, she placed her hand on my chest. "Beau?"

"Yeah?"

"My bikini fell off." She blinked, as if she was in shock. "I'm naked. It's gone. Blaine's gonna kill me. I lost her suit."

She wasn't worried about being naked, which nearly made me laugh, but I didn't want her naked. We were surrounded by boats; they'd see what was only meant for me.

Diving under, I tried to see if I could spot it underwater, but saw nothing but us treading water.

When I surfaced, she was watching me curiously. "Anything?"

"No." I shook water from my eyes. "Are the bottoms gone too?"

She reached down. I should have offered to check. "No, got those. Just my top." Slumping against the side of the Jet Ski, she made sure to keep her body below the water. "This weekend has sucked."

I stared at her like she'd lost her mind. "How can you say that? You met me."

"Oh, sorry." She laughed. "But it's been a disaster. I smashed my head and my body looks like I've been inside a dryer with rocks." Her arm flung up in my face, smacking the side of my head. "Look at these bruises. And I met you, but now I gotta leave tomorrow."

"You don't have to leave. . . you could come with me to Montgomery."

I threw it out there, hoping she'd take the bait, only I doubt she heard any of it with her rant.

Not knowing what else to do, I swam over to a nearby boat. "Hey, my girl lost her top jumping." And every girl on their boat was topless I might add. "Do you have a towel she can use?"

Surprisingly, they did. "Damn." The man who handed me the towel smiled over at Bentley. "I wouldn't let her have the towel looking like that."

"Thanks for the towel." Douchebag.

Swimming back over to Bentley, I handed it to her. Silence settled between us as I kissed her once and then helped her up on the Jet Ski.

"Are you glad you jumped?" I asked when she kept saying she couldn't believe she did that, and that she lost her top.

I turned to face her, my lashes sprinkled with drops of water from my hair.

I crave you, baby, in an innocent, heart-pounding way.

She looked at my lips and then my eyes, smiling. "I've never in my life felt more alive than I have this weekend."

"Me too."

Chapter Nine

WHEN HE LEAVES YOU

BENTLEY

"SO WHAT, LIKE, your dad thinks you should work for him at the bar instead of pursuing your music?" I asked, waiting for Laney and Blaine to get their bathing suits on so we could go on the boat.

Luckily, Blaine had another one I could borrow after losing hers.

I felt exhilarated and on a total adrenaline rush since I jumped off that cliff, and I couldn't stop talking. As usual.

Beau laughed bitterly at the topic of his father, and I thought maybe I shouldn't have asked that. Maybe it was too much. "Not just that. He thinks I should work for him, and forget about *my* dreams. My Grandpa handed it down to him, and he thinks my brother and I should want that too."

"So he doesn't support your music then?" My legs dipped over the edge of the dock as I watched the ripples they created in the water, and then my attention was snagged by Gavin, Miles, and Wade loading beer onto the houseboat we would be taking out to the middle of the lake tonight. "Would you want to work with him?"

I was nervous about what tonight would mean. Or what might happen. For that reason, I was babbling about nothing, about anything I could think of. Would he want to have sex again?

I was leaving tomorrow morning, what would happen?

Beau was silent for a moment before he said, "Working in a bar, that's *not* me. Just because it's his business, his dream, doesn't mean it's mine. I have my own life, which doesn't revolve around him and that stupid bar. It's just a status for him. I don't even think he likes owning his own business, just that he does and he can call himself the owner."

"What do you want to do?"

"My music." He shrugged, trying to blow off the conversation.

"You're really good."

His head dropped forward, his hands tugging at his hair. "It doesn't matter if I'm good or not, Bentley." I wanted to grab his hands and wrap them around me, and make him believe he could have anything he ever wanted despite what his dad wanted for him. "But I don't know if that's ever going to work out."

"You're on a tour right now. Why would you say that?"

"It's not *my* tour. I'm opening for Sam Shaver." Beau reached down to chip at the worn wood of the dock. "It has nothing to do with me thinking I'm not good enough. It's me facing reality. Sure I could probably continue to do what I'm doing, but getting noticed by a record producer doesn't just happen like everyone thinks."

I gave him a sour look, my brows scrunched together. "You're right, and you won't sayin' crap like that. You're just setting yourself up for failure if you have a shit attitude like that."

Beau laughed, raising his eyebrow at me. "Yeah, okay."

He was bitter when it came to his dad, I was gathering that much. In a sense, I could relate to that. My dad left without so much as a goodbye when I was a teenager. Not that he was present in my life much before that, but it still hurt.

We stood, ready to head for the boat, tired of waiting on the girls, when Miles' black lab came loping down the dock and lunged into the water after a snake. I jumped back when I saw it, squealing.

"That fucking dog hates me," Beau mused, watching Buddy eye us with the snake in his mouth. "I don't know why they call him Buddy either. He's nobody's buddy. I hope that snake bites him, too."

"He's not that bad." I laughed, backing up and wanting nothing to do with the damn snake.

"Wait until he bites your ass, you won't be calling him Buddy anymore."

"With everything that's happened to me this weekend, I'm surprised that dog hasn't bitten me."

Beau winked. "The nights still early. I might bite you."

"C'mon guys!" Miles waved to us from the deck of the boat. Somehow, and I don't know how, but the girls were already on the boat. We must have missed them. "We're ready."

I guess I was so caught up in Beau talking, I hadn't realized the girls walked right by us.

With a sigh, Beau stood. "Let's go, pretty girl. Time to party."

"Man, how many toys does his family have? Do his parents know he has parties like this?"

He helped me up, probably so I didn't fall. "He has a boat, that houseboat monstrosity, Jet Skis, and a few quads. His parents are loaded. They own a couple restaurants."

"I see."

"They spend the summer in the Bahamas, or someplace like that, and don't give a shit what he does."

When we reached the boat, I took in the vast size of it and all his friends. "So we're going on this thing for the night?"

Beau wrapped his arm around my shoulders. "Yep. Sleepin' on a boat tonight."

"Only sleeping?" My face burned, remembering vivid and amazing details.

Taking in everything, I wasn't sure what they had planned, just that we had sleeping bags and enough alcohol for a frat party.

Beau groaned, twisting his head to bury it in the crook of my neck as he took a closer. "Not if I'm lucky."

"I think you've already gotten *lucky* this weekend, buddy."

"Baby," he pulled back, kissing my cheek once, "you have no idea."

He was right, I really didn't have any idea.

I had an idea of what he was doing to me, but he hadn't said much about what he felt for me.

We were on the houseboat with around fifteen others, Payton being one of them. I wasn't exactly thrilled because of the close quarters, and I couldn't exactly jump off the side of the boat. I was done with jumping into water all together after the cliff and the missing top.

The boat was nice, much like everything Miles had. It was even equipped with an upper deck where you could sunbathe, or as Beau said, watch the stars. Apparently, we were sleeping up there tonight.

Beau tipped his head to the deck of the boat, noticing the way it held my attention. "You wanna dance?" Handing me a beer, he then pushed a shot my direction not long after we found a good place to stop in the middle of the lake.

I would have agreed to anything if it meant his hands would be on me and my hips. The dance floor held my attention, mostly because there were some girls desperately trying to show off their bodies for him, repeatedly asking him to dance with them. Every time, he said no.

While I enjoyed the liquid courage in my hand, I wanted to dance with Beau, I did.

It was apparent Beau was the life of the party on the boat and the reason the majority of these people were here.

He was the man with the voice that could melt any woman, including me. Every step he took, women surrounded him, and

I began to notice he was either oblivious to it or numb to their advances.

Embracing me when I stood, his eyes remained on mine, never giving the other women a glance. His hand found my stomach, and his finger ran along the edge of my bikini bottoms, stopping near my belly button. The touch made me squirm and want to do more than dance with him.

Since last night, we hadn't really talked about us having sex. Not that I wanted to, but I did wonder how he felt about it. Part of me wondered if he regretted it, but the other part didn't want to know, wanted to believe anything but reality.

Beau tossed back a shot, handed me one, and I did the same. The fire burned, and before I knew it, his mouth was adding to that delicious feeling, creating an ache from deep within. Whistles broke out, probably from Miles, only I was so caught up with the way Beau's mouth felt against mine.

"Don't pay them any attention," he told me, before deepening the kiss.

Judging by the fact he kissed me in front of everyone, maybe he *was* feeling what I was feeling.

The hum, the ache to touch him again, was something I couldn't stop thinking about. I could stop myself from overanalyzing his feelings, and talking too much, but I couldn't stop the desire.

Every time he touched me, I felt the raindrops on my cheeks from last night and the weight of his body, a reminder of what we shared. It may have been a one-night thing, or whatever, but the memories, the vivid details my mind held onto was worth it. I focused on the ones where he whispered

my name and the desperation in his movements when he came
and the way he held me all night.

I twisted, wanting the contact, *needing* that contact, I
wrapped my arms tight around his neck. I wasn't sure if it was
the alcohol talking, but it took all I could not to attack him
completely and wrap my legs around him.

Every eye in there was on us, I could feel it as we made our
way to where everyone was dancing.

Since last night, the passion between us was about as
intense as the humidity, heavy and constricting, and there was
no way it went unnoticed.

I was surprised to hear the song playing was actually a Katy
Perry song, one you could do more than a line dance to.

Beau's head remained down as our bodies came together.

Gliding my hands over his bare shoulders, he smelled so
good, and I couldn't get close enough to him, even with my
body welded to his.

Running his nose along the curve of my neck, his breath
was hot, sticky, and consuming. The small deck on the
houseboat was crowded and probably at its maximum weight
limit. Sweaty bodies grinding against one another in the
confined space.

With his red baseball hat on backward, Beau's left hand
moved from my hip, his other holding the bourbon he was
slow-sipping on. Pressing his hand to my face, he trapped me
with his intensity. The beat thumped in my chest, but not as
loudly as my heart.

Swallowing, Beau drew in a deep breath and then pulled
my face to his. Lips hesitated, making whisper touches.

"You still taste so sweet."

I took his hat and put it on me. "You taste like bourbon."

Beau chuckled, lightly, smiling against my lips.

We swayed, the beat changing, but Beau poured a lot into that kiss. If he was trying to reassure me with the intimacy of the kiss, that last night meant more to him than I initially thought, it was working for me.

As I was bumped from behind, my teeth knocked his, but that didn't stop him. He kept his lips on mine, slowly tracing my mouth with his tongue. Just when I thought he was going to pull back, his hungry lips would reclaim mine, his hand tangling in my hair. Every time, it left me burning and craving more.

When we weren't kissing, Beau's eyes often remained down, watching my hips move against his.

"Are you relaxed now?" His voice was low, but still heard over the music.

"Is that what you were going for?"

Our eyes met. "No, not really. I just wanted to kiss you."

"By all means, don't stop."

And he didn't, at least not during that song.

THE SUN SET, unwavering fiery red slowly sinking on the horizon. The lights and music from the nearby boats lingered in the distance, as did the twinkle lights wrapped around the top deck of the boat. It was a reminder many were doing the same thing we were, letting go and having fun.

I couldn't tear my eyes from the sunset and the pure, natural beauty it held. First orange, then red, and fading into dark blue, another day melting away only to be replaced with sequin-silver stars glowing in the night.

I loved everything about the night and couldn't wipe the smile off my face.

Beau was at the bar again, refilling his drink, glassy-eyed and laughing with Miles and Wade as I sat next to Blaine.

I giggled when Beau stumbled, leaning against the side of the boat for support. "He's really drunk."

"Don't let Beau have tequila tonight." Blaine kept her gaze on her brother while taking a bite of her hot dog.

"Why?"

Setting down the half-eaten hot dog, she rolled her eyes. "He turns into an asshole."

"Good to know." I brought the rum and coke mixture I had been sipping on for the last hour to my lips. "I've heard a lot of people turn into dicks after drinking it."

Had to say it was true for my dad too. I guess in some ways I wasn't much of a drinker—aside from this weekend—because of him. No way did I want to be like him.

"Does Beau drink it often?" He had the bottle in his hand, talking to Miles and pointing at it, maybe giving him some elaborate drinking story.

"The only time I've seen him drink it, he punched Jensen in the face."

"Oh." I couldn't imagine Beau being physically violent with anyone, but I also saw the way he was watching Joel tonight.

About an hour ago, Beau overheard Joel ask me to dance, and shoved him back into Miles and Gavin, but said nothing.

Joel didn't seem to mind, laughed it off and asked Blaine to dance. Joel seemed determined he would get me to dance sometime. For an eighteen-year-old kid he was harmless, although extremely flirty.

Something also told me there was a side to Beau he didn't display often, but when he did, it wasn't pretty.

He set down the bottle of tequila, and I could hear them talking about some concert in Memphis when Payton approached Beau as he moved closer to me, now within earshot.

"Hey," she looked right at Beau. "I'm gonna sing a little." Then she leaned forward, saying something in his ear, only to have him shake his head no and back away from her.

What the hell did she say to him?

Beau told me he was going to play later tonight, but hadn't said anything about anyone else. I didn't even know Payton could sing.

"Payton sings too?" I asked Beau, when he returned to sit next to me on the couch, his mood changed completely from the laughing I'd just witnessed, to a set scowl at Payton.

Beau nodded to my question, but said nothing.

All the blood drained from my face. *Fucking perfect.*

I was dying to ask what she said, but didn't. "I can't sing," I noted, my word vomit returning. "I sound like a cat dying."

He nodded, again, giving me a wink, but still, said nothing, his body rigid and tense.

Of course she sings. Damn it. I hope she sucks. She needs a flaw.

I thought it was great when she played "Any Man Of Mine" and had Blaine and Laney dancing around. Payton sounded surprisingly a lot like Shania Twain.

I wasn't sure what to expect after that, I mean, she got the party started, but was shocked when she began an acoustic version of "When He Leaves You" by Shania Twain.

My first thought when she glanced at me several times was "What have I gotten myself into?"

My other was that I found her flaw. Jealousy. Why else would she have chosen that song?

"Fucking bitch," Beau groaned under his breath, but I heard him. Downing the rest of his drink, he seemed annoyed with Payton in the opening lyrics that were directed my way.

Part of me was stunned to hear him talk that way about her.

Beau looked like he was going to explode. With a sniff, he stared her down with fire-lit eyes.

I had a feeling their breakup wasn't exactly pleasant judging by the hostility in him right then.

During the chorus, her eyes remained on mine, revealing a pain deep within, and maybe even caused by Beau.

Was she singing that to me?

Hell yes, she's singing to you.

Was she warning me?

Probably.

I no longer had good, kind thoughts about Payton.

Nope. They were gone when she gave me that vindictive smile and sad eyes.

Beau said absolutely nothing during that song, but he also never moved his arm from around my shoulders, which I appreciated, but still, that song was a warning, even I knew that.

I glanced at Beau and then Miles, who was laughing at Payton when the song was over. She flipped him off and walked away.

Unsure what just happened, my stare found Beau again, and when he felt me watching, he smiled halfheartedly, his breathing increasing.

I guess he didn't know what to say.

There was a long pause before he spoke again. "I'm sorry."

"Why did she do that?" I asked, even though I knew what it was, I wanted him to tell me.

She wanted to let me know this was her man I had been messing around with, and maybe she was trying to stake claim, again, or let me know what they had was still there.

I couldn't tell you if it was still there or not, because I didn't know myself. All I knew was they broke up, and since two nights ago, my dream had come true.

"I'm not sure," Beau mumbled, and then stood. "I'll be back in a few minutes."

He then left, walking over to Payton. I silently wished he was going to be a jerk to her for that.

Despite not eating most of the day, my hunger escaped me after hearing Payton sing, along with any comforting thoughts I had of Beau only having eyes for me. I couldn't compare to someone like Payton, no way. They had a past together. We had one night. Or two.

A few minutes later, Beau returned and took his guitar from its case, never saying anything to me.

What did they say to each other? Is he mad at her now?

As Beau was setting up to play, I stared at the hamburger in front of me, unable to eat. I couldn't understand why either. It was either because I was so worked up over Payton, or my own internal lunacy. Whatever it was, it felt like butterflies were attacking my heart.

"You okay?" Miles asked, seeming to notice my lack of appetite or maybe he observed the way I stared endlessly at Beau.

I shrugged, picking at the sesame seeds on the bun one by one, trying not to make eye contact with Miles since I was close to tears.

"Yeah," I sighed. "Just too much to drink," I lied, thinking me being drunk was always a good excuse for anything out of the normal.

"Ah, I see. Well, if you've drank too much, then eating is good. Soaks up the alcohol. . ." he bumped my shoulder, "but if you're upset about Payton, which it seems like that's the winning ticket here, she's nothing to him," Miles spoke with sincerity I didn't know someone like him could have. "Actually, they've been broken up for over a year."

Immediately, I wanted to know why they broke up. I wanted to be a fly on the wall in that conversation and know every single detail about it. Everything.

"He really likes you a lot," Miles noted. "You know that, right, Legs?"

I lowered my eyes nervously, feeling uncomfortable being near Miles. "We just met the other day."

"Yeah, I remember," he teased, ribbing me playfully as though we were best buds. "You landed in his lap. Fate, huh?"

My smile took over. "Stop it."

"Do you have any more of that rum we had last night?" Laney asked, taking a seat on Miles's lap. "That stuff your uncle left?"

He grinned and licked her cheek. "Yep, it's on the counter." He then gestured to the galley of the boat where it was pretty much impossible to get into.

Confused, I watched Laney on Miles's lap with a joint in her hand. I wasn't surprised to see her smoking; she did it a lot. What I couldn't understand was what she was doing this weekend. She came with Gavin, but yet, she was hanging on Miles? Although, I wasn't surprised. In the four years we spent at Auburn University, she had a lot of visitors.

Out of boredom and absolutely no life, I used to keep a log, but eventually ran out of paper and interest.

Miles seemed like a good person, just incredibly flirty with everyone.

To my right, when I found Beau again, he and Payton were deep in conversation, and he didn't look too happy with her, his jaw clenched.

I didn't think Payton liked me, but it seemed she didn't like many people here, including most of Beau's friends, like Miles. Which was strange to me. They all seemed nice.

"She's a bitch," Miles huffed as Laney got up to find the rum.

"Who's a bitch? Lane?" I asked him, noticing the way he was watching Laney and then Blaine dancing with Gavin and that Joel guy. At least he found someone to dance with.

Miles chuckled and turned to face me. "No, I was talking about Payton. . . she's a bitch."

"I thought you guys were all friends?"

"No, we are not. She and Beau are friends. . . or used to be." He pointed to himself. "*I* am friends with Beau, not her, not that slut." He shivered as though he was disgusted by her very presence, but he was also stoned, so he could have been exaggerating on the matter entirely.

I couldn't say I felt any different.

"Why is she a slut?"

"They broke up and she fucked all his friends."

I raised an eyebrow, shaking my head in disbelief. "All of them?"

"Uh-huh. We were all victims of a hate-crime."

"I'm pretty sure that's not the term to use."

"Oh, well, I'm sure it is. She hated him and used us against him. All I had to say was 'I love you, I have a condom' and she was all over my dick like it was a lollipop."

I rolled my eyes, laughing, and not at all surprised by anything he was saying. "You could have said no."

"See, that's expecting too much from a man. Lower your standards, darlin'."

The more Miles talked, the more entertained I became. Or maybe it was because he had a bottle of rum with him and he was helping ease me out of my self-loathing pity party.

As Beau leaned against the side of the boat, guitar beside him and Payton walking away, he drew in a deep breath and hung his head, picking up the guitar and making his way to where they had the microphone set up near the bow.

Beau's mood before was energetic, but now he seemed a little more on edge, vulnerable and shifting into something else entirely. "You wanted me to sing, here's something I'm sure you all know." He gave a nod to Wade, who was playing a guitar beside him, chuckling as he took a drink from his cup. "It's one of mine. . . and if you're not a fan, get off the fuckin' boat then."

Everyone laughed, except for Joel who smarted off with, "Who the hell are you?"

Beau's glare shot to his, leaning into the mic. "You can *definitely* get the fuck off the boat."

Joel laughed it off. Beau didn't. I was positive Joel knew exactly who Beau Ryland was.

"This song is called 'Don't Tell Me That You Miss Me'." During the opening notes, Beau caught my eye every once in a while, and every time his expression was something I couldn't place. His mood was off. What had Payton said to him?

As I sat in the corner with Miles, I noticed Beau gripping the mic, his body swaying, slightly rocking from one foot to the other.

As the music went into a riff, his eyes found Payton's, but he kept his head bent forward, almost more menacing that way.

"Don't tell me that it hurts, how's that supposed to make me feel? You were the one that said goodbye. Left me all alone to deal." Through the darkness, I saw the sky blue that could give you chills and tingles at the same time, glaring at his ex-

girlfriend. *"I gave you everything I had, you mislead me all along. Don't tell me that you miss me and go on about all your heartache."*

Whoa.

"This ain't water up on water, this is gas poured on a flame and the last thing that I needed was for me to hear you say, this face is what you wanted. But I know what to believe cause you left me for him." As the music sped, his voice became louder to the point where he was practically screaming. *"Don't pretend that I'll listen, when you're the one that's lonely. Oh, don't tell me that you miss me. Now that you come here beggin', pleadin', wishin' wanting me back around. I don't need to hear how sorry you are now."*

Looking at him now, I'd never seen him play like this before, so dejected, so angry. He had an intensity that seemed even darker than the lyrics to the song.

He rocked from side to side throughout the third verse, his hand tight on the microphone, one in his pocket. *"I don't need to hear how sorry you are now. Don't tell me that you miss me."*

Across from me, Miles smiled. "Told you he doesn't like her."

WHEN HE FINISHED singing, Beau picked me up, swinging me around with him as he kissed me passionately and then whispered in my ear, as if nothing happened, "I hope you don't have plans the rest of the night."

"Why?" I was a little tipsy and giggling, red-cheeked and swaying, faking nonchalance.

"Because I plan on taking this bikini off with my teeth," he said in that gravelly, seductive voice with a glint of mischief in his eyes, setting me on my feet.

"What are you, a dog? Who uses their teeth, and how is that even possible?"

There I went talking too much again.

He pulled me away from the party and into the bathroom, alone. "I'll show you."

While I had no objections to being alone with him, I needed to know where I stood in all this and what was going on.

Nervously staring at my hands, I spoke slowly. "What are we doing? I don't want to get in the way of you two."

"What?" he gasped, his fingers touching under my chin, forcing me to look at him.

"I just figured—"

"You figured what?" he demanded an answer, and a jolt hit my gut at his sharp tone.

Great, I pissed him off.

"That you were with her."

He closed his eyes and leaned in, pressing my body into the door, his bare chest hard against me. "You thought wrong."

"About what?"

Apparently, I was mental again.

"Me. Her. . ." he swallowed, "us."

"Beau. . . ." I paused, feeling like I needed to say this now, right now. "I didn't go into this weekend, or the last day, thinking it would go anywhere. I don't even know how this happened or what's happening."

Shaking his head, he cupped my cheeks, kissing slowly and tenderly up the side of my neck, lips as soft as feathers dancing in the wind. "You thought wrong. . . again."

I didn't want to be led on or confused, and now I felt like I was. What the hell did any of this mean?

My hands moved to his shoulders, his dropped from my face to my hips, curling around the backs of my thighs to wrap my legs around his waist, before settling on my backside. "I want you again. . . *really bad.*"

As I slid my hands to his hair, he spread my legs farther and let out a low grunt when our bodies came together. "Come back with me to Mountain Brook. I'll take you home in the morning and show you want I mean."

His erection made it difficult for me to respond.

And when he grinded into me, pushing my bikini bottoms aside, I gave up trying.

Then he entered me and nothing more was said.

"WHERE'S BEAU?" Payton asked, looking around, at me mostly, but never talking to me directly.

Well, he was just in the bathroom with me having sex.

I did not say that. Mostly because I wasn't *that* girl, and no way did I want someone like Payton mad at me.

"In the bathroom. . . ." Miles threw his arm around my shoulder, my cheeks flushing as he did so because he knew Beau and I were in the bathroom together a few minutes ago. "I'm sure he doesn't need company."

"What?" Payton seemed annoyed by Miles tonight when last night they were all over each other. She glared at him, adjusting her strappy sandal shoes. She was wearing jean shorts, her bikini top, and a flannel tied up around her waist. I was wearing my bikini and Beau's flannel, which hadn't gone unnoticed by her.

Wade, Beau's cousin, stuck his head down from the upper deck over the railing. "Miles, can you come up here for a second?"

Miles looked from me to Payton and then at Wade, but got up. "I'll be right back, Legs." He seemed to think he needed to protect me from her.

Payton wasted no time at all in sitting next to me. "There's a lot to him, Bentley. He's complicated, and he needs someone who understands that."

"Who? Miles? He seems normal enough," I stalled, knowing exactly who she was talking about.

Payton laughed sarcastically. "I'm not talking about Miles. I'm talking about Beau."

I decided to be brave for once in my life. "What about Beau?"

"He needs someone who can understand him," she said flatly, looking in the direction of the cabin behind us. I had a feeling she was keeping watch for Beau, who really was in the bathroom.

"Are you saying I can't do that for him?" My brave front faded just a little.

"Yes, I am. He only just met you, and you have no idea what he's like or been through. Bentley. . . ." She smiled, and if I didn't know any better, I'd say it almost looked tender and she was trying to be my friend. "Beau isn't always the good guy. He's just *the* guy. The one you'll never forget no matter what."

I didn't know what to say to that, because I had a feeling she was completely right. He was certainly nothing any song would capture. He was everything my heart needed that weekend.

In all my worshiping I did of Beau Ryland and my obsession with him over the years, in reality, I knew very little about who Beau was on the inside.

For that reason, I was no competition for someone like Payton, someone who knew Beau and everything he kept hidden.

"So what," I laughed, trying to keep my voice even. "Is this like your way of telling me to back off?"

"No." Payton stood when she noticed Beau approaching. "It's just me letting you know if you fall, for him, you'll never get back up."

I had no idea what to say to that because in many ways, even after the two days I'd spent with him, I knew exactly what she meant. There was something about this guy that you couldn't shake.

BEAU CAME BACK, his mood completely different from our time in the bathroom when he noticed Payton walking away from me. Seated near the bow of the boat, I focused on the rippling water below, unable to see much else but the way the twinkle lights above me reflected off the dark water.

"Why did you and Payton break up?" I blurted out when he put his arm around me.

"Uh. . . ." I could tell Beau wasn't exactly comfortable talking about him and Payton as he shifted his weight into me, squeezing my shoulder. The way he started fidgeting with the cup in his other hand confirmed my theory.

I realized I was probably invading his privacy a little and backed off. "It's all right, you don't have to explain."

Beau shrugged, the motion relaxed yet suggestive to his demeanor surrounding the subject, and scratched his jaw. "It's not that. . . it's just. . . I don't even know what happened."

He certainly had a way of playing it cool, didn't he?

"What do you mean you don't know?" My eyes darted over his face.

He didn't respond right away. Instead, his expression was lost, as if he was in deep thought. He didn't want to tell me.

Reluctantly, he explained. "I left a few months after graduation and she came with me. Being on the road does things to people, and she wanted to go home. So she did. And. . . I made some bad decisions."

"And by bad decisions, you mean?" Hundreds of scenarios played out in my head—women. . . drugs. . . alcohol. . . all of the above?

"I slept with other women. I was honest about it, and we stayed together for a while, but it wasn't the same and she eventually left. For the last year and a half, we've been hooking up on occasion." He swallowed, taking in my reaction. "I told her three months ago I was done and couldn't keep living that way. She never had any intention of us getting back together. She just wanted to hurt me."

I never thought Beau was that guy, one who would have cheated on his girlfriend. I think in some ways I saw him in a little bit of a different light. In some ways, it was a letdown to hear that.

I could tell it bothered him too; it was in his pensive stare and the way he waited for me to say something in return, and the way I never did.

For the first time, I had nothing to say. I certainly didn't blame him, people made mistakes, and it finally made sense why they were so hostile toward one another.

Chapter Ten

WILDFIRE

BEAU

"WHY'D YOU GO and talk to her?" I asked Payton when Bentley snuck away to the bathroom. I'd just told Bentley I cheated on Payton. The last thing I wanted to admit to Bentley was that I was someone who would do that to a girl.

"Oh, Beau, it wasn't meant to be mean. And what, are you afraid she'll find out your eyes wander a lot on the road?"

"You know, I was nice to you about the song when really I should have been an asshole. Feeding her bullshit is where I draw the line." She challenged me with those pouty green eyes that used to work on me. "You broke up with me, remember?"

"I do remember. And I remember you cheated on me."

"And you fucked my brother. . . and all my friends, so don't act like this when I'm. . . ."

"You're what? In love with the clumsy girl who tripped over you? Jesus Beau. . . ." Her head shook, as if she was disgusted with me. I knew the fucking feeling right now, only it was her I was disgusted with. "You've known her what, a few hours?"

"Don't act like I'm the *bad guy*." I clarified wishing she was a man so I could shove her. Not that I would, but I wanted to. "You. . . ." I was pissed, my breath expelling in frustration. "You fucking show up when you want something and expect me to just drop everything. Not this time. I let you string me along for the last year. Not anymore."

The truth was, when we broke up, yeah we did the hook-ups and I silently hoped she'd take me back. Then I realized what she was doing to me while fucking my friends on the side. She was a vindictive bitch and she knew it.

She challenged me, taking in my stance, my hands on my hips. "Jesus, Beau, you don't have to be a jerk about it."

Payton knew she struck a nerve when I stared at her, fire in my eyes and words. "I'm the jerk?"

"Yes."

"You know what?" I didn't even want to deal with her anymore tonight. "Never mind. You go do whatever it is you came here to do, but you and I are done. For good."

I didn't wait for her to say anymore and made my way through the crowd, wanting to get back to Bentley.

I found her standing with my sister and Laney, doing shots. I wasn't sure how she'd react after me telling her what a piece of shit I was. Would she want nothing to do with me now?

She noticed me and turned around, looking adorable with glossy eyes and her hair pulled back in the messiest bun I'd ever seen. Wrapping my hands around her middle, I drew her into my bare chest and threatened to jump in the water with her.

"Don't you dare, Beau, I can't afford to lose another top."

"You're right." I leaned in and kissed her neck, once. "I don't want anyone seeing you naked but me."

We moved to a more secluded portion of the boat, and I had one thing on my mind, pressing my hips into her. After last night, and the quickie in the bathroom, I wanted more, wanted to show her she had all my attention tonight despite how many times we'd gotten interrupted.

"Beau. . . ." She teased, trying to maneuver herself back, playing hard to get, and pointed her finger in my face. I tried to bite it. "What's with you?"

"You're half naked and sexy." Slowly, I kissed her soft, sun-kissed skin, heating it to degrees she'd never felt before; I was sure of that by the way she squirmed under my touch and gave more, felt more, was more.

I felt almost domineering in a sense, the way I controlled her moves and breath, a strength only she gave me.

"I still can't believe this is happening." It was a quiet, throaty whisper that made my bones shake.

Maybe she'd let go of my confession and accepted I was only human?

My breath caught in my throat, my pulse beating louder than before. "Believe it, pretty girl."

She knew *what* I wanted, and I certainly knew what she *wanted* and needed now.

"We don't have to end this tonight." I kissed the side of her neck with intention, tracing the gentle curve with my tongue. I whispered and begged, never wanting to let her go. "I want you to come back with me."

"Why?" she asked, so tender, so sweet, her words as soft as summer rain. There was no more space between us, our bodies melting together.

Because it's different with you.

Slipping my hands under the flannel, my palm spread over her back, teasing skin. There was this heat between us, stronger than the night's air, one I hadn't noticed until I had her alone like this. "Because I want you."

She nodded, lips moving over mine, and her dark, pleading eyes locking on sky blue.

With no hesitation, I slid my hand lower to her ass. "I have a bed there. I could take my time with you and show you how good it can be, alone with me, in a bed."

"Is that so?" she whispered, her heartbeat speeding with every quick breath as her arms tightened around my neck, her hips shifting against mine.

Pleasure shot through me instantly when our bodies rubbed against one another. I never wanted it to stop. Instinctively, I angled her hips to drag her over my erection. "Will you, please?"

There was no air for words, so she nodded, giving into me, or into my movements.

Removing my hand from her backside, I hooked my arm around her waist, sliding her from my lap. With one hand cradling her head, I laid her back against the wood so I was at her side.

Lips at her ear, my free hand wrapped around the back of her head, my other hand made a slow path between her legs and inside the bottoms of her bikini. It was a brave move, considering we weren't the only ones up here, but it was dark enough no one knew exactly what I was doing but her.

"I can't stop thinking about you," I said, so quietly she barely heard me. Rubbing slowly, every touch building the intensity in her as her eyes drifted closed and her knees fell open for me. "That's it, let me take care of you."

Her eyes, so heavy, opened at my words and found the stars, her body arching at my every movement. Gripping onto my shoulders, she let me take her higher than the stars above her.

"*Whiskey-lit and holdin' on, I whisper, don't be afraid. Baby, look up and get lost, take in the night,*" I sang softly, trying to tease and tempt her, letting my voice draw out into a growl, my hardness pressing into her hip. "*Make a wish on everlasting light.*"

I had no idea what I was singing. I was lost in the words of something I was making up on the spot for this girl in my arms.

Her hand moved from beside her, to over mine pushing it harder against her.

I chuckled, my breath catching. "More?"

Licking her lips, she nodded shyly, her eyes finding the stars again. "I need more. Don't stop."

"Do you know what you're saying?" Had she realized I couldn't stop now, even if I wanted to?

The problem was she didn't know what she was asking for. Not when it came to the two of us and what was developing here.

After I knew she'd come, I moved between her legs. "Just let me show you how good it can be." I could barely catch my own breath before my mouth was on hers, trying to convince her through my kiss if she came back with me I'd make it good for her. "Come back with me, please."

You're about to fuck her on a boat with people surrounding. Nice, Beau. Classy.

Bentley wasn't that type of girl though and pushed against my chest. "We can't, Beau." She panted against my lips. "Not here. There's people over there."

My stomach flipped and I looked up, they weren't paying us any attention. In fact, it was Wade up here on the other side of the boat with Laney, and by the looks of it, they weren't just talking.

"Are you sure?" Pulling back was hard, but I had to, for her.

I sighed, and then breathed in deep a breath of humid starry-night air, my hands on her hips moving her against me. "Come on, Bentley, just let me. I promise, I'll be gentle with you."

Jesus, I sound like a horny kid again begging to get laid.

She giggled. "Oh I'm sure you will, but with my luck, we'll roll off the top in the process and either drown or everyone will see me naked."

"I'd catch you. I won't let you fall."

When she started to wiggle underneath me, I kept her there and pressed my hips into her once more.

"Come on, baby." I was begging now, especially after seeing her get off just moments ago. "We'll be quiet." Drawing back, I sat on my knees, moving her hips so our bodies were aligned, and then I pressed forward again, letting her see how bad I wanted it. My stare was low, between her legs, feeling the dampness seeping through her bikini.

She wanted it too, only her palm came in contact with my chest, gentle touches and firm pushing. Her lashes fluttered, seeming uncomfortable under my gaze. "Not here."

Bentley trapped me in her midnight eyes and I took a deep breath, swallowing the thick air like she punched me. I had to respect that. I wished the sun was out so I could have seen her eyes in the light; only in the sun could you see the flickers of copper in her dark brown irises. They were breathtaking.

"Then say you'll come back with me."

Sitting up, she kissed me, once. "I'll come back with you."

Chapter Eleven

CLOSE YOUR EYES

BENTLEY

"CALL ME WHEN you get to Michigan."

Laney smiled, hugging me tightly to her chest as we said goodbye Monday morning. "I will." And then she whispered, "I'm proud of you for taking the jump."

Grinning, I couldn't help the way my face heated, watching Beau over her shoulder.

I was proud of me too. Only took me twenty-four years, but I finally did something for me.

As I stood there, my bag on my sunburnt shoulder, Beau's flannel tied around my waist, he gave a nod to his truck. "You comin' pretty girl?"

I was leaving with him. I couldn't even begin to describe the giddy feeling that gave me.

Maybe it was the lake and the feeling *it* gave me.

Maybe it was *him* and that easy grin.

I have heard people say when they think of summer, they are, or were immediately reminded of a boy and where it all started. It didn't start with a boy. It started next to a fire staring up at the stars. But it was going to end with a boy, I knew that much.

Beau invited me to his apartment in Mountain Brook.

He rented a place with Wade and Gavin. I had no idea he lived with them, but from what I could tell, he didn't stay there often. He spent most of his time in Nashville with Sam.

I learned from Blaine, after graduating high school, Beau moved to Nashville for a little while, intending to play where he could and in any bar that would have him. He'd been writing his own songs since he was a kid and wanted to get them out there.

He wrote a few for Sam Shaver, who had a number one billboard spot with one of his songs, but Beau had yet to get the attention he deserved with his own music.

"So tell me." Beau leaned toward me in the cab of the truck, turning down the music and keeping one hand on the steering wheel as we made the hour drive back to Mountain Brook. "Am I gonna have to fight off any hometown boys when I bring you back with me? That Joel kid seemed hell-bent on getting your attention. Any others?"

What? Why would he ask that?

"Uh, no. Don't have boyfriends. I told you that."

His brows scrunched, probably seeing the truth in that statement. "Like ever?"

"Nope." I felt ridiculous. "The closest I've come to a boyfriend was my lab partner freshman year. We had sex during study sessions."

Beau's chest shook with laughter, but it was tense, the muscles in his arms flexing. "And who was this kid?"

"Like his name?" I blinked, and he smiled again.

"Yeah, what's his name?"

I swallowed nervously. Why did he want to know this? "Nathan. Why would you want to know that anyway?"

Beau tipped his head, acknowledging, and then giving me a side-eyed glance. "Just because."

Weirdo.

"Your dad owns Rusty's, right?" I was getting good a conversation jumping on him.

Beau let out a breath I didn't know he was holding. "Yeah, my brother Jensen works there, too."

I remembered seeing Jensen around school. He actually went to Auburn University the first two years I was there. I passed him on campus every Tuesday morning, but he never said a word to me.

Probably because I never tripped around him.

"Are you close with Jensen?"

Beau took a deep breath, acting like he had to think about the answer, or maybe wasn't sure how to word it. "No, I'm not."

"Not like you and Blaine?"

"Nope. Jensen is three years older, and has two kids, Mason and Memphis. . . we just don't have a lot in common."

"Do they come to any of your shows?"

"No, well, Tiffany, his wife, has brought the boys a couple times, but my dad has never come to one yet."

"Why?"

"I think. . . well, he's never been encouraging of my music. I think he feels if he comes, he's giving me approval to live a life he thinks is just a hobby."

"But you make money doing it, so it's not like it's still a hobby, right?"

"I make enough I can eat and have a place to live, but I'm certainly not rich." His brow furrowed, as if he was done talking about this, and then asked, "How long is your internship at the hospital?"

"Well, I start on Monday next week. It's for six months, and then I might be able to get a job at one of the assisted living centers in Birmingham or even Nashville." *Oh Jesus, that was pretty fucking subtle Bentley.*

"Where?"

"There's a few different ones I've looked into." I didn't want to tell him I knew he'd lived in Nashville at one point and I looked into jobs there. I didn't want him to realize my obsession bordered on stalker levels. None of his business, right?

He nodded but said nothing else, his eyes on the road again.

"When do you go back on tour?"

"I have to be in Montgomery tomorrow night, then I'm in Atlanta on Friday. I think we have seven more shows on this tour."

"That's exciting."

No, it's actually depressing.

"It is." His answer seemed almost. . . sad.

He loves you. He wants to never leave you again.

I'm clearly crazy.

"Does it get lonely being on the road?"

That got him. "It does." And then he smiled, his arm draped over the back of the seat and touching my shoulder lightly. "Too bad you have the internship. I'd kidnap you, take you with me."

Goddamn real life!

I wasn't sure what to say, so I switched the conversation randomly back to him.

"So you don't get to see your nephews then?"

If he was annoyed by my questions, he didn't lead on and continued to answer them. I just wished I could stop myself from asking them, but I couldn't. Probably because, for being his number one stalker, I knew very little about him personally.

"I see them on holidays and birthday parties."

"That's sad."

He shrugged. "What about you? Siblings?"

"I had an older brother, Corbin, but he died when I was five. I don't remember much about him."

Beau's eyes were desolate, like he felt regret for asking but wanted to know. "How'd he die?"

"He had a really bad cold and got a respiratory infection from it. The infection went to his blood. He was only nine."

"Jesus, that's awful." He cleared his throat, a slow shake to his head. "I'm sorry."

"Don't be." I waved him off. "It was a long time ago."

"How'd your parents deal with it?"

"They didn't very well. My dad was an alcoholic. He finally left when I was fifteen, and I haven't heard from him since. . .and my mom went into protective mode. If she could have wrapped me in a bubble, I think she would have. She cried for two months after I left for college. She was in a really bad car accident when I was a sophomore in college and she's now in an assisted living center because she's so forgetful."

"Fuck, man." He shook his head, seeming depressed. "That really sucks."

"It does. I remember seeing Corbin sick and coughing all night, and then the next morning he went to the doctor with my dad and never came back. I went through this fear about going to the doctor because I thought when you did, you didn't come home."

"Wow, I had no idea." His posture changed, tensing. "Is that why guys moved from Jacksonville?"

"Yeah, my mom couldn't stand to be in that house anymore, so we moved to Mountain Brook."

Nodding, Beau focused on the road, never saying anything more. Not wanting him to think he upset me, I rested my hand on the inside of his thigh.

That resulted in a trip down a country backroad.

"Never in a million years who I have thought I'd be doing this in your truck, with you."

Kissing up the side of my neck, he pushed forward, the truck rocking with him motions. "Don't say it like that."

I froze thinking I'd upset him. "Why?"

"You're giving me a complex and I'm not sure I'll live up to it."

"You've already exceeded it when you kissed me for the first time." Closing my eyes, I stared up at the headliner when he buried his head in the space between my neck and shoulder, groaning softly.

"How so?"

"A guy like you would have never looked my way had I not fell in your lap."

"You're wrong," he breathed, never stopping. "I would have noticed."

If he did, or didn't, or wouldn't, none of it mattered because I was here with him now.

THE NIGHT HAD arrived, Tuesday night, the moment I would see Beau live in concert.

We drove home from Mountain Brook on Monday, stopped off long enough for us to grab a change of clothes and then we were onto Montgomery with Blaine, Miles and Wade in tow.

Before the show, Beau had me backstage for a moment. I gently kissed his lips, only he had other ideas and deepened the kiss. Letting go of my hands, he cupped my face with both of his hands, palms on my cheeks. "Miles and Wade will take care of you. Stay away from the guys or I'll jump off stage and beat some ass."

Throwing my head back, I giggled as he kissed my neck, seeming like he just couldn't part himself from my skin. "You're kind of cute when you're jealous."

"I'm dangerous when I'm jealous," He warned, kissing me with a few more lingering pecks to my lower lip. Pulling away, he kissed my nose once. "Enjoy the show, pretty girl."

Miles, who'd escorted me backstage helped me back into the general admission area where Blaine was waiting.

When she noticed me, Blaine put her arm around my shoulder. "Do you like my brother? I mean, I know you two are fucking but do you like him?"

It was a simple question. An obvious one, but simple.

"I've had a crush on him since I was fourteen and he winked at me. I was obsessed from then on. He was like Prince Charming and unattainable. A fantasy really. And then, bam, I trip and land in his lap. And now here I am, still feeling like I'm in dreamland."

Stop talking. She's going to think you're a weirdo.

"Okay, so are you convinced my brother's into you yet?" Blaine looked over at me as she spoke, smiling, and this time her blues didn't bother holding anything back. She wanted me to believe her.

At the mention of my feelings for him, though, I wanted so desperately to fight anything I felt, in fear it wasn't going anywhere, I smiled.

When I fell into his lap, I never thought I'd experience what I had so far. It was like a dark gray morning when the sun finally crept through, broken cracks sparkling honeyed rays. He was lighting up beauty I'd never imagined before.

Leaning into Blaine, I whispered, "I'm really not sure. But I couldn't get much more *into* him unless I was physically part of him."

She grinned. "If my brother doesn't love you yet, I do."

We were standing in the front row at the Montgomery Performing Arts Center, awaiting Beau to come on stage. The first opening act was currently playing.

The stage lights were bright, bursting around the stage, creating heat all around me. Reflected from the white lights, the stage seemed so vast in comparison to the men standing on it.

"Beau's after this guy," Blaine noted, staring up at the stage, squinting, but refusing to put her glasses on.

"He's been playin' amazing on this tour," Blaine murmured, ignoring Wade when he spit chew in her direction, coming to stand next to us.

"No, he hasn't," Wade mumbled, already drunk and looking down at Blaine with mischievous eyes. "He's playin' like shit."

Wade definitely reminded me of Beau. He had the same Ryland blue eyes and that silly smirk they all seemed to hold at bay when they wanted. They could have passed for brothers.

"And what would you know, nut sack?" Blaine took her beer and dumped it on him, like that wasn't anything new for her. It wasn't, because in the few days I'd officially known them, Wade had worn at least four beers.

"More than you," Wade teased, shaking off the beer now covering the front of his black T-shirt. With the heat, he didn't seem to mind being wet.

There was such a rush around us, bodies swaying, the vibrations of live music, and it was easy to get lost in the energy. I could definitely see the appeal being at a concert held.

EVERYONE WAS CLAPPING as Beau took the stage, the venue erupting with screams. Finally, it was the moment I had been waiting for.

Beau's head was bent forward, but I noticed the smile tugging at his lips from where I was, center stage at his feet like a true groupie would be.

He looked around before approaching the microphone. "Hey—" there was another fit of screams, some from me, some from the group around me "—I'm Beau Ryland."

The noise was somehow dimmed by a steady drumbeat, everyone beginning to feel the music even before it really began. Beau turned and smiled at the bassist to his right. I really wasn't sure what to expect when he invited me to Montgomery with him, or how seeing him in concert would be. Surely it would be different from the lake, and I was right already. Not only that, I was impressed to see how relaxed he was up there.

After they exchanged a few words, followed by laughter, Beau turned back around as he adjusted his guitar strap. He played a few notes and then stopped, grinning that crooked smile he had. "I've got some family here tonight, and my girl too." He winked down at me. "And ya know, this is Bentley Rae's first concert. Whatcha say we make it one she'll remember?"

Everyone cheered, but I just stared up at the stage in shock. He called me his girl and singled me out in front of everyone.

My face was immediately on fire. The swarm of high-pitched screaming girls near the stage went crazy.

Beau looked at me for a brief moment, knowing my reaction. His smile, crooked and powerful, made it hard not to spill my heart on the ground before him.

He leaned into the microphone, our eyes remaining on one another. "She doesn't think I'm charming. . . ." The crowd ahhh'd when he stuck his bottom lip out.

"You're not!" Blaine yelled, her hands around her mouth to carry the sound.

He frowned, shaking his head at Blaine. "My sister's here too."

While Beau played the first riff of the song "Nothin' Wrong," his eyes were downcast. He looked up and my breath caught in my chest.

Holy shit.

Beau's voice rose above the shrieking crowd, both hands clutched the microphone, pouring out words that came from deep in his soul. *"We all got more than this nowhere town in common. It aint much to talk about, but here we are talkin'. . . we don't got a lot of money, but that won't be what stops us from havin' a good time and livin' the good life."*

I gasped at the intensity, having never seen this side of Beau before. It wasn't like around the fire or the boat; this was his life, band and all, with lights and screaming fans. . .I found it hard to breathe with the feeling of the bass in my chest and his voice surrounding me.

I couldn't take my eyes off him, the liveliness in his performance and the desire he put into it, leaving every girl in here wishing they were going home with him.

Well, maybe everyone but Blaine.

During the chorus, his eyes were drawn to mine as he sang just for me, my breath stolen with every word. "*We got the moonlight. . . and we've got some cold, cold beer. . . And that bonfire ain't the only thing burnin' here.*"

His hair was damp with sweat, his white T-shirt clinging to his body, his face contorted as he sang with such emotion it was clear to see this was his passion.

His voice was straining, his rasp cracking with the way he pushed out the lyrics. It was all perfect, the way the music amplified his voice, the intensity the crowd provided, and his rapt attention on me, only me.

The music soared through the venue, taking with it the souls of everyone in here, listening to his words poured from his chest.

When the song ended, my ears were ringing from the screams and I couldn't believe this guy I crushed on for so long was a rock star and I hadn't even knew this side of him.

Beau chuckled into the mic. "Okay. . . I take it y'all liked that one. This is a new one I've been playing around with." He flashed a sly smile. "It's a dirty one so. . . you know. . . fuckin' deal with it." He winked at the crowd, who went wild.

Beau burst into the sexiest lines I had heard yet, and left Blaine pretending to gag beside me. "*Slide on over, I'll be gentle but if you want more, we can get a little dirty.*" He started laughing, barely taking the song seriously, but the crowd loved it despite the roughness. "I feel like I should be naked singing this one."

When Beau saw how everyone was getting into his music, he fed off the crowd and upped the intensity of just about everything, from his passion in the lyrics to his interactions with the crowd, and eventually took his shirt off for the crowd, or maybe for me.

I definitely wasn't complaining one bit.

I think I lost my voice twenty minutes into him playing. I even reached out to him when he fell to his knees in front of me at one point.

I had officially become what Blaine told me was a groupie.

"Montgomery knows how to party," he noted, looking to the band and laughing at how loud they'd become. He lifted his shirt to wipe sweat from his face. I watched the muscles in his honed physique as they flexed with each breath.

I was becoming morbidly obsessed with him.

"So, I said my sis is here too. . .and the first song I ever learned to play was one she loved called "Hey, Hey" by Sawyer Brown. This goes out to Blaine."

Blaine leaned into me, her lips at my ear so I could hear her over the crowd. "He used to play this for me and I'd dance around my room when our parents weren't home."

My heart pounded in my chest with the piano and Beau standing in front of me, just three feet away, both hands holding the mic.

Blaine and I danced to the song, but still, I kept my eyes on Beau.

When the song finished, he was back to talking to the crowd. "I have one more song for you. Y'all probably want something you've heard before, right?" Everyone screamed in response as Beau raised his hand to calm the crowd, and then turned his hat around backward.

The band went into the opening beats of a Big & Rich song as Sam Shaver came on stage on with him.

"Give it up for Sam Shaver!"

They did all right, as he was the reason most of them were here.

Blaine and I danced to the song, as we did to every single one of them.

The beat slowed down, the crowd quieting when Beau dropped to his knees before me, his voice a growling harshness that could melt the panties off any girl. It sounded like a moan, one I'd surely remember forever. "Save a horse. . . *ride* a Schow girl."

Did he really just say that? Yep. He did. He altered the lyrics of "Save A Horse (Ride A Cowboy)" to include my name.

My idea of a country concert was nothing like what I envisioned it would be. Beau was talking to the crowd way more than I expected. He even sat down at one point, threatened to strip down completely naked, and shot-gunned a beer with a dude out of the front row.

It was nothing like I expected a country concert to be, but then again, this was more of pop country with a mix of rock and roll. Nothing like I'd ever heard before.

"Thank you guys! Thanks to Sam for having me on tour with him." He waved to the crowd one last time and then walked off stage.

"WHAT DID YOU think of your first concert?" Beau's eyes twinkled with excitement as we stood in the parking lot.

I grinned, spinning, feeling so alive, and I wasn't even the one on stage tonight. I felt like I'd been smiling more than I ever had before. "That was. . . AMAZING!" I shouted.

Laughter broke out around me, probably from everyone in the parking lot who heard me screaming, my heart thumping in my ears. With blurred vision from my excessive drinking, I could faintly make out Beau's full on cheesy grin. "I had no idea you could sing like that! Have you always had that in you? I mean, Jesus, Beau, you've got talent!"

"Thank you," he mumbled humbly, letting his eyes wander over my body as we stood outside his truck. "But you knew I sang, how was this different?"

I let out the breath I was holding, and he smiled. "This was *so* completely different. You're a *fucking* rock star!"

"You're drunk, pretty girl," he said, reaching for me. "Adorable, but very drunk, and I'm beginning to think I might be a bad influence on you. Did you even drink before you met me?"

And I couldn't argue with that. I wasn't much of a drinker, but since I met him, I had been drunk every night. "Nope, not really."

Before I knew it, I was on the bed of Beau's truck doing my own guitar solo as he tried to help me down.

"You want me to get up there with you?" he asked, running his hands up my thighs and pulling me to the edge of the tailgate.

I nodded, but he didn't comply. Shimming myself back, I laid down and he finally came with me.

"Let me take you back to my place." His arm gave way and he settled his weight on me, all of it, every hard line. I felt the cool metal against my back and my bare legs.

"Why do you want to take me back to your place so bad?"

Beau pulled away again. Sitting up on his knees, he gave me a smile and then laid down in the bed of the truck beside me. "I really want to get you back in a bed," he said in a low strained voice. "Please."

Feeling the spins, I stared up at the starry night. Beau lay beside me. His hands rested on his chest as he stared at the same sky, his breath light and relaxed, like there was nowhere else he wanted to be.

"You know I always wondered how they figured out the constellations. Like, why did they pick the stars they did? Is it because they were the brightest? Or were they playing connect the dots with the stars and just happened to come across the designs." I couldn't stop talking, no matter how hard I tried. "And those constellation designs are so random. Are they in a different language or just completely random. I don't get it. The only things I actually get is the Big Dipper and the Little Dipper because they actually look like a big pot and a little pot."

Beau smiled, his quiet laughter shaking his chest.

The parking lot was empty now, or maybe I just didn't notice anyone else, but what I saw, or thought I saw, was a clear night with lights sparkling above me, hopeful wishing stars that told me I could have anything I ever wanted.

"How did I never know how truly amazing you are?" I asked, keeping my eyes on the stars.

He didn't say anything, his breathing light, body peacefully content. Sighing, his breath tickled my skin when he whispered in my ear, "Maybe you did."

"Why would you say that?"

He sighed again, the sound strangely comforting. "Something kept you interested, and I'm thankful for that."

He leaned forward, capturing my lips. I eagerly sought out his, kissing along the salty curve of his lower lip. Feeling bold, I sucked on it softly before running my tongue across it. He deepened the kiss, and I had no complaints.

Turning on our sides, I wrapped my arms tightly around his sweaty neck, leaning as far forward as I could. Our kisses heated rapidly as they always did. The heat from the day had faded, but the heat between us was soaring high on the adrenaline he still had.

"I want you," he whispered against my lips, his hand reaching down to drag my thigh up over his hip. Warmth spread throughout me, sending a tingling sensation of anticipation throughout my body. "Let me show you how much it meant to me that you came here with me. Let's go back to the hotel room."

How could I deny him?

IN THE ROOM, the lights were dimmed and lit only by the moon. Wrapping his arms around mine, I was slowly lowered to the bed as he moved between my legs, his lips moving slowly over mine.

The adrenaline from the concert had slowed, easing like the night. Everything felt so natural between us, I couldn't imagine being anywhere else but with him. I wasn't thinking about what next week would bring, or if he felt the same way about me. All I wanted to focus on was this.

My skin felt toasted from the day, and when the air conditioner kicked on, swirling cool air with his warm breath, it became a little easier to take in air around him.

Moving to his knees, Beau hovered over me, his hands on the sides of my hips at the waistband of my jeans. His eyes were dark, full of feeling as my hands slid to his bare chest, pushing back slightly.

It was then I felt his pulse racing, his breathing just as heavy as mine.

"Are you okay?" I asked, sitting up to circle my hands around his neck.

His entire frame was shaking—arms, legs, and chest. "No, I'm not."

"What's wrong?"

He tried to be gentle; his kiss, his touch, all hesitant but needing. He clearly wanted something, but what he wouldn't say.

His movements were harsh, never remaining in one spot for long—at my lips, my neck, my chest, and then moving back to my lips.

With his grip tight, he was hard, pushing against me sometimes, but never taking the leap to actually take my clothes off.

"Beau," I whispered, kissing the side of his face when his hips moved again.

He didn't say anything, and then he moved back, his eyes catching mine as if he had to know the answer. "Do you want this?"

My eyes squinted, watching the emotions on his face. "Us?"

"I mean after this next week when your internship starts and I go on tour?" His voice shook, never more vulnerable as he was right then. "Do you want any of this past right now?"

I want you so bad it's the only thing my heart knows.

"Yes," I answered truthfully, struggling to keep my voice even. "I mean. . . if you do."

He swallowed and then pressed his lips to my forehead. "Me too. I don't think I could watch you walk away."

There was a burning sensation in my chest at his words

I was feeling so much more than I ever realized for Beau Ryland.

Like a shot of the hard shit, I knew it was something strong.

I would always remember that weekend on Lake Martin. I would. I swore by it. Some say there is one summer, or even a day, they would always remember because of how their life changed, an awareness of where their heart belonged.

Everyone had a moment like that, too, as if their soul was now imprinted with the memory, and was never letting it go.

That weekend, today, tonight, tomorrow—it would be my moment that was imprinted inside of me.

Chapter Twelve

RIDE

BEAU

PERFORMING LIVE WAS exhilarating. Having Bentley there watching me made me twice as nervous and the high twice as hard to come down from.

I laid there awake for hours, watching her sleep, knowing when we left this hotel room, things might not work out. We both agreed we wanted it past this week, but could that really work?

I knew in my heart I wanted it to.

The idea that she felt the same way made my chest tighten. For a moment, I could pretend she felt something more for me, even if the only words were yes, she wanted whatever this was to continue.

The drive back to Mountain Brook was long, only because we stopped twice, both times for close to two hours.

Back in Mountain Brook, Bentley wanted to see my dad's bar, and meet him. I wasn't at all excited to take her there. Mostly because I knew my brother was working and I didn't want that judgmental asshole making her feel nervous.

"Well, look what the cat drug in," someone at the bar hollered as soon as we stepped inside.

Here we go again.

I gripped Bentley's hand a little tighter when I noticed my brother at the bar, watching me take a seat. "Hey, Jensen."

He gave a nod, too good to even give me a hello.

He was a fucking prick.

"What brings you in here?" Dad asked, giving me a nod, much like the one Jensen offered.

Bentley and I took seats at the bar. "Just passing through. Thought I'd show Bentley around town."

Dad looked over at Bentley. "You must be the latest groupie?"

The phrase *fuck you* rested dangerously on the tip of my tongue any time I spoke to my father. I was ready to walk out right then. Fuck it, she didn't need to be subjected to their bullshit.

And then I began to wonder why I even brought her here in the first place.

"Shouldn't you be on tour or something?" Jensen asked, giving me that same scowl he always wore. "I am on tour. Thought I'd stop by and say hi." I reached for Bentley's hand, again, ready to leave. "I can see it's the same shit as always in here though so fuck off, nice to see you again."

My brother was only remotely approachable or tolerable for that matter when he was sleeping. I was sure of that. I don't know if he was tortured or something as a child, but he was completely different from Blaine and me. He was a cold hearted prick is what he was.

Jensen's eyes flashed with anger, he hated when I called him out. "You know what, Beau, fuck you." My eyes shot to his, fire and ice. "Fuck you, just because you're some hot shot rock star with pussy thrown your way every night doesn't mean you're better than everyone else in your family or too good to talk to your own brother. Don't put your shit on me."

None of what he said even made any sense.

I wasn't sure what I was thinking, maybe because he didn't have enough respect to keep his mouth shut in front of Bentley, or just that I hated him that much but I reacted.

I spun around to face Jensen, grabbing him by his shirt over the bar to yank him forward. "Don't you *ever* act like I'm the one too good for my family. I've done nothing but be there for mom and Blaine. You and dad, yeah, well you're *hardly* family." My voice was sharp but wavering, I hated reacting like this in front of Bentley but no fuckin' way was I going to let him walk all over me again. Dad stepped forward and attempted to push me away, but he got right back in Jensen's face. "Whatever this is between us, this hostility, the hate I feel anytime I see your goddamn face. . . It's because of *you*. Remember that, this was because of *you*!"

When I let go, I offered a few more words in his ear that I knew Bentley wouldn't hear, "I hope fucking my girlfriend was worth it, because you and I will never be brothers again."

I meant those words too. We shoved away from one another. It wasn't the first time this happened—Jensen and I getting in each other's faces—and I was sure it wouldn't be the last.

"I'm sorry about that," I told Bentley when we were outside. "They're just. . . ." I wasn't even sure how to explain what they were, other than judgmental assholes.

"Nothing like you," Bentley finished, backing me up against the side of my truck and fisting my flannel in her hands. "Don't listen to them, Beau. Don't."

"I never have before."

The fact that she understood spoke volumes. Payton never did, but she also held a soft spot for my brother.

After all, she fucked him first, not me.

WHEN WE WERE alone, nothing stopped Bentley and me once we made our way back to Mountain Brook, or maybe it never could from the moment we met, and I couldn't separate myself from her. We were living off the intensity of whatever this was between us, and the utter consumption it gave us.

We were in my bedroom, her legs around my waist as I carried her to the bed.

Dragging my kiss, my tongue, my body against hers, I didn't ease up. I couldn't with the adrenaline overriding me tonight.

No, I pushed harder than I ever had with her. A strange pulsation ran through my veins thinking our time was almost up and it made me angry.

This girl was mine, and I didn't want to ever let go.

This, right now, these screams she was giving me, they were mine. The way she curved into me, mine too. Tonight it was all mine. My lips brushed over her skin, never wanting to stop. How the hell was I going to leave when the tour was farther away?

I sat on the bed, her on my lap. As I ran my hands up the back of her thighs, coming to rest on her ass, she smiled at me. "I'm ready to kidnap you. Fuck your internship."

I couldn't deny it now. I had a possessiveness for her, and I didn't want her alone, without me. Didn't matter where we were or what we were doing, I wanted this girl with me. "Is this what you want?" I asked when she ground down on my erection as she peeled off her shirt and let it fall to the floor.

There was more meaning behind my question, and I think she understood that when she nodded.

"I do," she hummed, her lashes fluttering closed.

She felt unbelievable against my skin. The heat, the noises, her scent—I craved it.

I wanted, I craved, and I fucking needed.

Once our bodies joined, her hands became frantic with the same desire I felt deep in my bones like the lyrics of a song that kept me awake at night, restless until I bled their beauty into a verse. My breath, my movements, and my thoughts were controlled by this obsession I seemed to have and my inability to let her go. Sliding my hands around her waist, letting them go lower to her ass as she rode me. Her sexy curves, from her tiny waist to the gentle curve of her hips, were breathtaking.

Bentley tipped her head back. "God, Beau, you feel so good."

"Bentley. . . fuck. . . ." I was getting close, my restraint fading. The way she watched me made my fucking knees shake, made me want to beg and give her anything she'd ever wanted. Her breath took the air from my lungs and gave me chills, that kind of shit. It took my world and crushed it, knowing it would never be the same after this last week with her.

"Fuck, pretty girl, the way you move," I whispered, rocking my hips with her movements, mesmerized watching her body take all that mine was giving her.

Like a song that kept me up at night, I gave every miserable ounce of frustration and aggression that I had shouldered all my life into making love to her, the only girl now.

Running my hands over her body, I closed my fist around her neck, giving her a gentle squeeze.

She moaned, looking down at me with her sexy dark eyes, and I couldn't stop myself. She liked the roughness but was afraid to ask for it.

Using a little more force than I would have liked, I flipped her over onto her back and hovered over her, leaning in to kiss her passionately. "All you have to do is tell me you want it."

She said nothing, words trapped in her throat.

"Just ask," I said softly against her shoulder.

I knew she wanted it, she did, and if the flushed cheeks and passionate stare didn't tell me enough, her wetness gave it away. She was soaked, all for me.

Stilling for a moment to salvage my composure, the sensations of being inside her was almost too much for me. With my head against her shoulder, I closed my eyes, fighting back the orgasm that was bubbling under the surface. I didn't want to spill my shit before she got what she needed.

"Please, Beau. Fuck me," Bentley finally pleaded and I almost couldn't believe what she had said or how it would make me feel to hear her say that. It was erotic as hell to hear those words out of her beautiful innocent mouth.

"You want to be fucked, Bentley?" I asked, gritty and raw.

"Yes." She bit her lip, moaning as she nodded, and completely undid any restraint I had left.

Pulling out of her, I vigorously thrust back inside. I used one hand around her waist to draw her flush against my chest, arching her off the bed and into my movements.

"Oh, my God," she panted out, clawing at my shoulders, giving my mouth access to her neck.

That same possessiveness swelled because it was my body causing this reaction from her.

I felt like I could fucking explode at any moment, but I desperately wanted to get her off.

I had been with women who wanted it rough, but half the time, they had no idea what rough was. Bentley didn't either, but she wanted my grip tight, tight enough that she felt my passion through my touch. She wanted the relentless angle of my hips giving her an indication that I couldn't get enough, that I was using her body to give me pleasure.

Well, I wasn't using her for my own need. I was giving her all of that and then some in an attempt to make this beautiful girl in my arms see how much she'd gotten to me in a week.

"I'm so close. . . fuck. . . so good. . . ."

Fuck yeah.

Before I could say anything in reply, she screamed out in ecstasy, her legs tightening around my waist. I couldn't stop myself, grunting loudly, completely overpowered by the sensations.

I faintly registered Bentley crying out against me, her fingertips dug forcefully into my skin, holding me against her. The tidal wave washed over me, crumbling but I could feel *every* sensation. It was by far the best orgasm of my life.

"Don't stop," she begged. "Don't let go of me. Not tonight."

"I'll never let go," I moaned, pushing deeper once more, shaking my head against her shoulder. "Tell me," I whispered between pants. "Lie to me, tell me. Just say it."

"I won't let go either."

I was fucked. I'd never be able to let this girl go, and if I wasn't convinced then, I was in the morning when she wanted more.

"Oh, God, Beau. That was. . . . Holy shit. . . ." Running her hands through her hair, she panted heavily as I kissed her perfectly flushed skin. "Amazing. You're so good, like really good, and I haven't had sex like this. . . . I should be quiet now. Why are you so perfect? I vomit words all over the place and you seem to know exactly what to say, all the time."

"I'm not perfect." I kissed her cheek, emotions scrambling through my chest, unable to process their meaning. "I can be selfish, like wanting you to give up your internship to be with me, and I make things harder than they need to be. I may know what to say, but I'm *not* perfect."

"So no one's perfect and you're a selfish, well-spoken jerk, aren't you?"

I scowled, rolling her so she was on my chest. "I never said I was a jerk, you added that."

She laughed. "I did, didn't I?"

"You forgot to add charming." Kissing her lips once more, I knew I was fucked. This girl who rambled on and smiled sweetly had just burned every idea I ever had that I should be alone in this life.

"Keep dreamin, boy."

Yep. Totally fucked.

Chapter Thirteen

WAITIN' ON ME

BENTLEY

A MONTH HAD passed since that weekend at Lake Martin.

A month of me falling for everything that was Beau Ryland. His heat, his intensity for living and singing, his charm, as he said before, he could get a lot with that charm and I knew that very well. He could.

I still hadn't told him he was charming, but there were some things Beau didn't need to know. I didn't want that pretty head of his getting any bigger.

I felt increasingly comfortable around Beau since the concert and our relationship moved fast.

My life felt boring before I met Beau, but now I was living life in the fast lane and dating a musician, and all the twisting curves of emotions that forced me to follow the journey with him.

I started my internship with the hospital and hated it. I had always had no problem getting along with everyone, but there were two other interns with me who were making my life hell. And now I was questioning becoming an assisted living assistant all together.

Did I really want this? Everything about the job, from what I was seeing, was so much more political than I thought it would be.

A few days before Beau left for a two-night show in Jackson, he and I picked apples from his yard. I was giddy almost because it felt like a couple thing to do—clean up the yard. He was living in Mountain Brook still with Miles and Wade, and I was living in a tiny apartment about five minutes from him.

Looking down at the apples in my hand, I smiled while setting them on the counter. "We should make apple pie out of these."

"Okay, we could take it to your mom."

"Uh, Beau, you don't want to meet my mom." My mother was the whole reason I wanted to be an assisted living assistant. She was in a car accident that resulted in a brain injury and couldn't live on her own because she tried to burn the place down a few times. I believed the whole reason was because she had a crush on a local firefighter.

She also had some dementia, but it hadn't progressed enough that she didn't remember me.

Beau smiled, boyish and trouble. "Why is that?"

"She's crazy."

He leaned in, kissing the end of my nose. "I like crazy. I'm dating you, aren't I?"

I rolled my eyes. "And you wonder why I keep telling you that you're *not* charming."

Digging out a baking dish and ingredients he surprisingly had, I began to make the pie.

"Prepare yourself. I'm an amazing cook," I told him, peeling the apples.

"My mom makes the best apple pie ever. That means nothing to me," he turned slowly and smiled, measuring out flour and sugar for me. "So this better be impressive to me or else."

"Or else what?"

Another coy smile, tugging at the edge of his lips as one hand ran down the scruff on his jaw. "You'll see."

Part of me wanted to ruin the pie so I'd know exactly what he was talking about.

When he was finished preparing the ingredients, he hoisted himself up on the counter, grinning wider, watching me peel the remaining apples.

I told him about my mother and all her crazy stories, how this was the second assisted living home she had been in and that she was a klepto. He followed along with my every word, nodding in agreement, but I knew he was mocking me, teasing and torturing me like he enjoyed doing. And eating all the ingredients.

He shoved apple slices in his mouth as soon as I chopped them, despite me swatting at his hand with a knife.

"Beau, if you don't stop, we won't have anything for the pie." I tried my best to sound irritated. "Either that or I will chop your fingers off."

He threw an apple slice at me. It bounced off my nose and into the bowl. "Score!"

"Really, Beau?"

He threw another.

It became a war until his kitchen was covered in what would have been apple pie if not for the food war.

When he was out of ammunition, I had a bowl of apples covered in cinnamon and flour ready to pour on his head. "Don't test me, charm boy."

His hands flew to the air, begging for mercy. "I'm sorry."

I let my guard down, set the bowl on the counter, and put my hand on my hip. "Chicken."

"Face it, you just said I was charming." Beau tackled me to the floor where we laid flat on our backs, laughing, the kind of laughter that made you nearly pee your pants.

"No I didn't. I called you charm boy, there's a difference."

He licked sugar off my arm, eyes on mine. "No, there's not."

Wade came in, wanting to know what the hell we were doing on the floor.

Beau stood and helped me up. "Making pie."

"Uh-huh, sure looks like you're making pie."

After retrieving a beer, he left us to our apple mess.

Surprisingly, we still had enough apples for pie. I gave Beau the first piece before we took it to my mom.

"Pretty great, huh?" I stole a bite from his plate only to have him swat my hand away.

"No," he said, mouth full of sugar-sweet apples and fluffy dough. "It's awful."

"See. . ." My hands wrapped around a cold glass of milk, drinking slowly before adding, "You may be a rock star, but now you're just being rude."

His brow pulled together. "Don't do that."

"What?" I sat back in the chair, unsure what it was I did wrong.

"Act as if I'm not a regular person."

I waved him off. "Regular person, rock star, country-boy charmer, I don't care. If you don't tell me my pie is amazing, I will punch you."

He huffed out a breath, rolling his eyes while taking another bite. "Fine, but for the record, you said charming again."

I stole his pie plate from him. If he couldn't admit it was good, he had no business eating it. "You are so single-minded. And I said country-boy charmer, as in *you* think you're charming."

"I just don't see why you can't accept the fact that I'm charming." He took the pie plate back. "It's like you're in denial."

"Kind of like you and how good my pie is."

His smirk took over. "Oh, I know your pie is the best in town. I keep eating it, don't I?"

"That was surprisingly really dirty sounding."

He burst out laughing. "I know."

As we sat around that table in his kitchen, laughing about simple things like making pie, I knew every single memory I had with him would hold some sort of meaning for the two of us.

They were significant to me, mattered to me, and held me there with him.

Standing, he reached for my hand. "Come on, let's go give this pie to your mom. I bet she thinks I'm charming."

Knowing my mother, she probably would.

Around seven, we loaded up the pie into Beau's truck and headed out.

She was living in Birmingham at a place called Greenbriar. It was only about a half an hour from Beau's house and the pie was still warm when we arrived.

Walking through the front doors, my favorite old man was there waiting.

"Harry, what are you doing up this late?" Harry was a dirty old man, who used to fly fighter jets with the Air Force and now just dirty.

A nice guy though, if you didn't mind his naughty side. I paid him no attention.

"Did you bring me a pie, Legs?" He patted his lap. "Come sit with me, darlin'."

Beau glared at Harry and whispered in my ear, "If he wasn't in a wheelchair, I'd kick his ass for saying that."

I pushed Beau's face away with my free hand, ignoring him. "You'll have to beg Mae for a piece, Harry."

"I've been begging Mae for a piece for years," Harry mumbled, his head tipped forward, as if he was going to take another nap. "She never gives it to me."

I gave a tug on Beau's arm when he stared at Harry, glaring.

"I don't understand what makes old men think just because they're old, morals go out the window. You're young enough to be his granddaughter and he was flirting with you."

"But I'm not *his* granddaughter."

"So?" He gave me the look that said I was crazy again, you know, the one where his pretty blue eyes widened and his lips turned down. I loved the look. "It's not the point."

"Stop it and open the door."

"Which one?"

I pointed to the red door. "The one with the wooden M on the front."

Mom was in her room with Shep on her lap, petting him. "Oh, Shep, you hush," Mom scolded, setting him on the floor.

Beau leaned in and I had to laugh. I knew exactly what he was going to say. "Uh, that's a fake dog."

Placing my finger to my lip, I winked at him. "Shhh, it's real to her."

He nodded. "Gotcha."

"Hey, Mama, how are you feeling tonight?"

"I'm good, sweet girl," and then she noticed Beau standing beside me. Probably because I'd never brought anyone with me to visit her besides something stuffed. "Who's that?"

"Mama, this is Beau Ryland. Beau, this is my mother, Mabel, but most call her Mae for short."

Beau reached out to shake her hand. "It's nice to meet you, ma'am."

"Oh, dear boy, have a seat." She offered him a seat on the couch beside her, which he took. "Are you her boyfriend?"

Beau grinned, stretching his arm across the back of the couch like he was completely relaxed around my family. "I am," he said proudly, the words ringing in my ears like music.

Boyfriend.

I had a boyfriend.

The next thing I knew, Beau and my mother were watching Jeopardy together and he had Shep on his lap, petting a stuffed dog and listening intently to Mom tell him about me as a kid.

Watching him with her made me fall for him even harder and I knew she liked him too by the way her eyes lit up with his southern drawl and charm.

"How did you two meet?" Mom asked him, looking to the both of us for an answer.

Beau grinned. "She fell in my lap."

Mom burst out laughing. "She's so clumsy."

"You got that right, but I'm glad she is, gives me a chance to rescue her like prince charming."

"I like him." Mom sighed, about the same as she did when the firefighters would carry her out of her house because she told them she couldn't walk.

"Okay, Mama, we should probably get going." I was practically pushing Beau out the door. "I have to work in the morning."

She leaned into Beau and kissed his cheek. "Come back soon."

The look on his face was priceless when she did that, a mixture of pride and nerves. I knew exactly what he was going to say to me. She thought he was charming.

Focusing on the red mark on his cheek, I smiled. "Well, you won her over."

"*She* thinks I'm charming."

"Shut up." I punched his stomach, reaching for the door handle.

"So what's the story behind the stuffed dog?" Beau asked when we were outside the door, wiping bright red lipstick from his cheek.

"I found she was happier having him there. Gives her something to do during the day."

"Why not get her a real one?"

"Because she'd kill it." I giggled, tucking my arm in his. "I once gave her a doll and she thought she was babysitting for the weekend. I'd never seen her so happy."

Beau breathed in deep and kissed my temple. "You're a good person, Bentley."

"Thanks, I try to be."

At the end of the hall, he steered me the other way. "Is there a backdoor?"

"Yeah, why?"

"Because if I see that dirty old bastard again, I'll hit him."

I knew him well enough to know he wasn't jealous, but it was still cute seeing him be a little possessive.

"Some people would call that charming."

"What? Being jealous of an old man?" Beau nodded and I had to laugh. "Some people would, yes, but I'm not some people."

"Hmmm." He kissed my forehead. "You're right. I'll try harder."

I had no doubt he would.

EVERY MOMENT BEAU and I were away from one another, we were texting and calling, and falling. I couldn't believe how fast it was happening. By the end of July, Beau told me he loved me. And I was sure I fell too. It was easy to do, country boy charm with a rock star style.

I remember the day he said it. Exactly four weeks to the day I fell in his lap, and maybe that was too soon for what society thought, or anyone else, but it was perfect for us.

We were in his truck, clothes coming off just about as fast as the song playing on the radio.

"I love you, Bentley," Beau said, cupping my cheek like he finally understood the meaning behind the words and the impact they'd have on me.

Everything went cloudy when those words left his lips. They were words I always wanted to hear, but convinced myself I never would, not from someone like Beau. I couldn't move, let alone breathe in fear if I did anything, he'd take back the words.

But he didn't.

He wasn't going to.

Staring back at me, he waited, nervously.

The weight of the words settled over me, sinking way down deep. And then I felt the sudden pang of insecurity they held me to. I wanted to believe those three words would change my life and I could have Beau in all the ways I wanted, but my future was unknown.

"I love you too," I told him, finally saying the words out loud to him. "But you already knew that."

"I did." He smiled, and I believed him, though our future was unknown, there was some confidence in that smile.

You couldn't resist Beau if you tried. I didn't want to be that girl who fell immediately, but I fell for Beau a long time ago, long before I knew what it was like to find myself within him. That statement may not make a lot of sense, but it did to me because of what I was learning about myself, while I was with him.

A few weeks after the concert in Nashville, Beau was approached by Colt Records, the same company who signed Sam Shaver. They wanted Beau to start recording an album when the tour was over. It seemed everything was happening for him all at once.

And then came the surprise in late August. I knew when it happened too, the only time we ever forgot a condom, caught up in the adrenaline of his show in Nashville. The same night he told me he loved me.

On the bench seat of his truck and foggy windows on an old country road, I got pregnant.

In the bathroom at work, right before sneaking out early on Thursday to catch his show in Atlanta, I took a pregnancy test. Damn thing turned positive before I finished peeing on it.

I'm pregnant with Beau Ryland's baby?

The news wasn't exactly exciting for me with the internship and Beau still on tour. Not only would he start recording his first album, but the tension was already in the air because it would mean weeks apart. And the last thing I wanted to do was cause more stress for Beau.

The idea that I was going to have a baby with Beau, a part of me and him together, was exciting.

For a while, as I drove to Atlanta with Blaine talking my ear off, I went back to my coma theory. Had I hit my head again?

"What's going on with you?" Blaine asked an hour into the two-hour drive. "You're quiet and I'm doing all the talking."

"I'm pregnant and I have no idea how to tell Beau." It was surprisingly easy to blurt the words out to Blaine.

Blaine's eyes about bugged out. "I'm going to be an auntie?"

"Uh, yeah, but what do I say to Beau? You know him pretty well. Will he be mad?"

"I doubt it." I wished I believed her confidence. "You should see him with our nephews when he gets to see them. He's great."

When I didn't say anything, she turned down the radio. "Are you going to tell him tonight?"

My stomach dropped at the thought. "Should I?"

"Yes! I'm telling you, he'll be excited."

I drew in a deep breath, trying to calm my nerves, my heart beating so fast. "I'm just nervous. So much is changing for him with recording an album, I just don't know where I stand."

"You stand with him."

Okay, well, she had a point, didn't she?

"Do I tell him before the show or after?"

"After. I don't think we're going have time beforehand and you'll want him alone, not surrounded by fans and his band."

Another excellent point.

A half an hour outside of Atlanta, Beau sent me a message saying he missed me and couldn't wait for us to get there.

Smiling at the screen, Blaine noticed my excitement. "Is that my brother?"

"Yeah."

"Ask him if Miles and Gavin are with him?"

I did and then laughed at his message.

Beau: Yes, but I got us a hotel room. Alone.

"He said they're with him."

"Ugh." She groaned, slumping against the steering wheel but, thankfully, staying on the highway.

"What's wrong?"

"I don't want Miles there."

"Why?" I tucked my phone back in my bag, setting it on the floorboard again.

"Gavin and I are. . . you know. . . and Miles is being weird about it."

"What?" I gasped, shifting in the seat to face her a little more. I needed some details on this one. Over the last month, Blaine had definitely become my best friend. We were working at the same hospital together, and anytime I wasn't with Beau, I was with Blaine. "When did that happen?"

"Few weeks after the concert in Montgomery." Reaching for her soda in the cup holder, she gave me a side-eyed glance. "Hey, did you know that friend of yours slept with Gavin, Miles, *and* Wade that weekend?"

"No. But I'm not surprised by that."

"Sheesh, was she like that in college?"

"Yep. Different guy every week it seemed. I could never be like that," I mused, unable to understand Laney and her ways.

"I know what you mean. I feel weird that I slept with Miles and Gavin, since we all roll in the same crowd."

"Was Beau mad you slept with his friend?" I wondered what Beau thought about it, but no way would I bring it up to him.

"Oh yeah, fucking pissed off like you wouldn't believe." She laughed. "He's pretty protective."

"Well, you are his twin."

The rest of the drive to Atlanta, I thought of ways to tell him. This would ultimately being changing both our lives forever.

"I'M PREGNANT, BEAU," I told him when we were in the hotel room, the words leaving my mouth before I could worry about the impact they had on us.

Again, it was easy to just blurt the words out.

Never looking up, Beau set his guitar down on the floor and then took a seat on the edge of the bed. I saw the grin tugging at the corners of his lips under the shadows his hat provided.

I waited for him to say something, and when he didn't say anything, my anxiety soared. "Say something about it."

"Are you happy?" He turned his hat around backward so I could see his face.

I nodded, taking in his steady stare, my heart beating so loud while a lump rose in my throat, thinking the worst.

I wanted to stop him, make him look at me and face this, us, what was changing. "Are you?"

"Well, I wasn't expecting it," he answered.

"You knew when we started having sex this could happen."

Word vomit, shut up. Don't say anything else.

A strange look crossed his face. Leaning back on the bed, he lifted his legs and wrapped them around the backs of my legs, pulling me toward the edge of the bed. His smile, that smile, heated every inch of my already heated, frustrated skin.

When he did say something, his words were delivered slowly, his Southern drawl present. "Do you think because I'm not jumping for joy, that I'm not happy?"

"What? No. I didn't say anything like that."

"Is that really what you think?" he asked, and I could hear the edge of anger in his voice. "That I don't give a shit about anything but music?"

I thought before I answered. "No, I never said that. I just wanted to know what you thought. I know we didn't plan on this and we haven't been dating very long."

"I don't know what to say," he mumbled, shaking his head, the sharp tone fading. "I guess I'm a little shocked."

"I was afraid your reaction would be like this."

"Is that so?" He seemed to struggle with his choice of words, almost disappointed I would think he wouldn't be happy, and then he moved on. "I don't know what I have to do to convince you I've fallen for you and I want this relationship, but it never seems to be enough. You just have it in your head I'm just here for now, not for good."

I blinked, not sure what to say.

"You don't believe me still. . . hmmm?" He arched an eyebrow, his position changed, and he grabbed me, forcing me on top of him, and then rolling us over so I felt his weight. "Then how should I convince you that you're my girl and I want to have a baby with you?" His mouth moved closer, pulling at the collar of my flannel. The cool air hit my skin, scorched by his teasing mouth. "Should I show you?" His voice lowered, a seductive shake in his words. And then his hand moved from my hip to my stomach, fingers fluttering touches over the miracle inside me. "Or would you believe me if I said this baby shows my love for you?" he smiled, drawing back to see my reaction.

Well.

He had a way of making me feel like those words were everything I needed to hear. "Yes." I blushed.

"Do you love me?" His question held vulnerability, so much it couldn't go unnoticed.

"I do love you."

He drew in a whistled breath, shaking his head with his eyebrows raised, as if to say I was screwed. "That could be trouble, honey."

"Shut up." I grabbed him by the shirt, kissing him hard. "You're trouble."

Drawing back, he kissed down my body, stopping at my belly. "I had plans for a wild kinky night."

Running my hands over the curve of his shoulders, I watched him moving over my body. "What's stopping you?"

He placed a gentle lingering kiss just above my belly. "I think I need to show you how much I care, and how I'm always going to be there."

I had no words. My throat tightened up and the only response I could come up with was to kiss him with as much passion as I could.

Our story changed that day. We were no longer a summer romance, and we never would be again. We would forever be bound by this life we created. No matter what the future held, this would be the link between us.

He could sense there was something still wrong when I had tears in my eyes. His hand rose to touch the side of my face. "What's the matter?"

"I'm nervous."

"About what?"

"Being a mom. I have no idea how to be one."

Beau chuckled, relaxing against my side. "It's okay. I don't know how to be a dad. Together we can wing it."

"I'm pretty sure you're not supposed to wing parenthood."

"Every parent does, honey. Every single one of them."

Chapter Fourteen

STRIP IT DOWN

BEAU

FOR A GUY LIKE me, given my relationship with my own father, I wasn't sure how to feel about Bentley being pregnant. I wanted kids someday, and I certainly wanted them with Bentley, only I wasn't expecting it be this so soon.

I knew when it happened, as did she, in my truck on a country back road.

It was also the night I finally told her I loved her.

I knew I loved Bentley simply because she fell for me when I couldn't love myself.

I was never one to believe in first love, the kind that you never forget, so they tell you. I believed in second love, because they're the ones who made you believe love existed in the first place.

After all, they loved you when you were sure no one else would again. And that was exactly what Bentley did for me. She loved me when I wasn't sure anyone else ever would.

I had a feeling my parents wouldn't be thrilled with Bentley being pregnant. Scratch that, I had a feeling my dad wouldn't be happy about it. I didn't have the greatest relationship with my dad or Jensen.

Jensen was the perfect son, the one who followed in his old man's footsteps and did what he was supposed to do. That wasn't me. I went the direction he asked me not to.

For that reason, I didn't have much in common with either of them. Telling my father Bentley was pregnant wasn't something I felt I needed to do, but Bentley made me, saying she needed my family to know while I was in Nashville.

Her biggest fear about all of it was thinking we just met and fell in love quickly, so people would assume she was trying to trap me. For that reason, she refused to marry me.

I knew when she got pregnant. And honestly, I wasn't surprised when she told me. Probably because during that amazing sex with AC/DC blaring in the background, I realized I hadn't put a condom on.

Did I stop when I knew my slip-up?

Nope.

"Didn't think you'd come back here after bringing that girl in," Dad said when he noticed me take a seat at the bar. It was empty inside, as it usually was this time in the morning, just a few lingering locals.

"Yeah, well, it's not that I wanted to."

He snorted, his hands on the edge of the bar with a rag thrown over his shoulder. "So why are you here? Need money?"

"No, I don't need your fuckin' money." I stared at the bar as I spoke, fidgeting with a coaster and annoyed my own father made me nervous. "Bentley's pregnant."

He laughed. "And that's my problem? You're twenty-five."

"No, it's not your problem." I stood, shoving myself away from the bar and knocking the stool over. "See ya around, Dad."

Dad was straightforward and asked as I reached for the door, "So where does that leave them while you're off pursuing your dream?"

It pissed me off that he reacted that way, quick to think I'd drop my responsibilities as a man for the sake of my music.

"I see them with me, *supporting* me," I said, walking out the door. I didn't care what he had to say after that.

Inside my truck, I wasn't so calm and gripped the steering wheel tight. "God, he's just. . .fuck him. He never fucking gets it. Everything has always been about him," I told myself, trying to get it out of my head I needed his approval for anything.

"When are you gonna give this hobby up, Beau?"

"Music isn't a career; it's just noise."

How could he think I wouldn't support my family?

TELLING MY MOM was easier. Mostly because Blaine had already blabbed and told her. I was expecting her to be knitting a damn blanket or something.

Knowing she'd be home, I stopped by on my way out of town. My mother didn't work. She did when we were younger, odd jobs here and there and used to do the books for the bar. That all stopped two years ago when the bar was audited. Dad fired her.

Piece of shit. Who fired their own wife?

Russell Ryland did.

"Hey, Ma," I yelled once inside the door, wondering where she was at.

"In here, honey," she chimed from the kitchen. Rounding the corner from the family room, I noticed her at the kitchen counter, keeping a grin at bay by sipping from a coffee cup. "What's brought you by?"

Removing my baseball hat, I sat it on the counter; she didn't like me wearing my hat in the house.

I looked up and laughed. "Blaine's got a big mouth."

Mom squealed, setting her cup on the counter. "I'm so excited! How far along is she?"

Scratching the side of my head, my grin widened. "How long ago was that concert in Nashville?"

"A little over a month ago."

"About that long then."

"Beau Grayden Ryland." I was about to be scolded like a kid again. She used my middle name. "Did you get that sweet girl pregnant in your truck?"

I waggled my eyebrows. "Maybe."

"You're bad."

"Yeah, well, she's not as sweet as you think. She's actually kind of naughty."

Mom took a dishrag from the counter and threw it at me. "Stop that."

We laughed about it for a few minutes, and then she had to bring him up.

"What did your dad say?" Obviously she knew I'd tell him first. Mostly because I didn't want that conversation in my head the entire drive to Nashville. I always found it easier to get those kind of conversations over with quickly.

"What do you think he said?" I reached for my hat, picking at the frayed fabric on the side.

"Sorry, honey." She reached out, placing her hands over mine. "He's just—"

"Don't make excuses for him. You shouldn't have to. I'm old enough to know his reasons for being an asshole are about him. They're not about me."

Mom nodded, smiling tearfully at me. "You're absolutely right." Leaning into the counter, she stared down at her cell phone. "Hey, did you hear Wade and Lindsey filed for divorce?"

"No, well, yeah, he mentioned something about that a few weeks ago, but I already knew it was heading that way."

"How?" She looked at me in disbelief and I had to remind myself Wade and Lindsey had put on a pretty good show the last year trying to make everyone think they were happy, when in reality they weren't.

"He messed around."

I was honest with my mom and Blaine about what I did to Payton. Neither judged me, but still, I didn't feel good about it.

Maybe because it wasn't just one time. It was a string of nights over a month, and a few different girls. Cheating was cheating.

I know. Asshole.

And here I was upset with my dad about firing my mom and I fucked around on my girl.

To be fair, we weren't married, but that still wasn't an excuse. Being on the road was lonely and I finally understood why people cheated.

For me, it had nothing to do with sex. They craved closeness. They sought out what they couldn't have. Who really knew what the fuck my reasoning was? I don't even think I did.

"Beau," my mother's tone was concerned, drawing my attention to hers, "now that you're back on tour and—"

"I know, Ma." I cut her off again. "And I'm not the same wild kid I was back then." I felt incredibly small when she said that, like she knew what a mess I was just a year ago.

She laughed. Laughed. My own mother.

"That wasn't meant to be funny."

"I just hope things work out with you and Bentley. I really like her."

"I know you do, and I do too. I love her."

Tears welled up in her bright blue eyes that mirrored Blaine's. "Maybe you have grown."

"Damn straight." I stood, reaching for my hat. "But I'm late. I've gotta meet Sam in Nashville, and then we're heading to Kansas City."

"Good luck." Mom leaned in, kissing my cheek. "And tell Bentley I'm excited and here if she needs anything."

"You tell her."

You would have thought I told my mom we were having twins at the way her eyes lit up. She was never close with Payton. I wasn't sure why, they just never had a real connection. "What?"

"You can call her, or go by the house. She stays there on the weekends with Blaine."

"You don't mind? Or she won't?"

"Nope." I let out a laugh and stretched my arms over my head, then dropped them down to hug my mom to my side. "She'll love to hear from you." I kissed her cheek. "Love you."

"Drive safe!" she yelled after me.

Once I was on the road, I called Bentley to hear her voice one last time.

"Told my parents," I said, holding my phone to my ear and using my knee to steer. "They said we're on our own."

"Really?"

I laughed, finding humor in my joke. "No, my mom is knitting blankets as we speak. I'm sure of it."

Bentley paused, clearing her throat. "And your dad?"

"No comment."

"I'm sorry."

I sighed. "Don't be. When are you going to the doctor?"

"I had them do a blood test at the hospital. They said I'm for sure pregnant and due March fourteenth. I guess they said I'm eight weeks."

"Yep, Nashville, huh?" I gloated, feeling proud and a little more attached to this truck.

Bentley giggled. "Of course you take pride in knocking me up in your truck."

"Mmmm." I sighed, loving the sound of that giggle. "I can't wait to get home on Saturday. I'm gonna find out what this pregnant sex fuss is all about."

"I think maybe you'll have to wait until I'm not throwing up. I've been so sick this morning."

I panicked a little, my heartbeat quickened at the thought of her throwing up alone, without me there to hold her hair. "That's normal though, right?"

"Yeah, from what I hear. I have an appointment on September third to hear the heartbeat. . . can you make it for that?"

I tried to rack my brain, thinking if I had any shows scheduled for that day and realized I'd be coming back from Phoenix. "I think I can make it."

Fuck, I hoped I could make it. I really wanted to be there for her through this, show her I never thought she trapped me and I love her.

"Okay, well, I'm at work now. Call me when you get to Kansas City?"

"I will."

"Okay," she hesitated and then said, "bye."

I laughed, not ready to hang up. "Bentley?"

"Yeah?"

"I love you."

She breathed in deep, as if the words washed over her. I could almost picture her smile right then, sweet as a summer day with her long tan legs dangling over my tailgate, leaning back with the honey rays beating down on her.

"I love you too, Beau."

Closing my eyes, I breathed in myself, wishing we were back at that lake together.

Her words struck me in my chest, bringing up the same questions I asked myself every day. Was it worth it to be on the road so much?

It was because I could provide a life she never dreamed of, for her and our baby. I wouldn't be lying if I said it scared me to become a father. I could be a tough guy, but I could also break down and this had the capability of doing that.

Mostly because of the insecurities I knew it would make me feel, never being enough for the two of them.

I just hoped I was enough for her.

Chapter Fifteen

I'LL WAIT FOR YOU

BENTLEY

5 MONTHS LATER

MY PREGNANCY MOVED fast.

With Beau being gone up in Nashville during most weeks and me working full-time, I felt like before I knew it, Christmas came and went and we were preparing for the birth of our child in the March.

I had been feeling cramps all day at work to the point I went home early to an empty house. Beau and I were living together now, in a duplex with Blaine and Gavin on the other side.

After work, I planned to call Beau to check on him after I saw the news reports on the snow, and then I was going to beg Blaine to stay the night with me. I hated being alone.

I finished out my internship, and instead of working as an independent living assistant, I was offered a job at Midland Metropolitan Hospital in the Care Management Program where we assisted patients who had long-term conditions.

The one good thing about that job was working with Blaine. She was one of the nurses while I worked in the office.

As I dialed Beau's number, I walked by the picture of us on the fridge taken weeks after I told him about the baby. It was the two of us outside the doctor's office proudly holding the sonogram with the little bean on the photo. I loved that photo, but just looking at it now, no way you could capture the excitement and love in our eyes just by taking a snapshot of that one moment.

I had a plan in the beginning, a way I thought my life would venture after college, and it wasn't anything like what I had initially imagined. Somewhere along the way, probably when I tripped, it deviated from my plan.

One thing about the plan I had, Beau had taught me a little something about his theory on "You gotta jump sometime."

It was okay to just jump.

So we did, and now here we were, expecting a baby in a six weeks.

"Hey, babe," I said when he answered, sounding extremely tired. I settled on the couch, watching the flickering flame of the fire.

"How're my girls doin'?"

I giggled at the roughness of his voice. He sounded like he'd been gargling nails. "Wow, all those late nights are doing a number on your voice. I wish you were here to whisper in my ear."

"Me too." He cleared his throat. "God, I miss you, baby." Beau sighed. "I'm jealous my sister gets to see you every day. I fuckin' miss you so much right now. She better not be in bed with you every day."

I laughed. "Only when I'm cold. She really likes my noodle."

"Your what?"

"My noodle. That pregnancy pillow, remember? The one even you were cuddled up with while watching football last Sunday?"

"Oh. . . yeah. Didn't realize it was called a noodle."

"As much as I love your sister, I would prefer to see *you* every day."

He laughed and I could hear the faint sounds of music in the background and knew he must still be at the studio, another late night for him. I don't think anyone, even me, realized how much work went into recording an album.

"Will you be home this weekend?" I asked, digging through the freezer to find I still had some ice cream left. Score for me.

He seemed distracted, rustlings noise coming from the other end of the line followed by tapping. "I'm trying to be, but with this storm coming in, I'm not sure."

Stupid snow ruining my plans. One thing about being pregnant was I wanted sex all the time. The moment Beau would come through the door I was all over him. And you know, not once had he complained about it. All he ever said was when this baby was born, he was knocking me up again.

"That sucks."

"I wish you could come here and be with me during the week," Beau suggested.

Beau was constantly suggesting we move to Nashville. I thought about it, but I had a good job now at the hospital and I didn't want to leave that behind. Especially with the baby coming, I needed the medical insurance they had.

"I'd like that. . . but we can't."

"You're unreasonable," he teased lowly, and despite him being annoyed, his voice still made my breathing increase and my heart flutter in anticipation.

God, I wished he was here.

"I know, but I can't. Kevin would kill me if I just up and quit."

I hadn't noticed the clicking sound until Beau stopped, seeming to have been tapping something against the table, whatever it was that he was obsessively clicking, he had stopped.

"Kevin? Who's Kevin?"

"You know, Kevin," I stammered, smiling to myself the conversation went this way, "my boss."

Wrapping a blanket around myself, I frantically racked my brain to remember if I'd told him who Kevin was before. I could have sworn I had.

Shit, maybe I didn't tell him.

"Um, no. I know every man's name that has come out of your mouth since we met, and not once have I heard Kevin. I've heard mine a lot, mostly in my ear, moaning, but nope, no Kevin."

Of course he went there.

"Oh, well, Kevin is my boss," I spoke nonchalantly, not knowing what else to say, and opening the container of ice cream with my legs up on the couch, the fire going, all I needed was my man, or Blaine, to cuddle with.

"Does he know you have a fucking boyfriend?" Beau demanded.

"I'm sure he does. I am *eight* months pregnant."

"That doesn't mean shit." His tone was defensive and I wanted to laugh. "You told him you have a boyfriend, right?"

"Are you for real? Why does it even matter? What were we originally talking about?"

"I don't remember. You distracted me bringing up another man. I'm more *concerned* with this Kevin guy. I don't trust him. You should quit."

"Why would you even be *concerned* about him?"

"He knows not to fish in the company pond, right?"

"Yes," I sighed, getting annoyed he was pushing it this much. "I'm pretty sure he does."

"Like you're pretty sure he knows you have a boyfriend," he snapped. I knew Beau well enough to know he wasn't the jealous type, but it was actually cute and funny to see him this way. It reminded me of when he was upset about Harry offering me a ride on his lap.

"You're being irrational. You never act this way."

"No, I'm not," he defended. "And now, I'm definitely coming home tomorrow. I'm going to pick you up from work and meet this boss man," he said with a hint of finality. "I may even propose tomorrow in front of him."

"No, you won't." I laughed. "And I have tomorrow off. You'll have to save your epic proposal for another day."

He didn't let the marriage part go when he asked, "So are you going to finally marry me sometime soon?" Beau had been saying for months he wanted to marry me, teasing of proposing, but hadn't actually done it.

At his question, I instantly remembered that night at the lake and my cheeks heated with the memory. *"So are you going to let me kiss you sometime soon?"*

"I wasn't aware you wanted to." I used my same answer I did back then.

"Fuck that." Beau laughed, the sound throaty, and so incredibly sexy. "Yes you were. I think you are well aware of the fact I want to make you my wife, Bentley."

"Hmmm, maybe I did, a little."

"You knew," he hummed out a throaty sound that made my cheeks burn remembering what it sounded like against my skin. "You did."

We were quiet for a moment, me watching the snow and wondering if he was doing the same. "I can't believe this snow."

"I fucking miss you so much." He groaned, and then made an umph sound like he fell back against something. "The things I'm gonna do to you when I get home should be illegal."

"In some religions I bet they are, naughty boy."

"Like the Amish, they would *definitely* throw my ass in jail."

I laughed so hard at him it hurt my stomach. "Ow."

"What?" Beau was immediately at attention whenever I complained.

"I'm cramping tonight." My voice was a little strained from the pain, the dull ache that seemed to settle over my entire swollen stomach. "I think it's like Braxton Hicks contractions or something."

"I don't like the sound of that. You sound like you're in pain." His tensed voice made me realize how protective he'd become over us. "I should drive home tonight."

"No, Beau, the weather station said they're calling for another foot tonight. I don't want you driving home in this weather. Just wait until it eases up."

"I'm gonna come home in the morning. It may take me all day, but I'm coming back." I could almost hear the pain etched in his words.

"Okay," I finally agreed, because I wanted him here.

WHEN I WOKE up Friday morning, something felt strange. I'd been cramping all night, and finally I felt like it was time I called the doctor when I couldn't get her to move around. Usually, I would gently push on my stomach and she'd squirm. Now, she did nothing. And then I noticed a few spots of blood and really began to panic.

Sitting in the kitchen with a cup of tea, I waited for the nurse to call me back, staring out at the thick blanket of white snow and trying not to freak out. It hardly ever snowed in

Alabama and, of course, the one weekend I really wanted Beau here, a snow storm had to hit. There had to be at least two feet of snow on the ground now.

Looking down at my stomach, I touched it gently. "Are you okay, little lady? Move for Mommy and tell me you're fine. Please, baby."

The nurse finally called back and I explained what the cramps felt like and how the baby wasn't moving much. She instructed me to go to the hospital immediately and head straight to the ER.

After getting dressed, I went next door to knock on Blaine's door, hoping she wasn't working this morning and could drive me to the hospital. No way was I trying to drive in this snow when I was nervous like this.

Gavin answered in his underwear, his eyes wide when he took in my appearance and me holding my stomach. "Bentley, are you okay?"

"No, I'm not." With my heart pounding hard I was in tears by then. "Something's wrong. I need to get to the hospital right now."

Gavin reached for his keys on the hook beside the door. "I'll drive you."

He stepped out the door and I stopped him. "Clothes, Gavin. You need clothes."

Smiling, he looked down at his half-naked body. "Right."

Blaine came running downstairs, pulling on pants and a sweatshirt. "What's wrong? Gavin said something's wrong with the baby?"

"Something is wrong. I need you guys to take me to the ER."

Frantically grabbing at shoes and her purse, and then Gavin, Blaine helped me inside Gavin's lifted F-350. "Does Beau know?"

"No, I came right over here. I'll call him on the way there."

The wind picked up, blowing sheets of white crystals in my face, slapping at my skin like tiny pieces of glass.

Fuck, it was cold.

Huddled up in the backseat with Blaine, Gavin drove us to the ER, careful of the roads covered in a thick layer of snow. It took us ten minutes just to get out of the driveway and I had a feeling the roads from Nashville to here were even worse.

Please tell me he's on his way home.

With my phone in hand, the tears kept flowing, thinking the worst—I was going to have her early and Beau wouldn't be here for it.

I called him, only he didn't answer, and I was afraid to leave this kind of message, but I had to. "Beau, I'm cramping and bleeding. The nurse told me to go to the ER, so Blaine and Gavin are taking me now." I gasped, my tears overtaking my words. "Beau, I need you. Please."

WHEN WE ARRIVED at the hospital, they had me immediately hooked up to a fetal monitor in the emergency room and then the doctor came in the room, did an exam, and looked up at me. My heart fell before he even spoke.

"You have what is called a premature rupture of the membrane. We're going to send you over to labor and delivery and give you some antibiotics and some medicine to try to the stop the labor. There's minimal fetal activity, which leads us to believe the baby is in distress. We are going to run some more tests and see where we go from here."

Where we go from here?

"What?" I gasped, covering my mouth as tears surfaced, my mind spinning. My baby's in trouble? In that moment, when those words left the doctor's mouth, my heart felt like it weighed a thousand pounds.

Blaine clamped her hands over mine tightly, giving me support without saying too much. The doctor left the room without another word.

Refusing to let me walk, I was transferred to another bed and wheeled over to labor and delivery with Blaine holding my hand. "Beau just called Gavin. He's on his way. They apparently left an hour ago. The power went out and Beau's phone is dead."

I wanted him here so badly. The anxiety welled up, and my vision blurring into the white walls and ceiling as they moved me to a different room. All along, I thought something was going to go wrong. No way would I be granted a life like this with Beau. And when I was, I'd thought it was a miracle.

And now it was all spiraling out of control. I was waking up from that coma and inside of the worst nightmare ever, without him by my side.

"Does he know about the baby?" I asked Blaine.

"Gavin told him."

I used the sleeve of Beau's jacket I was wearing to wipe my eyes. "What did he say?"

"Nothing that I know of. The connection was really bad and I think he was out of range."

They got me into a room, in a gown, and then laid back in bed with the monitors hooked up. If I wasn't panicked by then, I was when I stared at the monitors and the ultrasound screen as three nurses huddled around. Commotion was all around me, but I focused on that screen, my baby girl, not moving.

They wanted to know where Beau was. "Is your husband with you?"

"We're not married, but no, he's not here with me right now."

"Can he get here soon?"

My voice shook. "He's on his way."

Placing my hands gently on my stomach, I looked down at my baby bump, teardrops splattering on my shirt. "Hang in there, baby girl. Please be okay. Mommy and Daddy love you so much."

Gavin stayed in the waiting room with Gale, Beau's mom, who rushed over, while Blaine remained by my side.

I refused to let Blaine out of my sight. If Beau couldn't be here, I had the next best thing, my best friend and his twin sister. At least I could look at her and find comfort.

"Don't leave me," I told her when we were inside the labor and delivery room.

In tears herself, she pushed her dark messy hair from her face, rubbing my arm. "I'm not going anywhere. Even my brother won't be able to kick my ass out. I'm staying."

Another nurse came in, long blonde hair and a perfect smile, and noticed Blaine. She looked familiar, but I couldn't place her name, or if I even knew her. "Hey, babe, what are you doing here today? I thought it was your day off?"

We were at the same hospital we both worked at, so naturally we were going to run into people we knew at some point.

"It is my day off." Blaine handed me another pillow, staying right by the side of the bed. "This is Beau's girlfriend, Bentley. She's in labor. Bentley," she nodded to the nurse, "this is Tabitha. We went to school together."

"Oh goodie! A little Beau baby." Tabitha gleamed. "I heard he's coming out with a CD in April, is that right?" Before I could answer, she went over to the bedside computer. She let me know she would be my nurse while I was in Labor and Delivery and then began staring at the screen.

"Great, and yes, his record comes out in April," I mumbled, waiting for her face to give me an indication as to what my chart said, my face falling right along with my heart.

As she read the notes, she began talking, the color in her face draining. Something was wrong. "So it looks like they're waiting on blood work." Her eyes darted through what I assumed was everything said to me in the emergency room, and it hit her. She swallowed, as if her throat was suddenly dry. The dread of what she was seeing washed over me like the snow outside, cold, bitter, clinging to your skin, refusing to let up and gnawing at every other sensation you had.

"I'm just going to call the lab on the blood work and I'll be right back, okay? Can I get you anything?"

I said nothing and gave a blank stare.

"Blaine, can I talk to you for a minute?" Tabitha gave a nod to the door.

Blaine stood and I reached for her hand, looking over at Tabitha. "Don't do that," I snapped, ready to break down completely. "I know what you're going to do." Tabitha's lips turned down at my words, her cheeks heating with the faintest shade of pink. "You're going to pull her outside and tell her my baby isn't going to make it, aren't you?"

Tabitha drew in a deep breath, visibly fighting back her emotions I was sure she'd become numb to over the years of being a nurse. Making her way beside me, her warm hand touched over my stomach.

I was afraid to meet her eyes, thinking she'd tell me right then I shouldn't have hope. "I was only going to ask where Beau was. If he was on his way." I nodded. "Okay, so, hopefully, he gets here soon and we can go from there."

"Why?"

"Because I don't think the medicine is going to work. The baby is in distress."

"Okay, so get her out now."

"That doesn't mean she's going to survive. I'm so sorry, Bentley. We can only hope for the best."

AS I STARED at my phone in my lap, hoping Beau would call and say he was here, an hour passed with Blaine and Tabitha by my side. I had no idea what to think when the doctor came in, only I feared the worse by his brashness toward me.

"Good morning, Bentley."

Fuck you. My baby is dying. There's no good morning about it.

The douche of a doctor wouldn't even look at me. "As I said before, there is still minimal fetal movement, we see the cord is wrapped around her neck at least once and your blood tests came back abnormal. I'm very sorry, but the chances of your baby's survival are very low." And then he left, not saying another word to me.

Was he serious?

I stared at Tabitha. "What the fuck is he talking about?"

She sat next to me and took my hand in hers. "What he means, and can't be subtle about anything, is your baby is in severe distress. We're giving you some antibiotics and steroids since you're thirty-three weeks, but with the minimal fetal movement and abnormal blood tests, it means her chance of survival is low."

An indescribable guilt knotted in my chest when I thought about my baby in distress. This wasn't happening. It couldn't be happening. Not like this. No.

I stared at Tabitha, praying she wasn't telling me this. Her eyes darted to Blaine. "Have you heard from Beau yet?"

"He's on his way, but his phone died and with all the snow. . . ." She burst into tears. "I don't know. I imagine the roads are horrible."

I wasn't settling and wanted to get out of the bed, so I started to. "I'll go to a different hospital then." The tightness in my chest took over and I gasped, another wave of emotions taking over. This could not be happening.

"I'm very sorry, Bentley." Tabitha urged me back in bed, never letting me get up.

"STOP saying that!" I screamed at her, shaking my head frantically, trying to make her take back the words. "Do the ultrasound again. You have to be wrong. She was fine yesterday. Maybe she's just sleeping. Just, please, do it again."

Taking my hand, Tabitha whispered, "Bentley, this is the best hospital for you to be at for your situation, and if you leave now, you may jeopardize your own life as well. You may think at this moment Dr. Doushan, is a douche, but he is one of the best."

"He said my baby won't make it," I cried. "Obviously he's not the best if he can't save her. I want to leave."

I didn't know if it was my crying, but something went wrong and the monitors went off, alarms whistling through the room.

I panicked, feeling pressure in my stomach. "What's happening?"

"Her vital signs are dropping." Tabitha turned to another nurse. "Page Dr. Doushan!"

The door to my room swung open and following a string of four nurses was Beau, eyes wide and glaring as if he'd been through hell trying to get here.

I exhaled at the sight of him, so relieved that he made it.

"Bentley!" He gasped when he took in my appearance. Immediately he was beside me, one hand on my cheek, the other over my stomach. "What happened?"

"I'm so sorry, Beau." I sobbed into his chest, fisting his jacket in my hands. "I did something wrong. She's not moving around. It's all my fault. I'm so sorry."

He snapped back searching my eyes. "What? What are you talking about?" His sudden hostile glare moved to the doctor who came in. "What's wrong? What's wrong with my daughter?"

Dr. Douche wouldn't answer him.

"Tell me she's fine." Beau began pacing the room, maybe in attempt to keep from hitting him. Watching him, I drew in a shuddering deep breath. "Tell me she's okay and that she's going to be fine!"

Dr. Douche sighed, as if he couldn't believe he had to clarify anything. "Now is not the time for us to discuss this. The baby is in distress and we need to get her out or we could lose the both of them."

That set Beau off completely. Tears pooled in his eyes, but they didn't let go, grief and despair seemed to be holding them off. "What happened? Someone better tell me, because two days ago, she was fucking fine, and now you're saying my daughter is dying?"

"Ms. Schow came in cramping and bleeding. She had what we call a premature rupture of the membrane. The baby has the cord wrapped around her neck and she's suffocating. So you tell me, Beau, would you like to talk about this or would you like me to try to save your daughter? It's up to you." The doctor crossed his arms.

I looked at Beau through my crying. Taking in a deep breath, I held it in for a moment. "Meet Dr. Douche."

I don't know why I said that, maybe to try to calm Beau down because I wanted him here with me, not in jail where I was sure he was going to be thrown out for hitting a doctor any minute.

It was then Beau finally drew his eyes back to mine and realized how bad I was freaking out. "I'm sorry, Beau. I came first thing this morning. I didn't. I should have!" I burst into another wave of tears, my body shivering though my skin was burning up.

Beau looked at me and then the floor. And back to me. His eyes spoke volumes for what he couldn't say with words. Confused, hurt, angry.

And then it hit him, hard, pounding him into the ground like it did to me.

"Baby, you did nothing wrong," he whispered, kissing my tear soaked cheeks, both of them, and then my lips, forcing me to look at him. "This is not your fault." Tears were falling down his cheeks, one after another.

"But it is. I'm her mother. It was my job to keep her safe inside of me and I didn't do that. What if it was the ice cream I ate last night? Maybe she doesn't like ice cream."

"It's nothing you did. Sometimes things happen without any explanation," the nurse tried to assure me, again.

In a rush, they prepared me for delivery.

When the doctor finally spoke, I wished he would have kept his mouth shut because the words he spoke weren't ones I ever expected and hadn't prepared myself to hear. "If she is breathing when she's born, she won't make it long. I'm sorry." He ordered nurses around and it was a blur as the prepared to do everything they could to save our daughter. "I need to know if you want us to try and save her, or if you want to hold her."

With every word, blood pounded in my ears as I shook my head violently. I refused to accept it, refused to listen to his words. Fire pushed through my veins, stealing my breath, landing in my heart and constricting it.

How the fuck did this happen? HOW?

My heart was sinking fast, fearing the worst, but holding onto the possibility there was no way this was happening. It couldn't be. Not to us.

Maybe they were wrong.

Maybe.

Please, God, give me a maybe. You gave me Beau, please give us our baby.

Please.

"I. uh. . . ." How could I make that kind of decision?

"I need to know right now what you want me to do." The doctor between my legs barked only to have Beau snap back at him.

"Don't fuckin' talk to her that way," he warned.

The doctor returned Beau's glare. "I'm trying to either save your daughter, or give you a chance to hold her. You might not ever have the chance if she doesn't decide right now, and if she doesn't start pushing right now, Bentley could die."

It's just a dream. It's not happening. You're going to wake up and this nightmare will be over and she'll be fine.

The problem was it wasn't a dream.

My heart felt crippled, suffocated by his words. I couldn't breathe; the ceiling felt like it was collapsing around me.

"Save her," I cried against Beau's shoulder, feeling the need to push again.

They wanted me to have an epidural, but I refused. I wanted to feel this pain, any pain but what I was feeling in my heart. In the end, I had no choice. They made me get one in case they had to rush me to surgery.

I felt nothing now.

No pain but the crushing suffocating feeling biting at my lungs.

Beau said little, because really, what could he have said? Nothing would have helped me, or made this okay.

As I pushed, he looked livid and on edge, his hands shaking, as if any word by someone would have set him off. This was his baby too. I couldn't discount that. He was in pain as well knowing she might not live.

Might. A maybe. We were holding onto a maybe.

"You can change your mind at any time," Tabitha whispered. "If you decide you want to hold her, just tell him."

Unfamiliar voices and a series of images haunted me as I pushed and cried. I tried to lift my head, but I was too weak. All I could do was stare at the wall, watching the clock, second after excruciating second.

A wave of nausea hit me so strong I thought I was going to vomit all over Beau. I looked at him, the worry evident in his face.

The room was quiet and Beau was watching me.

Waiting.

My throat felt dry, like sandpaper, my lungs so heavy I feared drawing in a breath would hurt and never be enough.

Anger flickered in Beau's eyes, knowing how painful this was, his jaw clenching, narrowing his stare at the doctor between my legs.

A pressure built in my hips, the doctor and nurses around him moving quicker. "Give me one more push, Bentley."

Looking up, my eyes were drawn lower, gripping Beau's hand so hard I was sure I was hurting him.

And then she was born, blue and not moving, her body limp. "She's breathing," the doctor mumbled, to a nurse.

They were going to take her away and I knew right then there was no saving her. Something inside me snapped seeing her in the arms of someone else. If she was alive, this second, we had her for a moment. A moment is all we were going to have. I knew it in my heart. This was the end.

"Give her to me!" I screamed, holding out my arms, crying out in utter devastation, my body pulsing in wrenching waves of pain. "Don't take her away. Give her to me!"

The doctor looked to Beau for confirmation and he nodded, knowing we didn't want to prolong her suffering or put her through anything unnecessary. Trying to save her for the sake of our own wants wouldn't give us a healthy baby.

We could, however, enjoy her final breaths.

They had Beau cut the cord, with shaking hands. Our eyes locked on one another and then the baby.

Placing her motionless body on my chest, so tender and true to what she was, a precious angel given to us if even just for a moment. Her eyes were closed, her color a pale blue, but she looked healthy, with little rolls around her wrists and thighs.

Beau climbed into bed with me when they handed us a blanket to place around her, his right arm around my shoulders, his left around our daughter.

She was beautiful. Absolutely beautiful and perfect in every single way.

I memorized everything I could about her in those seconds, everything from her perfectly sweet pouty lips to her nose, eyes, tiny delicate fingers that wrapped about Beau's pinkie when he touched her.

And then she breathed, once, her chest rising slowly, labored, letting go.

I breathed in deeply, for her maybe, because she couldn't.

She looked identical to Beau with his dark hair and my nose. Even though her eyes were closed, I knew they'd be his bright blue, something deep inside told me so.

I knew Beau was crying; his chest shook mine as he wrapped his arms around the two of us, trying to hold on. "She's beautiful, pretty girl," he whispered, his words shaking and breaking. "Just like her mama."

Blaine, who had been in the room the entire time, holding my hand right along with Beau, let out a sob, covering her mouth as she stared down at the baby. "I'm sorry," she breathed, making her way out of the room, unable to hold the emotion back any longer.

There was heartache, and then there was devastation in this world. My happiness in those moments with her was marred by the fact that those would be my only moments.

I no longer had a maybe. I had a memory.

Nothing could have prepared me for the way that would feel. The pain, the loss, the remorse I felt for thinking it was something I did wrong. I was her mother, I was meant to protect her and keep her safe even inside me, and I didn't do that.

She was there, our baby girl, with us, until God took her back, giving us at least that much, her touch.

I guess, as awful as it felt, I was thankful for that, the breaths she did take, the touches she did give, and that feeling, the one of knowing what it would be like holding her.

"Please, wake up, baby girl. Please wake up for us. Open your eyes," I begged through my tears, unable to accept it.

Only she didn't.

I knew the moment she stopped breathing. I felt it in my chest, like my breath was sucked from me all at once.

Make it stop.

Make time stop.

Make the pain stop right now.

Give her life. Take mine. Give it to her.

I'll sacrifice the very breath in my lungs, if you just please give it to her.

My baby was gone.

I SPENT four hours holding her. Blaine held her. Gale held her, and finally, Beau held his daughter. It was the first time I'd seen him sob as if nothing in the world could capture his pain. I knew the feeling.

A photographer came in and took some photographs of her. We were able to bath her, hold her, kiss her, and I apologized endlessly to her for not being able to help her. It was my fault. I was sure of it. I had done something wrong to cause this, to have her taken from me.

"What should we name her?" Beau asked, his words breaking at the end, the pain evident in his voice, his face blotchy and red from crying.

Taking in a deep breath, I held it for a moment and then kissed her cold forehead. "Dixie Mae." I loved the name when Beau suggested it not long after we found out we were having a girl.

At the mention, my mind flooded with memories, one right after another, flowing into the next of the last eight months and all the wonderful memories we had preparing for her.

And now this.

Why?

What had I done for this to happen?

"It's perfect." Beau kissed my temple. "It's perfect for her."

They said I could stay the night in the hospital, but I saw no need. I didn't want to be there any longer.

I also couldn't bear to leave Dixie, in that hospital, alone, without me.

The longer we waited, the more her body deteriorated in my arms. I wanted to die with her. I no longer wanted to live if I couldn't have this, her, us. My life had ended when she stopped breathing.

As the nurse took her out of the room, away from me, I sat there, drowning in a horrible, agonizing grief, after holding my dead daughter and cursing God and everyone else for taking her from me.

It wasn't fair.

It never would be.

Chapter Sixteen

DON'T TAKE THE GIRL

BEAU

DIXIE MAE RYLAND breathed in one precious breath, and then never again, as though she granted us that one, as if it was her gift to us.

She wrapped her tiny hand around my finger like she was pinky promising me, something, only I didn't know what.

As Bentley cried in my arms, begging her to breathe, I wanted to tell her it was going to be okay, that I would make it better, but there was nothing I could do for her, or Dixie.

They discharged Bentley around midnight, six hours after our daughter was pronounced dead. They wanted her to stay overnight, only she wouldn't. She didn't want to be in that hospital another minute if Dixie wasn't with her.

As I we made our way out, we passed by the lobby where our family had been waiting.

Bentley didn't speak to anyone and cried in her hands as I wheeled her to the automatic doors.

Pausing next to Blaine and Gavin, I wanted to thank everyone for waiting.

Miles looked up at me and then to Gavin. "I'll catch a ride with Gavin and Blaine. Do you guys need anything?"

"No, I'm just going to get Bentley home." My voice was low and raspy. I felt like wanted to fall to my knees and sob. I couldn't even comprehend what happened, let alone how to deal with it or go through the motions of what came next.

Blaine cleared her throat. "Do you want me to come over when we get back?"

"No, not right now." No way did I want anyone around but Bentley.

AS WE LEFT the hospital, I didn't say much. Neither did Bentley. There wasn't anything to say. No words would do what we went through justice.

We walked slowly to the truck, trudging through the thick bank of snow I parked on, I think we were both waiting for the other to say something.

Anything.

Or maybe. . . nothing.

Maybe nothing needed to be said right then.

After helping her inside the truck, I blew into my hands, trying to warm myself up. Out of the corner of my eye, I could see the tears streaming down Bentley's cheeks.

Why?

Why had this happened?

The lump in my throat rose, the tears fell slowly, quietly, as if nothing I could possibly do would stop them at a time like this.

We had just gotten on the highway, the blizzard raged on, a silent storm of screaming silver. The roads were quiet, and white oversized flakes that looked like crystals fell heavily like our tears, obscuring my view completely.

It had taken over four hours for me to get to the hospital this afternoon from Nashville, and I had a distinct feeling the twenty-minute drive to our house would take over an hour.

Bentley let out a sob, clutching her stomach with her arms wrapped around her. "Why can't we. . .I want her back!"

I jerked the truck over, skidding to a stop on what I assumed was the shoulder of the road and unbuckled my seatbelt. It was more than likely dangerous, but I didn't care in that moment.

Unlocking her seatbelt, I slid her across the seat over to my side.

"Don't, Beau, please. Don't touch me or hold me. Don't!"

I wouldn't listen to her. I couldn't. Roughly, I grabbed her by the shoulders and forced her to my chest, trapping her in my embrace. "I'm sorry."

"Don't." In her anger, she slapped me. "I don't want you to hold me!"

I felt nothing, though I glared back at her. "I'm sorry," I repeated, wondering when she was going to see I was hurting too; it wasn't just her.

She fought me for a while, and then she gave up, her weight sagging into my chest, finally allowing me to be there for her.

Bentley cried as if there was no controlling it.

I felt her pain, swirling like the blizzard outside, unable to make sense of anything as the angry wind picked up. She was clinging to the idea that maybe this was all just a horrible nightmare.

I was too, but I knew it wasn't.

"Make the pain stop," she cried, over and over again. "Please make it stop. It hurts so much."

Make it stop.

I wanted to.

Fuck, I want to take her pain away so badly.

I desperately wanted to.

"I wish I could, baby. I want to." I could barely get the words out I was trembling so badly.

Nothing I did, said, or felt was going to bring her back.

I didn't know loss, and certainly couldn't understand it until I loved her, a baby who I'd never even felt the softness of her touch until a few hours ago. You don't understand that kind of pain until you've seen it firsthand, had it ripped from you without so much as an answer.

That was devastation.

That was loss.

For an hour, she let me hold her alongside the highway.

When my body began to grow tired, my arm tingling from where she was laying on it, Bentley moved, focusing on the obscured windshield and the white reflecting off it.

Looking at me, her eyes were threaded with scarlet, her body limp against mine. "I want to go home, Beau."

Kissing her once more, I then pulled back, searching watery eyes. "We're gonna be okay, pretty girl."

She didn't answer me.

I guess, I wasn't sure if that was the truth.

Maybe we wouldn't be.

When I had Bentley back at home, she wouldn't leave the bathroom that morning.

Wouldn't let me hold her again.

Wouldn't let me do a damn thing.

I sat on the porch, staring off at the white blanket of snow covering the driveway. Blaine came out of her apartment and sat down beside me in sweats and black boots that crunched against the ice like breaking glass. "Is she okay?"

"No," I took in a deep breath, wishing it was enough. "She's not okay." Turning, I looked at my sister who'd been there for me through everything before today, and here again if I needed anything. "I don't know what to do, Blaine. Everything happened so fast last night. We had her and then we didn't. I don't even know how to comprehend this and I can't take her pain away." The tears flowed now, knowing my sister would never judge me for crying in front of her.

Wrapping her arm around my shoulder, she held me. "I know, Beau. I know."

Sitting with Blaine for close to an hour, I went upstairs to check on Bentley. She was on the bed now, curled up with the blankets over her head.

"Can I get you anything, honey?"

She wouldn't answer me or even acknowledge the sound of my voice.

Chapter Seventeen

SISSY

BENTLEY

MY MIND WAS a jumbled mess of thoughts I couldn't decipher in the days following that cold winter day.

Thousands of wants, nevers, couldn'ts, wouldn'ts. . .they all swarmed me, swallowing me whole, as if I never had a chance to stay above water to begin with.

I should have gone to the hospital sooner. I should have known something was wrong with her.

What hurt most was I never got to hear Dixie cry. I never saw the color of her eyes. She was silent and perfect. Beautiful and missed, every minute, every hour, every day.

The next step was to plan the funeral. Beau called his manager and they agreed to give him some time off, as did my work.

When we were arranging the funeral, they told us we could choose a burial site, as if we wanted to do that. They also said it would be cheaper to bury her under a tree because she wouldn't disturb the roots, as if having to pay less for the burial site would make us feel better.

I didn't want to plan a funeral. I wanted nothing to do with it. Thankfully, Blaine and Gale did that for us. I wanted to hold my precious, beautiful, sweet baby girl in my arms as I rocked her in the chair Beau's granddaddy gave to us, the one Beau was rocked in as a baby.

I wanted to watch her grow and spit foods like mashed sweet potatoes back in my face or scream because I set her down. I wanted to change dirty diapers and run after a toddler as she cackled down the hallways buck naked. I wanted to kiss tiny scratches and swipe away tears with my sleeve.

I wanted to watch her sleep on Beau's chest and take pictures of them together like the obsessive photographer I would have been. I wanted to paint her toes and take her shopping, cry over her first broken heart with her.

I wanted all of that for me, and I suddenly realized how selfish that sounded, but I didn't care, because none of that was going to fucking happen.

I wanted to be selfish, for today at least.

DIXIE MAE RYLAND was laid to rest inside of a pearl white casket on a cold winter day in late January, one week after she passed away.

For me, I thought maybe there would have been finality in having the funeral.

There wasn't.

If anything, it hurt more because of that finality. I would never hold her again.

Inside there, she held my heart inside of hers.

I cried the entire day, unable to function. I even had to get on medication, just to make it to the funeral. I didn't want to go. I wanted to curl up in the corner and die.

We had a small funeral, just close family. I think there was maybe ten people, and I couldn't have told you who. If it hadn't been for Beau holding me up, I would have collapsed the moment I saw that casket.

My life and the world around me literally stood still in that moment as I thought about her. My future, my dreams for her, dissolved into the frozen red clay we were about to lay her in.

Every day I was pregnant, I had these images of what it would be like having a daughter, pictures I'd created in my head of what our lives would be like. Now I had nothing.

I felt like nothing. I wanted to be nothing.

Please, just let me die so I don't have to feel this pain anymore.

People tell you that becoming a mother is the greatest thing in the world, an experience unlike anything else. The love you feel for that baby couldn't even begin to be described or even be confined to a word like love.

It was so much more than that. So much.

And then that love was ripped away, torn from my chest, pried out of my bloody grasp as I begged on my knees for another chance, one more moment to love.

To feel.

To believe it was there in the first place.

I didn't get my moment.

I got a single breath.

It was a nightmare I was sure would never end, the image I had of her body, cold, helpless, lying in the dirt in a box, as haunting as that seemed.

Beau had no idea how to deal with me, or what to say to make it better. So he just held me.

I didn't know how to make it better.

What hurt was the *would not* about this. All those wants I had were big fat would nots.

We wouldn't be able to hold her when she cried.

We wouldn't watch her grow into a child and hold her hand that first day of kindergarten.

We wouldn't be able to go to her ballet recitals or teach her to play the guitar.

We wouldn't be able to see her go to prom or walk down the aisle.

Why?

Why wouldn't we?

What I wasn't prepared for was the could not's that came after the would nots.

I couldn't eat.

I couldn't sleep.

I was afraid I couldn't love.

I couldn't let Beau touch me.

Every time I looked at him, I saw Dixie with her hand wrapped around his pinky. If I even glanced at Beau, I broke down.

I couldn't help that. My world stopped that night. There was a black hole inside me I was afraid would never heal.

I finally understood my parents' pain, the pain they told me was unforgettable and unable to explain.

For so long, I thought 'You still have me, what about me?'

I remember being angry with them that they didn't take that into consideration, just that they were mad they lost Corbin.

But I never knew the feeling of being a mother, or a father, and having that love ripped from your hands.

Nothing could ever take that love away.

IT WAS MONTHS after the funeral and Beau was on his way back to Nashville as he had to be back in the studio. Life, unfortunately, had to continue, despite it stopping for me. He was gone for three days.

I cried for three days straight in Blaine's arms.

I hadn't gone back to work, and I wasn't sure I could ever step foot in that hospital again.

I feared seeing anyone. What would I say to them?

What would I say when they asked what happened? Or told me they were sorry?

When he returned on Friday night, I could tell he was drunk and wanted sex, as if that would solve our problems. I knew eventually he would want it, but I couldn't be close to him like that without breaking down.

I pushed Beau's shoulders. "Stop," I told him. "Your phone's ringing. You should see what Miles needs."

Having no idea if it was really Miles or not, I was still relieved at the interruption.

I was avoiding being with him in this way, and he knew it.

It had been almost eight weeks since Dixie passed away and I barely let him touch me since then. Every time he did, I'd cry.

Despite me pushing back, Beau didn't stop. He kissed up from my neck, around my jaw again, continuing to ignore the sound of a third call from Miles.

"Beau, stop," I said again, stronger this time, squirming under him. "Just answer your phone. What if they need you?"

Pulling away abruptly, Beau stood beside the bed, reaching for his phone, and when he found it, he practically jerked the battery out and tossed both pieces across the room. "You stop," he warned, meeting my eyes. He wasn't angry. He didn't raise his voice, but he was serious. He grabbed my hips and pulled me closer to the edge of the bed. "None of that shit matters right now. Be with me here like you love me. I want you to *need* me."

There was so much to that comment that I felt it in my gut. *I do need you.*

Swallowing, I held onto his hands, feeling him hold onto me. My thoughts, my feelings, the blue in his eyes, so real and begging, with the gray in the room, everything swirled at his touch. "I'm trying." I nodded.

He seemed to struggle for words and then looked at me, hurt and confused, his eyes glossy, a gamut of emotions swimming in them. "You still love me, right?"

"I do."

He swallowed too and leaned back down, pressing his lips to mine again. His kisses were heavier this time, his touch on my skin harder. His hands glided down my thighs, gripping and squeezing, alternating between tight and gentle. "I miss you so fucking much." His words blew over me like a summer breeze, warm, soul-healing and beautiful, just like him. "I just want you to need me."

It felt right, it did, but then again it felt wrong.

I tried not to think, or feel, or do anything but be with Beau the way I wanted because I wanted to be reminded of the magic between us.

We may not have been having sex, yet, but there was a passion between us, a spark still present that wasn't going to be put out easily. I knew that. But it was still hard for me. Anytime I looked at him, I remembered Dixie.

"Be here," Beau breathed raggedly against my skin, the smell of liquor prominent. He spoke low and soft, sure words, but he sounded tortured underneath his careful tone. "Please. I need you."

"I am here," I told him, trying to make myself, even as my heart was telling me there was something in his words that I might have been missing. "I'm here," I said again, trying so hard to believe myself.

"Then fucking be here," he quietly scolded, knowing, hushed and threatening as he gripped tighter and pulled me closer, knowing me well enough to know I wasn't here completely. I might never be again.

Moving down my body, pushing the sheets and his flannel that I was wearing aside to reveal bare skin he hadn't kissed in so long, he brought my right hip under his lips and closed them over me. I cried out at the roughness of his kiss.

Groaning, he sucked and bit, digging his teeth in. It was evident by the way my body was responding to his touch, I missed him. Humming against my skin, he groaned and breathed hot over his mark, playing my body as well as he did the crowd at his shows. He knew exactly what he was doing and how to make me want more from him.

Just as quickly as they were hard, his hands and lips softened, and I let go of my hesitance and let the adrenaline he lit in my veins run its course.

Tugging on his shoulders gently, my brain and heart spun into emotions. Hurt and needing him, I surrendered, letting him remove my panties.

I *wanted* him. I wanted to forget my pain somehow.

"Beau?" I whispered so quietly I barely heard myself. I blinked and my eyelashes felt wet. I didn't mean to cry. I couldn't help it. I couldn't. It just. . . happened.

"Shhhh, don't cry." His voice was strong and soft at the same time. "Don't cry." He moved up my stomach, kissing me as he made a slow path. "Be here with me."

I nodded, holding his eyes with mine as he settled between my legs and covered my body with his, just like I needed and didn't even know.

He warmed me.

He melted me.

Through icy blue storms he calmed me just by being so near in the eye of our storm.

"I love you," he told me, whispering words that felt like raindrops against canvas and a night filled with sparks that rained down on us. "You know that?"

I nodded. I did know. I also knew he was suffering too and together we felt an emotion no one truly knew the meaning of but us.

Devastation.

Two hearts.

Two souls.

Suffering the same unimaginable loss.

"I know," I promised, holding onto him so tightly as he entered me for the first time since our daughter passed away. "I love you too."

We stared at each other in silence for a long minute, lost in a moment neither one of us tried to surface from. We were okay drowning; we were okay lost at sea, as long as we were clinging to one another, right?

ANOTHER SLEEPLESS NIGHT for me as Beau snored gently beside me. I wished I could sleep like him. Instead I was constantly left staring at the damn wondering how my life got like this.

Unable to comprehend the moment it went from good and fairytale like to this, sleepless, tears rolling down my cheeks watching a man sleep. The one man who'd give anything to take that pain away.

I wouldn't let him though.

As I watched the slow rhythm of his stomach and chest, I was jealous he'd found the peaceful bliss of sleep.

All I ever had was nightmares.

I watched him for hours, knowing exactly why I fell in love with him, and not understanding why it wasn't enough anymore.

It should always be enough, right? Love could build a bridge right? No, The Judds were liars. It built a bridge all right, one you could hurled yourself from.

"I HAVE TO go back to LA for a week." Beau said the next morning. "You can come with me if you want."

We should have been healing together; instead, Beau was recording and I was at home.

Staring at another message from Laney, asking if I was okay, I ignored it. I couldn't answer her because who really wanted a big fat no every time I talked to them?

"I don't want to go," I told Beau, setting my phone aside.

I don't want to live.

"Did I upset you?" His words were so unsure, so hesitant, that I wanted to lie to him.

I closed my eyes, preparing for the conversation and attempting to redeem myself from the mini nervous breakdown I seemed to be having.

"No, you didn't upset me," I told him as we sat on the edge of the bed. "I just wish you could be here. You're only here for a day or two, and then you're gone again."

"I wish I could too. You know it's hard for me, right? I don't like being away from you." His eyes were careful; the way they were when he was hiding something.

When I didn't say anything, he continued, his lips pursed as he nodded once and hung his head. "You don't think it's hard for me?" he asked shrewdly.

"I guess I feel like you have this life now—a life that I'm not a part of. You're healing and I'm just here, hopeless."

I turned my body to face him when he didn't speak, surprised by the pained expression he wore.

"You are a part of everything I do. You're more than just a best friend or a girlfriend to me, Bentley. You're a part of me, whether you want to be or not. It's just who I've become."

I smiled as a tear slid down my check. He always knew exactly what to say to make me feel better, but it didn't make me feel all that better because it didn't change the fact that he was never here. I needed more than a friend in him, someone here on occasions and in passing.

I had Blaine as a friend. I *needed* my boyfriend.

The words were there, I wanted to speak them, to tell him how much I loved him. Tell him I needed this lifestyle to change, but chariness rooted me. I couldn't form the words.

There was a droning silence with Beau's phone vibrating obsessively before he leaned over and kissed my check.

"I have to go, honey." He pulled back, his hand rose to my cheek as his thumb ran over my lower lip. "I'll be back on Friday night."

I nodded, unable to choke out anything else, and he once again opened his mouth as though he was going to speak and then sighed.

He wanted to say 'come with me,' but he knew I wouldn't.

I didn't want to do anything.

We were healing in different ways, only I wasn't healing.

Just so much as going to the grocery store was difficult for me because I'd see diapers and cry.

Or baby food and want to knock them all off the shelf because I had no baby to feed.

Beau took a deep breath and then pulled away completely, standing and reaching for his hat. This time he didn't look back. He grabbed his bag and left.

I tried to be normal. I did.

An hour after Beau left, Blaine came over and sat on the couch. "Why didn't you go with Beau to LA?"

"Because I couldn't."

"He wants to help you, Bentley."

I knew he wanted to help me, but how could he help me when I didn't even know how to help myself.

The reasons as to why I didn't go with him had more to do with me being nervous about what his life was becoming. Concerts, touring, record deals, it just felt like he had this life outside of our bubble and I didn't know how I fit into it.

Chapter Eighteen

FALLING

BEAU

THERE WAS NO next time, tomorrow, time out, stop and look around.

It was now or never, hold her, love her, give her anything you could to make her see.

They say tragedy defines a moment in your life when you go one of two ways.

What if you're stuck in place?

What if you're rooted to the one moment you couldn't escape?

Watching Bentley sleep that night, when I arrived home from LA, her hair spilled over the white pillow, lips pushed into a pout, I wanted to press my lips to her thick, dark fluttering lashes that never seemed to dry. I wasn't sure what the future held for us now, but I wanted to find out, and it was as if she was slipping away from me completely.

More than anything, I wanted her to see I could be there, if she'd let me.

I wanted to take Bentley's pain away, carry it for her. I couldn't. She wouldn't let me. "I'll take care of you," I whispered against her forehead as I kissed it tenderly.

I will love you 'til the end.

I hated that I had obligations with the record company, but I promised them twelve songs, and in turn, they were producing the record, marketing music videos, recording time, all that.

My problem wasn't even the songs, it was praying those songs were what they wanted, what everyone wanted to hear. If I didn't give them what they wanted, and the record tanked, I'd probably have to give back the advance they gave me and deal with the fact that my father was right, this was a hobby.

I had so much riding on the album, for me, for Bentley. . .

It was that night, with my face buried in the pillow, I thought of the lyrics to "Forgive Me" and wrote down a few lines.

When my blood is all but bourbon
I give my pain the numbness I'm given
It's the only way I know
Empty and hollow
I can't get you out of my head
I'm haunted by the tears you've shed

Chapter Nineteen

THE DAY THAT SHE LEFT TULSA

BENTLEY

WHEN I THOUGHT about becoming a mother and what that would mean, I thought about waking up in the middle of the night to feed Dixie and holding her while I sang quietly to her.

And when I thought about it, even for a second, my face would automatically be wet with tears, silently rolling down my face before I could stop them.

I still woke up in the middle of the night, only now it was because my arms and heart were empty.

I had no baby for them to hold, to feed, to care for or love.

I had the tragedy I was given, a life granted, and then taken just as quickly.

"Are you ready for lunch?" Blaine asked, peeking her head inside the door of my house, hanging on by the doorframe.

A warm breeze followed her, the fresh scents of spring and freshly mowed grass coming with it. It was now the beginning of April and past my original due date with Dixie.

The seasons were changing, the bitter cold letting up and spring flowers replacing dried leaves.

If only it was spring for me, a fresh new beginning. Beau was in Memphis, doing promotion for his album that was set to release in June, and I was going shopping with Blaine. I still hadn't returned to work, and I was finally at the point where I was thinking of going back.

Since Dixie passed away, I hadn't been eating much, or doing much of anything else, and needed some clothes that actually fit me. I thought for sure it'd be good for me to go out and have lunch with my best friend and go shopping.

Blaine and I were intent on getting me some clothes and her a dress for Tabitha's wedding.

Blaine had become the one person I could confide in and talk to for hours. Though she didn't know the pain I held deep inside, she did everything she could to help me.

I never wanted to forget Dixie. Not that I would, but Blaine kept her memory front and center for me with little heart-warming gestures.

Reaching for my purse on the floor, my hair tangled and caught in the necklace she gave me with a cross on it surrounded by angel wings and a cursive D charm attached to it. I wore it every day.

Blaine peeked over the roof of her car at me. "Did you decide where you want to eat lunch?"

I shrugged opening the car door. "I don't care. I'm not overly hungry."

"You need to eat. Your legs are too long for you to be that skinny. Makes you look like bones with sticks for legs."

"Uh, thanks." I smiled, buckling my seatbelt.

Blaine started the car and shifted into reverse, looking over her shoulder as she backed out of the driveway. "Does Beau come back tonight or tomorrow?"

"I think he said tomorrow night." My eyes dropped to my phone and his text messages this morning. "Yeah, tomorrow. His flight comes in at six."

"So let's buy you something sexy and you two can have a wild night together tomorrow. I want to be able to hear your naughty sex noises through the wall like I did when you first moved in."

"That's weird that you'd want to hear your brother's noises."

"At least they're better than the ones coming from his room when he was thirteen." She shivered. "My room was next to his."

Laughing, my cheeks warmed at the thought. Beau and I had begun having sex again, and it was easier since that first time, but it wasn't the same anymore.

I feared sex never would be the same, and with him starting another tour, then what?

I trusted Beau, I did. I didn't fear he would look for it elsewhere even though he did with Payton, but I did fear I wasn't making him happy anymore.

I couldn't even make myself happy, let alone him.

How was that fair to him?

THE AFTERNOON BLAINE was nice, we laughed, had lunch, did all the things I remember doing with her before Dixie.

That was until she was trying on dresses and I was waiting outside the dressing room, only to hear Payton on her cell phone looking at dresses behind me. Payton of all people. Beau's high school girlfriend who sent me a get well card after Dixie died.

A motherfucking get-well card. Like I had the damn flu or something.

"David is freaking out."

My head whipped around when I heard her voice. I hadn't seen her since the lake, but I knew that voice anywhere. I knew from Beau that Colt Records had also signed Payton as a new artist, and she was going on tour with Beau as his opening act. I wasn't pleased by it and had some fears thinking they'd fall back in love, but I wouldn't allow myself to think that.

Hiding behind a rack of evening gowns, I maneuvered myself in them so she couldn't see me and listened to what she was saying.

"He thinks the album is gonna flop since Beau's attention has been elsewhere and they still don't have the final track ready. They already had to push the release until June because it wasn't ready after all the time he took off." Payton sighed, as though this was her problem, flipping her hair over her shoulder. "They wrote a duet for Beau and me to do, but he keeps refusing, saying Bentley wouldn't like it. He hasn't even heard it and won't consider it. I just don't know. . .he's sacrificing his career for her." She paused, listening to whoever she was on the phone with. "I know. I'm opening for him in Atlanta and then the rest of the tour and he won't even agree to do one song with me. If only she saw what she's doing to him. I *get it*, they lost their baby, but still, he's throwing away everything he's worked for over the last ten years on this. Well, no, but come on. Maybe I'm heartless, but I don't get why she's so broken over it. It's not like she had the baby and could fall in love with it that fast. The baby took like one freaking breath. She's been moping around for months. From what Miles says, she won't even talk to him about it. They just don't talk at all. Oh. . . wait. . . ."

Crap, did she see me?

But then again, if those words wouldn't have hurt so badly, I would have stood up and hammer punched her in the clavicle.

They hurt.

They hurt far worse than I expected.

Did people really think this about me? That I was moping around grieving the death of a child I should have never fallen in love with?

I don't care if I had her for two seconds or twenty years, her death still hurt me. Tucking my feet in tighter to my chest, my heart started to pound, the familiar bile rising in my throat.

Here it comes. Right here in the middle of a store I'm going to break down.

"Beau's calling me. Maybe he's reconsidered. I'll call you back later."

He's calling her? Why?

The floodgates opened in that moment and I lost it.

I wasn't sure where Payton went from there, but she left and I couldn't move, as if my numbness and pain had rooted me in a damn department store.

Blaine came out of the dressing room, saw me huddled up with the dresses in tears, and frowned. "What are you doing? Did you want to go to the wedding with me as my date? If you do, you're wearing the tux. I'm far too curvy to play the male role in our relationship."

When I began to sob, she knew it was more and dropped to her knees beside me. "Do you want to go home?"

I nodded, filling my palms with the sadness I couldn't shake. I still felt 100 percent at fault for what happened with Dixie. I should have gone to the doctor sooner when I first felt like something was wrong.

And now my sadness was affecting Beau and his career he worked so hard for. I mean, he was releasing an album in a few weeks and he still had a song he hadn't finished?

The last thing I wanted to do was hold Beau back from anything in his life. If anything, I didn't want to be that burden. The poor depressed mother of his child who passed away.

I felt like that was all I'd ever be since we lost Dixie.

Lost?

It wasn't like she was misplaced. She was in heaven, lying on the pearly white clouds looking down on her mother who couldn't move on.

I wanted the pain gone.

Completely.

I just wanted it gone for one goddamn second so I didn't have to feel.

Did I feel like I was holding Beau back?

Yes, I did.

He was making a life for himself, and I was lost at sea, rocking with the waves and waiting for the rescue boat.

Only the person I thought should have been rescuing me, or treading the stormy waters with me, had found his own life preserve.

WHEN BEAU RETURNED the next night, I knew then, I needed to let him go. He came home and was packing his bag to head back to Nashville in the morning when he saw me sitting on the end of his bed with my bag packed.

"What are you doing?" His eyes shifted around the room, taking in things he'd been missing, the life he'd left behind during the week. "Are you finally coming with me?"

I wanted to whisper my reply, tell him the bad news gently. He deserved that much.

"I'm. . . ." My reasons, my emotions, they all swirled in too glossy eyes and a too heavy heart. I could barely think about leaving, let alone say it. "I don't even know," I whispered, searching for words and an answer to make the pain go away.

Why was I doing this?

I was doing it because I didn't deserve him in the first place. I waited, my body tensing, anticipating his reaction to my words and waiting for him to react.

Only he didn't give me anything to go on. His reaction was, well, guarded. Leaning into the doorframe, his eyes were on the floor while he waited for me to say more, give him a reason.

Beau sighed, his gaze moved over mine like the changing of a season, slow, distinct, and then gone like the leaves falling from a weathered tree, finally letting go after months of hanging on.

His season had changed. Mine never would again. My heart was frozen in winter surrounded by ice I would never thaw.

His gaze left me wondering.

What now?

What would he say to me?

Would he be angry with me?

"You're not coming with me, are you?" His voice was barely above a whisper, as if he wasn't sure he wanted me to hear him.

I swallowed against the lump in my throat. Taking a deep breath, and then another, I gained the courage I needed to speak. When I looked at him again, his eyes seemed darker than ever before. "Beau. . . I can't do this anymore."

Oh, God, what was I doing?

Was I really breaking up with him?

"Do what?" The pitch in his words let me know he didn't want to be having this conversation right now. He never wanted to talk about it.

"This." I motioned around the house and then to him. "Us."

His eyes went to the mountain of tear-soaked tissues next to the nightstand. Tears he knew were for him, for us, for Dixie, and then to me, processing what I said. Running his hands over his face, groaning, he seemed torn at what he wanted to say. He wanted to say something.

He waited, as did I.

"Don't do this," he pleaded, his deep voice, raw and etched with pain I would never truly grasp, shook around the words, trembling with every crack in our hearts. "I'm begging you."

He wouldn't look at me at first, and I had a feeling he hadn't looked at anyone recently. He paused, meeting my eyes. The betrayed expression he wore made me feel guilty. Like shit, absolute shit for doing this, but what choice did I have?

"You really have no fucking clue, do you?" He dared me to answer him with pleading eyes and mournful shoulders.

He knew I was lying when I said it was over.

It could *never* be over between us.

"I know you love me, Beau." I began to cry, despite begging myself not to. "It's just. . . we can't keep fooling ourselves. This isn't working. You're gone all the time, and I'm left here to deal with this myself. I think it's best if we go our separate ways."

His furious eyes washed over me, crushing my heart with just his gaze upon me. "I've fucking *begged* you to come with me!" he shouted, his face turned pale, every breath shaking his frame. His lips parted, intent on saying more, but then it passed, and his eyes darted around the room again before locking with mine. "Don't go." His tone was softer, pleading.

"I have to." I couldn't even look at him. I was breaking his heart, letting him believe this was something he did wrong. "I can't live here. . . like this."

"Is there someone else?"

Of course he would want to know that. "There will *never* be anyone else for me."

"Then why are you doing this?" His voice cracked, his eyes fire. "Tell me."

"I have to." It was the only answer I knew.

"You have no idea how I feel, Bentley. No idea," he said, eyes fierce and determined as he picked up my bag from the floor and tossed it against the wall, never breaking our stare. "But I'm done with this shit where we step around the topic of Dixie dying. It happened. It fucking sucked. It was fucking awful, the worst day of my life. I love you *so much* and it fucking kills me inside to think I couldn't bring her back for you. I would have if I could. I can't lose you too." He drew in a heavy breath, and then another, as if no amount of air would be enough. "You think I don't care, don't you?"

"Sometimes, yes," I admitted with shaking words, looking down at my feet.

Beau came forward, kneeling before me. His hands shook as they reached my cheeks, my glossy eyes swimming with emotions I couldn't even begin to comprehend. "How could you ever think that?"

The situation, the dilemmas inside my head made me cry, constantly, with no escape. Only Beau didn't see this because he was gone all the time, so I was left to deal with it alone. He had no idea what it was like for me.

With a frustrated sigh, wanting to get up and leave, my forehead leaned against his, powerless to the connection I had with him, the connection I would *always* have to him now.

"I don't know what we're doing anymore, Beau."

"Look at me," he demanded, mournfully gasping out the words.

Unable to control my sobs, I shook my head, refusing. "I can't. It hurts so bad to look at you."

He stood and lifted me to my feet before placing me on the center of the bed and covering me with his body.

I was so tired, of everything, my eyes dry and swollen from crying so much, so often that I closed them hoping that maybe by resting them, denying myself from seeing him, this wouldn't hurt so badly.

He kissed me then, an act of possessiveness if you asked me, but he did it anyway, harder than he'd ever done before. Maybe he was trying to show me we had something worth fighting for, or maybe he just wanted to. I might never know. I might never *want* to know.

"Do you think I want it to end like this?" he whispered, pulling back, his eyes finding mine. "Is this really what you want?"

"I do." It was the only lie I'd ever told him.

Lifting his lips from my neck, he covered my mouth, not waiting for my answer. "C'mon, honey. Don't do this. I fucking love you." I knew he was crying, I could feel the tears falling from him, but I couldn't bear to open my eyes and look at him, reminded of that night in the hospital bed holding our angel and the way his tears felt soaking my neck.

"I have to, Beau. I need to. Just go to Nashville," I begged, knowing this would kill the both of us inside. "Nashville is where you need to be."

When I reached up to push him away, my hand on his chest, he moved it to kiss the inside of my wrist and then my elbow. "Please," he whispered. "Please."

The tip of his nose glided up the side of my throat and I wanted to erase our mistakes. Feeling his touch shattered fragments of love gone wrong.

"Please what?"

He placed his hands beside my head, supporting his weight as he looked down at me. "Don't do this." And then as if he wanted me to feel him, he laid down on me completely.

His weight made it hard to take a full breath, but it seemed easier, this breathing under pressure. "I need to go, Beau, get up."

He moved away, as if he couldn't take hurting me. Removing himself from me, he stumbled against the wall and slid down it. He looked around, at me, and then at the floor with his face in his hands.

"I'm sorry," I said softly, wondering if he even heard me.

He looked up, unable to meet my eyes, afraid, hurting, feeling everything I'd been feeling too. "If you were. . . you wouldn't push me away when I still love you."

I stared down at him. "It's the only way, Beau. You have a life and a tour to start. I don't fit into that world."

He shook his head like he didn't want to accept that. "It doesn't have to be that way. I want you with me. We could start over in Nashville."

"I don't want to start over." I took a step toward the door, reaching for my bag he threw earlier.

If there was one thing I'd never considered, it was that Beau felt the same pain. Of course he did. How could he not?

Beau's head bowed, his eyes on the ground where his heart was. "I can't let you walk away."

"You have to."

Life had the power to change in a heartbeat, a split fraction of a second. A moment when everything was taken and we were left with a memory of what it was like.

That was what I had.

Only a memory.

Chapter Twenty

GOODBYE IN HER EYES

BEAU

HER MOUTH WAS moving, words spilling from her shattered, relentless heart full of pain, only I couldn't make sense of anything she was telling me. I knew it was over when she looked at me. It was the hallow eyes and the distant way she moved.

Sliding down the wall until I was sitting on the floor, I rested my arms on my knees.

She couldn't be serious, could she?

Had I turned my back and let this happen?

Taking a deep breath, I rubbed my forehead. "We can make it."

"I'm not sure we can, Beau. Too much. . ." she choked on her tears, a gasped breath leaving her chest, turning to face the door.

It hit me then, that breath, the tears, all of it. I was angry, fucking livid, but what could I have said?

Bentley was fragile, delicate, not in a way where I could show her my anger, even if it was killing me inside.

I wanted to send my fist through the wall, give my pain an outlet, a reason, an answer she wouldn't give me.

Before she made it out the door, I stood, following her, hoping she'd reconsider. At the door, she turned, reaching for me one last time. "Honey, please. It's the middle of the night. Where are you going to go?"

"I'll stay with my mom."

With her hand on the door handle, she paused when I asked, "Do you love me?"

Come back to me. Don't leave.

Letting out a cry, one she attempted to keep hidden, I asked again, hoping maybe it would be a reminder enough that she couldn't leave. "Do *you* love me?"

"I will always love you, Beau," she whispered into my chest, sobbing so badly she couldn't breathe.

Let her go. You have to. If she wants to leave, let her.

"Then I will consider myself a lucky man," I told her, never wanting to let go. Though I had her in my arms, it was over. She said it was.

I looked at the purple under her eyes and I told myself it wasn't that bad. Only it was that bad. I'd lost her completely to her own guilt. I didn't want her to be sad anymore.

I didn't want either of us to be sad.

We were two people both silently trying to find ourselves again when we couldn't. I felt like nothing we did worked out anymore, and then finally, she put an end to it.

Blaine came over when she heard glass breaking and me standing the destruction. "Where's Bentley?"

I fell to my knees in the kitchen, holding my head in my hands. "I don't know. I don't know," I kept saying, as if I didn't.

I didn't know. I didn't know anything anymore.

I TRIED CALLING her before I went back to Nashville, albeit drunk and sitting in the aftermath of what was my house, which I destroyed after she left, only she didn't answer, so I left a message like any grieving drunk boyfriend would. "I'm begging you, Bentley, please don't end it like this. Come with me to Nashville. We could start a new life there, together."

She never returned my call.

Two days later, I moved to Nashville without her and moved in with Miles and Wade.

I had this photograph of Bentley, and it was the only reminder she was still there with me.

When I looked at that photograph on my phone, it didn't do the moment justice. You couldn't tell by looking at her lips they were a bright cherry red and her cheeks, so pink and hot. Her eyes were the color of midnight, and that smile was one of happiness.

The picture was taken the weekend we met.

It may have seemed silly to everyone else, but every time I looked at my phone, I was reminded of her and it didn't hurt as bad. I still had this. For now, living inside a photograph, I could still pretend. I could still fall for her, even if I was only a memory.

Chapter Twenty-One

WHISKEY LULLABY

BENTLEY

IT WAS LATE May now, four months after Dixie passed away and weeks after Beau left. Or I left. Either way, I was left with one single word.

Gone.

Not like Dixie, but gone from my life. Like a memory in the wind, he blew across my life in every way possible.

How could I heal, or even move on, when my heart was with Beau and Dixie, and I'd lost both? It was more than the loss of Dixie, it was the loss of having something perfect and then it was gone again.

I went back to Beau's theory on jumping. You gotta jump sometime. I had to heal. But how could I truly heal when I felt so guilty?

Unfortunately, now that Beau was living in Nashville—probably with Payton—I had to get up and go to work. I was now living in an apartment with a girl from work, Heather.

Every morning, I would get up and stare at myself in the mirror. I stared at my freckles where he used to connect the dots, and my golden hair he twirled around his fingers right before he kissed me.

My midnight eyes stared back at me, not completely convinced I wouldn't ever see him again and wishing I hadn't let him go in the first place. I didn't know what part of me hurt, or why I was feeling that way; it was just an all-consuming feeling that destroyed me, crushed my bones into dust.

When I finally went to work, usually rolling in twenty some minutes late, I didn't make eye contact with most people, and it wasn't out of bitchiness. It was out of insecurity. I didn't want anyone to know me.

If they knew me, they'd see who I was. The girl stuck on a summer and her daughter who died at birth. I couldn't let go, because he wouldn't let me. She wouldn't let me.

Kevin would never say anything when I came in late. He'd look up at me, weak-smiling and give me a nod, saying nothing.

I also passed by the inconsiderate asshole who delivered our mail in the mornings too, and he'd pop of with the same phrase every day: *Smile, it can't be that bad.*

Yeah it could be, fuck face!

On my desk sat a calendar with daily inspirational quotes Blaine left for me. I'd crumble them up and toss them in the garbage next to the coffee I drank half of, then discarded. I felt discarded. Like life had completely discarded anything I wanted. I was left grieving and trying to make sense of what the fuck had happened to my life.

A LONELY FRIDAY night, a month after Beau and I broke up, among many lonely nights when Blaine felt like she needed to jump in and save me from drowning myself. Probably literally because I was in the bathtub when she came barreling in my bathroom.

I blamed her recent going back to school again. This time it was psychology. Seemed fitting since her best friend was so messed up.

Blaine sat on the edge of the tub. "What are you doing? You forgot the hair dryer in the water with you."

"Couldn't find one."

"Let's get drunk tonight or order Chinese food and fat girl it up."

I stared at her. "Do I know what that means?"

"It means eat junk food."

"Ah, well, I'm enjoying a bath."

"No, you *were* enjoying a bath." She reached in the bubbles and pulled the drain. "Now you're going to get out and get dressed and come down to Rusty's with me."

"That's your dad's bar. I'm *not* going down there."

"Fine, we order Chinese food and eat."

I sighed. I hated Chinese food. "Fine, bar it is. Beau won't be there, right? This isn't some kind of setup, is it?"

"No, it's not. Knew you'd reconsider," she mumbled as she walked out of the bathroom and into my room, passing Heather in the hall.

"Can I come with you guys?" Heather asked when I had my towel wrapped around my body, running a brush through my hair.

Blaine looked to me for an answer, and then to Heather. "If you want, but are you allowed in bars?" Heather was a recovering alcoholic. Probably not the best decision for her.

"Oh, right, probably not." Her sad eyes dropped to the floor, drowning in her mistakes. I knew those mistakes and suddenly felt like I could help her.

"You could just drink water though." I smiled toward Blaine. "Right?"

Heather perked up. "Yeah, I could."

We left an hour later and headed to Rusty's, a place I hadn't been since I was there with Beau, because of the memory it held. Him. A time when I was in that very bar with Beau. Drinking was my only answer. I thought for sure if I was drunk, it wouldn't hurt so badly. Maybe Heather was onto something.

Eventually, though, the night led to where I knew it would, dancing in the arms of someone else named Cowboy. I was sure his name wasn't Cowboy, but it didn't matter to me. No other name mattered to me but Beau.

The alcohol had gotten the best of me, as did his thick accent, and I found myself contemplating going home with him.

What the fuck is wrong with me?

He was all hands-on. I enjoyed the fact he seemed turned on, so desperate that he fumbled around, but I couldn't get Beau out of my head. The problem was, I thought about that night in the tent, belt buckle clanking and the sounds of rain on canvas. I fucking thought about it so much, his face close to mine, breath on my neck, grunting with each push, his hands on my body, so rough with need.

If anything, it should have been a memory I forgot. But that same boy was also the one who held my first love, the father of my baby girl, and for that reason, he would never ever be forgotten.

I was right when I said I would love him forever.

"I will always love you, Beau."

"Then I will consider myself a lucky man."

Fucking memories.

I couldn't be with guys like this cowboy mauling me, as hot as he was, because I was constantly mind-fucked by Beau's memory.

I gripped the bottom of the cowboy's T-shirt, pushing him away. Everything he was doing felt wrong. Wrong touch, wrong name, wrong everything.

"I can't," I told him, stepping back.

He stopped instantly, like the gentleman he probably was, putting a good two feet of distance between us. "Okay, sorry."

And then Cowboy stared at me, blinking in disbelief that I was telling him to stop. I was pretty sure, positive almost, this had never happened to him before. Any other time, in another life where I wasn't me, the girl in love with a memory, I would have probably given into his slow southern drawl, but he wasn't Beau Ryland.

"It's not you, it's clearly me," I told him, thinking he needed to know.

He nodded. "It's alright, Darlin'." And then he walked away.

A good part of me felt bad for denying him, but then again, I had to. Sometimes I wondered what the fuck was wrong with me and why I couldn't brainwash myself into curing the gaping hole in my heart, but then I realized you couldn't heal a broken heart until it was ready. You just couldn't.

Back at the bar, I watched Cowboy leave—surprisingly alone—and then turned to Blaine. "I'm ready to drink more."

"That's my girl." Giggling, she motioned for Jensen to come over with a bottle of whiskey.

"Anything but bourbon. I hate it. I hate the way it tastes and lingers in your mouth."

Jensen stared at me, his brow scrunched in confusion but said nothing.

Beside me, Blaine snorted. She knew why I hated bourdon.

Just like that bourdon lingering, Beau's memory surrounded me and I saw Beau in Jensen's features and it pissed me off. I waved my hand in his face. "Stop staring at me. You look like him."

His brow scrunched. "I'm nothing like Beau."

"I know that." Anger gnawed at me. I couldn't understand how he could hate Beau over a situation he caused. "And it's sad really, because he's amazing and you act like he's not even good enough to be your brother. Jerk face."

Jensen rolled his eyes and reached for the whiskey on the counter. "I think you've had enough."

It was then I noticed a George Straight song playing in the background, "Easy Come, Easy Go" and I slapped my hand down on the bar. "What's with the sad shit? Change it to a more exciting station."

"My bar, my station," he replied simply, as if that were the rule.

Blaine snorted. "Your bar, Jay? More like dad's bar he makes you run."

He ignored Blaine completely and moved around the bar to flip the neon sign in the window off. "Closing time." He gave a nod to the door. "Let's go."

"Jesus," I turned to face Blaine. "You're *absolutely* right. He's an asshole."

She burst out laughing.

In the taxi on the way back to my apartment, we realized we had lost Heather.

"Shit, I didn't see Heather leave, did you?" I began to panic and looked in my purse for my phone to see if she called. There was a message she went home with the cowboy and not to come home for a while. I turned to Blaine. "Can I stay with you?"

"Yeah," and then she sprung into telling me about her dream last night where she was running through a hotel lobby in Vegas holding her own shit in a towel. The bellhop outside refused to get a taxi for her, so she threw her shit at him.

Then she asked about the cowboy. "Who was that guy you were dancing with?"

"Cowboy? I called him Cowboy. And now Heather is with him."

"There really shouldn't be a question in that answer," she reminded me. "But, damn, that guy was fine, and I'm engaged."

The word engaged stuck with me because I wanted to be engaged. I wanted a life with Beau and all that was ruined because of me. But drunk me blamed Beau. "I fucking hate your brother, Blaine. I think I need therapy," I said, taking a drink of water from the bottle I stashed in my purse earlier. "I can't get him out of my head."

"Well, if we're being honest, I hate him, too. He stole my favorite flannel before he left." Blaine shook her head, as if this was a major disappointment in her life. "Little motherfucker."

"It was his flannel and there is absolutely nothing little about your brother." I waggled my eyebrows suggestively.

Blaine gagged. "Bullshit. I wore that flannel all the time. It might as well have been mine. At least he could have given it to me. I am his twin."

I laughed, really laughed for the first time in a really long time. Over nothing but a flannel shirt and Blaine.

Was it making me feel better?

Not really. I thought it was helping with the healing process, though. With every smile, every laugh, a weight was lifted.

I ended up spending the night with Blaine that night, and it was really hard being next door to where I used to live with Beau. Now there was apparently a single mom and her two kids living there.

Still felt weird, but since Heather had Cowboy at home, I didn't want to go back there.

"I can sleep on the couch," I told Blaine as she made me get in bed with her. "I feel weird sleeping in the same bed you two have sex in, with Gavin on the other side of you."

Blaine rolled over in the bed, Gavin snoring in her ear. "Bentley. . . can I ask you a question without you being mad at me, or breaking up with me too?"

"Sure." Adjusting the pillow under my head, I tried to get comfortable despite feeling the spins.

"Why did you break up with Beau?"

Maybe she knew, since I had been drinking that I'd answer her truthfully. Any other time, I avoided the topic of Beau. Mostly because it hurt too bad to know I broke his heart. "He. . . ." I stopped and realized what I had done. Leaving Beau had nothing to do with him. It was all me and my shit.

Yeah, he was gone all the time. Yeah, Payton was a bitch, but I never told Beau she was the reason. I never told Beau my reason for leaving was because deep down, I never thought I was good enough for him. I walked out, so no, the reason would never ever start with him.

It started and ended with me.

"I was afraid I was holding him back."

"You weren't though. And he's not doing good, Bentley. He's a mess. He's really. . . just not good."

I wanted to ask details but I knew if I heard any of it, just like hearing his voice, I would run back to him, and that may not have been what either of us needed.

"I know it's hard for him, and it's hard for me too. But I can't heal from this and be with him while doing it. Every day is a constant struggle for me. I have days when I feel good and I can go on. And then I have the more depressing ones where I want to die and wish I could, so I didn't have to feel this pain inside."

Blaine seemed relieved, somewhat, by my confession. Something I hadn't told anyone before. I wasn't sure if any of it made any damn sense, but maybe it did, in an awkward round-about way.

Gavin made a noise, something between a groan and a growl as he turned over cuddling into Blaine's side, his hand on her boob.

Laughing, she moved it, only to have him move it back. "Can you promise me something?"

"Maybe."

"Well, two things. . . hear me out?" I gave her a halfhearted smile. "When you're ready. . . give him another chance. Talk to him and explain. . . and see a therapist. Someone who can listen to you and give you some tools to help you."

"That's a lot of demands." Rolling, I looked up at the ceiling. "And why can't you be my therapist? Isn't that what a psychology major would do?"

"Well, yeah, but I'm certainly not a good one. My answer tonight was to get you drunk. . . and now you're in my bed. Pretty sure that goes against privacy laws, or something."

As I laid there staring at white walls, I thought about what Blaine had said, and Beau not doing good. I needed to do something to change this.

THE WEIGHT BEGAN to lift, peeled at the edges like a sticker being pulled off the strongest glue, I began seeing a therapist, as Blaine requested. I wanted to be better, I did. I just wasn't sure how to do it.

Before seeing Dr. Tori for the first time, I stopped by to see my mom, who was up and watching television while holding Shep.

My mom knew enough that she understood what happened with Dixie. She may not have remembered to brush her hair in the morning, but she understood pain in a way I didn't yet. And she gave me probably the best advice anyone could have given me.

"You don't see yourself clearly, Bentley. You think losing Dixie has defined your life as a mother who lost her daughter at birth. How you handle it, how you move on, what you learn from it, that defines you."

I wasn't alone in my depression. I knew that much. Just like what my mom went through depression with Corbin, I wasn't alone. I began to understand people who didn't smile, or worse, the ones who smiled too much, like my mom. She was hiding a pain no one knew.

Had she been able to comprehend my life now, she would have understood my pain and anxiety over it.

I began to realize the ones who put on a front were struggling the most. I knew one thing, if she could survive, so could I. It was for that reason I started going to therapy.

Not only did I have the burden of feeling like I had done something wrong to Dixie, I now had the guilt of walking out on Beau because I thought it was best for us. I needed help, and from a professional.

During my first session with Dr. Tori, she handed me a notebook at the end.

"What's this for?"

Her kind eyes shifted to mine. "When my daughter passed away, I found it comforting to write her letters. Anything to get the pain out."

Feeling the canvas outside of the notebook, the corners of my mouth lifted at the memory of a tent and a boy. And then it was immediately replaced with pain. "Like write something to Dixie?"

"Yes." Dr. Tori stood, handing me a tissue when she noticed the tear rolling down my cheek.

"About what?"

"Write about anything. Give your pain an outlet."

Dr. Tori said my pain?

Or did she mean my regrets?

I let her die.

I pushed away the only man I'll ever love.

WRITE MY PAIN.

My therapist said it'd help to write down the pain inside. Give it an outlet, a reason for haunting me in the first place.

What if I was haunting myself?

She wanted me to write down everything I was feeling from the pain to the guilt. Maybe then I could live with myself and be at peace with what happened.

I wanted to remember every detail about Dixie from the softness of her skin to those precious pink cheeks and tiny features. I wanted to remember every memory like it was yesterday, a chance to relive the only moments I had with her.

I had this pain, this unbearable guilt I carried around with me, and the only way to get rid of it was to write about it and give it an outlet. A reason for holding me captive. I never wanted to give the pain power. I wanted to let go of it.

At first, I wasn't sure I wanted to relive any of it, or feel that heartache that had been drowning me, but once I started, the act of putting the words on the paper became therapeutic.

When I was six years old, I learned to ride my bike without training wheels. I fell and skinned my knee; I had a scar to remind me for weeks of what that pain felt like.

To this day, I still remember falling because not only did I have a scar to show for it, but something about that spring morning was memorable. Couldn't tell you why.

When Dixie passed away, my heart was broken so severely I would more than likely remember it forever, despite not being able to see that scar. This pain was so deep it was in my blood and bones, aching every day with no cure in sight. I never thought I could move on from it.

In reality, I didn't want to. I wanted to remember my tiny piece of perfection I had for the moments we were able to hold her.

But writing provided me a certain amount of closure.

At night, when I was lying in bed staring up at the ceiling with my pen in hand, attempting to write that first letter to her, it was then Beau's memory, his touch, the way he made me feel burned through me like thousands of stars dusting the night's sky. Everywhere I looked, he was there, reminding me of what I let go.

Him.

Us.

And in many ways, her.

Dixie Mae,

I don't know what to say to you, baby girl. I'm surprised I can even write to you, let alone allow your memory to occupy my mind for so long, because it hurts so badly when it does.

Dr. Tori thinks that writing to you can heal me, help me deal with the pain. She gave me the idea of writing my story down, the exciting, yet sometimes painful parts from when I met your daddy to losing you.

How can I write down those things when I never got to finish telling your story?

I guess, in some ways, your story never having an ending is perfect because your memory is never-ending with me.

It feels wrong that you're gone, and so is your daddy.

I pushed him away when I didn't think I could love him the way he needed to be loved. He had a life going for him, and I couldn't get over you in order to see him in front of me.

Somedays, the ache of you and him being gone feels numbing.

Somedays, I sit on the floor and I cry for not seeing the warning signs and maybe going to the doctor sooner.

Somedays, I cry for letting your daddy walk out of my life.

I'll never get to hear your story, baby girl. But I can tell you my story, how I met your daddy and how much he influenced my life, and, sadly, where it ended for us.

Maybe that's something you'll want to know.

Some would say I never had the chance to get to know you, so why does this hurt so much.

It hurts because I carried you inside me every minute of your life, and inside my heart for every minute after.

That's my explanation of it.

Just because I never had the chance to see you with your eyes open, this still hurts and I still love you with unending. Just because my pain isn't justified to them, doesn't mean I don't love you.

So I guess where this all began is the way to start.

My love for your daddy started back when I was fourteen. It seems so silly how infatuated I was with him, and how little I really knew about who he was.

It started with a wink. Isn't that how all good love stories begin? With a wink?

Years later, I fell into his life where the red clay danced along the water's edge and bursts of light rained down on us.

It was a night when the heat couldn't be escaped. As he whispered against my sun-kissed summer-sweet skin, "Baby, look up and get lost in that everlasting light," it was easy to believe it would last forever.

He gave me light that night.

He gave me everlasting light.

"What are you writing?" I nearly jumped out of my skin to see Blaine had let herself inside my apartment and was standing over me, her long brown hair fell neatly over her shoulder.

"Oh, I, uh. . ." My voice failed for a moment. Clearing my throat, I tried again. "Well, Dr. Tori had the idea that I should write to Dixie."

"That's sweet. What are you writing then?"

"About Beau." My eyes dropped to the pink tinted paper. "About her daddy."

Blaine smiled, rubbing my back, as if she would do anything to help me heal. "What are you going to do with it?"

"I was going to put it on her grave for her."

"That's sweet."

As I finished the letter, detailing what it was Beau meant to me, I finally understood how Beau could lose himself in writing songs. Here I started around noon and it was nearing dusk.

For a moment, I imagined him clearly sitting at the kitchen table, biting his thumb and bouncing his knee as he wrote from the heart.

Taking the letter with me, I went to see Dixie. I did exactly what I said I would. I left it with her, knowing she could help me.

Gently placing the letter on her gravestone, I left it there for her. "I miss you, sweet baby."

THE NEXT MORNING, I wanted to give her some fresh flowers, so I went back before work to find the letter gone. More than likely it blew away with the wind, but when I looked around and didn't see anything on the ground, crazy enough, I imagined, for some strange reason, she had something to do with it being gone.

What the hell? Where'd it go?

I searched the grounds on my hands and knees and then stood, staring at her headstone with the words, Dixie Mae Ryland.

Did Beau take it?

No, he's on the road.

What if God reached down here and took it for her? Or she flew with her little baby angel wings and snatched it to read?

I wanted to know she was still with me, and I constantly found myself talking to her like she was with me.

I felt crazy for believing she had the letter, that somehow it'd gotten to Heaven, but was it so crazy to believe that?

Chapter Twenty-Two

PLAYING WITH FIRE

BEAU

TIPPING MY HEAD back, I stared at the goddamn ceiling, again. It seemed to be what I did a lot now. Stare.

I felt, in many ways, lonely again. If that was what these emotions were.

Helpless. There was another emotion I felt.

Guilty. Another one.

Useless? Yep. Been there.

Confused? Always.

Another shot to drown the pain.

All right, another bottle.

No matter how many shots I took, I couldn't get her out of my head.

I kept the memories hidden, afraid of them.

Afraid to let myself feel them. It was like I filed them in a category of do not touch.

Only now—when I was drinking—the door was wide open.

Every minute of every day, I thought of Bentley and what it was I did so wrong.

She was always on my mind, there, giving me something to write.

I knew turning to drinking was a horrible idea, but so was falling in love with a woman like Bentley Schow. And I did that pretty fucking effortlessly.

Bentley was a beautiful misery I liked to torture myself with. I couldn't touch her, or even breathe her name now because of the pain I felt with just one touch, one glimpse into the pulsations she sent my heart into. Just the words passing through my lips, which used to worship her, wrecked me.

I wanted so badly to make her happy.

I wanted to be enough.

I wanted her to understand how that first night might as well have been my last.

I wanted to hold her.

I wanted to make those midnight eyes see the brightest of days.

I wanted to make her a mother and wrap my arms around the both of them and promise forever, together.

I sent Bentley messages constantly. All I wanted her to do was reply. Give me some kind of indication that she was okay.

Was that really too much to ask for?

Me: Please don't get over me, over us, say this is so. Give me something.

Those were the messages I sent her. Only she gave me nothing.

Staring at the bottle, the moonlight flickering into my room, wishing it wasn't my answer, and knowing this pain wouldn't let up until I had the pen pressed to the paper and my blood was bourbon.

When my mind wandered, I was given her memory.

And then I would immediately be reminded of what I had been denied. Our lives together.

Bringing the bottle to my lips, I knew one thing above all the rest. I was searching for a day when this wouldn't suffocate me. For now, I was dying inside with the idea that I'd lost what made me feel whole. In a lot of ways, I was. . . merely nothing. I was anything she held me hostage to.

It was that night, with the guitar in my lap and my head full, I wrote the beginning of another song.

Hide the sun
Give me the rain
To see you it'd be worth the pain
I don't think I can explain
~~But I wish I had a gun~~

I scribbled that line out knowing that wasn't wise, and then took another shot, slamming the bottle down on my nightstand. Sending another song crumbled up to the floor, I looked up and realized I hadn't left this apartment in days.

Surrounded by empty takeout boxes and wadded up paper all over the room.

There was a hole in the wall where I threw a baseball at it. Another in the door when I couldn't control my temper and threw my phone at it.

They were all reminders that I was nowhere near the man Bentley needed and maybe it was for the best she left.

I look in the mirror
And all I see is a man
nowhere close to who he wants to be
I'm finding out now
how it feels to be waitin' on me
To be waitin' on a stubborn
hard-headed quick-tempered slow to sorry
'cause he's too proud to ever admit he's wrong

Setting the pen down, I brought the bourbon to my lips. "I can't believe this shit."

I was angry that she never considered how I felt or what I wanted. Nights like this, I tried to hate her. Only I couldn't, ever. Not someone like Bentley.

Lying back on the bed, my head hit an envelope and a note from Miles: **Dude, check your mail every once in a while, and while you're at it, clean this shit up!**

The envelope was a letter, I assumed from Blaine. I opened it immediately, thinking only the worst news came in the form of a letter or text messages these days.

Folded around pages of pink paper was a white card from Blaine.

Please, Beau, help her heal.

My thumb ran over the textured paper and the words, some smeared from tears. I gasped when I read the opening words.

Dixie Mae,
I don't know what to say to you, baby girl.

What was this? My mind and heart were racing, scanning the words.

Flipping through the pages, my head spun, trying to understand what is was Blaine sent me.

I guess, in some ways, your story never having an ending is perfect because your memory is never ending with me.

The further I read, the more I understood Bentley had written a letter to Dixie. Tears I couldn't hold back fell slowly down my cheeks while reading her pain, a pain she would never tell me about, no matter how many times I begged her.

I'm going to leave this on your headstone, baby girl, in hopes that it finds you. Love you with all my heart.

After I read the letter, I was confused with everything. I wanted to drive to Mountain Brook and demand answers. And then I wanted to call Blaine and ask her why she sent it to me of all people. Was she trying to hurt me?

Why couldn't Bentley talk to me about it?

Drawing in a heavy breath, I looked at the letter again, my fingers running over the words, Love Mommy.

Maybe it went back to how I could pour myself into my music and express the deepest pain imaginable, but couldn't unless I was hiding behind the lyrics of a song.

She was hiding this, finding ways to give herself some closure. I was proud of her, the feeling swelling in my chest as a smile tugged at my lips.

I couldn't understand what Blaine had meant though. Help her heal. How could I do that? How could a broken heart heal another?

People say twins have a special bond. I agree. Blaine knew me better than anyone, and she also knew by giving me those letters containing Bentley's pain, she knew eventually I'd know what to do with them, even if I didn't right then.

Scrubbing my hands over my face, I set the letter by my guitar and walked into the living room. Reaching inside the liquor cabinet, I removed another bottle.

The bourbon didn't even have flavor anymore and neither did its effects. Nothing did. All I wanted was the relief it gave, but I couldn't even get that anymore.

That night I finally realized what I was doing, living my life in a memory of what we had; it hit me like a punch to the gut. She was doing the exact same thing.

She still wanted me.

The sun had set, a reminder of the lake days with Bentley, and I sat on the balcony outside my apartment in Nashville, slow-sipping and wanting to understand what it was I was feeling after reading that.

I had no answer and was thankful for the darkness around me, the dead of night. Mostly because if I had it my way, it'd be dark all the time.

It was a night when the heat couldn't be escaped. As he whispered against my sun-kissed summer-sweet skin, "Baby, look up and get lost in that everlasting light," it was easy to believe it would last forever.

And then, as I stared up at the silver specs of light, I felt judged. I felt like I'd given up, just like Bentley had.

Setting the bottle aside, I went back inside and read the entire letter again. Help her heal. Help her? How?

I called Blaine, I had to understand what she meant by that note.

She answered on the first ring. "You finally got the letter?"

"Blaine. . . what is this?"

She sighed, heavily. "It's Bentley. She's writing to the baby. Something her quaky doctor told her to do. So I stole it from Dixie's grave and gave it to you, hoping you could help."

I was silent, unable to understand, probably since I'd been drinking so much lately but I always did my best writing drunk.

"I just. . . I wish she could see that me and her together would help her. Not writing letters to her."

"She can't, Beau. She can't just yet. But maybe this could help. If you know. . . I know it's a lot to ask that you hold on, or the burden on you right now, but I knew you'd know what to do. I'm worried about her. She's not eating, she cries so much."

Fuck, those words hurt my chest so goddamn bad. It felt like someone punched my heart.

Did I know what to do? No, I didn't.

My blurry stare dropped to the sheet music crumpled in front of me and what I did have right in front of me.

Music.

Maybe I could make her see through that?

"How is she. . ." my voice cracked around the words, "I mean, other than crying all the time?"

What was I asking? My throat when dry. What if she was seeing someone?

Blaine knew what I was asking. "Beau, I'm lucky if I can get her to eat dinner let alone seeing anyone."

Not that I wanted her to be starving herself, but I was strangely satisfied she hadn't moved on.

It was the most hope I'd held in a long time.

"I HAVE THE final track for the album."

I started working on the song after I hung up with Blaine and around four that morning, I had the chorus and the bridge done and was laying down sheet music for it. Now all I had to do was get it recorded. I envisioned the song like an acoustic raw version. Just me and my guitar, pouring myself and her into one beautiful melody, our pain, together.

I didn't want anything fancy, much like Bentley. She was simple in that way and if this song could convince her of what

I felt, and that I was still here for her, then it needed to be this way.

"Beau," David, my manager, gave me a disappointed look. "We've already pushed the album once, we just can't. You and Payton will record 'Summer of 17' next week."

"No," I mumbled, standing against the wall. "I'm not doing a fuckin' duet with her. It's my album and I say what track is the final one. I'm not asking to push the release date. I'm asking to add 'Everlasting Light.'"

I didn't care what anyone thought. All I cared about was my pain and I wasn't going to do a damn duet with my ex-girlfriend. Imagine if Bentley heard that. No goddamn way. She'd think I was with her, and as far as I was concerned, I needed to remain single. She needed to know I was waiting for her and "Everlasting Light" was the perfect way to do it. I knew it'd take more than a song to prove my love for her, but it was a start.

Right?

Either that or she'd think I was a lunatic.

I was scared it wouldn't work. It wasn't that I didn't want to believe it either, like I said, I knew she felt that way, but I was scared. Scared of hurting her and scared of her hurting me.

David stared at me in confusion. "What about this other song you told me about, 'Pinky Swear'?"

"I want to add that one to my tour. I don't want to record it for the album."

"Is 'Everlasting Light' one you think can work with the rest of the album?" I nodded and David pinched the bridge of his nose, his elbows resting on his dark cherry wood desk. "It sounds fine. I'm not going to try to understand what you're going through, Beau, but we can't keep messing with it."

"Then let me add 'Everlasting Light.'"

Drawing in a heavy breath, his chest puffed out, and a subtle shake to his head as he adjusted his tie. "You have studio time today. I want to hear a rough cut of this song tonight."

Nodding, I was out the door immediately before he could give me any other stipulations.

Miles met me at the studio that afternoon. He was with me all the time and was now working on setting up his own studio, so being around Nashville was right up his alley.

"What are you doing?" he asked when he heard a few takes.

"What are you talking about?" We were taking a break, me drinking water and looking over the upcoming tour schedule, and him eating a hamburger getting ketchup all over the place.

"Well, the way I see it, you're hoping this song will make her see that you still love her. That's your plan, right?"

"It's a plan." I smiled weakly. "Think it'll work?"

"Well," he chewed slowly for a minute, then wiped his mouth with a napkin, "it's plan A, and you still have twenty-five more letters in the alphabet if that one doesn't work. You got time."

The thing was, I didn't feel like I had time. I needed her to see I couldn't do this without her. It had already been too long as far as I was concerned.

Chapter Twenty-three

THE DAY YOU STOP LOOKIN' BACK

BENTLEY

2 MONTHS LATER

SOMETIMES I WISHED Beau would have cheated on me, because then I would have had a reason to have pushed him away, instead of this empty space I now had from not having him in my life.

Or Dixie.

How could it be I had both, for such a short time, but yet they both affected me so much I didn't feel like living, or going on was worth it anymore.

As I stared up at the blue-lit, early-morning sky, I prayed for closure after another sleepless night. I breathed in deep and reached for the notebook beside me.

I still wrote to Dixie at least once a week. And every time I returned the next day, the letter was gone. I knew it was crazy to think she was taking them, but I felt crazy. I did.

Summer had arrived, and with it, the intensity of the heat, all reminders of Beau and that weekend that changed my entire life.

Somedays, I felt the pain more than others. It could be numbing and hopeless, like the last thing I wanted to do was get out of bed. Those were the worst, but I still got up.

Somedays, I would sit on the floor and stare up at the ceiling, whispering, begging, pleading with God to bring her back, and wishing Beau was there with me.

Somedays, I would be fine and the day was great. I would go throughout it and be okay. Not because I didn't miss her, but because I had strength that day.

Somedays, it didn't matter. Nothing did. Everything about life just fucking sucked and I wanted to give up.

I also knew it didn't matter how many letters I wrote her, and how many disappeared, nothing would bring her back.

A million tears wouldn't either, because I would know, I had shed about that many.

"You're not crazy," Dr. Tori told me when I was in her office, telling her about my letters disappearing.

She told me that *every* week because I asked her *every* week. I didn't know if I believed her, because I trusted my letters I was placing on my daughter's headstone were being delivered to heaven. I also bet it was her job to tell me I wasn't crazy. Probably some suicide prevention law. Don't tell your grieving patients they're crazy when they think their dead daughter is stealing their letters.

I bet it was in their textbooks in school. If that didn't spell out crazy, I wasn't sure what would. It was crazy the things I did to *feel* pain too. Anything but the pain in my chest.

I would fill the bathtub full of scalding hot water, submerge myself in it, hoping the feeling of my skin burning would make me feel something. It didn't. I was still left with the pain. Life seemed like a blur to me, every face forgettable but one, and at times, it seemed fitting.

Chapter Twenty-Four

SWEET ANNIE

BEAU

I WAS IN the studio, listening to the final cut of my album, biting my nails when "Everlasting Light" came on.

It was the first time I'd heard it like this. You never knew how it would turn out when you're in the studio, but it was pretty fucking amazing.

"Beau." David shook his head, breaking the silence in the room. "That is one of the best songs I've ever heard. Wow, you really put your heart into this one."

I put my life into this one.

It was a song about Bentley, for her, yes, but the way I sang it had more to do with me and everything I was.

I smiled and nodded. I knew it was because of what I put into it. The song was rough, raw, voice breaking, but it was fucking perfect the way it was because it was *me.*

And then came the letdown I knew would follow. "While this is good, I think 'Tail Lights' should be the demo, though."

"No." I shook my head. "First single needs to be 'Everlasting Light.'" I had arranged all of this ahead of time. Why he wanted to change it now didn't make a lot of sense to me.

"I think—"

"No, David." I stood, ready to walk out. "The first song released will be 'Everlasting Light'. You either give me what I asked for, or I don't sign."

Over the past few months, David had put up with a lot of crap from me, but I wasn't backing down. This song needed to be the single.

"I just don't see how that song is good for a demo," he explained, trying to make me understand. "We need something upbeat."

I snorted, uninterested in what they wanted. This song wasn't about them, or anyone else. It was about her. "I don't give a shit. It's the song I want."

"It's rough."

"It's me."

"I'll do what I can." David knew arguing with me wouldn't get him anywhere. "I understand you're trying to get your girl back, and this is your way, but you really need to start thinking about what it is *you* want, music or love. In this business, sometimes there's not room for both."

He had a point. I'd give him that much. It still wasn't enough to change my mind.

"You do it, or I walk." I knew David and Colt Records was my chance at making it, but if they were going to start changing shit on me now, how could I trust them later on when there was more money on the line?

David frowned. "I told you, Beau, I'll see what I can do."

In the end, they apparently saw it my way and "Everlasting Light" was released as my first single.

I mailed a copy of the CD to Bentley based on the address Blaine gave me and wrote:

Bentley,

I hope you listen to it. If you ever wanted to know how I feel about you, every word on this CD is for you.

I love you,

everlasting, Beau

THE DAY MY record was released during the last week in June, I started my tour the same night in Nashville.

I had worked for the last six years to get here, doing this, and it wasn't anything like I thought it would be. It felt wrong, like something was missing.

At night, even after I started my tour, when I was alone and forced to deal with the loneliness I felt, everyone tried to intervene. Probably because I was drinking so much.

Even Payton, who was an opening act for me said something. I should have been excited to have my own tour—it was my fucking dream for as long as I could remember—but now all I could think about was Bentley and the life I left behind for this. She may have left me, but I felt like it was the other way around. My other problem was I refused to play "Everlasting Light" on tour, a song I made them put out as my first single and was nearing that number one spot on the Billboard 100. If it hadn't been for the sold-out shows, I was sure the record company would have had something to say about that.

It wasn't my idea to have Payton on tour, but my manager's. I wanted to fire him for thinking it would be a good idea. For weeks, she'd been trying to get me alone. It was subtle at first and then downright blatant.

So when I heard the knock on my door after the show in Pittsburgh, I knew it would be Payton. She figured, and though I couldn't blame her, being on tour with me that we could pick up where we left off. It was why I didn't want her as my opening act. It was why I refused to do a duet with her.

No way did I want her thinking we'd pick up where we ended.

I tried to keep my thoughts focused on the tour and making sure everything was perfect. Last thing I wanted was for her to think there would be a chance for us.

There would never be anyone else for me. Only Bentley.

"Hey," I said, trying to offer her a smile, my cheek pressing into the doorframe. "What are you doing here?"

"You. . . look lonely." She reached up to touch my face, only I gathered her hands in mine and pushed away from her.

Not only did I not want this, Miles and Wade would be back any minute with dinner.

I was lonely, but there was nothing *she* could provide. No matter how hard I poured myself into anything, it never compared to the way I felt with Bentley. Even sex. Though I hadn't been with anyone since her, no one would compare.

I never liked one night stands and there was no way I was going back to that. Never saw the appeal, really. Sex was supposed to relax you, but any time I was with someone, for one night, I felt even more agitated and unsatisfied.

Sure, the during part was good, as was the coming part, but the after never left me sated. It was like I was on the edge, never quite experiencing all it had to offer.

There was times I even felt like crying, like somehow it'd destroyed a part of my defense and left me vulnerable, gutted and depressed.

Maybe it was because I was a man, but I wanted to *feel* something. As I looked at Payton, my stare dropped to her chest and then lower to her curves hidden behind a tight pink tank top and painted on jeans.

When she noticed my stare dropped, Payton wasn't going to give me a moment of time to reconsider and was pushing me inside the room and onto the bed.

It felt good. Physical contact had a way of reminding a person how badly you wanted sex.

When I groaned, ready to push her away, Payton shook her head and pushed against my chest, making me lay back on the bed. "Don't turn me down, Beau." Her breath blew over me, whispering and needing something she thought I could provide for her.

Flat on my back, she straddled me, her hips lining up with mine. Probably because it had been a while, but I was hard at the slightest bit of contact and she knew it.

"You missed me, didn't you, Beau?" Her hips rocked against mine. "I know you want me. What we have will never fade."

I didn't say anything.

I don't want you.

I want Bentley.

Her eyes searched mine, trying to decide if I was going to deny her and they saw a drowning man, I was sure of it.

My head fell back against the mattress, my hands scrubbing down my face, remembering Bentley and the fact that, despite her not being with me, I hadn't gotten over her.

I didn't think I needed to explain this to Payton. I didn't *need* to explain it to anyone.

Ripping my hands from my face, Payton's kiss was sudden, capturing my mouth with an intensity I hadn't felt in a long time.

At first, I returned the kiss, franticly even, as if just the feel of her mouth excited me and pushed me forward. Grabbing her by the hips, I rolled her over, pressing my weight into her. As Payton bucked her hips into me, pleasure shot through my entire body just at having the contact down there. My body shook from the need to take this further, but I was reluctant.

Payton arched her back into me, angling her pelvis again and rocking with a little more force this time, slow, with a grinding motion I found incredibly satisfying.

In that moment, I didn't care who was beneath me, just that I wanted it. I wanted sex in the worst way. Maybe then I could feel something.

Only what I felt was a memory of a girl I used to know.

He gave me light that night.

He gave me everlasting light.

Reality came fucking crashing over me as I heard the rain hitting the window outside my hotel room. It was a sudden flash of Bentley in the tent, and then again in my truck after Dixie.

Stop! Don't do this with her.

"Payton," I jerked back, gasping and sitting up on my knees. "I can't."

Her face fell with my words. "Why not?"

"Because a lot has changed since me and you."

Everything has changed.

"I thought she broke up with you."

"She did. . . ." I shook my head moving from the bed to create more distance between us. It didn't matter if she ended it. It didn't end for me. "But it doesn't change the fact that I love her."

And then her face was crushed, her expression shifting from sadness to annoyance because our love never compared to this, what I had now, or had with Bentley. If I could deny Payton now, maybe she'd finally understand.

"Fine," she huffed, adjusting her shirt I'd somehow had up around her breasts. "Take me to have a beer at least."

Miles and Wade walked in, lost in conversation and then looking from Payton to me, and then back to Payton.

Miles grinned, winking at her. "Me next?"

Payton snorted, rolling her eyes as she punched him in the stomach. "You're such a pig."

I nodded to the door, shaking my head at them. "Let's go to the bar downstairs."

No way was I drinking with Payton alone in fear of how that would be taken.

OVER THE YEARS, Payton and I had remained civil for the most part. I couldn't help but feel a little bad about the way everything had worked out between us, because I cheated on her.

I shouldn't have a problem talking to her either. The thing was, I couldn't talk about *this*.

I didn't want to talk. It was just the topic of how I was doing. "So talk to me. Tell me what happened."

I shrugged my shoulders and looked over at her, and then back to my half-empty glass.

Payton sighed, running her fingers over the condensation forming on her glass, drops of water dripping onto the coaster in the process. "Did you cheat on her?"

"No." I snorted, knowing damn well she was going to throw that in my face. Why wouldn't she?

"Explain then."

I shook my head. How could I explain something I didn't understand myself?

Disappointment washed over me, a twinge of pain rippling in my veins. "I wasn't there for her when she needed me the most."

It went down to that, it really did.

"She hasn't been there for you, either."

Chuckling at the irony of this, I sipped my beer. "Thanks, but don't make it about her." I set the glass back down. "If you want to talk, we can, but not about Bentley."

Shifting my eyes to hers, she gave me an odd look and then smiled weakly. "Fair enough. But can I ask you one question?"

"What?"

"Why her?"

Why her? Hell, even I didn't know the answer to that. If I did, maybe then I could figure out why, even after we broke up, I couldn't move on. But I couldn't.

"I don't know the answer to that."

I wasn't lying. I didn't. All I knew was my heart was taken that first night when this clumsy girl fell into my lap and there was no way I was getting it back from her.

IT WAS EARLY July and the last place I should have been was at a bar outside Talladega, contemplating going to Bentley's apartment and begging her to talk to me, to give me an answer.

It was everything I could do *not* to bang down her fucking door and demand she hear me out, give me another chance.

The record company had me scheduled to sing the National Anthem at the NASCAR race in Talladega. Of course, I jumped at the opportunity.

"We need to get you laid," Wade said beside me, as if this was something he'd finally decided on.

I couldn't even look at him. "Why is that your answer for everything?"

"Because sex fixes everything."

"Or it complicates it." I took a drink of my beer. "How'd that work out for you when your ex-wife left you?"

He sighed, heavily. "You're depressing."

"You're a bad influence." Retrieving his phone from his pocket, he strolled through his Twitter feed. "Did you look at the Billboard Top 100?"

I couldn't hide my smile. "No, but David sent me a message at midnight last night when it hit number one. It's pretty cool."

It felt rewarding to see her song topping the charts. Now if only she'd listen to the damn thing.

Since we were so close to Mountain Brook, I wanted to pull a John Cusack 1989 *Say Anything* move and stand outside her room with a boom box. Or do one better and stand outside in the pouring rain with my guitar like the lovesick lunatic I'd become until she heard the song.

A girl like Bentley, she'd find humor in that and give me some rambling speech about how the rain felt against her skin while avoiding the reality of the moment.

Smiling, I remembered us in the back of my truck and her talking about the stupid stars and how they made no sense to her.

"See." Wade waved his hand at my empty beer. "Order another one. We should be celebrating with poon and beer."

"Then go find yourself some poon. I'm good with beer."

Wade let out a whistled breath when he noticed a busty blonde ordering two pitchers of beer. "See what I mean, man."

Maybe I was blind, I wasn't sure, but I didn't even look anymore. Bentley had brain-washed me. It had been since the last time I was with Bentley, since I'd been with a woman.

Physically, though, the need was there, the desire simply wasn't. Some piqued my interest, I was still a man, but nothing I ever acted on.

Wade went to the bathroom, or who the hell really knew, and left me at the bar when the conversations around me became louder.

"Go ask him for me, please?"

"No, you go over there. I'm busy."

"Doing what, drinking? Get off your ass and get me his autograph."

"Jesus, woman," the man huffed and I could hear footsteps behind me, and then a man was beside me, adjusting his hat. "Sorry to bother you, man, but you're Beau Ryland, right?"

I nodded, never looking up.

"My wife wants your autograph. She apparently loves your song 'Everlasting Light'."

I wouldn't turn her down, so I twisted in the chair to face him and instantly recognized who he was. Jameson Riley, a famous NASCAR driver. "Yeah, sure."

He didn't have anything for me to sign, and I didn't have a pen. I wasn't exactly prepared for this kind of thing. Patting the pockets of my flannel and jeans, I frowned. "Do you have a pen?"

"She probably does." He gave a nod to his wife. "I don't have anything for you to sign."

"Sign her tits!"

We both turned at the same time to see another man raising his beer in the air as it sloshed on the table, barely able to stand.

Jameson shook his head, glaring at the burly man with black hair. "Ignore him. He's crazy." And then he leveled me a serious look. "You're not signing my wife's tits."

The woman, his wife, who wanted the autograph, stood and waved at me, clearly having a few drinks in her as well and held up a napkin. "You can sign this, Beau."

She smiled when I approached her, avoiding eye contact as her husband wrapped his arm around her.

I felt a twinge of jealousy when they embraced, an ache vibrating in my chest. It wasn't from the fact that he was touching her, but from not having that type of contact myself any longer.

Closeness, warmth, love, I was alone now more than ever.

"What's your name?" I knew her name, only because of Jameson Riley, the man who had won the last, what, six NASCAR championships, and this woman was constantly photographed beside him. The fact that she wanted my autograph, when Jameson Riley was her husband, had me a tad nervous.

"Sway."

I scribbled a thank you Sway on the napkin and then signed my name before sliding it across the table. "Here ya go, ma'am."

The man to my left, the one who yelled 'sign her tits' gave a nod to the table he was now seated at with a blonde next to him. "Have a beer with us."

"Thank you, but I'm heading out soon. I'm actually singing the National Anthem tomorrow at the race. So you know, I should take it easy tonight."

"That's awesome!" tit guy said, high-fiving me.

I thanked them again and made my way back over to the bar where Wade was.

"Was that Jameson Riley?" Wade turned to look, and then stared at me. "That NASCAR driver?"

"Yeah, his wife wanted my autograph."

"Holy shit, that's awesome." And then his voice lowered as we took a seat. "His wife is hot."

Laughing, I shook my head at him. "And married."

Two glasses of whiskey and I was feeling brave again and contemplating a quick one-hour detour back to Mountain Brook, trying to come up with a plan when this kid sat next to me. "Hey, aren't you Beau Ryland?"

Not this again.

At least it wasn't some chick. After every concert I played, there was a line of them waiting. I gave Wade and Miles—my thank you to them sticking by my side through all my moodiness—their choice of rock star pussy.

"Yeah, I guess," I mumbled, giving the bartender a nod for one more.

"You don't gotta be rude about it." He snorted, but then took a seat. I already wanted to knock him off that damn stool.

"I'm not." I shook my head, wishing he'd get the goddamn point. "I'm trying to get drunk and you're talking to me. That's not rude. That's real."

To my left, Jameson and his family were starting to get rowdy, doing shots and shot-gunning beers.

Turning back to the glass now placed in front of me, I forgot the kid next to me until he said, "Aren't you that guy who used to date Bentley Schow?"

All right, now he had my attention.

"Why?"

"You left her too, didn't you?"

Now that I was looking at him, I knew exactly who this kid was. Then it hit me. Joel. That fucker from the lake.

I wasn't in the mood for this. No way. And what the hell was he doing in Talladega at the same bar as me?

"Bentley is none of your business."

He snorted, stumbling and leaning with his arms on the bar. He'd had a little too much. So had I.

"So what, you leave her after your kid dies?"

Yep. He crossed the line.

"You son of a bitch." I didn't wait. I had the kid with his face pressed to the bar, my forearm across his neck. "Don't you ever fucking talk about Bentley again, or my daughter."

He must have had too much because the stupid fucker shoved me. Commotion broke out all around us and the bartender began yelling at me to stop, but I didn't.

The only reason I did was because Jameson came over and broke it up.

"Hey," he raised a hand, motioning the bartender over, "can I get a round for me and slugger here?"

"You don't need to buy me a drink." I really just wanted to be left alone, but I didn't want to be rude to this man either.

"I think I do."

"Fine."

We drank in silence for what seemed like eternity when he asked, "You okay?"

"I'm fine. That guy just doesn't know when to keep his mouth shut."

Jameson snorted, flipping a coaster in his hand, over and over again. "I know plenty of guys like that."

I didn't say anything else, just nodded when he slid another beer my way. "Girl problems?"

"Yeah."

He nodded, again. "Wanna talk about it?"

I wondered if he really cared. Here was a professional athlete talking to me like I was his friend, when he didn't need to. "I uh, my daughter. She died at birth. From then on, my girl wasn't the same. I was on the road all the time and I guess I wasn't there when she needed me. So she left me." There was a hell of a lot more to it than that, but then again, there wasn't.

That was the simple version.

We made small talk, the best I could being drunk but then Jameson stood, maybe knowing I wasn't in the mood for talking but he offered one last piece of advice I took to heart. "No matter how great it feels to succeed and be the best, if the girl isn't there, none of it really matters, does it?" I nodded, knowing how true those words were. His hand clasped over my shoulder. "If you want her back, and I think you do, give her a grand gesture, go all out and prove to her she means something to you."

I thought I had with the song. Only she wouldn't listen to it.

What else could I do?

"Thanks for the beer."

Jameson smiled. "Any time, kid."

"I WANT TO make a small change to the tour."

David groaned, probably getting tired of my frequent demands. "Like what?"

"I'd like to add a show, a small one on Lake Martin on August first. I want it for Bentley's birthday."

David raised an eyebrow. "At the lake? Like a private showing?"

"Yes, it's where Bentley and I met."

I sounded like a lovesick fool.

"What day is that again?"

Shoving my hands in my pockets, I stared at my feet, waiting for him to deny it. If he did, I'd find a way to do it myself. If she wasn't going to listen to the radio, Blaine could get her to that concert and she could hear it. "August first."

He nodded, jotting down some notes. "So you're thinking if you play there, she will come."

I'm transparent, too.

"I have hope she will."

Hope was all I had.

"Are you planning on finally playing 'Everlasting Light' live?" I knew David's thoughts on me holding out on that one, and, eventually, I would have to play it. People wouldn't wait forever to hear it. Though it was creating quite the hype of when and where the first live showing would take place. I had to say every concert was sold out and I gave them the performance they deserved, minus one song.

"If she shows up, I will."

Gavin, Blaine, *and* Wade had all told me Bentley hadn't even listened to the CD, let alone heard "Everlasting Light," a song that was specifically written for her based off that first letter I read.

She had no idea I couldn't move on from her no matter how hard she tried to push me away. I liked to think Dixie had something to do with that. She knew where her daddy's heart belonged and it was with her mother.

"How many people do you think you can have there?"

"Well, my buddy Miles, he has a house on the lake with an empty lot next door. We can set up the stage there. . . I don't know." I scratched the back of my head, taking a seat at the table with him. "Maybe like five hundred tops. I need ten tickets for my family."

David made some notes. "I'll see what I can put together."

AFTER I LEFT David's office in downtown Nashville, I had a radio interview to do. The interview was held at a local station, but the same series of questions flowed as they usually did. This time one caught me off guard.

"If you could pick one person who has influenced your music, who would it be?"

I hesitated for a moment, leaning back in the seat. Looking at Miles and Wade, who stood near the wall, I should have said them, two guys who never left my side these days. Or Blaine, she was at every concert. Only I didn't write songs about them, not the ones that held the most meaning.

I couldn't say it was one person who influenced my music because it wasn't *just* one person. It never was in music. Every person I encountered influenced me in some way, whether it be me, or my music.

"I can't say just one person has helped me," I told him. "My mom has given me so much emotional support over the years, and my sister, Blaine, she's always believed in me and my music. My cousin Wade, and my best friend, Miles, they're always there for me. . . but as far as influencing my music and the songs I write, it's Bentley, always will be."

What fuck kind of answer is that? Now they're gonna ask who she is and how are you going to explain that?

I wanted to kick myself for saying that.

"Who's Bentley?"

"Oh, you know, everyone's got that one girl they can't shake," I said with a laugh, trying to sneak some humor in there.

I could feel the interview getting more and more personal and my theory was confirmed when he asked his next question.

"Now I hear you're single? Is this Bentley girl in the picture?" I wasn't sure how, but somehow Bentley and I, our relationship had stayed out of the media, and so had Dixie. I knew eventually it would come out, but I wasn't ready to tell the world about Dixie.

It wasn't until after she was born that I was thrown into the spotlight.

Shifting uncomfortably, I knew the women who had been faithfully following me on Twitter and every other social media outlet was eager for my response.

"I uh. . . I've never been one to date. I am single." *No you're not. You never will be.* I felt like I needed to clarify that a bit so I added, "But I *don't* have time for dating right now with being on the road."

What the fuck kind of answer was that?

"That's what I hear. Tell us about this new album of yours."

Oh thank God.

And just like that, I avoided the personal questions and had the conversation back on my music, the way it should have been.

Nobody needed to know I was in love with Bentley and she had basically shut me out of her life after our daughter passed away. Nobody needed to know what "Everlasting Light" meant but us.

I would always love Bentley. Even if we were never allowed to be together again, she showed me who I was, who I wasn't, and who I wanted to be.

For that, I would love her until the day I died.

"DID YOU GIVE her the ticket?" My hands were shaking holding the guitar as I sat on my bus, unable to meet Blaine's eyes.

David had managed to get everything together in time. On August first, I returned to the familiar red clay where I met a girl who changed my whole world.

"I did, she said she would come, but she wouldn't come with Gavin and me."

I knew what that meant. She wouldn't because she was afraid if she did, she'd be forced to show up, and hear me. If she came alone, she could chicken out.

"Are you ready for this?"

I nodded, trying to appear calm. I'd been on stage hundreds of times now but this had nothing on it.

This was different.

It was where I met Bentley, where I fell in love with her, and now, where I was trying to make her see this was all for her. The only way I could show her I still loved her, and have her hear me. I would always love her, even if she didn't love me in return. I believed in loving someone, even when they couldn't.

Blaine stood from her place across from me, rubbing my shoulders. "I'm trying to help, Beau, I am. It's why I gave you the letters. You did your part, it's up to her now."

I knew how badly Blaine wanted to help me and Bentley. My mother was the same way, trying everything she could to make Bentley see she had support. All she had to do was look up.

The concert was to begin when the sun dipped down over the lake. My mom came in the bus, giving me a gentle smile when she saw the bottle beside me. I hadn't realized how obvious bad my depression had become.

She gave me that concerned motherly tone. "I know you can't see it, and I know you miss her and Dixie, but everything will work out." Reaching for the bottle, I frowned when she took it from me. "Jensen has a drinking problem. Your father has a drinking problem. Please don't turn everything to drinking for everything."

"I just...." I didn't have an answer. At least not one anyone would find acceptable.

"What?" she asked, waiting for me to give her an excuse.

"I miss her. I miss them," I admitted quietly. "It's like there's a hollow ache inside of me. I can't see how I can do anything without her. I've tried to show her I'm still here for her, but how can I do that when she won't even hear me out?"

My mother had always been a spiritual woman. She believed in having her stars read, daily horoscopes, all that. "Beau, your story, it's the reason you were meant to be Dixie's father. You can't fix Bentley. It's not your job to. All you can do is be there for her in any way you can. Even if it's being a friend for her. You can't fix her. Nobody can. Nobody should. She lost her baby, just like you did. It's okay to heal separately. I know eventually you two will find your way back."

"How? She won't even talk to me."

She smiled and held on to my hands. "You will find a way."

Glad she was so confident.

Just before I went on stage and the sounds of the opening beats of "A Little Bit More Of You" played, Miles tugged on my arm, his expression one of concern. I didn't think he wanted me to go out there unless I was prepared for the letdown.

"Maybe. . . it's time you move on," he said quietly, trying not to piss me off.

"I love her," I said slowly taking in the crowd and excitement surrounding me. "I love her so much that I can't move on. I can't." I stared at Miles, unable to explain what it was I couldn't let go of. I don't even think I understood it anymore.

"You know she might not come, right?"

I sighed, thinking about how that would feel. "I know." I looked back down at the guitar adjusting the strap. "But she might, and I'm holding onto that might."

God, please let this work.

I had been on stage countless times in the last year, in front of thousands and even the Grand Ole Opry. Nothing prepared me for that concert at Lake Martin and the stirring need in my chest to see her. It was an anxiety I couldn't quite explain, something gnawing, a need deep inside my chest.

I wouldn't sing "Everlasting Light" unless she showed up.

I couldn't. That was her song. The first time it was played, she needed to be there.

As the sun set and the sky painted with bright sweet colors, I took a seat on a stool and played Dixie's song for her, for the first time live. Tears were streaming down my face, as they were rolling down my mothers and Blaine.

I couldn't promise your first breath
And I couldn't give you one more
I can promise to love you
A pinky swear made true

Chapter Twenty-Five

DANCIN' AWAY WITH MY HEART

BENTLEY

I COULDN'T LISTEN to the radio or watch television. Despite anything I told myself and lack of sleep, outside of my bubble, the world continued, as did Beau's career. He had mailed me a copy of the CD, and I wanted to listen to it. Told myself I would, but just the mention of his name and staring at the cover with him on it, his head down, staring at a guitar, sent a stabbing sensation to my chest.

Imagine if I heard his voice.

Imagine that pain.

When Blaine gave me the tickets and basically told me we were going, I wanted to. I did. And I had every intention of going.

I wanted to get out of the car and hear that voice, the one that held me close and whispered in my ear when I needed him the most. Only I couldn't.

I even drove out there and listened to the muffled sounds coming up from the lake. I just couldn't actually get out of my car, my hands shaking on the steering wheel as the tears fell over heated cheeks, a reminder of the heat, and the way he made me feel. Even in my car, my heart knew he was close.

That night, I finally sent him a message. It was the first one since that day in April when I left him.

Me: *I'm so proud of you. I'm sorry I couldn't make it. It's just. . . hard.*

I wasn't lying, I hoped that.

He sent one back, almost immediately.

Beau: *I hope someday you will give me a chance again. I love you.*

Staring at his message, I immediately wished he was there with me, holding me. I wanted him so badly my body ached like the first day of a cold, head pounding, throat sore, ready to give up. I wanted his gentle touch—a heartbeat like mine, warm, not cold like this car and my fears.

There are parts of this world that will tear you apart. Things that happen to you that break your faith in love and the ability to move on. It doesn't happen right away. It happened slowly, like that cold, then before you knew it, you woke up and felt like a train hit you.

I was never more than those letters, suffering alone beside a headstone, reliving my pain where black ink touched pure white. I was lost in words, sparks of heaven bursting down and carrying me away.

I have looked at a cloudless sky and thought of one man as he whispered in the darkest of nights, *"Kiss me under the stars, love me and they're ours."*

Maybe I would never love anyone the way I loved Beau, but I was okay with that. I had lost myself completely in this grief but then again, did I ever really know myself at all?

I went from the girl her parents had forgotten about, to the girl whose dad up and left.

Then I was the girl whose mom wasn't all there, because she got in a car drunk and made a really bad decision.

Then I was the girl struggling to make something of herself on her own.

And when I did, I met a boy who changed my world.

The time I had with him was worth it.

I still felt like my life started the day I tripped into his arms and met him officially.

When I made it home that night, I wrote another letter to Dixie and placed it on her grave the next morning before work.

If anything, maybe she could help her mama out and make me see what it was I was missing.

Chapter Twenty-Six

A THOUSAND MILES FROM NOWHERE

BEAU

I TOOK ONE last look at the stars. *Here's to the night we felt alive.*

She didn't show.

"Thank you for coming everyone," I said, before exiting the stage. I was sure some were disappointed they didn't hear what they wanted, but I gave them one hell of a show, I was sure of that.

They wanted "Everlasting Light" and I didn't play it. Refused to. If she wasn't going to listen to it, I refused to play it live.

I caught a lot of crap for not singing my number one single, but how could I when that was her song, meant for her, and she wasn't there?

It was a piece of me and her, together, and if I was going to sing it live at Lake Martin, it needed to be for her.

I told myself I would wait for her. A girl like Bentley was one you waited for, but now I was starting to doubt myself, and my plan because it didn't work.

For months I had poured myself into my music, obsessing over every single lyric as if somehow I could make her see I was there for her still, if she would just listen to me.

Inside my bus that night with Miles, Wade, and Gavin hanging out, I nearly dropped my phone on the ground when I saw there was a message from Bentley.

Bentley: *I'm so proud of you. I'm sorry I couldn't make it. It's just. . . hard.*

My stomach churned thinking of her. The cold grabbed my insides again and again as I tried comprehending what she had sent.

I tried to picture her face, wanting to burn the image into my brain, never forgetting how perfect she was, the delicate twist of her mouth when she smiled, or the way her eyes lit up when I would sing for her.

Me: *I hope someday you will give me a chance again. I love you.*

With tears in my eyes, I moved back to the bedroom at the rear of the bus to be alone, leaving the guys drinking, and stared at the letter in my pocket, crumbled around the edges because it was the one I couldn't bear to take out of my wallet, I never would.

The way I loved your daddy was the type of love that only came around once in a lifetime. It was the kind of love that didn't know any better, foolish love that soared high above the night. The kind of love that smelled like a summer breeze through an open window.
The reality was, he changed me, completely. I live my life differently because of him. I was learning to live in the moment and never for the future again.

If she meant that, why didn't she show up!

What was stopping her?

I stared at myself in the mirror that night, asking myself if I should let her go and why I was doing this to myself. I told myself to forget about her, but I couldn't. Bentley was my heart, and how could you move on without your heart?

I made her a promise. I told her I would always love her and I meant that. I would. If anything, if she wouldn't come back to me, the least I could do was keep my promise to her.

The one I wanted to keep, the one that I would take care of her, bring back Dixie, I couldn't keep.

This one I could.

Chapter Twenty-Seven

EVERYWHERE

BENTLEY

NOVEMBER

GAVIN AND BLAINE PLANNED a fall wedding, to which I was a part of. I knew Blaine getting married meant she'd invite her twin brother.

I wasn't in any way prepared to deal with that. I had to think back to how long it had been since I last saw him. April.

I hadn't seen him since April and here it was November. Seven months.

The exact amount of time I was pregnant with Dixie.

"Is Beau singing?" I asked Blaine as she got dressed that afternoon.

"No, he asked that we not have him play at the wedding." Blaine stared at herself in the mirror, probably second-guessing that damn dress.

"Why?"

Blaine shook her head, reaching for her make-up bag to touch up her lipstick. "Because it's my day and he doesn't want any of the attention on him."

Goddamn him, why's he gotta be so damn sweet?

I had no idea what to expect when Blaine asked me to be her maid of honor. I had never been in a wedding, and I also wasn't sure how their family would treat me.

After all, I broke up with their son. I definitely wasn't worried about Beau's father, he could take a flying leap off a cliff for all I was concerned with. It was his mother I worried about. Would she think I was a complete bitch for that?

The wedding was done up as fall country theme complete with hay bales next to whiskey barrels and twinkle lights hung up. It was beautiful and if I was getting married, I'd want something like that.

What wasn't as beautiful was the fact that I had drunk an entire fifth of Fireball since I arrived at Gavin's parent's house in Montgomery because I knew Beau was going to be there.

It terrified me to think of us in the same room since I broke his heart.

With that fifth of whiskey came my spunky clumsy side.

Not only did I feel completely out of place, but I was ready to cry myself to sleep next to the hay bales in my self-pity.

Blaine felt the same, and it was her family and wedding. Poor girl. She'd been crying all morning and looked pissed at her husband-to-be for making her have a wedding instead of getting married in Vegas, which she literally begged him to do, and then threatened to shove a candle stick up his ass if anything went wrong.

As I watched her that morning, I felt bad for her.

I'd be pissed, too, if I had to wear that dress. Apparently it had been passed down from his mother and it was a tradition the bride wear the groom's mothers dress. I had never heard of such thing. It sounded like some crazy cult religion if you asked me.

Which no one did, because I was the drunk girl no one would even look at. Blaine resembled the Michelin tire man with all those ruffles. She wasn't impressed, that was obvious.

I was in the living room with their relatives, most of whom I didn't know, aside from Beau's grandma.

I was pretty sure I was supposed to be doing something, at least I thought I was, holding a bouquet of flowers and all, but no, I was holed up in the corner, leaning against Blaine's grandma, doing shots with her.

The wedding would be starting shortly outside the Koche home, followed quickly by the reception, all in an attempt to get it in before the weather changed. I felt like the weather tonight. Impending doom.

"How do you say Gavin's last name?" Grandma Edith smirked, knowing what I was going to say.

"It's pronounced Cook, but to me it sounds like koo-chee."

We both broke out in giggles and passed the bottle back and forth. My eyes kept scanning the crowd, unsure of what to think when I noticed that dark hair and those eyes I still dreamt of.

It was then I noticed him, tall dark and handsome standing next to Gavin, his hand clasped over his shoulder as if to congratulate him.

Stupid. No one should look that good.

And look at me. I was a drunk train wreck in my lilac tear-stained dress.

It was a wedding after all. Wasn't everyone supposed to be drunk?

As I sat there beside Grandma Edith and our booze, Beau came over.

Oh shit, really? He's coming over now?

He was walking toward me, the way only Beau Ryland could walk, making sleepy, slow steps look sexy. After all these months my heart remembered him immediately, the beat speeding and my skin burning.

Before he reached me, his mom was standing in front of him, nodding to Jensen to his right who was also drunk. Like I said, everyone drank at weddings.

"Just talk to him, Beau," his mom said, shoving at his shoulder. "He's your brother."

"I have nothing to say to him," Beau returned, looking back at the bar set up to his left. He hesitated for another moment, looking at me and then chose the bar, not ready to come over to me yet.

Thank God!

Staring at me, blues so deep and tortured I feared they'd never be free, he hesitated again as he reached for his drink the bartender handed him.

How badly had I hurt him? Like bad enough he'd never talk to me again?

After the concert he texted me a few times, but still, we hadn't actually spoken, and I didn't go to the concert he specifically scheduled for my birthday at the exact place we met.

Asshole move on my part for sure.

Beau moved away from the bar, back at least a foot, and then looked at me again, sighing, before he turned and walked outside with Miles.

Blaine came rushing out, crying, and holding her Michelin tire dress, like the crazy emotional bride she was today. "Bentley, get your ass in here! I need you right now."

I swayed slightly holding onto Grandma Edith's fragile arm for support. "You know, I've been thinking. Maybe I'm not bridesmaid material today."

"Well that's a good thing because your drunk ass is the maid of honor." She stomped her foot for dramatics. "Now get in there right now!"

"You should have had Payton do this."

She rolled her eyes. "Yes because we're such *good* friends."

I was actually glad Payton wasn't here. It'd be too soon if I never saw her again.

I suppose it was about time I started my duties as the maid of honor.

As far as I was concerned, and let's face it, I wasn't exactly a good person to be making decisions right now, but my duties as maid of honor meant taking a few more shots—or at least that was a duty for myself.

Blaine had other ideas when she said, "I need you to walk down the aisle with him."

Was she fucking serious?

"No way." I shook my head. "Not happening. I'm not the one getting married. Are you insane?" I was shaking my head so much I was making myself dizzy. "Are you sure you want to marry him anyways? Your last name will be Koochee. I could call you B-koochee. You didn't think that through, did you?"

"He's one of the groomsmen." She was ignoring my teasing all together, and hit me with, "I thought I told you that."

My eyes narrowed. "No you didn't fucking tell me that. This feels like another one of your plans to get me to talk to him, or be near him in hopes we will talk."

Blaine raised an eyebrow and lifted her dress in an aggravated motion. "Do you really think you have any room for negotiation today?"

Shrugging, I slouched against the wall where I was sitting trying to apply make-up. "I guess not." I stood up, swaying a little, but standing made me appear more stable. At least I thought so.

When we were downstairs and the wedding was just about to begin, Blaine cornered me again, pointing at Beau standing against the wall, his head hung, staring at his feet. "Walk with him, or I will never forgive you for this." She pointed to the bottle I got out again.

"Walking." I took another swig from my bottle only to have Grandma Edith walk by and take it, mumbling something about bullshit traditions before dumping the flower girl's basket of flowers out on the floor.

I really liked Edith. I knew where Beau and Blaine got their humor from.

Blaine looked at me and pointed, as if I was a child who refused to listen to instructions. "Get over there. I'm not telling you two to talk, I just want you to walk together, that's all. And then you can go back to *not* talking."

I did as she said without another word, though I knew she was lying. She wanted us to talk.

Beau stepped toward me, and as I hooked my arm around his, I looked around.

Oh God, we're touching. Don't trip. Don't breathe. Don't do a damn thing, or say anything.

My lungs felt like they were going to freeze up any moment. Then he was beside me, keeping my gaze much longer than I felt comfortable with. The warmth of his body felt like acid on my skin, though he was barely touching me. He was still that shining star in the dark I couldn't look away from.

Fuck, look at him!

That jaw, that scruff, the eyes against the black tux.

I'm a fucking idiot for letting this go.

I tried to breathe through my frustration when the music began. Blaine noticed and glared. I winked at her, pushing back the bile rising and trying to force a smile.

Beau looked over at me, smiling tightly, like he wanted to say something, but it pinched, hurt too much.

So I spoke first, though I told myself to remain quiet.

"You had to show up looking like this, didn't you?" I asked him as we started to walk down the pebble stoned path leading to the archway. The sun was setting now over the field, little slivers of chalky pink and purple peeking through slate gray. I hated it because of the reminder of the nights I spent with him at the lake.

Beau tilted his head toward me to listen, but he continued to face forward. "You're just as pretty as I remember," he replied, low-toned and turning slightly.

"That's cliché." Shaking my head, I sighed. "The Beau I remember would say something charming right now."

Beau laughed, mostly under his breath. He nodded, checking our surroundings. Now wasn't exactly the greatest time to be having a conversation. "Okay," he said easily, tightening his elbow to his side to pinch my hand in place.

Never let go of me. Please.

Touching his body, even if it was just his arm, felt unfamiliar and inaccessible, like a lost shoe suddenly found months later, only to find it didn't fit anymore or wasn't nearly as comfortable as you remembered.

He wasn't unfamiliar and inaccessible. He was warm, a security I craved knowing I'd never fall with him beside me.

When we reached the arbor, Beau let me go, and then there was the awkward staring at each other since we technically had to face one another.

I felt nauseous. Like any minute I was going to spew cinnamon whiskey over Blaine's entire wedding.

Thankfully the ceremony was finished in a matter of ten minutes, and I barely could focus, what with trying to avoid puking all over the bride, until I saw the expression on Beau's face when the minister asked them to repeat after him.

The pain in his eyes was clear. Again, his stare held me. I couldn't look away.

Why did I let him go? Why did we lose Dixie? Why was this so fucking hard?

And then I puked.

Luckily we had walked back down the path and had returned to the house so I made it to the bathroom just in time.

As I sat there on the edge of the tub, trying to get myself together for the sake of Blaine, I thought about his face again and what it was he was feeling.

Just go out there and tell him you love him.

I wasn't in that bathroom five minutes and Blaine was looking for me. After today I was sure I was up for the worst best friend ever.

She handed me a cold rag right before the reception started. "When you get married I'm going to drive my car through that motherfucker." I knew she wasn't serious, but if she was, I deserved it. "Don't come out of here until you're sober."

Twenty minutes later I emerged.

The reception was in the backyard. All the chairs from the wedding had been pushed aside and made way for a makeshift wood dance floor and a small stage where Beau was standing with Miles and Wade, his back to me.

Everyone was concerned about the weather so things got started pretty early, but it was pretty damn funny that everyone's hair was a mess from the humidity and the women's dresses were blowing up from the wind. Strategically placed white umbrellas offered a little shielding.

If I hadn't been so drunk, I probably would have laughed.

Instead I sat there and drooled on myself.

Although when Grandma Edith's dress blew up to reveal her garter belt, I did laugh.

Beau eventually took a seat at the table, hands clasped with his elbows on his knees, head hung. It was as if he was trying to decide on something, only what I wasn't sure.

I hadn't actually moved from the table Blaine sat me at after the wedding. I wasn't sure I could. It seemed like a lot of work, and I was sure I would fall face first if I tried to move.

Who gets drunk on their best friend's wedding day?

Me. I did that shit.

Poor Blaine.

God, I'm a horrible person.

"Here." She handed me a cup of coffee. "Drink this and don't move."

She was about ten feet away when I yelled after her, "What if I have to pee?"

Blaine shot me a glare, picking up her dress. "Piss on yourself!"

She wasn't serious. We'd get through this. She loved me. I knew we would. I still felt like an asshole, though.

When Beau heard my voice, his head whipped around, but he didn't get up. Instead, he focused on his mother and aunt seated next to him.

The night had settled into an easy pace now. Country music came from a DJ to my right, friends and family all celebrating the joining of two great people. Part of me was incredibly thankful Beau wasn't singing. Had I heard him now, I wasn't sure how I would react.

After Gavin and Blaine's first dance, everyone made their way to the dance floor.

Beau was walking to me now, a slow stride set by his indecisiveness that held me steady.

Shit, this is it. He's gonna wanna talk and you're going to have to explain yourself.

He was nervous, I knew that much. I could hear my heart in my ears when he approached me, his suit jacket had been removed, white dress shirt rolled up to his elbows.

I panicked and stood, suddenly, as if I had somewhere to be.

My only problem was when I stood, I sent the coffee in my hand flying and all over a lady in a cream dress.

Fuck!

Not knowing what else to do, I turned, quickly, as if nothing happened and sat back down, red faced and sweating.

"There's the clumsy pretty girl I fell in love with," Beau whispered, his lips dangerously close to my neck.

I jolted back, head-butted him and then gasped, inhaling spit.

Why can't I be normal around him?

Rubbing my head, I don't know why I thought I could *ever* be normal around him. He was Beau Ryland. I just couldn't.

"Dance with me," he said quietly, his hands on the edge, leaning forward but not looking at me; he was looking at his hands. The top few buttons of his white shirt were undone, giving me a peek at his skin beneath the cotton.

Focusing on the words, the statement, it certainly wasn't a question. It was demand, one I wasn't sure I could ignore.

"No. I can't. My armpits itch. And I've had too much to drink, clearly. I might trip."

He smiled, remembering the night we met and I tripped, and glanced over at his parents on the dance floor before looking back at me.

"Dance with me," he whispered under the wind, his voice resilient, biting so much back.

When I didn't reply, his voice came stronger.

"I'm not asking you, Bentley. Get up and dance with me. You've ignored me for months, don't you think it's the least you could do."

Wrong choice of words bucko.

"The least I could do?" I snorted. "Why do you want to dance with me?" I could tell when his hands gripped the edge of the table a little tighter and his knuckles turned white, he hated that I would even hesitate. His disappointed eyes told me so. Mine moved from his, quickly avoiding him.

"I want you to dance with me because I have some things to say to you." He gripped the table tighter and hit his fist against it lightly, enough to shake the wine glasses. "And I don't want us separated by a *fucking table*. Get up."

My heart started pounding because I was speaking a truth neither of us wanted to hear.

He surprised me when his voice came a little louder, determined even. "Bentley, *I called you,* I called you *over and over* again, only to have you *not* answer. I won't sit here and tell you it was easy to leave. It wasn't. I know I left but you told me to. I also sent you tickets to my concert, and you didn't show. So please, I'm practically fucking begging here, please dance with me."

I stared up at him, giving in. "What if I trip?"

"Then I'll catch you." As he winked, I looked down at his extended hand, and then his face, and there it was, the fragile hope in his eyes and the nervous set of his mouth that I would deny him.

I couldn't say no.

I kept wondering if his being away from me had any effect on him at all. Now I certainly had my answer. His bloodshot, swollen eyes told me he had at least been thinking about me lately.

"Okay," I finally said, placing my hand in his, our fingers curled around each other, fitting together perfectly. It reminded me of the first time I took his hand at the lake, and the day we buried Dixie.

The reminder of her sent a shot straight to my heart, knowing she tied the two of us together.

As we swayed, I caught sight of Jensen, drinking with his father, both of them wearing the same vacant stare. "What happened between you and your brother?"

"Same shit as always." Beau's brow pinched together. "He's an asshole and always will be."

"I'm sorry." It wasn't needed, but I felt like I should say it. *I'm sorry for so much more.*

"Why didn't you come to the concert?" he asked, his mouth at my ear as he pulled me to his chest.

"I couldn't hear you sing." I looked at my hands instead of his face, because it was too much, too invasive, as I tried desperately to shut down and not care about anything he was about to say to me. "Not with the memories your voice holds for me."

Your voice is everything I hear. It haunts me at night.

His head tilted slightly, a wince to his features as his hand squeezed mine.

"Can you ever again?" Beau asked, his tone still low, a reminder of what it felt like to have him whisper words to me.

"I don't know, Beau."

How can I hear you sing when I can't let you go, and you don't need me. Clearly.

Look at me. I was the girl who lost her daughter, broke the love of her life's heart, and then took a giant crap on her best friend's wedding. Great life plan.

"I miss you," he finally said, our bodies swaying slightly to the music, but not enough that we were actually dancing.

"Beau. . . ." He silenced me with one look, knowing I was going to tell him I didn't want to talk about us right now.

Now seemed like the worst time to talk about us. There I was in my lilac dress, barefoot, splotchy, and tear-stained because I still couldn't get my shit together and he wanted to talk about us.

I write to our dead daughter and dream of you every single night.

I hate you in some ways, because you haunt my memory of the happy ever after I was denied.

I felt as if the air was still, my focus entirely on him.

Fuck, did I say that out-loud?

"I miss you, Bentley," he said, again, voice breaking as he opened himself up and waited for me to give him something, an indication I still cared for him.

"I miss you, too," I whispered, feeling the tears welling up. Any moment they were going to let loose in front of everyone.

For a moment his arms tightened around my waist, and we were both silent, but I could tell by the tension in his body he was working himself up to say something, finally.

He pulled back, his eyes watchful. "Will there ever be a chance for us again?" he begged desperately, hopeful that I was going to give him the answer he wanted.

"I don't know," I said, barely a whisper. The truth was, I didn't know. I wanted there to be, but I couldn't give him an answer right now. I wasn't at that place yet. "I want there to be, someday."

Nodding, he blew out a huge breath, like he was completely ridding his body of oxygen. "I still love you." He mumbled the words, like he couldn't give them anymore sound than he had. "I've never stopped."

My mouth went dry looking at him. He was taking large even breaths now, warming himself up for me letting him down, again, or maybe settling his nerves.

Fuck Bentley, tell him! He's right here, it's your chance to give him something! You love him and he needs to hear it.

Beau frowned, looking frustrated. I could tell he was struggling to express himself this way. He dropped his head forward, like he was giving up.

"I'm sorry, Beau I just..."

His eyes lifted to meet mine and the agony in his face knocked me sideways. "Don't worry about it."

I nodded, my voice hitched when I said, again, "I'm sorry."

He tipped his head to the side, like even breathing was painful for him. "I'll uh. . . ." The way his voice trailed off had my heart in my throat again and my skin prickling. And then he said, "I'll see you around."

My heart jumped when he let go of me, my eyes swollen, filled with that sadness I knew too well and had let control me for too long.

"Okay," I said, trying to stay strong and not burst into tears. I knew I wasn't going to be able to hold back much longer.

As he started to walk away, his hand on the back of his neck, he turned slightly to look back at me and I looked away. I couldn't deal with the vulnerable side of him; it made me feel vulnerable, too.

He didn't leave, as if he couldn't. Something was holding him here, a force he couldn't ignore. "I know you love me, Bentley, even if you can't say it. I'll never be sorry for the time

I was granted with you. . . and her." He reached out and cupped my face as he inhaled loudly, my breath in my lungs exhaling just as harshly. "The way I feel about you hasn't changed. It *never* will."

I took in a ragged breath, though it gave me nothing in return. What he was saying and the *way* he was saying it held such honestly I had no choice but to believe him.

He turned his back on me, and it wasn't out of hate or regret. It was him giving me space. He was leaving me with those words, as if he had to say them now, or else he never would.

A familiar ache stirred in my chest and weaved around my throat. I started to panic thinking I was going to have an attack right there.

My eyes closed, and I felt my chest heave as the tears slipped down my face, wanting to tell him how much I loved him. Drawing in a deep breath, I couldn't pry my eyes from his departure.

He made his way over to Blaine, danced with her and then left with Miles.

When he was gone, I took a seat at the table, watching Blaine dance with Gavin.

Still not thinking clearly, I approached the two of them, wanting to apologize to both.

Wrapping my arms around Blaine's middle section, I pulled her against my chest. Immediately, she turned and hugged me despite my shitty behavior tonight.

"I'm sorry," I whispered against her neck, starting to cry again.

Blaine untangled her arms to place her palms on my cheeks just as she had done the night I went out with her to the bar, and had my breakdown then. "You will always be my best girl, Bentley," she said, tear-soaked, same as me. We were definitely having a moment. "I mean it though, when you marry my brother, I'm driving a truck through your wedding."

I found it funny she thought I'd marry Beau, but not surprising.

Part of me thought, maybe, there would be time for us later.

Chapter Twenty-Eight

I MET A GIRL

BEAU

"WHAT DID SHE say?" Blaine wrapped her arms around my waist as we said goodbye.

"She still can't, but I think she's close."

Blaine feared I'd give up on Bentley only neither of us could. "Don't. . . I mean. . . are you done? Are you giving up?"

"I didn't come here thinking she'd even talk to me, so I guess maybe we made some progress."

"I'm sorry, Beau," Blaine looked completely dejected, thinking her plan failed. "Tonight turned into a disaster. I had no idea she was going to get a hold of that fireball."

"I thought she was pretty funny. Grandma did too." I chuckled running my hand through my hair. "You have to remember how nervous she would have been knowing I was going to be here."

"I know."

"And you're married now. Dad stayed sober enough to walk you down the aisle, so it wasn't a *complete* disaster."

"You're right." She smiled at Gavin with Miles in a headlock. "It still seems crazy to think I married him and I didn't even like him at first."

"I'm just glad you didn't marry Miles," I teased, winking at her as I placed my arm around her shoulder and held her to my side, willing myself not to look in Bentley's direction. "Then I would have objected to the wedding. I'm happy you two found each other." Pressing my lips to her forehead, I whispered. "Thank you for trying. Enjoy that honeymoon." Letting go of her, I winked about the time she started laughing.

"Will you be home for Christmas?"

"Just for a day." I took a step away from her, nodding to the driveway as if to say I was leaving now. "And then I'm heading out on tour again. I think I finish at the end of January."

Blaine adjusted her dress, fidgeting with the ruffles. I knew what she was going to ask. "Have you played 'Everlasting Light' yet?"

"Nope." I took a step back toward her, not wanting our conversation heard by anyone else. "And I'm catching a lot of shit for it too."

"Are you really not going to play it until she hears it?"

Shrugging, I backed up a step. "She needs to hear it live, first."

I wasn't sure it was going to work that way, but it was still my plan.

"Is she uh—" My eyes deceived me and snapped to Bentley as she sat a nearby table sipping water. That girl, the one barely able to make eye contact with anyone could never be anything but mine. I knew it for sure. "Has she wrote anymore letters?"

"Not that I've seen."

After saying goodbye to my mom, I met Miles at my truck where he was leaning against the door. "Well? I saw you dancing with her," he opened the door when I unlocked it. "What did she say?"

I waited until we were inside the truck before I answered him. "Wouldn't say much. Just that she couldn't listen to the song, or me for that matter."

"Man," Miles groaned, a slow shake to his head as he smoothed out his slacks. "How long are you gonna wait for that girl?"

"I'll wait forever if I have to." I started the truck and began to pull out of the driveway.

"I don't know how you do it," he mumbled. "Seems like a lot of fuckin' work for pussy."

I rolled my eyes.

The truth was, I didn't know why I held on either, just that I couldn't let go of her. Something tied me to her and it was stronger than anything I'd ever felt before. It had me holding on even when I thought I should let go. I met a girl and everything changed. Everything.

Miles was passed out before we hit Mountain Brook, snoring away, so I stopped by Dixie's grave and placed some flowers on her gravestone for her.

Please baby girl, if you can hear me, help me find a way to convince your mama she needs me.

Chapter Twenty-Nine

BREAK YOUR PLANS

BENTLEY

JANUARY

WHEN I BEGAN writing letters to Dixie, I never realized how much writing to her would have helped me.

I would never forget Beau or anything we had been through, or what Dixie had taught me in just minutes. What I would let go of was the grief I tied to him, the hurt, the frustration to blame myself for what happened to Dixie.

Through those letters to her with silly drawings and countless acts of love, was a love for her and Beau that I poured my soul into.

Writing helped me.

I couldn't say it healed me, but it certainly helped.

For a while, my soul had been crushed beyond repair. But with writing to Dixie, a tiny flicker of hope arose within me. Hope that I hadn't lost everything and I could go on and accept that, yes, I did feel guilty for losing her, but I couldn't let it control my entire life.

I knew I wasn't healed completely, but looking back on the months from where I began, I knew now I could at least survive.

For me, I had decided those memories with Beau, that weekend with him, and then the ones of Dixie, wouldn't consume me forever.

Would they always be a part of me? Yes, but for myself, in order to heal, I wrote them down, carried them around with me for months, reliving every detail as if they held answers I wasn't sure I even needed anymore.

Relief came after Blaine's wedding, when I realized maybe I didn't *need* the answers; just remembering and purging those memories to paper was enough for me.

"I know you love me, Bentley, even if you can't say it. I'll never be sorry for the time I was granted with you. . . and her."

I realized what it was that little precious angel gave to me, and what she was trying to bring me back to. Beau. Had she somehow had an influence in that?

I believed she did.

Now I was more aware of that than ever, but I felt something else entirely, something she didn't give me, but *showed* me. I was still her mother. She taught me parts of this world no one had ever shown me before, including heartache.

But I taught myself how to live with that heartache and give it an outlet.

Older, not necessarily wiser, I did learn from what I wrote. I was one step closer to being me and seeing what I needed to see.

All of what I wrote to her was true. They were my thoughts, memories, doubts, confessions, demands for answers, and my summer with Beau before winter took it away.

Believe me when I say that writing it, I felt everything real was slipping away. Hello, I thought they were being delivered to Heaven, when in reality, they probably weren't.

In truth, if I hadn't wrote to Dixie, I feared I would carry that heartache forever, but I was ready to let go now.

The day Dixie would have been a year old was hard, and with it brought a pain I didn't know I could still feel that real. Pain I thought would have gotten easier.

Beau sent me a message.

Beau: I love you, pretty girl. Still. Always. Forever. My heart is with you today.

I sent him one back that said: **My heart hurts so badly today, but there's comfort in knowing someone feels that same way.**

I wanted to tell him I loved him.

I wanted him to wait for me.

I wanted him to move on, and not put himself through this.

I was thankful he hadn't.

I struggled for so long not to feel the pain of losing her, and the reality that I let Beau go, when I knew he was the best thing for me. Maybe it was because I needed to heal on my own. I wasn't entirely sure what my thought process was on that one, but feeling was what I needed.

Like my mother always said, "Whatever your struggle is, sugar, own it. Feel it. Life is messy, so just deal with the shit and smile. You're not perfect, and you're not alone."

I'd like to think I was better and I wouldn't have days where even breathing hurt, but I did. I knew, no, I wanted to believe there was beauty in that too.

Now what was I supposed to do? Live my life again? How was that even possible?

I spent Christmas alone, despite knowing Beau was in Mountain Brook with his family. He didn't call, and I didn't either. All I could focus on was I didn't have a family right now.

On New Year's Eve, I made a resolution I was going to change. The change came for me when I spent the evening with my mom, watching television when everyone else was out partying. It was somewhere between The Voice and Grey's Anatomy when she asked about Beau.

My mom knew about Dixie and that Beau and I broke up, I wasn't sure though how much she comprehended it.

"He's on tour right now," I told her, kinda hoping she'd leave it at that.

Beginning to panic a little, the rush of emotions that always seemed to flood me came back in full force.

Standing, I made my way over to her cabinets in search of a water glass and found a firefighter's helmet in there. "Mom, did you steal this from the fire department?"

"No." She picked up Shep and laid him gently on her lap. "I'm sure he'll be back for it soon."

Crazy woman, stealing stuff just to get them to come back.

"When are you going to bring Beau back? I miss that charming country boy."

Me too, Mama. Me too.

I laid my head against the cabinets and mumbled, "Not you too."

I always wondered if it was really Corbin dying that tore my parents apart or if it was something else. They fought constantly growing up and I always assumed it was just them. Until losing Dixie I couldn't comprehend how life changing it was to lose a child.

"Hey mom." I sat next to her again, taking her hand in mine, her dark eyes tender. "Do you think if Corbin hadn't died, you and dad would have been okay?"

After Corbin died, my father was a drunk, crazy and violent at times. I didn't know him all that well. When he was home, he was in the garage, drinking, tinkering with his truck or out back on the tractor, and probably hoping to fall off the damn thing.

One day, he never came back.

Death destroyed families.

I didn't ask where my father went, neither did my mother. Maybe it was some unspoken reality we were both avoiding, I might never know.

Mom's eyes drifted to a photograph she had of me and Corbin standing next to an old Buick, big cheesy smiles on our dirty little faces. "I never thought your father was someone I should have married in the first place. He was the rebel from the wrong side of town and I was the preacher's daughter hell-bent on pissing off daddy. I loved him dearly but you're right, losing a child changes who you are inside. We changed in opposite directions."

Had Beau and I changed in opposite directions?

I didn't think we did. I pushed him away and he was hanging on.

"You and Beau are different."

Of course she would say that.

"I'm scared I won't be enough for someone like him."

"Is that really why you broke up with him? Because you never thought you were good enough?"

"That among other reasons."

"You are good enough."

Was I? Did I deserve someone like Beau?

I wasn't so sure.

EARLY FEBRUARY

IT WAS ANOTHER Saturday night and I was laying on the couch, alone, watching movies when I heard a knock at my door. Peeking out the window, I noticed a black car I'd never seen before.

As I opened the door, I saw Payton standing before me. "Why haven't you listened to his CD, or returned any of his calls?"

"Oh, hey, Payton, so nice to see you."

She looked confused. "Really?"

"No, fuck off." I was about to close the door when she stopped me, her hand on the door.

"Okay, I deserve that."

Stupid twat waffle. You deserve more than that.

"Yeah, you do. If I had a dick, this is where I would kindly tell you to suck it."

Payton smiled, shaking her head as she tucked a strand of her silky dark hair behind her ear. "Now I see what Beau liked about you."

Funny, I don't know what he saw in you. Maybe it's your winning personality. NOT!

"There was always *more* than my looks."

"I deserve that too."

"Why are you even here?" I wanted to slam the door in her face. "You don't like me."

"I didn't like you before because I was in love with Beau and, well, he was looking at you like he never looked at me."

Very true, beauty queen.

"So?" I opened the door and let her in. I guess I'd hear her out.

"You look good. Boney, but good."

Rolling my eyes, I offered her a Coke, only to have her decline. "Not everyone can have Dolly Pardon tits. And what, are you too good for Coke?"

"Do you have diet?"

"Yeah, it's called water. Would you like some?"

She nodded, and I handed her a bottle of water from the fridge. There was a moment of silence between us and then she sighed, a heavy but jagged breath that caught my attention.

"I'm sorry I let you believe there was something between Beau and I, and there wasn't. It ended a long time ago, maybe even before he cheated on me."

My eyes found glossy green. It was easy to see why Beau was attracted to her and how much he loved her back then.

But I was still mad at her and she knew why.

"And I'm sorry for those things I know you heard at the store. . . about Dixie. I've never lost a child, and I had no right to pass judgment on your pain."

She was getting somewhere, but not yet.

"You're right, you don't get to judge me." Breathing in deep, I stared out the window, unable to look at her. "I'm sure you're not perfect."

"Beau wasn't my first." Payton couldn't look at me now, a nervousness she usually never presented in the pink that rushed to her cheeks. "Everyone in town thinks he was, but he wasn't."

"Who was?"

"His brother, Jensen, when I was only sixteen and Jensen was eighteen."

Figures she'd do something like that.

"Does Beau know this?"

Payton breathed in deep. "It's exactly why he and Jensen don't get along."

"So you cheated on him?"

"No," she whispered, "we weren't dating at the time. We had broken up because I wanted to date other people for a little while. All I had ever known was Beau, and I was curious as to what else was out there."

We had sat there in silence for a while, when I sighed. "I still don't understand *why* you're here. Beau and I broke up. That's great you wanted to apologize, but you and I will never be friends."

"I'm going to the Grammy awards tomorrow. . .with Beau."

Is he seeing her? Are they. . . fuck, they're having sex. Goddamn it!

The rush of emotions that swarmed me was more than I expected. I stood, pointing to the door. "I'm not surprised, you whore. Now please leave."

Payton refused to leave, crossing her legs like she was getting comfortable. "I deserve that."

"You *deserve* a lot more than that, Payton. And Beau and I broke up, so you're free to go with him. I hope you two are happy."

"Are you?"

"No." Sighing, I scrubbed my hands over my face and then let them fall in my lap. "Just go, Payton. I don't. . .want you here."

She waited for our eyes to meet. "You guys didn't break up, Bentley. You may have parted ways for a while," she said with all-too-sad eyes, a portrait of a woman who had given everything to one man, and now he wasn't there. "You've broken him, though." Payton swallowed, like she couldn't bear to tell me this, but was. And then I wondered if Beau knew she was here. More than likely, he didn't. "You need to tell him he still has a chance."

"Why?"

"Because it's destroying him and it's not fair. For months I've watched him drink himself into what he believes is normal and functioning, when in reality, he's killing himself."

"I didn't break him." I'll admit, my response was snipped. I felt like she was accusing me. "*Life* broke *us*."

"It's *not* fair, none of it, losing your daughter, all of it and I know you still love him. He did *everything* for you, to make you see his love for you, and he was nominated for a fucking Grammy because of it," Payton said. "But you haven't once made an effort for him. Make a damn effort."

A Grammy? Holy shit!

He was doing this for me?

But why?

Why not for him?

Payton seemed to understand my confusion. "He wrote that song for you because he loves you and he was trying to make you see it."

It was then I started to go into all out panic mode. As if suddenly it all made sense and what he said at the wedding.

"The way I feel about you hasn't changed. It never will."

"What if he's moved on? It's been nine months."

Payton scurried over to me, sensing her opening to convince me, taking my face between her hands. "He's waiting for *you*."

"I doubt that," I said, unsure of what I was saying.

"I can tell you without a doubt, Beau loves you." She held my stare, begging me to see. "That song he wrote, 'Everlasting Light' you know the one that's been number one for so long, it earned him a Grammy, and he wrote it for *you*."

As she spoke, I wanted to tell her she didn't understand and her theory was wrong. Only, I didn't know. She could have been right. Maybe that was why he wanted me at the concert so badly.

When I didn't say anything, Payton rolled her eyes. "Bentley, he's performing at the Grammy's tomorrow, and for the first time ever he's playing 'Everlasting Light' live, and you're going to fucking hear that song, and he's going to sing it like it was meant to be heard if I have to drag you by your hair to get you there." Stunned by her verbal lashing, my eyes about bugged out when I noticed Blaine in the driveway, now standing outside Payton's car now with a bag in hand and sunglasses.

Had they planned this?

Was this their intervention?

"I got us a redeye flight to L.A. which means we'll get there in the morning. The Grammy's start at five. Nine months has been way too long. Now get your boney ass inside that damn car. We have a long flight and still have to make you look like you're alive." She pushed me toward the door. "You're too pale."

I was rushed out of the house in my sweats and messy hair in a bun with barely enough time to put shoes on. Once inside the car, Blaine peeked over the seat where I was sitting in the back. "I'm sorry, but we had to do something."

I wasn't sure how to respond and then she patted my shoulder.

"And don't be mad at me after you talk to him."

I whipped my head around to face her. "Why?"

"No reason."

My nerves skyrocketed. Was I really heading to LA to see Beau perform live?

NINETEEN HOURS LATER, I was standing in a dark parking lot outside a limo behind the Staples Center, all by myself. If I had nails, they would be gone. I'd thrown up twice, brushed my teeth three times, and had enough makeup on I was afraid to smile in fear I'd crack it.

When Payton returned, breathless, she drew in a couple calming breaths. "He's backstage right now in the dressing room. Miles said he could get us back there."

I flattened my palms over my black dress that clung to every curve I didn't have and made me look ten feet tall. I felt absolutely ridiculous wearing it, but then again, this was the Grammy awards. Clearly my usual attire of yoga pants wasn't going to work. "Is he okay?"

"Yeah, he's just nervous. Back there biting his nails and pacing the floor. He was nominated for Best Solo Country Performance, Best New Artist, Record of the Year and Song of the Year." And then Payton eyed me and the dress I was wearing. She and Blaine had spent hours on me and this black dress. "You look great, a little bony, but great." She clapped her hands together. "What's your plan?"

Was she serious? We flew here and she wanted to know *my* plan?

"My plan?" I gasped, my eyes wide. "I thought you had one?"

She started to pace the parking lot. "I do. . .I think. Let's get in there and well figure it out. He won for best solo country performance."

"Really?" My eyes stung with happy tears. "He won a Grammy?"

"Yep. They already announced it, but he's backstage at the moment. He's performing in a few minutes, but you need to get in there and get in my seat that way he sees you when he performs."

"Why?"

She waved in my face, like I shouldn't concern myself with the minor details. "Because it's like a grand gesture. He'll never expect this. Not in a million years."

The nerves hit me like a punch to the gut. "What if I waited too long? And what if he wants you there and not me?"

"He'll want you there, believe me. He hasn't said a single word to me all night. He loves you. He never gave up on that."

Stepping toward the building with her, I prayed.

Don't trip.

SOMETIMES I WONDERED if I had moved on, mostly because I couldn't even listen to his music. Unfortunately for me, that hadn't happened. I might have set down the pen, I might have thought I was moving on, but there was a good part of me that, after seeing Beau at Blaine's wedding, still hoped there was a chance for us.

Seated in the front row, directly in front of the stage he was about to perform in front of, I was shaking so bad I looked like there was something physically wrong with me.

Thankfully no one paid me any mind.

"Performing his hit single 'Everlasting Light' for the first time live off his latest album *Tail Lights*, here is Beau Ryland."

The crowd around me cheered, the applause shocking to my already ringing ears.

As the lights of the stage dimmed, I spotted Beau walking forward wearing dark jeans and what appeared to be a black shirt just a few shades lighter than his jeans. His hair was messy, no reason to the madness but it fit him so well. Around his neck was the same necklace he always wore, a simple cross.

He looked amazing. Slimmer than I remembered, the muscles in his arms appeared defined, like maybe he was leaner than before.

A single light shined down on him standing in front of a microphone with his guitar as he started a slow rhythm I knew was going to make me cry. There was a reason why I hadn't listened to this song before.

Behind him was a small band, playing softly, but appeared this was an acoustic performance and nothing fancy, just like our love. Simple.

I couldn't move. Frozen.

Holy fuck. It's really him. I'm really here about ready to hear him sing.

Shit. Breathe.

No seriously. You need to breathe.

When he scanned the crowd, his eyes swept over me, and then darted back when he saw that familiar blonde in a seat where there should have been a brunette beauty.

I wanted to wave, do something, but I was just as frozen as him.

He stared down at me like I wasn't real, wide eyes taking me in from my face to my feet. The look on his face was pure shock, but then just as quickly, he blinked the look away, smiling at the cheers around him as he began to play his guitar. Every few cords, he'd tap his hand to create a unique rhythm.

I thought, hoped, that my feelings would have changed for Beau. I wanted them to. But they hadn't, and in that moment, I realized they probably never would.

He was the father to my baby girl.

He was the man who I fell for in a matter of hours, and erased from my life just as quickly.

Like it or not, part of me was still holding on to that summer and his smart-mouthed Southern drawl I knew him to be.

Now, here I was, waiting for him to acknowledge me, to give me hope, or not.

Feeling the sudden panic rise, my hands and heart trembled as I decided what I would do next.

I really, *really* needed to relax, but I was running on adrenaline. And, suddenly, before I knew it, I was living my life through memories flashing in my head, fourteen again, sky blue passing in the halls, and living for a boy with a guitar in hand, sun glowing, the days long and hot, sticky and heavy—everything his memory was—beating down in rays so hot you couldn't breathe.

Beau was visibly nervous when he stared down at me, his breathing intensifying like the muffled roars of cheers around us, his hands shaking as he reached for the microphone in front of him.

He looked down at me as if the world stopped for him and it leveled me. I'd forgotten how it felt to have him look at me like that, and the power it held.

And then he began to sing. *"There's a girl I used to know. Under the stars I gave her light. We sparked a fire in the night."*

When I heard his voice, I was reminded of what we were. We were two hearts. Two souls. Devastated by the same loss.

My heart ached when I saw him on that stage, in front of thousands. I didn't want his voice to be one I used to know.

I wanted it to be everlasting, like our love.

The tears I'd been so desperately holding onto broke free.

"She took my breath with that kiss, gave me her heart. Maybe I'm to blame." His face was pure agony belting out the lyrics with force, as if when this song was written, he was ready to give up. *"Because, honey, somehow that smile is one I used to know, one I'll never let go."*

Hearing him sing with such raw emotion that he couldn't keep his voice from shaking, made me understand that he, too, had gone through the same pain. There was beauty in his imperfections, displayed only in these lyrics. He'd captured everything we were.

A fire burns all around us
Headlights dancing in the dust
We're whiskey-lit and holdin' on
I turn to you and whisper, don't be afraid
Baby, look up and get lost, take in the night

Make a wish on everlasting light

His brow scrunched, his eyes glossy as he sucked in a breath and belted out the bridge. I felt the air sucked from my lungs right then as a strangled cry fell from my lips, my hand over my mouth.

Baby, I wonder if you think of me now
Tell me, can you hear these words
They own my soul
I can't let go, I want you so bad

When he looked down, it was as if at any moment his knees would give out and he'd fall to the ground and beg me to never leave.

Maybe we were blind
I know our love was one of a kind
Trust me this one last time
Open your eyes
Give me a chance to right the lies

A fire burns all around us
Headlights dancing in the dust
Whiskey-lit and holdin' on
I turn to you and whisper, don't be afraid
Baby, look up and get lost, take in the night
Make a wish on everlasting light

Beau's eyes found mine again, but now, here right now, they told a different story from the one I knew when he left. It was a story that split my chest and bared my own soul for him to see the hope, adoration, happiness, trust, belonging, softness, love, and forgiveness.

Sometimes, I felt like we were pulling a rope, but neither one of us was pulling the rope at the same time. Now we were both fighting for what we wanted, at the same time.

I thought loving someone was doing what was right, but also doing everything wrong. For a long time, I struggled with how to do that, because before Beau, I had never loved anyone like that.

Looking at Beau now, it was all there.

It was in every word being spoken. It was the guilt behind his eyes and the purple below them. It explained the way he wouldn't give up on me and the way he wasn't running from anything. It was in the way he held his smile at bay when he was teasing. It was in how he always knew what to say to me, even when he didn't say anything. It was in the way he kissed me the night we met. It was in the life he would have thrown away for me. And it was in the way his heart was beating for me.

Beau's voice broke, and I knew there were tears he wouldn't let go of, holding them back. His head hung as he sang the next verse.

Baby, please, just look up, make a wish
Give me something
Hide the sun

I'll take the rain
Give me your pain
I'll do anything, just let me explain

Don't be afraid, look up, take in the night
Make a wish on everlasting light
Baby, please, just look up

I was looking up, at him, at our lives, at Dixie, all of it for the first time. When the song was over, Beau gave me one last look and turned, walking off stage.

I wanted to go back to the moment he first noticed me, that first wink. I wanted to go back to him scooting me closer and begging for a kiss under silver-sequin stars. I wanted to go back to that night just for a split second.

And that song did it for me. Hearing his words, I was trapped like fireflies in a jar, reliving every beautiful moment I had with him, surrounded by his broken raspy voice. I wasn't sure what tomorrow would bring, or even later tonight, but I knew one thing. I wouldn't push Beau away. I never would again.

His manager, David, approached me during the intermission. "He's backstage. Would you like to see him?"

I nodded, eagerly, though I wasn't sure.

With David's help, I was able to get backstage to see him face to face. I never thought I would be next to him like this. I assumed I didn't deserve to. Especially after letting him walk away, again, at Blaine's wedding.

When I made my way backstage, I was met with the man who held my beating heart in the palm of his hands. It was everything I could do right then not to cover my mouth with my hand, admiring the way he looked, up close, as he leaned into the wall twenty feet from me, a slow smirk tugging at his beautiful lips, holding a Grammy.

We looked at each other as he ran his hands through his hair and tugged at his tie.

The moment between us, the stillness, the bloodshot eyes and the bleary stare hurt so badly.

He looked up at me, and my heart soared. I knew then, for sure, I would only ever love Beau Ryland.

Walking to me now, a slow stride I remembered. He was nervous, I knew that much. I could hear my heart in my ears when he approached me. He was looking at me and the nervousness ran up my spine wildly causing me to shiver, maybe in anticipation of being this close to him.

And I itched. Fucking itched to no end just like seeing him at the wedding. Maybe from the dress, or maybe, my nerves again.

"Hi," he whispered, waiting for my reaction. My stare was drawn to his, framed by thick dark lashes as he spoke.

I sighed, my palms sweating, my armpits feeling itchy, waiting, wondering what I should say to him after all this time. "That song was. . . just amazing, and I can't believe I didn't listen to it sooner. I'm so sorry." Brushing my hands over my cheeks, I knew my make-up was smeared. "And I can't stop crying, or sweating." I fanned myself, feeling the heat rising. "And this dress is *way* too tight. I can't breathe."

Stop talking!

I could barely contain my crying when Beau gave an emotional chuckle, pulling me into his arms. "Still the same girl I remember." He smiled, his own eyes teary as his chin quivered. Nodding, he tried to compose himself. "And you came. That's all that matters right now. On the biggest night of my life, you came for me."

He said the words as if he didn't believe them, as though he was stunned, but appreciated that I made the effort, finally.

"Is it too late? Am I too late?" My voice was exactly how I felt, awkward, timid, and wavering as I cried into his chest.

Beau exhaled loudly, drawing back, forcing a smile. "I wanted to let you go. I told myself that a lot and even tried to a few times. But there was *always* something that kept me hanging on." His eyes lifted to mine, watching my reaction to his words. "I believe it was Dixie, and then Blaine who gave me those letters and I saw you were still holding on."

Blaine what?

My brain scrambled back to my conversation with her in the car. *"Don't be mad at me after you talk to him."*

So that's what she was hiding.

I panicked, my heart in my throat, palms sweating all over again as I recalled what I wrote in there, all the detailed feelings surrounding Beau and my love for him.

How could she do that? She knew I thought they were going to Dixie and she let me believe it?

"Don't be mad at her," Beau mumbled, staring at his feet as he buried his hands in his pockets. "She was only trying to help us."

"That *jerk*." My eyes fell to the floor.

I should have been mad at her for it, but then again, Blaine was trying to help me. And she knew exactly how to. She let me believe those letters were going to Heaven and it helped me. If it hadn't been for writing to her, and believing with all my heart she had those letters, I would have stayed in bed longer, smiled less, and never laughed again.

She gave them to Beau, and in turn, it gave him hope I was still holding on to him.

"I thought you were fine. You had moved on and was on the road. I really did feel all alone, like I shouldn't have been so sad. And then I overheard Payton talking, and she questioned how I could be so upset over losing Dixie when we barely even had a chance to see her."

When I didn't say anything else, Beau moved closer, sadness rolling down his cheeks, his jaw clenching in what could have been anger. "I was never fine." Our eyes met and I was shocked at what I saw. He was, one, crying, and, two, angry. Probably because I never considered how he felt until now. "I *wasn't* fine. I didn't think I could make you happy if you were incapable of being happy."

He was absolutely right. He couldn't make me happy when I wasn't ready to be. "I'm sorry I never considered how you felt, and that you were struggling too. All I focused on was my pain, and it was selfish of me."

When I looked at Beau now, in this light, I didn't see the boy who winked at me and I fell hopelessly for someone I didn't know. I didn't see the man I met later and tripped into.

I saw the man who struggled to tell the truth in his lyrics and accept his father would never approve of his career choice.

I saw the man who loved a woman so deeply he never gave up on her, even when she gave up on herself.

I saw the man who opened up to me in a song for the world to hear, and fought to get me back. There was something about his determination to be more that made him who he was.

His hand raised, the backs of his fingers brushing against my tear-soaked cheek. "It's okay."

"I'm sorry I didn't listen to the song sooner," I said feeling like it needed to be said.

"I'm kinda glad you didn't. I like that you heard it the way you did."

He was right. Somehow, hearing it this way, in person when his eyes never left mine had a far greater meaning than it would have had I heard it on the radio.

"Beau?"

A smile tugged at the corners of his mouth. "Yeah?"

"I love you."

Beau heaved in a heavy breath and then crushed me to his chest, holding on so tight I could barely breathe. "I love you too. . . *God*, so fucking much."

"YOU WANT TO come back to my hotel room with me?"

"I just want to be alone with you," I breathed, feeling like no amount of time with him would ever be enough. I wanted to be alone with him more than anything right then.

Beau made the faintest groan when I pressed my body into his side as we walked, leaning in to kiss the hollow spot just below my ear. "Me too."

He couldn't leave just yet, but after interviews and photographs, which he made me take with him, we were finally alone.

He smiled, again, his hands in his pockets as we walked to the limo. "Bentley?"

My heart beat faster, so fast I had to draw in a deep breath. "Yeah?"

His smile grew wider, into the one I missed, the one that made my heart beat in my ears when he spoke like this. "That song was pretty *charming*, wasn't it?"

I rolled my eyes, trying to play hard to get, even just for a second. "Maybe."

He raised an eyebrow, running his hand down his jaw. "Maybe, she says."

I remember thinking at one time, when I was at my lowest, that Beau would have moved on. Sometimes I wondered why he hadn't. Why did he wait for me for so long when I couldn't give him anything in return?

And sometimes, I was thankful he did hold on, because I was here now, with him because of it.

City lights brightened the car, my heart thudding in my chest as we reached the hotel, the moon lighting up my eyes. The limo pulled up to the hotel, near the entrance where the driver opened my door and reached for my hand.

Outside the limo, Beau stared at my hand now in his. Bringing it to his mouth, giving me the lightest kiss.

I couldn't process all of this, the feeling settling in my bones that I had him, here, now. I might have only had the smallest slivers of time with him and I was going to enjoy it.

If losing Dixie taught me anything, it was that nothing in life was guaranteed and if you had the chance to say something, you should say it, be it, and believe in it.

Once inside the room, Beau whirled me to face him before I had a chance to set down my purse. His rock-hard body pressed to mine, his hands running up the length of my torso and to my neck where he angled it, and then kissed me. "I'm sorry. I couldn't wait any longer to kiss you."

I said nothing audible, lust and emotion I'd kept buried for so long overwhelmed me and I wasn't sure how to process it.

Beau sighed against my lips, shaking his head slowly. His breath against my skin felt scorching, yet the feeling was so familiar. "You want me to tell you a secret?"

I nodded, I wanted his secrets and I wanted anything he'd give me.

His face buried in my neck as he gave me another kiss and then drew back. "You've healed me."

Chapter Thirty

DIE A HAPPY MAN

BEAU

BENTLEY'S HANDS ROSE to my face as I crawled up her body, pressing my weight into her. The touch sent a jolt straight to my groin, my need stirring immediately. I think she knew by the soft groan that fell from my lips as they parted over hers where my mind was heading.

My hands were trembling. I was nervous she would either push me away or tell me to stop. She could at any moment and I would stop for her. The way I explored her body was evident of our time apart.

"I can't believe how amazing you sounded tonight."

I wanted to cry, overcome with such emotion that she heard my heartache for the first time. I didn't know how to respond.

When I read those letters from her to Dixie, she talked about me like I was a man who changed her life, but left her when she needed me the most.

How could I have ever. . . well, left her like that? I know she told me to leave, but I did. I could have stayed and worked harder, made her see I wanted to be there.

I didn't.

"It was all for you, baby." I kissed her temple, my lips lingering, afraid to pull away from her. Touching her skin now stirred thoughts inside of me I desperately tried to ignore. Surely she noticed the reaction I was having to her being this close. "I love you."

Nothing physical, Beau. Don't push your luck.

"I thought you moved on," she whispered, her eyes on me when I laid next to her, her smile laced with sadness I finally understood as she threaded our hands together.

How could she have ever thought I moved on?

The answer was simple. I never told her and she never listened to the song.

Reaching across my body, I touched my palm to her warm cheek. "Now you know, my heart was breaking along with yours."

I watched her face contort with the emotions overwhelming her, eyes closing. Feelings and memories rushed to the surface. Her skin, her smile, her scent overwhelmed me.

With sadness falling from the corners of midnight stars, she admitted, "I never stopped loving you, Beau."

You will never have to doubt my love.

I wanted to hold her and promise I would never let anything happen to her, but I knew I couldn't. A promise was nothing.

I knew I was going to take my time with her, become reacquainted slowly. Maybe we wouldn't necessarily make love, but she was going to understand my love for her tonight. A love that soothed the rough edges of this broken life and the ache inside of us. Or maybe she didn't want anything sexual, and I would be okay with that too.

It's been nearly ten months. You're not okay with it.

But I would be, for her.

The last thing I wanted to do was to expect anything would happen tonight outside of talking, despite the kissing on the way to the hotel room.

I hadn't been with anyone since Bentley, and to say I was ready for it to go beyond talking was an understatement.

My lips lowered to hers. She didn't move or try to stop me, so I pressed them to hers once, and then pulled away. Her eyes were tired and I realized she had to have been exhausted, only she wasn't pushing me away.

I never wanted this to end.

"You can sleep."

"Beau?"

"Yeah?" I hummed against lips I couldn't pry myself from.

"I was kinda hoping for more."

"Really? I didn't want to push it, but I'm all for more." She nodded and I rolled the two of us, pressing my weight into her. That was all the encouragement I needed. Believe me when I say I didn't need much encouragement any more. "Thank God," I mumbled, deepening the kiss.

Legs spread, bodies tangled, our clothes were carelessly discarded. My soul and my heart were laid bare for her.

My hands grasped, needed, moved, tugged, and gave way. It took me a while to get the condom on, and then I was fumbling, like some kind of kid and not a man.

"Beau?"

"Yeah?"

"That's, uh, the wrong um. . . you. . . that's the wrong hole." She giggled, her body shaking against mine as she tried to help me out.

Laughing, I moved, positioning myself. "Sorry, it's been so long I must've forgot."

My body screamed in approval. Entering her, I knew then I was still the only one. Something told me. Her movements, her gasps, her eagerness told me it'd been just as long. Reeling at the thought, my hips moved on their own, pounding into her.

"Beau?"

I laughed, shaking the both of us. "Yeah?"

"Kiss me," she whispered, long lashes lowering as we moved as one. "Please kiss me."

I did.

I poured everything I had into those kisses, wanting her to *feel* the love I had for her. I would always give myself to her, now more than ever.

I held her hands above her head against the pillow before hitching her leg further, my head dipped down to whisper low and seductively in her ear. "I've waited so long to remember this feeling." I panted as I slowly began to move. My orgasm was nearly there. I fought hard, not wanting my time to end with her.

My hips moved languidly for a while as she caressed the length of my back, feeling the taut muscles. My body tensed at her touch, or from the sensations, each movement slower than the next for fear that at any moment this would be over.

"I missed you," I confessed, grunting with each movement. "I missed you so fucking much." My hands curled around her shoulders, pulling her into my movements.

"Me too, Beau. *Me too.*"

"You feel so good," I grunted as my movements sped on their own volition, needing the release.

She tightened her embrace, wrapping her legs around my waist, and I lost all sense of existence. We fell together, crashing into one another as our orgasms surfaced.

Handling her with care as my breathing slowed and my shaking started to calm, I let out a long breath and eased her body from mine.

She exhaled deeply, sliding to the side, but I wasn't letting her go. Pulling her closer, I wrapped my arms around her waist, bringing her flush against my chest.

We lay quietly, our eyes connected, remembering everything we'd missed about one another. A sweet smile spread across her face, lighting her up. "I love you."

There was no definition for what we were right now, and for once, I didn't need it. Not with Bentley.

I knew we needed very little in life to feel wanted, loved, and needed.

With Bentley, she trapped me inside of her, made me feel those things even when we weren't together. Made me believe it was possible not to feel lonely anymore. To believe there was someone out there for me.

"Shhhh. . . sleep," I whispered against her temple. "I got you."

Love doesn't wait. Love grabbed you in an instant, taking a hold of your heart, forcing you to see what you needed, take what you wanted, and hold onto what you cherished.

I held on. Though she didn't think she did, Bentley held on, too. I once asked myself, how could a broken heart heal another?

Easy.

Together.

IN THE MORNING, I let Bentley sleep in as long as she wanted.

Me? I was amped. I'd gotten my girl back, won a fucking Grammy, and felt the happiest I'd been in over a year.

"Will you go someplace with me today?" I kissed her temple just as she was waking up, tempting her awake with a cup of fresh coffee because I couldn't take that she was still sleeping and I felt this alive.

"Where?" she yawned, stretching her arms up and knocking me in the jaw. "Shit, sorry!"

Rubbing the side of my face, I winked. "Back to the lake."

Our eyes met, memories of last night evident in our movements, and the way our bodies were reacting being this close. "I'll go anywhere with you."

Anywhere was in bed, for another hour as I remember everything I missed about her.

IT WASN'T THE first time I had been to Dixie's grave since the funeral, though I hadn't been as much as I should have.

I wasn't sure how to react, or what to say when we went to her grave. The two of us sat in silence, memories of the day I had to hold her up, watching the pastor say a pray for our angel.

Only today was different. It was calmer, the emotions not quite as intense. It still hurt, and I knew Bentley felt the same way, but there was a year of difference now.

On our knees in front of her grave, we remained silent until Bentley drew in a breath. "Is it so wrong that I miss her the way I do when I only had her for a few minutes?"

"No," I held her closer, my arm around her shoulders as I brushed my lips to her temple. "She signified a greater meaning in both of us. She wasn't *just* our baby girl. She was a part of us, and it was taken from us before we had a chance to understand it."

Bentley drew away slightly, but I pulled her back, never wanting to let go. "Beau, what if I'm not that same girl you fell in love with?" Her tears slipped down her cheeks. "That song. . . I just. . . what if *we're* not the same after Dixie?"

"You are." Twisting her to face me, my hands framed her face. "We are."

"I don't think I am." Bentley looked down, her lashes fluttered before she looked up at me, eyes wide, searching for forgiveness she thought she didn't deserve. Her lips brushed the inside of my wrist placing a tender kiss against my skin. "You're different."

I guess in some ways I was.

I took an uneven breath as her eyes moved over my face. "Then I'll love her, too. And I hope you can love the man I am now."

Leaning in, our lips finally touched. "I do."

AFTER LEAVING MOUNTAIN Brook, we made the trip back to the lake. Sitting on the edge of the dock, I gave a relaxed nod to the house behind me. "Miles's parents sold this place."

"Oh really? Crap, are we trespassing?"

"Yes, but I'd gladly spend the evening in the back of a cop car with you."

"Beau, be serious. We should leave."

"I'm sure the new owner won't mind," I hinted, wondering if she would catch on.

She peered over my shoulder, wide eyed at the house. "Do you think they're home?"

Taking her face between my palms, I slowly kissed her. "They're home now."

"Beau," she gasped against my lips, finally understanding what I meant. "I couldn't let them sell it when I had so many memories here."

Closing my eyes, I let out the breath I'd been holding. I wanted to ask her what she was doing for the next fifty years, and if I was in her plan.

"So what's next for you?" Bentley asked, settling into my arms.

You. Us. Making lots of babies.

"I just finished out my tour and I was thinking of relaxing a little. What about you?"

"I'm still working at the hospital and living with Heather, but I have been taking classes in writing, of all things." She giggled, as if she thought that was a silly thing to do. "I don't like working at the hospital. It's pretty sad I'm still paying on my student loans and I'm going back to school."

"Sometimes life takes you in a different direction. Look at Blaine. She's still going to school." We both laughed and then came the awkward silence. The kind that always presented itself when you knew there was something else that needed to be said, but both parties were stalling. I couldn't look at her when I asked, needing the confirmation. "Do you see me in your life?"

She didn't hesitate when she said, "I see us together."

I kissed her then, slowly, and then grinned.

"Can we *please* just admit I'm charming now?"

She frowned, a smile desperately trying to pull through. She cracked, and then burst into tears. "You've always been charming, and I should have told you sooner."

Wrapping my arms around her tighter, I kept her against my body. "As long as you admit it at least once, I'm okay with that."

"You're charming."

"Thank you. I can die a happy man now."

Her body tensed. "Wrong choice of words, Beau."

"I know, but I'm still charming, just so we're clear."

"You are."

Staring over her shoulder at the lake, the memories of her and I together swimming in my head, I knew one thing for certain. I'll never crave the waves of the ocean. I'll always need the gentle ripple of the lake.

Chapter Thirty-One

HAPPINESS PART I

BENTLEY

11 MONTHS LATER

"COME ON, PRETTY girl. You gotta push."

My face felt like it was on fire, every part of my body aching and burning. "I don't want to."

"You kinda have to," Tabitha pointed out. Yes, the same Tabitha that helped us with Dixie was now here helping us deliver our daughter. I'm happy to say Dr. Douche was nowhere in sight.

"No, I don't. Let's just keep her in there," I said, and then another wave of contractions hit me and I was sure I never ever wanted to be pregnant again. I grabbed Beau by the front of his shirt, and then his arm in the midst of one and screamed, "I'm *never* having sex with you again."

He gave me a look that screamed, "You're joking, right?" but said nothing in response.

I wasn't, but in that moment, I swore on everything holy, I was serious. Labor pains with Dixie weren't like this. With this little rebel child who kicked constantly and gave me quite possibly the worst heartburn I'd ever experienced in my life, she wasn't going to come out easily. That much was for sure.

It was nearing the time when they said I was crowning and the babies heart rate dropped that I really panicked. I had been doing good through the pregnancy with my fears of something going wrong, but that was when it hit me that I could lose another baby.

Beau and I exchanged a look and he immediately got in bed behind me, his arms wrapped around my chest. "We got this, honey. She's fine. You just need to push and she's fine," he whispered. "It's gonna be okay, she's perfect. You're perfect."

I wasn't sure I believed him. I wanted to but my own fears, the visions of his being in this same position just two years ago, they tore apart any happiness I thought I would feel and then I just burst out crying.

The doctors moved around me, Tabitha encouraged me and somehow amongst it all, it was Beau who calmed me down. "Look up, Darlin'," he whispered, and I did.

There in the doctor's hands was our daughter, all nine freaking pounds of her screaming like we'd thoroughly pissed her off. With sweat and tears pouring down my face, my hair matted to my cheeks, I looked up and got lost in the cutest chicken without feathers and covered in goo and blood. That was exactly what she looked like.

But she was ours, and healthy. I had to have reassurance as the doctor handed her to me. "Is she healthy? She's breathing?"

Beau laughed. "She's screamin' ain't she?"

And she was, but when she was set in my arms, she stopped crying almost immediately and looked up at me. "Hey, pretty girl," I cried, pulling at the blanket they wrapped her in so I could get a better look at her. She looked almost identical to what Dixie had looked like, only bigger.

Beau rested his head on my shoulder, kissing the side of my neck. "She's beautiful, just like her mama."

I wasn't sure if he remembered, but that was the exact same thing he said to me when he saw Dixie for the first time. I glanced back at him and saw the tears streaming down his face. I wanted to say so much to him right then but the hormones just had me crying. I wanted to thank him for never giving up on me and apologize for when I did.

But I couldn't. I couldn't do anything but hold this precious gift and thank her big sister for giving her to us.

IT WAS HOURS later when Beau finally got to hold her. We were laying in the bed together, the room cleared of everyone but us and I sat there staring at my husband holding his baby girl. Beau never looked so hot.

"Fatherhood looks good on you."

He smiled, winking at me. "Yeah, well, I'm pretty excited to say I'm fucking a milf now."

"Beau!" I yelped, shocked he said that in front of our daughter. "Watch your mouth around her."

Snuggling her closer, he laughed. "It's not like she understands any of this."

He was right, she wouldn't, and I was thankful for the laughing because seeing him holding our daughter brought back those same fears, that anxiety I couldn't let go of. Beau noticed and looked up at me. "She's healthy, honey. It's okay to be worried, but don't let it ruin this for you. She's ours and we get to keep her."

I nodded and looked down at her. It was hard to believe, to comprehend but every time I saw her chest rise and fall, my heart told me it was going to be okay.

"Is it wrong that I keep thinking something is going to take her from us?"

Beau laid his head into mine. "I think it's perfectly normal."

"Do you ever wonder what she would have been like? I keep imagining her in our life like she's here. Like any minute she's going to come in and meet her little sister."

Beau lifted his head and looked over at me, his eyes glossy and red. "She's here with us now. She gave us Willa."

I believed Beau. If there was one way Dixie could help us heal it was giving us a part of her.

Willa Rae Ryland was our gift.

HAPPINESS PART 2

ANOTHER 9 MONTHS LATER

I've heard the sound of "Mama!" screamed from a crib at two in the morning and held a wide-eyed little girl who wouldn't sleep. I've kissed tiny scratches and held a chubby hand as we crossed the street.

I've had my heart broken and filled again with a curly dark haired hell-raising, unruly little girl we call Willa Rae Ryland, or in some cases, her favorite nickname of Willa Bean given to her by her daddy.

I've held a precious, beautiful, sweet baby girl in my arms as I rocked her in the chair Beau's granddaddy gave to us while she cried herself to sleep.

I've watched her grow and spit food in my face, pulled my hair and threw herself down in a tantrum. I've changed hundreds of dirty diapers and run after a toddler as she cackled down the hallways buck naked.

I've watched her sleep on Beau's chest and took pictures of them together like the obsessive photographer I was.

After years of heartache and thinking I would never ever have it, I was doing everything a mother would do. It was the little things I appreciated now, like holding chubby hands and kissing rosy cheeks before bed. Sunday morning waffles and coffee on a country porch overlooking the lake that started it all for Beau and me. We had a closeness, something we never lost, but cherished. We had both experienced the same loss, suffered that unimaginable devastation, but healed separately.

It wasn't easy to come back from where we had been, and I still struggled with losing Dixie. I still had days where the pain felt like it would bury me alive. It was a struggle fought in minutes, hours, days and months, side by side with the one person who understood that same pain, fought those same struggles, and lived with the same heavy heart.

I don't think grieving should be a word. Grieving wasn't something you could define by a word. It was having you heartbroken with one breath. It was a pinky promise made by the tiniest of hands. It was pushing someone away, even when you loved them. It was sitting in a scalding hot tub to feel pain. It was thinking letters were going to heaven.

Losing a child showed me parts of myself. The really ugly parts I would have never known under any other circumstance. I never thought I would have pushed someone like Beau away, but I did.

"Here." Blaine handed a sleeping Willa over to me.

Breathing in Willa's precious scent, I smiled at my sister-in-law. "I don't know how you carried her all the way from the house sleeping with your belly in the way," I teased, rubbing her very pregnant belly.

"I don't know how you function with yours. I feel like you've been pregnant for the last two years."

"I kinda have been."

I got pregnant with Willa in April, just two months after the Grammy awards. Beau and I were married in June, on the same day I tripped into his life two years prior to that. Willa was born on January twenty-fourth, exactly two years from the day we buried Dixie.

We apparently had a thing about dates and making them memorable, despite the tragedy that had occurred. In May, I got pregnant again. Now here I was, five months pregnant and feeling like I'd been pregnant since I met Beau. He wasn't kidding when he stood up at our wedding, drunk, and vowed to our guests and me, he'd keep me barefoot and pregnant for the next five years.

Looking up with my husband's voice all around me, I memorized every detail I could from the way the air felt to the drum beat in my chest. Willa stirred in my arms when she heard Beau's voice, lifting her head from my shoulder to look up at him.

You know what healing was? It was staring up at a man on stage and knowing you were placed on that path, with him, for a reason. You may not have known what the reason was, but you were in it.

"This song goes out to a girl who stole a kiss in the south." And then he winked at me and went into the opening notes of "Something Bad," the song he wrote based on that damn shirt I wore the night we met.

Have you ever thought about when your life was changing paths? Do you see it happening or do you feel it? I didn't know my life would change in the ways it did when I met Beau. I could honestly say I would never regret tripping into him.

Beau stopped the music and began peeling his shirt off, eyeing the ladies in the front row. I wasn't jealous, because it was just him working the crowd, and me. "I should sing this one song without a shirt on. . . because why the fuck not, right?"

With the shriek of girly screams that came from the women in the front row, this was exactly why he did things like that. Naturally, I screamed too when I was rewarded with my husband, the man I dreamed out since I was fourteen, without a shirt on singing a dirty song he wrote for me.

Thankfully Willa had no idea what any of the lyrics meant, just that her daddy was performing on stage.

Smiling down at me, Beau winked at he sang, "*Come a little closer baby, let me lay you down. Come a little closer baby, let me show you something bad.*"

He was still Beau Ryland for sure. My cheeks burned and I remembered how his touch felt in the heat of a moment, the dirty things he would whisper and the way it felt to be loved by someone like him.

Me, that small town girl who tripped into his arms one starry night was now his wife and the mother of his daughters. How lucky did I get?

Blaine shook her head beside me. "He looks like an idiot up there."

"Yeah, well, he puts on a good show."

She gagged for effect, and then smiled at the screams around us. "You got me there."

IT WAS THREE HOURS later before I saw my husband again, his sweaty arms wrapped around a now sleeping Willa. "There's my pretty girls."

I'd never tire of hearing him say those words, or the feeling my heart gave me when he held the two of us, or I should say three now.

Adjusting our baby girl in his arms, he lifted my hand to his mouth, kissing tenderly over the promise he'd only given to me. "I think I'm doing pretty good." A slight smile curved his lips. "I promised to keep you barefoot and pregnant for the next five years."

"Uh." I turned to argue with him, my hand on my belly where I was carrying our newest little girl. "No you're not. I think we should stop with two girls."

"Three girls." I smiled that he included Dixie. "And, yes I am. I want lots of babies running around. Little blonde haired Bentley's all over the place." I went to protest because Willa has dark hair like him, but again when he shook his head. He pressed his fingers to my lips, and then kissed Willa's forehead. "Look up, baby."

I did and thousands of stars lit the night, bursts of light raining down on the beauty between us. Stars had a new meaning for me now. Some people would say they're beautiful, but I don't think a word like beauty does them justice. It was like looking at a photograph and attempting to capture the magic of the moment. You couldn't. You only knew what that felt like because you remembered the experience.

"Beau?"

His lips brushed across my skin as he spoke softly. "Yeah?" The low resonance of his voice sent shivers down my spine.

"I love you, everlasting."

The End

Acknowledgments

If I do my job as a writer, it wasn't because you read my stories. It was because you believed in them.

I hope you feel that way after reading *Everlasting Light.*

When the idea for this book came about, I was staring at a near cloudless sky and the one tiny fluffy feather cloud in it. I thought to myself, if there was a baby in heaven, she'd be on that cloud there. So many families lose their baby before they ever have the chance to hold it, let alone show them the love they deserve. My mother lost my older sister when she was four days old, never had the chance to even hold her.

My good friend lost her twin boys the same way.

It happens.

This book was for every mom and dad who'd ever lost a baby before they could smoother them with the affection and love he/she deserved.

I have to thank my husband for constantly supporting me in this dream. Despite it being hard on the two of us, we make it work.

Thank you to my baby. Sweet baby girl, I'm so glad I've had the absolute pleasure of being your mommy, you silly stubborn, beautiful girl! I love you.

Thank you to Cody and Brynn Johnson for being on the cover and your amazing love for one another through tragedy.

Hot Tree Editing, I love you girls. You make my words make sense, because heaven knows when I give them to you, they do not.

Tracy Steeg, I know this cover took a lot of rounds, but it's absolutely perfect. Thanks so much for putting so much time into it.

Brandi Sorem, thank you for the beautiful photographs on the cover. They turned out amazing. It was such an awesome experience getting to do a custom book shoot for this one.

Adam Craig, thank you for allowing me to intertwine your music in this story.

Janet, Barb, Shanna, Marisa, Jill, Ashley's. . . Rachel, you girls are the best group to have around. Thank goodness for our group.

To the SheyNanigan's, I love you girls and thanks for the support of another release.

Meet the Author

SHEY STAHL IS A *USA TODAY* BEST SELLING AUTHOR, A WIFE, MOTHER, DAUGHTER AND FRIEND TO MANY. WHEN SHE'S NOT WRITING, SHE'S SPENDING TIME WITH HER FAMILY IN THE PACIFIC NORTHWEST WHERE SHE WAS BORN, AND RAISED AROUND A DIRT TRACK. VISIT HER WEBSITE FOR ADDITIONAL INFORMATION AND KEEP UP TO DATE ON NEW RELEASES:

www.sheystahl.com

YOU CAN ALSO FIND HER ON FACEBOOK:

https://www.facebook.com/SheyStahlAuthor

RACING ON THE EDGE

Happy Hour
Black Flag
Trading Paint
The Champion
The Legend
Hot Laps
The Rookie
Fast Time
Open Wheel
Pace Laps
Dirt Driven (TBA)
Behind the Wheel (TBA)

THE REDEMPTION SERIES

The Trainer
The Fighter

STAND ALONES

Waiting for You
Everything Changes
Deal
Awakened
Heavy Soul
Everlasting Light
Bad Blood
All I Have Left
How to Deal
Bad Husband

Love Complicated
Shade
Tiller
Burn
Untamed
Promise Not to Fall
Blindsided
Revel

THE TORQUED TRILOGY

Unsteady
Unbearable
Unbound

CROSSING THE LINE

Delayed Penalty
Delayed Offsides

Adam Craig Music

  I had the pleasure of collaborating with musician Adam Craig who graciously let me use his lyrics in *Everlasting Light*.

  To listen to his songs, visit his website at:

http://www.adamcraigofficial.com/

Or visit his Facebook page here:

https://www.facebook.com/AdamCraigOfficial/?fref=ts

Raise for Rowyn

The couple on the cover of this books means a lot to me. Not only are they a beautiful couple inside and out, they've experienced a tragedy like Beau and Bentley did in Everlasting Light. That wasn't the reason I used them for the cover, though the image who chose captures the heartache between them perfectly.

Brynn Johnson, the cover model, is the founder of the charity Raise for Rowyn, which most of my readers have seen I'm a big supporter of.

The Raise for Rowyn Foundation is designed to help families with that support whether it be funeral costs, counseling, anything to relief some of that financial burden upon the family and let them worry about what's important. Grieving the death of their child in a way that they can find peace within.

Brynn and Cassie have also began blogging about their struggles, as it's a constant struggle to remain positive and live life despite tragedy. I encourage everyone to read their posts. Though they're heartbreaking, the strength these ladies have is amazing. They have recently finished their novel *Life of an Angel*, which follows along with their struggle of losing Rowyn and how it's brought them closer together in their strength and faith. For information about their book, and charity, please visit their website of Facebook page at:

https://www.facebook.com/Raise-for-Rowyn-1525825754354063/?fref=ts

If you would like to donate yourself, you can do so at: http://www.raiseforrowyn.org/ to help local families who need financial assistance to families within the surrounding communities who are struggling with the loss of a child.